A Accidental Death

R.M. Winterbourne

This is a work of fiction. Names, characters, places, and incidents either are the product of the author's imagination or are used fictitiously. Any resemblance to actual persons, living or dead, events, or locales is entirely coincidental.

Copyright © 2021 R.M. Winterbourne

The moral right of the author has been asserted.

All rights reserved. No part of this book may be reproduced or used in any manner without written permission of the copyright owner except for the use of quotations in a book review. For more information, email hello@sprucepoint.net

First paperback edition December 2021

ISBN: 9798736436910

Published by Sprucepoint Limited
www.rmwinterbourne.com

To my book team, Sharon and Jon.

And also to Will, Rose, Harold and Judith.

Chapter 1 - Trust No One

Katherine arrived home and turned into the long stately carriage drive. The beauty of the towering beeches lining the private road and the honey cream stones of her ancestral home did nothing to calm her. She parked her shining car erratically, and emerged, a slight, elegant figure dressed in a light black wool trouser and cashmere turtleneck. She moved swiftly up the imposing staircase, and didn't stop to admire her home's architecture as she often did. She gave a sweeping glance only to the buildings flanking either side of the stairway, designs which spanned many periods of British history beginning with the foundation stones laid in 1450 during the reign of Henry VI. Today, her mind was elsewhere.

She fiddled with the front door lock which finally opened, dropped her leather handbag on the console and dashed up the curving staircase. She headed straight for Maisy's room to tidy up so she could then start on her new project - a project that had been waiting six weeks to begin.

It was a normal Tuesday. But the fresh breeze and bright sunshine was the nicest weather for over a month and Katherine couldn't help but feel refreshed by the crispness of the air and warmth of the autumn sun. She'd kissed Maisy goodbye about forty minutes earlier, and watched her four year old daughter enter her new school. It was still early in the term and she'd had to persuade her daughter to let go of her hand and join the queue. At the school she had waved a brief hello to Anjali, her closest friend and smiled quickly to the other mothers.

There'd been an energy in the breeze and she'd suddenly felt compelled to return home quickly and pick up the pieces that had been piling up since her mother's death. The drive home had been a perfect opportunity to think through what she had been putting off for well over a month now.

Katherine pushed open Maisy's door and despite the charm of her daughter's room couldn't help but sigh sadly. She finally had the energy to start again since her mother's accident six weeks ago. How could such an accident happen to someone as healthy and fit as her mother? Her mother had been 65 but still recognised as a beauty even as she reached her 'golden years' as one admirer in the paper called it. The worst was that still, no one knew exactly what had happened. The coroner had concluded that it was death by accident; that her mother had slipped on a large mossy rock as she took her morning swim in the river that wound its way through their family estate. The slip was fatal. She subsequently banged her head on the rock, fell into the water and quickly drowned in the flowing water.

Katherine shook her head as she tried to forget the scene that replayed and replayed in her mind. She focused on the room and the here and now.

Maisy's room reminded her of her own loving childhood. This had been her room, when she was young. Now, the room had sections of cream carpet and hardwood floor for soft play and art play. The furniture was slightly off white, and a playhouse took pride of place in the corner. A smile began to form. She loved her daughter and never regretted the time she took off from her career to become a parent.

Dramatically, it had taken sometime before Katherine was able to conceive Maisy. And that had presented its own problems. Katherine shuddered as her memory bleakly brought her back to those dark days when she was trying to conceive.

Thank heavens, thought Katherine, that she'd dissuaded her husband from enrolling Maisy in the boarding school his family had attended for generations. It may have been well-reputed, but Maisy was far too young and in Katherine's mind, it was an antiquated practice. Dropping Maisy off at her day school had been tough enough on Maisy given the sudden and tragic death of her grandmother a month and a half ago.

She quickly tidied the room and as she left her eyes swept across the room one last time. There was that teddy, that lovely rabbit she'd given Maisy on the day of the accident. She couldn't help but glance through the arched window, spotting the running river in the distance. She swallowed as an image of her mother cracking her head on the rock flashed through her mind.

Katherine squinted as she focused on the absurdity of the coroner's conclusion. She knew something wasn't right. She could sense it. She had too many unanswered questions: her mother's missing shoe, and the gash in her blouse. Another rush of urgency coursed through her and she felt that fresh desire again to visit her mother's study and look through her documents. It was a job she hadn't wanted to do up till now. She left Maisy's room and hurried downstairs to make her way to the west side of the house where her mother had lived for almost forty years since her husband's death.

As Katherine passed through the hallway she considered calling her husband, Colin, to ask if there was anything in particular regarding her mother's affairs that she should focus on first. She frowned instinctively. Colin was in China. If she somehow did get through to him despite the time difference, he wouldn't be interested in her issues. He liked to be left alone when he was abroad on business.

She remembered her recent discussions with Colin.

He didn't get her 'dissatisfaction' as he put it about the coroner's verdict. He was clear with her. He'd married 'her professionalism and reserve', and simply couldn't understand why she was emotional and reluctant to accept the coroner's conclusion.

He was also very grumpy that she'd dissuaded him from sending Maisy to boarding school this autumn. He believed their daughter was well on her way to growing up and liberating him from his parental duties. He was bothered that he had to collect his sick daughter twice from school recently because Katherine had been with clients and he'd been working from home. She steadied a sad frown; the last time he collected Maisy was the same day as her mother's death.

To Colin, her mother's death was unfortunate but explained. It also meant that he – or rather his wife – had another large property to add to their wealth. At this point,

Katherine was unsure what exactly she had inherited. She was clearly capable of understanding all financial aspects of her inheritance given her background in corporate finance, but being too stricken with the death she had let her husband sort it out.

Colin had confirmed that the house and associated estate remained hers.

Katherine pursed her lips in some distaste at her own conduct. Understanding her financial position was clearly important. Now was the time to kick back into action and appreciate the full extent of what needed doing, if anything regarding her mother's estate. Perhaps her husband had addressed everything, but post had piled up and Colin wasn't known for getting details done. He was always focused on big, flashy decisions. For now, she could begin to sort through the papers on her own.

The west wing of the house was quiet, eerily so since her mother's death and the start of Maisy's school term. Katherine passed by the sitting room where her mother had entertained guests linked to her professional horticultural work and headed straight to the study. The study was one of her mother's favourite rooms. A library in a garden is how Katherine described it. There were plants positioned in quiet corners and on tabletops. Some were huge and drooped with tropical vibes in the day and cast shadows by night. The walls were lined with shelves and book upon book about horticulture, architecture, garden planning and design. There were also numerous chronicles belonging to the family which detailed their long history and genealogy.

A tingle spread through her spine from her back straight up to her neck. This room epitomised her mother, everything was in place just as she had last left it. The beautiful swathes of thickly lined linen curtains with their hydrangea and vine patterns swirled from ceiling height into dramatic shallow pools on the floor. They were swept back from the grand french doors - four sets of them - and framed the view of the warm cotswold stone terrace outside the study. The room was bathed in light with the elegant french doors spanning one whole side of its perfectly square shape. The ancient stone floors had pale rugs of Oriental heritage placed warmly throughout the study and in reading spots under clusters of wingback chairs. Grey-painted side tables paired with Wedgwood creamware lamps complimented the comfortable chairs. The walls were hung with botanical sketches and landscape paintings from eminent artists and friends of the family throughout the centuries. Her mother had added her own personal touch to the study with paintings completed by both herself and Katherine. The study said it all: the family estate, Katherine, Maisy, and gardening had been closest to her mother's heart.

Her mother's writing desk was as tidy as ever with organised piles of projects she'd been working on. The most recent mail had its own growing pile. Katherine walked slowly to the desk and sat on her mother's embroidered chair, a lovely creamy linen with a pattern of pale green foliage & deep crimson roses woven through. She found herself affectionately rubbing the soft mahogany of the desk. She lowered her head to breathe in the smells of the wood polish and fresh flowers still placed there by Edward. Despite her death, he still arranged for her desk as he always had, a large vase of hydrangeas and roses. They were her mother's favourites. The scent of her roses, The Generous Gardener, seemed timeless. She felt so very close to her Mother.

'Miss, are you alright?'

Katherine lifted her head and whirled round, her eyes large with surprise at the broken silence. 'Oh Edward, yes of course, thank you for enquiring,' she replied to her family friend, the butler she had known all her life.

'Perhaps, tea? Shall I bring it in here?' Edward suggested.

'Yes of course, that would be perfect.'

He looked around and smiled at her. 'This room could do with some company. I'll return in a moment, Miss Katherine.' Despite her married name, Edward could never call her anything but by the name he had called her in childhood. To him, she was still the young Miss Katherine whom he adored.

The writing desk was perfectly positioned to enjoy the view of the expansive gardens. Her eyes followed the line of the lime trees down to the Orangery and the river beyond. What had her mother been thinking of? How could she have slipped? Katherine frowned and was about to stand up to reach for the pile of papers when her hand caught a loose piece of wood on the side of the desk.

'Ouch!' A loose piece of wood? That was odd. Katherine found the jagged edge and leaned closer.

Something had made a large indent in the desk leaving sharp wood slivers. She moved closer. Had someone tried to wedge open the drawer there? In fact, it was the faux drawer and so, that didn't make sense. There was no drawer to open, only a decorative drawer front. An unexpected shiver caught her off guard. Her home is secure, had always been secure so, what was this?

She wondered if her mother had left anything important in her main desk drawer. She pulled the large drawer at the front of the desk, but of course, it was locked. Her mother always kept this drawer locked. She reached under the table, to the concealed compartment under the faux drawer where the desk keys were kept. She checked that it wasn't open. No, all was fine.

She then returned to the side of the desk where it was damaged and pressed the keyhole on the faux drawer. The keyhole had a clever button that opened the hidden space. She heard the latch pop. She slid open the concealed compartment and sure enough the keys were there. She put the keys in the main desk drawer, turned and pulled, half expecting resistance. The drawer eased open smoothly.

As usual it was organised with her mother's special trinkets: a letter opener given to her on her 21st birthday; a selection of different sized scissors; glass paperweight, a gift from the Royal Horticultural Society years ago; a small sketch pad; a soft pale pink leather holder for sketching pencils which Katherine had given her one birthday and a small sewing kit that had been in the family for years.

At first glance there was nothing new there. With an air of mystery around her, she was slightly disappointed.

She did a double take when she noticed a loose piece of paper weighed down by one of the scissors. In fact, it was the scissors her mother had replaced in the drawer the night before her accident. But there hadn't been any loose paper in the drawer that night, of that Katherine was certain.

She moved too quickly brushing aside the scissors and the paper was shoved further back in the drawer.

She swept her hand inside the drawer. The paper tickled the tips of her fingers. She sat forward in the chair and stretched her hand to the very back. Gripping the paper with her fingertips she slowly pulled the paper out. With great anticipation, she unfolded the paper and read its contents.

She frowned. Katherine immediately closed the drawer, replaced the keys in the hidden compartment, and stood up to stretch out her tense feeling. Right, what could this note be? She walked to the french doors and stared at the blue sky for a moment, letting her mind rush through the possibilities.

Hearing Edward in the hallway, she tucked the paper into her pocket. Edward appeared at the study door with her tray of tea. She smiled at him as if nothing had happened, making pleasant conversation. When he left she immediately placed her teacup on the tray and pulled the paper from her pocket to read it again.

The writing, she didn't recognise, bar the last line which was in capitals. That last line was definitely her mother's writing, written in a different type of pen from the rest of the note. The other writing was firm and the font, dark, written in calligraphy. So not a quickly jotted message, she thought, but a considered note. The message itself was what perturbed Katherine. It was meaningful for sure, but not meaningful in a life that Katherine believed her mother, or herself for that matter, lived. It was polite but a threat, no doubt. And for her mother to possess such a note, and to hide this in her personal desk safe, was simply too odd.

Too odd, she thought, when there was a death? Katherine stared at the message, a vagueness of fear settling under her skin. It said:

Eco friendly as you asked. Rock solid.

1190563 srt 409456

No more niceties now, we are proceeding.

By end of play today. There can be NO DELAY.

Remember NDA and trust no one.

TRUST NO ONE

'Miss Katherine, would you care for a snack - I'm having one myself.'

Katherine crumpled the paper quickly in her palm and looked up at Edward who had returned at the door to check in on her. Time had simply disappeared as she deliberated the note.

'Actually, I do think I'll have more tea and a crumpet in the Orangery. I desperately need some autumn air.'

She tried a smile that was too stiff for her usual lightness and she swallowed quietly, a dry catch in her throat. Edward nodded and left to prepare her snack. Had he seen the note in her hand?

She watched him leave, then gave it a moment before folding the note smoothly and slipping it into her pocket. She headed straight for her handbag in the hallway and the mobile within it. As she began to ring a number, the full implication of the note weighed upon her. Her mother had written, 'TRUST NO ONE'. Could that have included....who? She dropped her mobile back into her handbag. For the first time in many weeks she felt immensely awake and strangely alert. What could all this mean, and did it have anything to do with her mother's death? It was best not to say anything for the time being about the note to anyone, of that she was sure.

Chapter 2 - Energy

James looked at his team around the table. He was immensely proud of them. They had made huge inroads in the race to identify methods of generating environmentally friendly energy, and had finally been recognised for their work. He smiled generously and, opening his arms to this small group of colleagues, he began to speak.

'Today is an important day for us. We've progressed our programme miraculously well given we're only six people. It's been fun, don't you think?' And he looked to the close-knit group for confirmation. They were smiling and nodding, but intent on hearing his next words.

'Look, it's been hard work, I know, with some disappointments and of course, real pressure from other companies who are aware of our work and are keen to downplay it, or for that matter, steal our new technology. Fortunately, as you know, the funding we received from a venture capital firm two years ago has allowed us to continue our research and development and to refine our technology,' he paused and looked around the room.

'And in the last few months we've been fortunate enough to have made an amazing breakthrough. We now have technology that will, this coming year hopefully, transform energy practices in Britain. It's likely that this technology could eventually transform coal dependencies throughout the world.

'When the dynamics of energy change, the dynamics of politics change and...' James' eyes grew serious and his voice sombre as he continued, '...this means that our discovery isn't just of scientific importance, but of national importance.'

James paced his spacious boardroom and he stared out at the countryside and the wind turbines spinning in the distance. He couldn't help but grin knowingly as he considered their success but also, associated issues. Hmmm, he thought, how things will change. He turned again to his small team and said in a formal manner unlike his usual, relaxed demeanour, 'What we discuss today is highly confidential. I've been advised that breach of confidence in this situation can result in a collapsed deal. With that impressed upon you, I'd like to invite our visitors in. Are we ready?'

He grinned at the team, but there was a determination in his eyes. All five employees nodded their heads solemnly and then, returned the grin. Energy 2 Embrace, E2E, was ready for their biggest breakthrough yet.

~ ~ ~ ~ ~ ~ ~ ~ ~ ~

Richard coldly took the tea from his assistant. He didn't notice her tired manner as she walked away; he didn't notice much about her for that matter. All he noticed was when his office wasn't tidy, or tea wasn't served on time, or if meetings were double-booked.

He was handsome and extremely successful, he knew, and very able to charm both men and women alike. Richard didn't need to pander or even be civil to the lower ranking people in the business. His ebullient and outgoing nature was reserved for the deserved. He once overheard a client, a mate in fact, say, 'If he wasn't so god-like handsome or dashingly appealing, he'd have a much harder time securing the funding he always gets and convincing owners to sell their companies to him!'

Richard was like an on/off switch. When he was 'off' he was hard-lined, stern and focused with no time for niceties. On 'off' he was serious and planned his acquisitions carefully. These quiet times he spent calculating, scenario-building, case assessing and his charmed manners were parked, allowing the whole of his mind to focus on the profit calculations or strategic opportunity of the deal.

Then, when it came to convincing senior executives, owners, board members, or City investors he turned the tap on. And the tap never dripped. When it was on, Richard's charm was second to none. It flowed, dazzled and enveloped the people around him so much so that the ambience was almost magical. In each negotiation everyone felt a player, intelligent and part of a much greater plan. And that was Richard's goal - the greater plan.

He had decided very early on how to secure enduring power in today's market - both the financial and political markets. The answer was energy. Energy was the key: it was the key to increased political control in Russia across Europe, invasions of the Middle East by the Americans in the past, and the interest in Canada's cold northern waters by several major powers. Energy too, was a key player in the growing trend for sustainability. To his mind, energy was something transformational that was about to happen in his generation.

In fact, it was about to happen because he believed *he* would be the catalyst. For a very long time he didn't know what would enable him to evoke this transformation. But in just the last few months it had all become clear. He personally had the means to throw a new technology into the works and shake up the powers that rule. There was no doubt that he could create a global cataclysm of power, because the innovative technology, he discovered recently, was on his doorstep and on his books.

Richard had a gold-star investment company, highly reputed and successful. But about five years ago, he set up a separate, small venture capital firm, a VC, to invest in tiny sustainable businesses mainly focused on green energy. These were very small businesses, with much needed upfront investment in research and development. They represented higher risk but with significantly higher returns if successful. Given the riskier profile of these investments, he kept this small VC separate to his established investment company and ensured it was unassociated in the market. He placed a trusted Director in charge. In fact, he thought his Director was the perfect form of himself, running the VC creatively and profitably.

A couple of years ago, his VC firm had invested in a small green energy company that had surprisingly, recently come up trumps. Richard had injected cash based on an off-the-cuff remark by one of his employees, a new recruit as it happened at the time, but now one of his superstar employees. It was an initial investment that Richard thought was risky but if it came good, the upside would be substantial. The company was scientifically well respected, even more so in recent years, and it had just happened to become, by the brilliance of its founder and majority owner, the absolute gem in Richard's portfolio.

Richard knew he was onto something good. Its revenue and profit potential were extremely attractive, but even more so was its actual technology. The technology was unique and exclusive, completely innovative intellectual property (IP) that could secure Richard significant control in a number of areas. His original investment had secured him 20% of the company, but now he wanted it all, to buy it outright. Such was the strategic importance of this company and his plans for it, that he code-named the programme, Project Gemstone.

The Project Gemstone programme to buy the company outright had been developing for sometime. His business plan had been aggressive with a tight timeline. His deadline to acquire was set for the end of the month; and once Richard put a date in a business plan, there was no turning back.

With a week left till the end of the month, he felt nearly there. He didn't want other companies snooping around to potentially lure the owner to accept other investment options.

He was worried that could happen soon, and was determined to sign the deal now before others recognised its value.

Richard sipped his tea like a gentleman and looked the part. His mass of boyish blond hair was classically cut and his suit impeccably black with a luxury white hand tailored shirt and gold tie. His desk was top designer material throwing off an image of power and success as did everything else in the room. His office was large - very large in fact, with a fireplace set in the wall between two grand floor to ceiling windows. A comfortable sofa set and coffee table were in a semi-circle around the fireplace. There were two other intimate and separate areas for sitting; one by the discretely hidden drinks cabinet and the other by the window with views to the city and the Thames. Even old Battersea Power Station was visible in the distance. He laughed, how humans progressed. And power? If anyone had wished to be impressed by power then they were surely not disappointed when meeting with Richard.

This morning he was focused on the numbers. At least, he was trying to focus. He took another sip of tea and gazed out at the Thames. He was annoyed but oddly, amused at the same time. There were several Gemstone meetings this week and he was quite sure they would convince the owner to sell, because the owner had a problem. He needed funding to develop his technology for large scale production and marketing; something that could be made accessible to governments and businesses through industrialisation and packaging. He needed to convert his new tech to a distributable product that would revolutionise the way people live and consume energy.

As usual, Richard had the answer. He had the means to do this, and he had the investor. Or rather, investors. Richard was very keen to buy the company outright, but he also had a backer; someone who he needed to further his plans, once the company was purchased. This someone was close to Richard - a classmate from his MBA days, Colin, who was as successful as Richard but by different means.

Colin's money had come from family fortune and his wife, Katherine, was from an aristocratic family. Ah, Richard smiled. Women. His friend's wife was glorious, beautiful, and titled. Remarkably, he thought, she was clever too, having created and nurtured a home lifestyle company. She was the visionary and CEO of a thriving business. Not unlike Colin, she also harked from landed aristocracy and she had only recently inherited a beautiful property - through the death of her mother.

He grimaced when he thought of the funeral. He hated funerals, hated the solemnity of death. Colin's wife had been the impeccable mourning daughter, and everyone had attended: titled families, politicians, and the media of course, given the mother's celebrity. It had been a very boring afternoon for Richard until he had spotted Thomas, Colin's brother and Katherine's brother-in-law.

At the time, his heart had skipped a beat; as Thomas came into full view he realised James, the owner of E2E, and Thomas' best friend, was with him. He strolled over and shook Thomas' hand.

'How's the family holding up?' he asked. He casually shook James' hand as well, but tried not to study him too carefully.

Thomas frowned somewhat. 'Well, not so badly from what I can see. Colin better than Katherine but you know how she holds out. Can't really ruffle Katherine. Colin's off to China in three weeks or so - some big deal,' Thomas stated then added, 'so he's got a limited amount of time to make headway through the family affairs with Katherine, then he's off.'

Ahh, Richard thought. Colin was off to China and had set the wheels in motion, as they'd discussed.

Thomas stared hard at Richard and when he'd had no reaction, adding, 'A bit untimely of Colin I would say, leaving his wife and daughter so soon after the funeral.'

'Yes, well in Colin's line of work, business runs at a pace,' Richard grinned absently. 'Katherine is strong, she'll be fine,' he added.

Richard turned to James, jostled his keys and casually asked, 'Is Anjali here?'

He looked around. Anjali was James' wife and Katherine's best friend. She was also one of Richard's key employees. Colin reflected on the friendship of this group. Thomas and Katherine, being the same age and neighbours, had been close since they were young. They met Anjali and James at Oxford during their University years and the four of them were always together. Many years later Anjali and James married and a couple of years after that Katherine married Thomas' much older brother, Colin.

Richard didn't know any of them until he and Colin completed post graduate MBAs in their thirties.

'No, Anjali isn't here, she's with her own mother who isn't well, and she also has the children – did you need to tell her something?'

'Ah, no, just wondered,' he paused casually and then added, 'how's business?'

'Yes, fine, thanks,' James was making polite conversation. He didn't much like Colin's friend. A muffled sob caught their attention and they watched Katherine across the lawn, gently comforting a tearful family friend.

Richard's attention turned to the couple. Katherine's husband stood by her side, reaching out to shake people's hands and thanking them for their words. He cut a striking figure but not as striking as his wife was in full black. She was beautifully elegant, just like her mother had been. Richard lifted his head high and took a breath in – with Katherine you could smell her beauty when you were close to her, feel magnetically pulled and attracted, one couldn't help it. Except perhaps Colin. He was certainly one who easily resisted the beauty of his own wife. A wry smile formed on Richard's lips.

And then, they were all moving almost en masse, slowly towards the black line of limousines. Colin ushered his wife and daughter into a limo then turned and caught Richard's eye across the mourners in black and they momentarily shared a faint grin with each other.

Richard sighed and pulled back to the here and now. Yes, Colin's wife was attractive, but he smiled competitively: his own love interest was far more sublime. Nothing could compare to the woman whom he idolised and had aspired to win over for sometime now.

Richard was single. And that was part of his allure. He was a target for women, single or married, and he knew it. But for a couple of years now - and that was telling, considering he'd never been matched to one particular woman for any length of time - he was deeply attracted to a unique and intelligent woman. This was completely alien to him and unlike his normal lovers. Typically, he dated women known in the main for their beauty and highly adept at entertaining and navigating social circles.

Although his love interest was a refreshing change to all of that, the situation itself wasn't so simple. It was in fact, very complicated and he knew that this only added to his obsessive desire to win her over. She had begun to work for him two years ago in a part-time capacity. Her brilliance he believed paralleled his own, and her work ethic was unfailing despite her part-time role and demands at home as a mother of two.

Being married and an employee were only the beginnings of the complications. Neither issue would have stopped his seductions in the past. Her character, comportment and professionalism appealed to him more than any other woman he'd known. And as to her physical attributes, to him she was simply, a beautiful creature. He appreciated fine art and recognised such exquisiteness in her cheekbones and exotic eyes. He frequently felt the impulse to embrace her when she smiled at him.

She was, he thought, divine material. Her graceful movements and delicate, fine-boned face were perfect. With her parents' mixed Indian and British origins she had such fair-coloured skin and thick raven hair that one couldn't quite place her nationality. And her voice was soft with an impeccable British accent.

Her marital status was a challenge which he took on with relish - he even adored her children whom he'd met a few times. He fancied the thought of taking on a paternal role to two such good-looking and well-mannered children. Well into his thirties he felt ready to take on a change in life and ready-made packages always did appeal to him.

But the final complication was the most interesting - and not one that he'd ever come up against. She was married to one of his clients, and at this very time, one of his most important clients. As a matter of fact, it had been a most unwelcome connection. He valued the input of his love-interest more than any other colleague or trusted advisor, but due to this unfortunate conflict of interest he couldn't involve her in one of the most important deals of his career. What contributed to her allure as well, was that she was unbelievably, innocently, unaware of his interest in her.

He took a sip of his tea and taking his eye off the numbers, checked his mobile again. He knew there was no reply message on it, but he couldn't help but check. He felt young again, young and confident and - dare he say it - in a place he rather liked; a place that could open a new chapter in his life. He laughed to release his tension and revel in the energy of the moment. If only she had responded to his text. He positioned his mobile to the side of his laptop and returned to studying his numbers.

Chapter 3 - Chinese Whispers

Colin stepped out of the hotel foyer and steeled his eyes for the whirlwind of activity in front of him. God, it's busy he thought, and slipped on his Gucci sunglasses. It was 5:30 in the morning and Zhongshan Road was already a hive of pollution - cars, buses, motorbikes, bicycles all pushing and rushing to work. The limousine was waiting; sleek, heavy and important. He smiled at the smartness of the car and ran his fingers through his gelled black hair. His heavy briefcase swung effortlessly in time to his boss-man walk. Tensing the frame of his wide and muscular shoulders, he re-adjusted his power tie with his free hand.

Colin smiled at the chauffeur and, giving him a slight wave that meant wait a moment, he decided spontaneously to cross the road and peer across the Bund to Huangpu River. The Bund was a section on Zhongshan Road with a cultural mix of architecture: Western Neoclassical, Art Deco and impressive modern design all jostled for attention. He normally had little time for admiring buildings, or river views for that matter, but today he was feeling ahead of the game, and generous with his time. Taking a deep breath he looked out at the odd collection of marine boats moving noisily by. In China it seemed, there was always noise even at 5:30 in the morning. The eclectic mix of boats was a story in itself: cargo ships a city block long or more and tourist ocean liners charged aggressively past old river barges and the delicate ribbed sails of Chinese junk boats. The dominant and powerful lined up against the considerably weak and insignificant. He likened himself to the former; he was part of that new culture - those new opportunities - enabling the Chinese to think about its dominance and future security. He was one of their enablers but as well he needed them to enable his success.

Today, he was in a mega-meeting, as he called it. A meeting that could make or break the deal. It had just about been on the brink of collapse a few weeks ago but was now almost all-go. Colin was a heavy-weight, a high profile figure, but he would need more than his reputation today. He was expected to provide scientific evidence over the next two days that the technology he represented was as advanced as he claimed, and that his and Richard's acquisition bid for the company that owned the technology was progressing successfully. He also was keen to ensure his Chinese partners were comfortable with the funds he was investing in their production plans. They had agreed a joint deal, and although Colin had ensured his part of the bargain was minimal - he also thought investment in this Chinese production facility could provide decent long term profit.

In return, Colin was looking for evidence of significant investment from his Chinese partners; investment to create mass production facilities for the new technology. They also needed to provide evidence of documented know-how to turn this unique and emerging technology into mass production. The last few weeks had been high drama for Colin, but he was now in a position to provide all the financial evidence required for his and Richard's side of the deal. And if it all fell to plan, by tomorrow he would have conclusive scientific evidence which the Chinese were keen to see.

He'd had an overall pleasant evening the night before with his Chinese hosts. The food was top notch, but that wasn't what had left him humming this morning when he woke up. It was the pleasures of the hostesses – one in particular – that even now had his pulse running, gunning him up for his dominance today. That kind of excitement, he loved it. The dare of finding the most alluring girl in the room and then enticing her. The coy flirting, and the power of changing the look in her eyes from professionalism masking distrust – even distaste in some cases – to a look of hope and innocence. It was a dangerous game: vying for the best girl when his Chinese counterparts were also eyeing up the most dazzling hostesses. But, he believed his success always commanded respect from his Chinese investors, if not a begrudging respect. In any case, he got a lot out of these meetings: inside information, quiet secrets and delicious entertainment. It always left him buzzed, on fire for his meetings the next day.

It also meant that he didn't suffer from the lack of passion with his beautiful, perfect wife. He sighed as he always did when he thought of Katherine. She was ideal posing beside him, and her pedigree added much credibility to his business brand. His business was a service that 'delivered investment strategy, driving long-term wealth and growth.' He chuckled at the strap-line and how often he dropped her family name into business conversations. Then, his mouth grimaced. Katherine had become a necessary pain in his life, as she grew closer to their only child and he, in turn, grew further away from her.

That child - such an effort he thought, although she was a beautiful little girl and completed his picture perfect family. The run up to conceiving her had been a nightmare, and had driven both he and Katherine in different directions. That, combined with Katherine's own business success had made it difficult for her to prioritise Colin in her life - and in Colin's life he was the only priority.

First born in a family of title, land and wealth, he'd always been the priority of his parents. He didn't take well to being second priority with anyone, especially his wife who had known him since they were children, and had always it seemed, till the latest years, looked up to him and his success.

The whole thing had become a necessary inconvenience, he thought. But he smiled - an inconvenience that was worth the wait - she had become a true asset recently given the situation with his own family fortunes. He left the sidewalk and returned to the chauffeur. He enjoyed seeing the chauffeur move quickly to serve him and open the polished black door. He grinned at the man and felt the power from the night before. This was going to be a good business trip. He knew it, and smoothly tucking in his tie and taking his seat, he settled in for the long drive ahead.

~ ~ ~ ~ ~ ~ ~ ~ ~ ~

Ahh, the crisp autumn air. And the sun - so incredibly bright and warm. Thomas dismounted his bike and pushed it up the Cotswold pebbled drive of Katherine's home. He always exalted at the energy the sweeping rows of beech trees gave him when he cycled between them. They were lordly and imposing but in a comforting way, not domineering. They protected the drive and grandly announced the visitors, preparing them for the palatial house perfectly balanced at their rounded tip.

He loved this home, almost as much as the Palladian home of his family where he grew up. Katherine's home had been built over many architectural periods. Its most recent addition, the 18th Century south front of the house and associated rooms were designed by Robert Adam and were the quintessential Neoclassical view that greeted visitors at the top of the drive. Sitting there too, grandly spouting, was an elaborate fountain fashioned after Greek mythology.

Although he appreciated the architecture of the house, it was because of the women who lived here that made him so fond of it. Or had lived, he sadly reflected. Thomas pondered on the past six weeks and the death of Katherine's mother. It was a crush to them all, except he couldn't help but notice as time moved on, to his brother. He frowned, as he often did with situations involving his brother. Colin was the eldest and grandest by far. His lifestyle was polished and shiny with success. He had a beautiful wife, a booming career in City investments and an adorable, healthy daughter. Colin also had had a celebrity mother-in-law, who was known widely for her garden designs, respected in their social circle and whom he leveraged whenever he could. But that had gone now, and in her place was a large property that Thomas guessed, Katherine now owned.

Thomas was uncomfortable with the situation. It was widely known that Thomas normally dropped in on Katherine, her mother and daughter, while his brother was off on his business trips. Thomas could manage this given he lived locally to Katherine, and his fertility practice was only a commutable train ride away in London. He would often accompany Katherine and her mother on the social circuit when his brother was abroad. With his own parents deceased for some time, he enjoyed visiting Katherine's mother, who had been a fond friend of his own mother. And he was absolutely besotted with his niece, Maisy, who loved her Uncle Thomas.

However, in the last few years with Thomas' reputation spreading globally, he'd spent more and more time lecturing across the UK and abroad, consulting on fertility treatments, best practice and his clinic's research. This meant he had less time to accompany Katherine and be with his niece. With the death in the family, he had cancelled all work abroad bar his most recent trip to the States. Going forward, he planned to spend a few months locally, so he could support Katherine.

Thomas rested his bike on the grand garden wall, and surveyed the deep border with roses trained along it. So perfectly clipped by the gardener each year. He followed a long and slightly twisted rose branch meandering several meters up the wall and his mind wandered as he thought back over the last few years.

Katherine's design hobby had blossomed into a growing online business and her busy life meant pressures and stresses. It had slowly become apparent that she and Colin were struggling to have the child that Katherine was hoping for. It was her mother who had suggested that Katherine seek Thomas' advice; after all she had said, 'he's a renowned fertility expert on our own doorstep, and a trusted family member'.

Thomas smiled as he remembered the hope in Katherine's face when she first visited his clinic. He squinted his eyes and ran his hand through his hair. Colin, however, had been less than keen. He'd reluctantly accepted his brother's assistance. He reflected on one of the private conversations Katherine's mother had with him, during the fertility treatment. Her eyes had been disapproving and she shared with Thomas that she found Colin's demeanour to Katherine and his consistent lack of support in seeking fertility expertise both odd and unacceptable.

Thomas' groundbreaking fertility treatment worked wonders on Katherine and Colin as well, but only after a year of difficult demands on Katherine. Thomas thought of the strain it had put on the couple's relationship. In that space of time, Katherine and Colin had grown apart, and Colin's relationship with Thomas had also become difficult. One brother's failure was the other's success, but not in the natural order it had always been.

He sighed. His brother appeared on the face of it so responsible, and yet, he was far from it. Thomas double-checked his bike wasn't resting on any plants and instead of heading to the imposing stairs leading to the front door of the mansion, he headed to the garden door set within the high Cotswold stone wall, about twelve foot tall. The roses arched impeccably over the door and he stood back a moment to admire them. He'd had a hard day, with some challenging cases. The abundance and fragrance of the roses worked their magic on him. He took a deep breath and the demands of the day slipped away.

He turned the heavy twisted metal loop handle on the garden door, testing it. The door was as usual, unlocked. Pushing open the thick door he stepped through - only to have a bird swoop in front of him. He pulled back, laughing, and smiled again at the freshness of the day. With Colin in China, and having returned himself from the States only yesterday, Thomas was popping in on Katherine to see how she was faring. He was concerned that she was still not her normal self when he left for the States a week ago. Typically very involved in her company, Katherine hadn't been to work since her mother's death. She'd also shown little interest in understanding the affairs of the family that her own mother had managed for so long, and that was very unlike her inquisitive nature.

But there was something else Thomas had noticed.

The funeral came to mind immediately. It wasn't a single action, or a single moment, it was, he realised, the whole funeral. There was a crack in the family veneer and in the sincerity of the funeral, and that was telling.

At the funeral, Katherine had behaved differently. Thomas recognised she was in sorrow but on reflection, he noticed that she wasn't so carefully gracious with her husband. She was distant, almost cold towards him. He knew she had tried – that she had tried to reconnect with her husband since Maisy's birth. She had genuinely worked to keep their relationship going. But at the funeral, it was obvious now to Thomas, she was completely feigning it. There was no warmth and in its place was an aloofness in her behaviour towards Colin. In fact, there had been a complete lack of touch. For someone as loving as Katherine, normally with her arm around her daughter or linked arms with her husband, he realised that he had not seen her touch her husband for the duration of the funeral.

Hmmm, he was definitely keen to see Katherine and make sure she was ok.

Colin wasn't due back from China till the end of the week so perhaps he'd invite her to dinner. He headed toward the Orangery where her home office was, hoping to find her there.

~ ~ ~ ~ ~ ~ ~ ~ ~ ~

Anjali was in a very still pose. Working from home, she normally had to remind herself to take breaks from her laptop. But today she couldn't focus and was distracted. Her hands hovered over the keyboard and her gaze looked out over the fields past her back garden. She had a strong intellect, terribly capable of focusing but today had been such an odd day so far, she couldn't focus on her research.

She'd been relieved to drop the children off at school so she could resume work and finish off her research. At school she'd seen Maisy and Katherine say goodbye. Anjali had lined Sara and Arun up in their classroom queues and had walked towards Katherine to check if she'd like a cup of tea when they collected the children later. But as Anjali was moving across the playground maze, Katherine had already waved a short hello to Anjali and was off towards her car. Anjali could take a cue, and had turned to walk the distance home. However, it was very unlike Katherine and she worried her friend was still in a difficult place with the death of her mother.

Later, whilst preparing tea at home, Anjali had received the most bizarre text message. Her eyes had opened wide as she read it and she carelessly scalded her hand on the kettle. She had to then reread the message. Double checking it was indeed from her director, she clicked her tongue, annoyed that she had misread its meaning.

And that in fact, was the cause of her distraction. Had she misread the meaning? Irked that she would even consider her boss might act in any way unprofessionally towards her, she wondered why he had texted such an odd message. Her boss had seemed different these last few weeks. She frowned as she searched for examples. He was obviously deeply involved in some business transaction. She could tell he was invigorated by the activity; the deal must be closing soon.

But she had also noticed his eyes, the change in his eyes. He looked at her differently, with more possessiveness than he usually did. And he was possessive. She was one of his key employees and none of the other directors were allowed to ask her to work on their accounts. He also paid her well, very well, after her initial pay 'wobble' when she'd shyly requested a revised remuneration package that valued her contribution to the business despite her part-time capacity. In any case, part-time was an illusion she had pointed out, given the demanding hours. Richard panicked that he could lose her and to ensure she stuck by his side, paid her more than she'd requested.

'Anjali great news, dinner at L'Esplanade this Fri. Late nite. Business of course.'

The text really, really made her uncomfortable. Why would he say 'business of course' other than to make her suspicious it wasn't 'business of course'? Anjali shook her head. She admonished herself for being so wrongly suspicious of her boss. In any case, not only did it jar against his always professional conduct towards her, but it was simply unimaginable that he would be inclined any way other than professionally towards her.

His taste in women and life in general was the complete opposite of what her life represented. Her life was comparatively simple, and she was a practical woman. Practical and down to earth in mind, dress and lifestyle. He was all about image - his personal shopper, his women, his lifestyle. And he was as well, let us not ignore the fact, Anjali pursed her lips, a very stunning individual.

She thought of him at their last City meeting. He was definitely a handsome person and she recognised that men as well as women were attracted by his demeanour and schoolboy looks. At the meeting, his black suit was tailored perfectly across his broad shoulders and he so effortlessly commanded the room, a room full of respected and experienced individuals. He was standing at the head of the conference table, looking at each person, pulling them into his story. He was electric and slowly they all bought into his vision.

Throughout the meeting, he would occasionally take a few steps sideways and lock eyes with Anjali, sitting at the presentation laptop. She was bothered but somewhat complimented that he often teased her that she was his muse. After that city meeting when they were later alone, tidying away the glossy papers, she congratulated him.

He flashed her a charming smile in response. 'Hey, you know, I simply look at your confident pose, and know that without a doubt all the background work that you've done, will make this deal a sure bet.'

Anjali thought back to the looks he gave her that day. There was possessiveness, as she had already thought but there was also fondness and sadness. Now, what was that about? Did he think she was going to a competitor? Ridiculous thought, she had no time to respond to competitor queries on LinkedIn, nor indeed to network contacts who invited her to lunch to 'talk over opportunities.'

Anjali decisively turned to her mobile and texted: 'Will check with James and get back to you. C u Wed.'

Wednesday was her sole day at the office, with Monday and today, Tuesday, being the other days she worked, but from home. She quickly texted James: 'OK if I meet Richard Friday night? Some big deal to finalise. Let me know. Love R.'

She parked her worries deep away in her mind, and returned to her laptop, looking for that elusive statistic she had needed.

~ ~ ~ ~ ~ ~ ~ ~ ~ ~

The city eventually fell away. Shanghai really had no suburbs, it was simply one huge heaving city. After several hours, the housing thinned out and the countryside emerged. Colin shifted his eyes from his laptop at this point, to look out over the fields of agriculture. What were they growing, he wondered? The limo parked to the side of a barely visible road, and slowed to a halt.

The chauffeur who he'd assumed didn't speak English, looked at him through his rear view mirror and said, 'I'm under instruction at this point to await another car which will drive you the final distance to your destination.'

'What for?' asked Colin.

'I don't question my orders, Sir. I can see the car now in any case.' And sure enough from this tiny lane emerged a perfect British Land Rover. The car pulled up in front of the limo, and the two back doors opened simultaneously. Two serious-looking men in matching suits emerged from the car. They looked of Chinese background and began to speak impeccable English.

Colin emerged from his limo and shook their hands.

'Come with us, we'll drive you to your meeting,' said one of the gentlemen, his face with the same unemotional and professional expression as his colleague.

'Thank you. Not sure why there's a car exchange,' guffawed Colin. He sat in the back of the Land Rover with the two men. A third gentleman was already behind the wheel. Slowly, the limo backed out of the tiny road and turned in the direction of the city, back from where it came. Precautions had been taken before when the deals were highly sensitive, but this seemed more careful than necessary.

'Sir, the travel must be confidential from this point. We apologise but we've been ordered to keep the location confidential.' The man to his right produced a black cloth. A blindfold thought Colin? The gentleman moved to wrap it around Colin's eyes. Colin couldn't help but react and instinctively blocked the man from nearing his eyes.

'Hey – is this really necessary? I'm not very comfortable with this,' again, Colin expressed his discomfort at the approach to secrecy.

'Sir it won't be too long,' was their singular reply. Colin realised his hands were tensed as well as his torso and he worked at releasing the stress he felt. Calm, be calm, he thought. He didn't want them to see his tension, so he laughed his reply,

'Right, if it's necessary, then please, proceed,' and they did, wrapping the cloth around his eyes. He was in total darkness. They sped off and drove for sometime. His initial tension eased and he felt himself slowly drift off to the rhythm of the car.

Eventually, they stopped. He awoke with a jolt as they fingered the knot on his blindfold. With the blindfold off, he blinked to a state of awareness and took stock. Colin had fallen asleep, for which he was thankful given the late night - but it meant he wasn't aware how long they'd been travelling.

The car was at the entrance of a large iron gate attached to what looked like a high-security walled fortress. On either side of the gate were concrete walls leading off for several hundred metres.

The driver showed an identity card to the gatekeeper who had a good look at Colin and then they swept through under the steel-framed gate. They headed straight for what Colin suspected was the main building.

They were waiting for Colin at reception: a group of five men that included three senior Chinese officials, he could tell by their suits. In fact, he thought he recognised one of them from the government ranks - was that possible? His two main hosts from the night before and previous visits, were there grinning at him.

Big smiles, but serious eyes, all five greeted him warmly with handshakes and murmured welcomes. He smiled extra wide at his hosts from the previous evening. They made quite a deal of him and he relaxed. He felt more in command, more domineering than dominated. They walked him to a discrete elevator off reception. One of the men placed his finger on the biometric sensor. The elevator doors opened and they waved him in first.

Colin's muscles tensed. The man he suspected to be from the government ranks had exposed a gun slightly under his blazer. Colin looked quickly to his main host from the night before. He'd followed Colin's gaze to the gun and locked eyes with him.

'You are not to worry. Protocol for secret service. We have much to talk about when we sit down.' Again he grinned at Colin, but it was an twisted, intimidating grin.

Chapter 4 - Secrets

James strode to the boardroom door and opened it to reception. Three professionally suited men sat in reception. He greeted them warmly by first name and shook hands. They were confident, approachable and expecting James to say something. He smiled. 'It's great news. They're on board.'

The atmosphere relaxed. The men smiled at James and were visibly pleased. They knew how important James's team was to him and how carefully he'd considered them in the decision he was about to make. He ushered his visitors into the boardroom then glanced around reception carefully to check no one saw them from the parking area outside. He let out a contented breath and closed the door behind them.

James introduced the visitors to his team waiting in the boardroom. Then, he proudly talked about his colleagues: their backgrounds, their contributions, their dedication. It was important to him that the team and each individual was valued by the visitors.

'I was just briefing my team on the business at hand. This is the first they've been aware of the situation,' he gave a friendly nod to his colleagues.

As the two groups exchanged greetings there was a tangible buzz in the air, of excitement and of nervousness too. James poured the coffee. This was an important moment. He was both relieved and exultant, now that it had finally come to this. James addressed his visitors, 'Perhaps you'd like to start the session, setting the premise for the day, and any protocol necessary?'

One gentleman nodded, put down his coffee mug and began, 'Today is a very important day for your business and recognises your work over recent years. It's also a momentous day in fact, for Britain.' He grinned at those around the table, all with earnest faces and listening intently.

'And this,' he pulled out a folder with documents within and looked to James, 'is where we start.'

~ ~ ~ ~ ~ ~ ~ ~ ~ ~

Edward was pulled from his newspaper with the 'pop' of the toaster. He stretched and reached for the Wedgwood dish to butter the crumpet; toasted perfectly as Katherine would like it. He thought about what he'd just read and was eager to read more. A snippet on the same subject had shown up on his mobile earlier in the morning, but it had not engaged him as much as this newspaper article did. He needed to know more about what was unfolding, as it definitely had an impact.

He glanced around the room. It was such a beautiful kitchen, even now he felt inspired when he was in the room.

Katherine had involved him in the kitchen redesign some years ago when she was first married. Together, he and Katherine had planned the complete overhaul. It wasn't just design, it was a house extension as well.

'Edward, I have this vision of a large, bright, timeless family kitchen. Perfect for children but for entertaining, too. Here, let me walk you through these,' and she had shown him clippings, photos, Pinterest, instagram, and of course her own designs.

'Pale grey cabinets, a marble countertop for your famous bread doughs, Edward, and a butcher block would all be lovely here. Simple lines. The dishes, pots and pans should be hidden away but easily accessible within wide drawers that have the softest open/close when pushed,' they had laughed together at the sticky drawers of the old pine cabinets in the kitchen the time.

Some dishes, her special ones from her mother, grandmother, great-grandmother, and indeed a remarkable number still remaining from her even earlier heritage, were to be displayed in two beautiful pale wooden cabinets with backlighting, flanking either side of the kitchen.

'Not old world country, more modern but with a timeless twist,' she'd shown him more of her own hand drawings, 'you know what I mean,' looking at him in total trust.

Those eyes! Such eyes - almost as deep and soft and trusting as her mother's. He'd gone on to work with Katherine on the full rebuild: the kitchen conservatory; kitchen bar and stool by the cooking section and of course, the oak frame extension for the kitchen dining area. There, she had wanted to keep the kitchen table from her childhood. Beams overhead were exposed and the whole effect was one of light, sophistication, and impeccable design. In fact, the kitchen had been the catalyst to her online success. Katherine had already set up a hobby design business whilst she worked at the investment firm in the town. It was a hobby, for friends and colleagues, and she delighted in the design work, more for the challenge, not the income. She oftentimes wouldn't charge for her design projects, but soon, the dynamics changed.

With the internet and social media, Katherine was quick to document her kitchen makeover on her small design website, as well as other key marketing platforms such as Pinterest, Instagram, YouTube and Facebook. She documented everything: her kitchen design thought process, her progress, Edward's involvement and tips for the 'perfect kitchen' from her 'perfect butler'. Before she realised it, people from across the country and abroad were following her on Pinterest, liking her YouTube videos and ordering her small selection of lifestyle products on her website.

In a very short space of time, once the kitchen was complete, requests came through to quote for kitchen makeovers and conservatories. When she documented her makeover of the garden Orangery, an iconic design of Robert Adam, she was overwhelmed by the fascination shown by her followers and clients. There were several requests for some breathtakingly grander versions still, as well as a significant demand for smaller versions of the Orangery. It was odd. She and Edward had thought that Orangeries were few and far between, but the requests for Orangeries were incessant.

There was demand for television appearances, coffee table books, product branding, magazine covers - it seemed she was a phenomena which her new followers simply couldn't get enough of. It wasn't surprising that shortly after her social media sensation, she left her role at the investment firm.

There had been career offers for Edward on the back of his involvement, but he was too busy with the family estate and his own affairs. Katherine's mother paid him handsomely and he was easily able to fit in his life-time hobby of playing the markets and investing. Edward's family had had such a long history of serving the family, he was content to stay with them. They loved him all the more for this.

He caught a sharp breath. Katherine's mother. Had she really loved him? She did have the capacity to love, one only had to look at her daughter for that. She'd been a hands-on single mother. Even in later years she was immensely interested and proud of her daughter's work. Having herself experienced celebrity status with her horticulture work - her publications, magazine articles, and several television appearances - she was able to guide Katherine through the onslaught of requests.

Edward remembered her remark, 'How different it is starting out now with social media, it's so constant, no downtime.' He thought wryly of how her early guidance to Katherine was to pace herself and not flood the media and market with too much. This gave Katherine more time to plan larger projects and indeed grow her lifestyle company as she wanted. Yes, her mother was a strong woman, loving to Katherine and wise.

His breath caught just above his lungs and tightened his breathing. Her death. He missed her presence deeply. Yes, she was wise, but not so very wise. He winced as he tried to repress the flood of panic he felt.

The crumpet. Edward was jolted to the present. He took a long slow breath, breathing with his stomach as he knew he should, and closed his eyes for some time. When he opened them the darkness at the edge of his sight came back into full vision and focus. Recovered from his moment, he went on auto-pilot. He embellished the cream plate with a small jar of local jam, a spot of clotted cream, and a few slices of banana. He placed the plate, a teacup and saucer plus a matching Wedgwood teapot with brewing tea all on a silver tray.

He set off to bring the tray to Katherine in the Orangery. He glanced with concern at the papers again before he left, checking the Financial Times headline and Investor Chronicle pages he'd left open. He thought he'd dealt with those issues, given his recent injection of cash. He frowned. He'd have to look into this further.

~ ~ ~ ~ ~ ~ ~ ~ ~ ~

Katherine was heady not just because of the perfumed leaves of the lemon, lime and orange trees in the Orangery but because of the tasks that lay ahead of her. She was finally taking ownership of her mother's legacy and her own inheritance, and had much to review with the family solicitors. Second, she most certainly had to get back to her senior management team at her company. Much had happened in the last six weeks and most of it required her input or sign off.

But, there was another new task: understanding and solving that note. It was the catalyst she needed to take on the coroner's decision and address the issues that had been playing in her mind.

She sat quietly in the Orangery contemplating the note. The building was originally home to the family citrus trees, and had stood still in time over the last two hundred and fifty years. Now however, it was home to the design inspirations for her company. It was maintained at a monitored temperature so that she and the citrus trees could live together comfortably over the winter months. For now, only the most delicate of the citrus trees joined her, the gardener placing them in their allocated spots, in fear of an early frost hitting the estate. Their elegance and Mediterranean allure complimented her working space perfectly and contributed to the indoor/outdoor look of the Orangery; a warmth of a home and the freshness of a garden working together. The remaining citrus trees were outside on the Orangery terrace and were a fine finish to the lime tree avenue that led visitors from the house to the Robert Adams designed Orangery.

Normally Katherine would have her etchings, fabric samples, and mood boards spread across her supersized Oval Table in the Orangery. This table was another of her designs: a pale beige wicker style with glass top that stood close to an arched window, for the best light. The table was sized for planning and designing, almost military-style one magazine article had reported, 'like a King Arthur's roundtable'. Indeed, the family since referred to it as 'the round table' when in fact, it was hugely oval. Katherine and her mother had laughed at that incongruous nickname, but delighted in it. Incongruity could work in the world of design and so, the nickname held. It was, after all, a special table.

But Katherine wasn't at her round table. She was sitting tensely in the grand wicker chair her mother had loved to sit in, when visiting Katherine at her work.

The note was so hard to interpret.

She squinted at the text, playing with the words and the numbers.

> *Eco friendly as you asked. Rock solid.*
>
> *1190563 srt 409456*
>
> *No more niceties now, we are proceeding*
>
> *By end of play today. There can be NO DELAY.*
>
> *Remember NDA and trust no one.*
>
> TRUST NO ONE

'Ok, let's start with the obvious,' Katherine thought out loud, 'an NDA is a 'non-disclosure agreement'. What would mother be so involved in, that required her to sign an NDA, as this message seems to imply? If she did sign an NDA she couldn't talk to anyone about this note or the information it alludes to. And why trust no one? Why would mother repeat this in capitals? She must have been very concerned about the situation.'

Katherine stared outside. What do they mean no more niceties? Do they mean mother being nice, or indeed, is this the author of the note saying he or she won't be pleasant anymore? And for sure, the author is expressing urgency.

'I know I saw her open her desk drawer in the study the night before her death, just before bed, and I certainly didn't see the note. She'd put some scissors in her drawer, alongside her other special knick-knacks. I surely would have noticed it as I did today. Even if the note was stuck in the back of the drawer, she would never have been as calm as she was. She didn't seem agitated or nervous when she opened the drawer,' she spoke out loud again and thought through the sequence of events.

That was Tuesday night but *when* had her mother received the note?

'End of day' was that Tuesday, or had she received the note on Wednesday? If her mother had received the note Tuesday, the day before her death, then was it possible she was unable to deliver whatever the author expected by the end of the day? And was her death the next morning, on Wednesday, an accident, or was it linked to events from the previous day?

She looked at the note again. Eco friendly, whatever could this mean? Mother was very keen to reduce plastics across the Estate, was it something to do with that? Someone helping her in her quest to be as environmentally friendly as possible?

The collection of numbers puzzled her: seven numbers, then 'srt' then six numbers. Again, she spoke out loud to seek clarity.

'A combination to a lock? A code?' Katherine couldn't understand how her mother would have become so involved in a situation where the author of such a note was outwardly threatening. Her mother wasn't secretive, at least not that she had ever known her to be. And she knew her mother very, very well.

Rock-solid. What did that mean? Fail-safe, low risk?

'Right, time to return to mother's study and check through her papers and laptop,' and she pushed herself from the supporting cushions to stand.

'Hello Miss Katherine, your tea and crumpet,' Edward announced his presence at the entrance of the Orangery with his silver tray and a pleased smile.

'Ah, yes!' Katherine squeezed her hand shut around the note. 'Here, let me make a space for that tray. Thank you, Edward.' She smiled gratefully and cleared the side table by the wicker chair. Edward elegantly deposited his tray and checked whether she needed anything else. His mind was distracted and he was keen to return to his investments and papers.

'I'm fine, Edward, thank you,' Katherine smiled gently. Edward returned the smile absently and left immediately for the house.

She closed her eyes and sighed. A bite to eat would be good. She'd been so spotty with her food over the last few weeks. The next few hours would be engrossing, best to have a bite here, now, and shake her thoughts out before going through her mother's papers and affairs in the study. She planned also to meet the family solicitors perhaps tomorrow. They had been keen to talk to her, but Colin had stepped in to help, giving her space at the time.

She put the note back in her pocket, to enjoy her tea.

The tea was just perfect, her favourite, Empress Grey. But it wasn't always called that. It was rumoured that the tea was an old family recipe from a tea holding in Sri Lanka that her family had owned for over 100 years. Although the property wasn't in the family anymore the background still entertained her mother. All those years ago, in the late 1800's her ancestor had created a special Ceylon blend for his wife.

Fast forward to a great royal event in British history. When the Tsar Nicholas II and his wife Empress Alexandra of Russia visited the British royal family at Cowes on the Isle of Wight in 1909, Katherine's ancestors were invited to the formal festivities. She remembered her 87 year old great-grandmother recounting the story to her when she was about ten years old. In 1909 her great-grandmother was only a one year old baby, but her parents would sometimes tell the story again at tea time as her great-grandmother grew up.

It had been an exclusive invitation. King George Vl knew Katherine's family well. With the invitation came an interesting request: to provide the tea for the Tsar's visit - specifically the exquisite tea gifted to King George VI earlier in the year. It was tea from their Sri Lankan plantation.

So delighted was the Empress with the tea, that she had several boxes of it returned with her, to Russia. Somehow, many, many decades later, a British high street retailer was looking for a niche tea offering. They happened upon the story and sourced the family tea from the Sri Lankan estate. Archives at the estate were researched and the tea blend resurrected. The tea company and the high street retailer agreed a commercial contract for the supply of this blended and fruit-infused tea which they called, 'Empress Grey'. And so this small interesting piece of family history was now a tea offered widely on the high street. Katherine's mother had found that history so entertaining....

Katherine laughed remembering her mother, and sighed contentedly sipping her favourite tea. She enjoyed her snack. The crumpet was perfect. It was all perfect, but she still felt sad as she gazed out towards the garden. Why couldn't she accept the death of her mother as an accident?

~ ~ ~ ~ ~ ~ ~ ~ ~ ~

From the garden doorway, Thomas looked towards the Orangery where he hoped Katherine would be, and paused to appreciate the landscaped gardens. His own family home was beautiful, although he rarely visited. Ownership had passed to Colin when his father died and then as Colin eventually established himself at Katherine's estate, Colin had decided to lease the ancient family property to a celebrity tenant. The estate came with two full-time gardeners and was ideal for entertaining. The grounds had been designed by Lancelot 'Capability' Brown and was a romantic landscape. But Thomas thought Katherine's garden, and the view from the house, although not as grand, were certainly one of the most picturesque in the Cotswolds.

Katherine's garden was renowned: it was hard to know where to focus the eyes and easier to simply sweep in the full grandeur and beauty of the design. The effort and care put into the many dozen landscaped sections of the garden was obvious to even those who weren't green-fingered.

There was the twelve foot high garden wall he had just been through, of pale creamy cotswold stone, clothed with the most common and adventurous climbers, fruit trees, and roses. Large sections of the wall had cool and then warm colours of herbaceous plants; borders 2 meter's deep in front of the wall. The wall continued for acres and was still maintained throughout the estate. The original garden design was by Gertrude Jekyll, with avenues of colour-blocked herbaceous borders and it still today, retained most features of her design. Thomas was familiar with Jekyll's design theory - she delighted in ordinary plants like lavender and old roses. She believed in hard landscape features so that certain plants could be better displayed, and shine in a variety of settings. To Jekyll though, everything was natural and not contrived - it was a philosophy that reminded him of Katherine's family.

His family's land on the other hand, with the Capability Brown landscape was, although 100 years older and with its own recognised natural beauty, was in fact, far from natural. His ancestors devoured the land based on Brown's design concepts, and moved hills, created lakes, and slightly unbelievably, relocated a whole village to accommodate the new landscape. Brown had designed a new Gothic-style

Church for his landscape design at Thomas' family estate. He advocated that by relocating the village, the view across the 'natural', romantic landscape would be untarnished. Thomas' family agreed and the village was moved. His family had always been about show - even to the present day.

He blinked to bring his mind back to the view that lay before him. There was the lime tree avenue from study to Orangery. Absolutely perfectly balanced, and minutely pruned for the length of the avenue. It was precisely 100 meters. The avenue always enthralled visitors. Halfway down the avenue were two openings opposite each other, framed with identical archways of wisteria and rose. The archways extended to pergolas structured ten meters in length, with many varieties of rose and clematis winding among the wisteria. Each of these pergolas ended in a formal sitting area amongst scented herbs, lavender, bay and olive standards.

The gardens on either side of the lime tree avenue were sectioned in half by the long pergolas - creating four enclosed sections of garden. Each quarter comprised pristine English lawns, with space enough for a large magnolia in the centre. The magnolias blossomed majestically in the spring and dominated in the summer. The family knew the magnolias to be 100 years or older and the effect in the spring was stunning. The base of the magnolias had elegant sitting areas and the lawns beneath the trees were radiant with circular displays of daffodils and then later, tulips and hyacinths in the spring.

In front of the Orangery, was a pathway to the right, which led to the kitchen garden. Much of this garden was walled, creating a warm microclimate. The stone walls of the kitchen garden reflected the heat for the summer fruit trees and berry bushes. It's organic produce graced the family's table and was shared with tenants on the family estate. There were also the stables, tennis courts, and of course more recently, the outdoor heated swimming pool which had been installed so Maisy could learn how to swim.

And then, beyond the Orangery was the lavender path to the river. Thomas unconsciously frowned.

He closed the heavy oak garden door behind him and plucked a fragrant pink rose from the garden wall. It had been baking in the sun and was warm. He then headed diagonally across the lawn towards the Orangery. He was hopeful Katherine would be there.

~ ~ ~ ~ ~ ~ ~ ~ ~ ~

Edward's mind was elsewhere as he returned from the Orangery to the house. He jumped when a sudden, 'Hello Edward,' was shouted out to him.

'Ah, Thomas, what a fright you gave me. I didn't see you there! You're back, how did it go?' They spoke as equals although Thomas perceived a slight hesitation from Edward. Thomas very briefly highlighted his travels and the numerous conferences he'd presented at. Katherine's mother and Edward had been supportive of Thomas when he was growing up, when his own parents had been much focused on his older brother.

Edward was interested, but it was obvious that he was eager to return to the house. Thomas was just as eager to see

Katherine. They wished each other a good day, and Thomas continued towards the Orangery.

Chapter 5 - Expectations

Colin emerged from the meeting. He was exhausted. It was a complex deal, and all the more complex now that they had involved officials and the secret service! They had not properly explained who the officials were exactly but it was a link to the Chinese state and it added a layer of difficulty. In fact, layers of difficulty.

This was supposed to be a strictly business deal, no politics, no state involvement, services or interventions. It was a difficult situation now. Should the British authorities get wind of this, it would be very tricky. God, he wished his partners hadn't exposed him in this way. If they had to involve state characters, it could've been done quietly, behind closed doors after the deal.

He knew there was a long return drive back to the hotel, the blindfold, the whole shenanigans. He was exhausted and annoyed as the challenges took shape in front of him, and the work he would need to do, to overcome them. For another person, the difficulty might have stretched beyond their ethics and code of conduct.....but to Colin, the difficulties were all in the complex negotiations which now had to take place. And he had to tell Richard. They ushered him off into the Land Rover, his blindfold on, and he was left to his planning, on the long ride back to the limo pick up point, then on to his hotel.

~~~~~~~~~~

Edward put duty first. He checked the AGA where his pie was baking, then popped on the kettle for a new cup of tea. He felt the excitement in his belly as he finally sat down to his paper. Yes, it was as he thought, it will impact him. He checked his mobile app to cross-reference his suspicions and determine the steps he could take. There were several. One of course, he had already tried. He paused and grimaced unwittingly. So options two or three were left - and he decided just now, on option three. The kettle had long-since boiled so he clicked it to reboil; this time he would drink his tea.

~~~~~~~~~~

Katherine relaxed a moment in the Orangery to eat her crumpet, and looked out across the lime tree avenue. She stretched her neck, and yes, her heart beat quickly, she saw a familiar figure appearing, tall, lanky, striding his way up the avenue.

She grinned happily and jumping up from her chair, walked towards the avenue. Thomas picked up his gate and with wide smiles they said hello and embraced closely for several seconds.

As they pulled away from each other, Thomas felt his throat constrict. This thing, it was so difficult, he thought as he looked at her face. She looked so well, so beautiful still, in spite of her stress.

Katherine was comforted by his reassuring embrace. She pulled back and checked him over.

'Well you look the same,' she teased. 'Those Americans haven't changed you yet, still British in your dress - and British in your accent?' she coaxed him to talk about his trip.

He presented the rose to her, and then they walked in step, back towards the Orangery. He filled her in on the cities he had visited, the lecture circuit, the Universities, the foundations. Katherine pulled his arm close and looped hers through his. She so loved his success and his work. It was meaningful and innovative and she loved his cleverness and ability to always push science. Since her own personal experience with the clinic, she had taken an even closer interest in his developments and success. It had made such a difference in her life, she knew it did in others too.

When they reached the Orangery, she popped over to a wooden cabinet and pulled another teacup and saucer from its display. She poured him his tea, and tried to keep the topic on his work although she knew what was coming. Thomas was always frank with her and open, so she was certain he'd come to visit not to talk at length about his trip, that wasn't his way, but to talk to her about her mother. And she had news to tell him of course, but she wondered, was it news she could share?

'And so Katherine, enough about me - what about you?' he gently nudged.

She sighed. It would be good to off-load her suspicions, and she turned to him with candour, hoping he might be able to help solve her concerns, as he often did.

'Look, Thomas, it's been difficult. You know me and there's no sense hiding this from you. I'm really struggling to deal with my mother's...' and here she paused not dramatically but painfully, 'my mother's death. My mind is also not focused on work, and I miss that as well. I'll be sorting that out shortly. I'll throw this in too, but I'm also worried about Colin.'

Thomas was watching Katherine closely. Her last comment surprised him, and he was careful to hold back until she had finished.

'I think if I'd been prepared it would have been easier to deal with the death; if mother had been unwell or unfit, but she was neither. And she was always careful. It plays over and over in my mind, her death, how could it have happened. And,' she glanced at Thomas to check his expression, 'I don't believe it, I don't believe there was an accident.'

Aware of what this implied she added, 'Not the way the police describe it,' and left her point, hanging. She waited for his reply half hoping it would be like her husband's, half hoping it wouldn't.

'Katherine if you are that convinced I think you should do something about it and find answers to the questions you have. To be honest, I couldn't believe it myself.'

Katherine breathed out deeply.

'However, I did ask the police a few questions and believed them and their evidence.'

Katherine digested the information then checked, 'What questions, Thomas, and what evidence?'

'The fact that they believe she slipped on a large mossy stone because a section of moss had recently been wiped away on that stone – the stone with her blood on it. The injuries she suffered to her face, shoulder and hip, all of which were indicative of a fall, scraping against rock. And of course, the concussion to her head. I asked the police if there was any other evidence, and if the evidence definitively pointed to an accident, of her own making. Their answer was conclusive. It was a terrible, unfortunate accident with no evidence of another party there.' Thomas looked soulfully at Katherine. He too had found it hard to believe. Her mother was so athletic and so familiar with the river, it seemed an unlikely accident on a warm autumn morning.

There were both quiet replaying the scene in their minds for a moment.

Katherine punctured the silence. 'But did they say anything about the location: like why she was found so far away from her normal swimming hole? On Wednesdays she always did a quick swim because afterwards, back at the house she would hold her morning calls for work. Why was she up river, as they said almost 500 meters away from her swimming hole, on a Wednesday when she didn't have much time – did they ever answer that?'

'No Katherine, they think she took a quiet stroll up river, before her dip, but that she never made it back...'' he trailed off.

Katherine felt back at point zero. Did she involve Thomas now, given he seemed satisfied with the police answers, or did she continue on her own? She thought about the note in her pocket – the note she would love to share with him, of all people. But then the warning in the note, 'trust no one', jarred her back to reality.

'Thomas you might be right, maybe you are right, the police must know what they're doing.'

'Hey Katherine, I'm not happy with the conclusion either. It doesn't seem plausible, it simply isn't characteristic of your mother, but that's what accidents are. They aren't characteristic, they are accidents. To be honest, I've wanted to go down to the river to look around myself but it was just too close to the funeral and then with the trip…do you want to have a look around together?'

The same for me, thought Katherine, I've also not been able to study the area properly. She looked at her friend's face, his honest eyes and felt herself defuse, gently, somewhere she was sizzling out of anger, like a slow leak of pressured air from a tire, and she felt herself gladly, opening up again to his companionship.

'Yes, that'd be great, thanks, Thomas. Is now a good time? I'd really appreciate going together. There are a few things I've wanted to check myself.' She thought to herself, like, where did my mother's other shoe go; and the rip on her heavy cotton shirt, could a rock have really caused that?

'Of course,' he replied seriously, up to the challenge.

What am I expecting to find down there, she asked herself. She worried there would be nothing to appease her or perhaps worse, that she might actually find something amiss.

~ ~ ~ ~ ~ ~ ~ ~ ~ ~

Richard checked his mobile for new messages, then oddly also checked his watch. Yes, his mobile phone and laptop were always at hand for the time, but it gave him great pleasure to lift out his arm, tug back his cuff-linked sleeve and check the time on his Rolex. It was a unique design and he adored it. He smiled and thought again about Gemstone. In the next half hour, he would have his Gemstone meeting with the Director of his VC firm. He was very keen to hear the results of the recent technology tests, and how the acquisition of Gemstone was progressing. It was critical that they reach an agreement by next week, preferably this week.

Shortly after his Gemstone meeting, he planned to catch up with Colin.

Richard had every confidence it would be good news, that Colin could easily get his Chinese partners on board and secure their investment in the production plan. Of course Richard would also then have the test results for Colin: the scientific evidence to back the performance of Gemstone's new green technology. Colin needed that evidence in order to secure the final signatures of his Chinese partners.

Richard leaned back in his leather swivel chair, pushed away from his desk, folded his arms behind his head and stretched back. It was a big, expectant, stretch.

Chapter 6 - Threads

Katherine and Thomas finished their teas, then left the luxury of the Orangery. They followed a lavender path down to the river, the very path Katherine's mother would have taken. Despite the autumn beauty of the day, and the lavender clouds of mauves, whites and deep purples on the path borders, Katherine and Thomas were both in their own, less dreamy thoughts.

They reached the low bank of the river. Rocks and fabulous stepping stones led to the river pool. It was so peaceful and calm. The coppiced acorn and hawthorn land border dipped down towards the river to start up again on the other side. It was ancient with twisted and overgrown roots running through the stone walls.

Although the willow and hazelnut billowed over the river, the pool itself was open and fully bathed in sun. Her grandmother had designed the river swimming hole when Katherine's mother was a little girl. The gardeners had, upon her instruction, widened the river into the river banks, and cut back the romantically arching trees to provide more space, more sun, and a perfect place to teach her young child how to swim. Although they were only two hours by motorcar to the beach, a seaside visit was a big excursion back then, and her grandmother was keen to teach her young child to swim at home.

Katherine could see her grandmother still in her demure bathing suit, and her mother's athletic body, both of them coaxing her into the water, her little three year old self. She smiled remembering the three of them laughing at the cold water and then, drying out on the large sun-warmed slabs the gardeners had placed for that very use; her mother towelling her hair dry, while her grandmother teased her mother that she had too many muscles for a lady. It was warm and it was happy and there was certainly no indication of the tragedy to which this site would eventually bear witness.

Katherine snapped back to the present - a witness. And this was the nub of her worry. She felt certain there was a witness to her mother's death, a witness who did nothing to help, and who had caused the accident to occur. She chanced a sidelong glance at Thomas who had begun to search the end of the pathway and was speaking.

'Did you wonder that Katherine?' he asked again.

'I'm sorry Thomas, what did you say?'

'I wondered why they found her dry towel up the river from this swimming spot, between here and up further where she hit her head. Did she normally swim further up in the river? And leave her towel by the side of the river?'

'No, she was tidy. Her towel always was placed on the slab, there,' and Katherine pointed to the largest slab, baking in the sun.

'She liked her towel warm for when she came out of the water. It had been raining for a few days. That's why the water was so high. But at that time in the morning, and on that Wednesday it was dry. In fact, that day it was bright, sunny and hot – this large slab stone would have definitely been dry.'

She repeated the fact, 'With the full sun, and the soft breeze, she would have left it here.' Katherine felt such a sadness in her heart, she really didn't know that she could do this.

'And no, she never swam further up the river. The water would have been fast and the stones at the side of the river would have been slippery with moss. It's much more shady up there and wooded. And why her towel would have been half way between here and where she hit her head, I simply don't know. I really have no idea why she would have been that far up the river in the first place, ' Katherine sighed sadly. She also was bothered about the shoe. The police had only found one shoe on her; they had never found the other shoe.

Thomas sensed her frustration. 'I'll join you along the river's edge, Katherine. Is there anything in particular you're looking for?'

She hesitated to answer, and then decided to share her suspicions.

'They only ever found one shoe, Thomas, the one that was on her,' she looked at him, with determined eyes.

Oh God he thought. What has she been going through? Of course, there was no mention of another shoe, but he immediately imagined the police must have addressed this.

'Did they tell you they couldn't find the other shoe?' He asked incredulously.

'Yes. When they told me they didn't have it, I asked them whether they could check again. The police thought it was a good enough question that they sent a few men out to look for it and any other evidence they might have missed. They found nothing,' and she opened her arms and then dropped them in a gesture illustrating how futile this was.

'Ok, Katherine, let's see if we can find that shoe, yeah?' He smiled at her, his deep blue eyes earnest and caring. She locked eyes with him for a few moments then slowly smiled.

'Shall we split sides, then?' she suggested.

Thomas jumped effortlessly from stone to stone and found his way across the river, without dipping into the pool. They both laughed, to relieve the tension, then continued their search up the river for a shoe they didn't know they'd ever find.

~ ~ ~ ~ ~ ~ ~ ~ ~ ~

Edward considered his next step. He calculated that Thomas and Katherine would be together in the Orangery for sometime. She needed to talk to someone, and Thomas would want to support her, that was for sure, as Thomas always did. This gave Edward some time. Perhaps a few hours he thought, and then Katherine would be leaving to pick up Maisy from school. He took the pie out of the oven, breathing in its great autumnal smells of blackberries and apples, and smiled as he rested it on the marble slab by the double Aga.

Edward went upstairs two flights, to his floor. It was the old servants' rooms but life had changed since his father's command at the house. Back then there were twenty servants running the estate and tending to the family. Now there was just him, several gardeners, plus a full time carpenter/handyman, and weekly visiting cleaning and washing ladies from the village. There was also a cook contracted in for grand occasions - a local woman who was well-esteemed and whose family had once cooked for Katherine's grandmother. Edward was able to deal with the day to day cooking and the family affairs for which he was responsible. It was certainly less busy with less excitement and gossip than in his father's day, but he liked it that way.

Katherine had renovated the top floor creating several fabulous guest rooms, all modernised with en-suite bathrooms. His area had been expanded into a large apartment. He loved it. There were very seldom staying guests and so he had almost without exception the top floor to himself.

With his approval and involvement Katherine had renovated and featured his rooms on her blog and website. She was careful to keep the cameras away from his bedroom, but the rest of the apartment was featured in several magazines as the ultimate bachelor pad. He loved the colours: grey ombre, warm whites, brown-beige and with the odd touch of burnt orange and faded gold.

He headed straight for his office, and opened his Mac. Signing in, he checked his portfolio page, and several websites. He flipped back and forth, then reached for his mobile. He was uncomfortable, but given the recent news, he thought it best to make contact. A woman answered. It was a voice he recognised and the two had a pleasant conversation for a few minutes. Then, she left to find the person he'd requested. While on hold, he twiddled with his beautiful calligraphy pen that had been his father's, a gift in fact, from Katherine's grandmother.

~ ~ ~ ~ ~ ~ ~ ~ ~ ~

They reached the area where Katherine's mother had been found. The police believed she had been washed down five meters by the bubbling river to this location on the lower bank. Further up from this spot, was where the police claim she had slipped and hit her head.

Katherine sat on a large, dry rock nearby to rest for a few minutes. It had surely been an hour, and nothing had been found. Her back needed a rest from bending over during her search. She was sure Thomas could do with a rest too, although she thought, he was perfectly fit from his cycling.

They had covered a lot of ground. In fact it wasn't just the riverside, banks, pathways, and parts of bordering fields they had covered, they had talked a lot too. But there was one topic they hadn't covered yet and that was Colin.

She wasn't ready to talk about him. Despite her disappointment in some of her husband's behaviour, and their growing distance over the past few years, she couldn't bring herself to be disloyal to her husband and take his own brother into her confidence. This problem she would have to manage on her own, and she was resolute and prepared for a long life of managing that relationship as best she could. She had Maisy's welfare to consider, as Colin was her father, and Maisy did love him despite his stilted love towards her.

She bit her lip as Thomas found a place to cross back over the river and sit nearby. She did think to share one thing with him about his brother. It was something she thought he should know. Something she had discovered before her mother's death. But how to broach the subject?

'I think we should spend another hour looking around here, then head back for today, what do you think?' he asked her. He checked his mobile phone and was surprised to see it was close to midday.

'Yes, that's a good idea. I'll need to pick up Maisy in any case. You know this is the spot where they found my mother?' she asked him.

He shook his head and said softly, 'I didn't realise this was the exact location. Where did she slip then?'

Katherine pointed about 5 meters away. It was the largest rock by the river, more like a boulder, and it stuck out defiantly. It was in shade from the overhanging oak branches, and was covered in thick damp, moss. He frowned and thought that even six weeks ago on such a warm sunny autumn morning it must still have been slippery with moss. Odd that her towel wasn't at the spot where she hit her head, or down by the swimming hole. He saw Katherine shudder. They both started to speak.

'Go ahead, Thomas,' Katherine invited him to speak first.

'It's hard Katherine, to make sense of events sometimes. For me, I struggled to understand why my father died so easily and didn't have the will to push on. But he was crushed by my mother's death. He also saw Colin, successful, able to handle the family affairs and finally settled with a good wife!'

He grinned at Katherine, 'And a wife who would keep him honest. Knowing his family's heritage was in good hands, and having lost his life's love, I think he just let himself perish. Sometimes we don't need to understand the why but just accept the events. Maybe he never had a chance anyway, with his weak lungs, but who knows? Sometimes we just don't know, and perhaps aren't meant to know. That's how I see this situation. Sometimes we don't know and can't know. Maybe an accident really did happen here.'

He looked at her carefully and waited for a reply.

She had been on the brink of saying something else entirely that wasn't about her mother but about Colin. She had to take a heartbeat moment to swap her response.

'Umm, yes, I understand what you mean. I, I was going to say the same type of thing, only, you beat me to it.'

She knew now she couldn't share the one thing she wanted to, about Colin, especially after what he'd just said. She would need to think that one through and be sure of her suspicions before she divulged anything to Thomas, if she could, on another occasion.

Chapter 7 - Surprises

It had been a long session. Straightforward, with a lot of material covered. James thanked his guests and led them out to reception.

He closed the conference room door and as there was no one else in reception, asked his guests what they thought of the team, and the day. Their feedback was positive. The calibre of his team 'was excellent' they stated. James smiled with pride and knew that the right decision had been made. These people understood the importance of individuals, of his team, and how necessary they were to moving the opportunity forward.

'It's important that the team keeps this completely confidential,' they said in parting. James agreed and opened the door to their waiting car.

For the second time that day, he checked his mobile messages. He'd had three texts: one from his wife and two business texts, all received around midday. His wife needed to go out on Friday, and given the progress today he imagined the negotiations could close early on Friday, so he could easily sort the children for the rest of the day.

He texted Anjali back: 'Ok, not a problem. Love James.'

The other two were related texts from his existing investors and he'd already replied to those during lunch. They mattered less now anyway, as in any case, the new deal would be done this week. He just needed to get the week finished.

~ ~ ~ ~ ~ ~ ~ ~ ~ ~

Colin was finally back at his hotel. On reflection he wasn't certain the day had gone well and that was very out of character. He always knew a good day, and the occasional bad day, but this day had been unlike any other. Was it good? He was certain his Chinese partners had the production capacity needed and the funds required to create these new facilities. They'd gone through all of that, with the documentary and photographic evidence. But it was bad, it was really bad, that the Chinese government and secret service had a whiff of this, and had representatives at the meeting. Should he let Richard know?

He settled himself back in his room and contemplated his dinner. There was no entertaining tonight, no dinner with his Chinese hosts. He sighed with relief, surprising himself.

'Hey, am I thinking of a night in?' He said out loud looking at himself in the mirror across the room. He grinned at the ludicrous idea, and called the concierge to book a seat at the top floor restaurant in the hotel for an hour's time. He'd wanted to dine there last visit and couldn't make it then, so this time, he'd take advantage of his night off. Sorted, he eased himself out of his tie and suit. God it was good to take that tie off, he thought.

The shower was perfect. On high, it pummelled his back and ran down him like a warm rainfall. He had ditched his own expensive toiletries in favour of the hotel shower gel. It was fresh and masculine with something like... ginger perhaps, that spiced up his shower and shook him free of his earlier concerns. He stepped from the shower and rubbed his body with the plush white towel. Yes, that felt good. He finished off drying the wet from his hair with another weighty and fresh-smelling towel.

Click...click, click.

His arm froze, suspended in mid-air. That was a noise in his room. A definite click.

Click, click. The noise had come from beyond his bathroom door. And again, just now, outside the door.

He looked at his body in the mirror. A strong body - wrapped in a luxury towel and his hair, spiked from the towel. Seeing himself like that, he realised how helpless he was. Did he need to defend himself? What did he have to defend himself other than towels - and toiletry bottles?? The meeting with a secret service official present must have spooked him.

Whoever was making the sound had stopped, was this because he was listening?

'Ok so where is that tooth brush,' he decided to continue casually but loudly, to scare away anyone in the room. He fiddled inside his toiletries bag and then heard a substantial click. That was definitely his hotel room door. He waited just a moment more then opened the bathroom door.

Ridiculous, he thought. No one here. There's no one here. He was annoyed with himself and didn't find the situation funny. God he certainly had been spooked. He looked carefully now, around the room.

He did spot one difference in his room from when he left to shower. Turndown service had been provided. His top linen sheet was folded slightly back and there were two chocolates on the satin border of the sheet. Ok, so it was staff. Caught out that he was in the room, trying to get the service done before he emerged from the bathroom. But that is extremely odd for a hotel of this calibre, he thought. He'd never before, in all of his travels, had a staff member in his room when he was the room as well. He walked to the door and put the double lock on before dressing for dinner. He thought to report housekeeping's error of judgement - whoever it was - to front reception. It wasn't appropriate. He didn't pay for that kind of sloppy service.

He dressed in his casual evening wear and checked his image in the floor length mirror by the wardrobes. He tucked his shirt in tightly then strode towards the room door. As he did so, he caught sight of his desk bin, still full with some of his tissues and papers. It irked him.

He carefully closed his door, checking the lock worked. He didn't know a lot about hotel housekeeping but he did know that turndown service often included an emptying of the bins. He cleared his throat and entered the elevator, where another man was already standing.

~ ~ ~ ~ ~ ~ ~ ~ ~ ~

Edward finished the call on his mobile. It had not been an easy call. But it was, he pursed his lips, a necessary one. He took a small key from his chain of keys tucked into his trousers, and opened a drawer in his writing table. From there, he selected a notepad. He ripped two pages from the notepad. The first page was already written on both sides with notes against several headings. The second page was empty. He dipped his father's pen in ink and wrote a simple message on the second note page. He blew on it slightly to dry it off. He replaced the notepad in the drawer and closed it.

A sudden jam brought his attention back to the drawer. He fiddled within and found the item which was stuck: a small envelope addressed, 'Dearest Edward' and an even smaller photo, paper-clipped to the envelope. He couldn't help the sadness that he suddenly felt. She was so beautiful, so angelic. And so, utterly unforgivable he thought. What was done was done. He fit the envelope back in assertively and locked the drawer.

The day had turned warmer and the sun heated the loft rooms despite the autumn weather. He refocused on the next set of events and put on a lighter jacket. The note was dry now, and he folded it, slipping it into a matching cream envelope. He placed his newly written note in his right pocket, and the single page with many notes, he pocketed in his left. Closing the doors, he moved with some urgency to the ground floor. It was Tuesday lunchtime, and he was expecting a visitor.

~ ~ ~ ~ ~ ~ ~ ~ ~

Richard reacted quickly to the knock on the door. He dropped his feet from the desk and moved his relaxed arms, from behind his head. 'Come in,' he commanded, in his perfect English.

'Ahh, great to see you!' He pushed back from his desk and stood up to shake hands with the Director from his VC firm. They locked eyes and Richard could see unfamiliar territory there, lurking in his colleague's eyes. A look of frustration clouded his normally implacable, determined face.

'Richard, hello. Well, what a day. I've had reports from the team about two hours ago around lunchtime and I've been round to see the usual interested parties. Gemstone is quite the gem – and acting quite precious in more ways than one,' he grinned sarcastically but his face was set. A stubborn set, that wanted the job done, not riddled with delays.

His Director continued, 'We've got to talk, I thought this was going to be an easy one,' he pulled out a chair and reached for his vaping cigarette. Richard didn't like the news, and didn't like the vaping. He despised vaping in his room; cigarettes and cigars were out but vaping, he was soon to make that a 'no go' area too. Not today though, not with a disgruntled exec sitting in front of him.

By the time Richard ushered his visitor out the door, several hours had slipped by. It wasn't the meeting Richard had envisioned. Project Gemstone was taking twists and turns he'd not planned on. He wasn't clear why this was the case, and he knew the project would come to a successful closure, but hiccups like these simply weren't welcome. It was Tuesday already and time to move on so that he could initiate the next steps. There was a fantastic business opportunity here at stake. The combination of massive profit and political clout this acquisition would give him, made him impatient. What if someone else nipped him at the bud?

~ ~ ~ ~ ~ ~ ~ ~ ~ ~

Thomas didn't need to see her face to know that something was still bothering Katherine. He was good at listening. She probably needed to talk and her mother wasn't around to talk to anymore. His mind jumped to his meeting with Katherine's mother the previous month.

A 'casual morning tea' had been her invitation. They'd had many of those over the years, but recently the meetings had become few and far between since his practice had become so busy, and he suspected, she'd not wanted to take up his time. And so, he was delighted to have the invite. The visit however didn't end up being a 'casual morning tea'. It was about a specific subject.

As the river gurgled by he cleared his throat uncomfortably, remembering the meeting.

Katherine pulled her eyes from her search and looked at him, expecting him to say something. She had only just heard him clear his throat over the river's hum.

But Thomas was already deep in thought, remembering what had been said that morning. He'd been uncomfortably surprised that Katherine's mother had talked so candidly about a personal matter with him. In fact, several personal matters. It had angered him - and Katherine's mother had never upset him before. Could she have meant what she said and was she right?

Her suggestions were deeply uncomfortable and he told her that. He'd left her upset but there'd been no chance to talk it through further. He was due that morning at his clinic with sessions he couldn't cancel. And so he'd left her home abruptly clearly angered by her requests.

He grimaced now, recollecting the situation. He'd never seen her so upset.

As usual, he'd put personal matters to the back of his mind. He knew he couldn't comply with what she'd asked of him. In his mind, life simply had to continue as it had, unless there was more evidence of her claims. Katherine's happiness absolutely stood in the balance.

He shuddered. There had been no second chance to discuss the issue.

'Did you say something, Thomas?' Katherine checked.

He was pulled back to the present and quickly responded. 'Ah, yes, I did wonder if we should arrange dinner sometime this week while Colin is away? With Maisy or just us two adults if you need the time to talk. What do you say?' He smiled at her.

'Adults, us two?' She teased him. 'I'm not sure, Thomas. I have this energy now,' she breathed in the sharp, fresh air of the crisp leaves and damp water, 'and I'd really like to dive into my mother's affairs, once I put Maisy to bed this week. Do you mind?'

'Of course not, that's great news. Let me know if you need my help with any of that,' he was pleased she was back on track.

~~~~~~~~~~

Colin smiled vacantly at the man in the elevator. There was something in his eyes that caused him to look again at the man. This time the man was staring straight ahead. They were both heading for the top floor. Ping. The man invited Colin to step out first, which he did.

The restaurant concierge moved forward immediately to greet both men, then asked, 'A table, for two?' Smiling awkwardly, Colin clarified the situation and was led alone, to a corner table overlooking the river some distance below.

The decor was sumptuous, luxurious with jungle vibes. The plants and flowers were exotic and green with sharp colours of red and yellow. The restaurant ambience, the quiet and immaculate service, ahh, he thought, this will do. Then, he took a deep breath, relaxing for the first time that day. One look at the menu and he settled into his chair, planning to pass a good few hours of dinner whilst he worked through his notes from the day and prepared for tomorrow's session. He glanced out over the restaurant and spotted the man from the elevator in the far corner, typing into his mobile.

Colin stared at him a moment longer, then he coughed to clear his throat and began his work.

~~~~~~~~~~

Edward descended the curved stairs just as the doorbell chimed. He hurried straight to the door, opened it, and smiled at his visitor. The two shook hands solidly, and then Edward led his visitor through to the library. He offered coffee, which his visitor declined, and they sat together at the old walnut table. Never would his father have dreamt such a meeting would ever take place. But times had changed, and Edward was as comfortable as he was sure, conducting the session.

'Thank you for meeting with me here, this time,' Edward said. 'I thought we might need to be here at the house, in case you had any details you wanted me to clarify, once you read through my information.'

'Yes, it was a good idea Edward,' the elderly gentleman smiled. He had a friendly face, and a gentlemanly demeanour about him. His eyes crinkled warmly when he smiled at Edward. He swung his heavy leather briefcase up on the table, and snapped it open.

'Well,' he turned to Edward, 'what have you got?'

Edward reached into his left pocket and pulled out the paper with many notes on it.

'Ahh,' said the elderly gentlemen, 'let's see what we have here,' and he put on some spectacles as he prepared to look at Edward's information.

He took his time to read through the contents, and then leaned back, pulling off his glasses and twirling them absently.

'I think I should say 'shocking revelations' having read that. But I find myself thinking outside of my usual role and don't know if that's what one normally says in these circumstances.' He had a solemn face now, and looked deep into Edward's eyes, hoping to find more answers.

'Is this all you know then?' he checked again with Edward.

'Yes,' Edward answered sadly. The gentleman pulled his eyes from studying Edward and reached for documents from his briefcase.

'This is of course, highly confidential,' he looked to Edward again, 'and certainly most unusual. But given the circumstances ...'

Edward felt himself wince while the visitor shuffled further through his papers.

'The firm and I think in this case, it is most appropriate.'

He found his first document and placed it on the table. He shoved it towards Edward pressing his fingers firmly down on the document as he held Edward's eyes.

'Read this please, and sign it. Then, we can proceed.'

He signed the crisp paper with his father's pen and then firmly pushed the document back along the table.

With the paper signed, the two men began to discuss the gentleman's documents and the contents of Edward's information.

Time passed quickly. 'Unfortunately we'll need to end our session shortly,' Edward glanced at the mantelpiece clock and sadly smiled at the elderly gentleman.

'Yes of course, however we have progressed much,' and he gave a confident smile to Edward. 'I know you'll be thanked for this - when, I don't know but I do trust Providence, and this will all come right.'

Edward respectfully led his visitor to the front door, and exchanged a solemn and solid goodbye handshake.

'I'll be in touch the usual way, once I work through these papers and digest the information you've provided. Good afternoon,' said his visitor. He carefully descended the outside stairs, an elderly gentleman with tall carriage and a confident stance. He opened the back door of his black sedan, placed his briefcase in, then opened the driver's door, and eased himself gently into the seat. He turned to wave goodbye to Edward, and then slowly the wheels of his heavy car crunched on the Cotswold gravel and eased out along the long drive.

Edward closed the door and turned for his final job of the day before preparing a snack for Maisy.

~ ~ ~ ~ ~ ~ ~ ~ ~ ~

Katherine studied the area carefully.

This was the spot they had identified. The spot where her mother had hit her head on a massive, mossy rock.

A few meters down is where her body had been washed to the side of the river. By the time Katherine had left her office and arrived at the scene of the accident, her mother's body had been moved higher up the side bank and covered respectfully.

Katherine had been at work that day with her team, reviewing the final pieces of next season's collection. The weather had been so warm, and the collection a bright summer palette for next year. She had been inspired by the collection and pleased. How that felt like a long time ago now.

She automatically looked to the bank where her mother's body had lain. She lowered her eyes as they swelled. Just then she noticed something white floating in the air, on the tail of a blustery autumn breeze wafting down from the meadow.

It was a small white piece of ripped fabric. She followed it to its landing spot and quickly grabbed it, before the breeze whisked it further along.

It was white cotton. She couldn't breath for a moment. It was a large enough scrap of cotton, to identify what it might have been part of.

She looked around and tried to remember the exact direction she'd seen the cotton floating from. She looked up, up towards the large oak tree directly above and then along to the base of its trunk where the meadow and sharp bushes were. The sun shone strongly into her eyes, through the golden leaves. She squinted further.

'Katherine, that was Edward, did you hear him? He's at the top of the path and asking if you'd like him to pick up Maisy!' Thomas shouted up to Katherine.

They had split over the last hour, searching different areas - she closer to the scene - and Thomas closer to where the path led towards the house.

Katherine squinted once more. Where did the cotton come from? But the sun was too bright. She pocketed the white cotton and felt devious, her heart thumping. She had to leave, now wasn't the time to investigate further.

She didn't like to miss Maisy's pick up times and had asked Edward to cover for her only on a very few occasions.

'Tell him not to worry! I'm coming,' she shouted. She subconsciously patted both pockets, checking their contents were safe: a note, and now some fabric. But not just any fabric.

She jogged to the path and joined Thomas who was waiting for her. He bowed and motioned her to lead the way as they made their return to the Orangery.

Edward was waiting for them in the kitchen conservatory. Katherine dashed to grab her purse and waved goodbye to them both. In her hurry she didn't notice Edward reaching into his right pocket and passing something into Thomas' hand.

~ ~ ~ ~ ~ ~ ~ ~ ~ ~

She heaved a huge sigh and pushed her chair from her desk. Done, done, done! Anjali removed her glasses and rubbed her eyes, Oh, that felt so good. And then she pinched the top of her neck. Aww, her back and her neck hurt. Her eyes hurt. Once again, too long looking at her laptop. But she had completed her research and the findings were as she had hoped. What an amazing opportunity! She couldn't wait to brief Richard on Wednesday regarding her recommendations. He was sure to love it.

God, her neck hurt. A big stretch and then she was down on the floor, arching her back like a cat, and then stretching her back down towards the floor as she looked up. They were back and neck exercises she was supposed to do each morning, but this morning, she'd forgotten.

Five minutes to go before she had to leave for the school run. She dashed upstairs to find a sweater for the walk to school. Great. She felt great.

She grabbed her mobile, to first check if James had returned her text regarding Friday night. In truth, she didn't expect an answer till later in the day. He was in important meetings today, she knew that much, although James had not talked about the specifics. He'd been quite secretive. She was used to that, as most of his research and work was so specialised and confidential they had agreed long ago that he'd be unable to discuss details with Anjali.

She was ok with that. She also often had to sign letters promising confidentiality, non-disclosure agreements (NDAs), before working on a deal, so she understood confidentiality. She knew generally what he was up to, and he knew generally the type of work she did, and they both were comfortable with that. In fact, they had little time to talk about work, given the demands of the children.

But tonight when he was home, and Sara and Arun were in bed, she was sure he would have great news to tell her.

She unlocked her mobile. He was fine with her Friday plan! Great!

So, Friday night was good to go. Fantastic! She quickly left to pick the children up.

Chapter 8 - Delays

Richard sighed, then asked his secretary to ring Colin and put him through to his office. Given the frustrating news from his VC director, Richard looked forward to connecting with Colin.

Colin was stretched out on his bed, almost asleep when his mobile rang. He'd had a five course dinner and wine to accompany it, and back in his room, had only just laid down on the bed to rest a moment. The ring startled him and left him light-headed as he sat up quickly to grab his mobile. He squinted to see the number, his eyes still unfocused.

Ah, Richard's number. He put his head down between his legs for a minute. God, he'd almost blanked out there, he'd moved so quickly. He checked the time on his mobile, 10pm, then answered the call.

'Hey Richard, how's it going?'

'Colin, lot's to catch up on. How are your Chinese friends, how are you?' replied Richard, grinning already at hearing Colin's voice. His chum had collaborated so well up to this point. There were only a few more steps to go. Colin had executed the most difficult step of the plan already. All that was well past now, soon they would be in the clear to transact openly.

'Yah, going ok. It's bloody hot and bloody busy I can say that!' He was also pleased at hearing his buddy's voice but regretted the information that he'd have to share.

'How did the negotiations go?' Richard was back in a relaxed pose, and had a small grin on his face, fingering a gin and tonic.

'Good and not so good, is how I can describe it,' Colin had decided to share the good and the bad - both - with Richard. Colin would surely have an opinion and some thoughts on the next steps.

'Huh, same here,' replied Richard referring to the meeting he'd just had, 'go on...'

'First we went through my papers. All the evidence was there regarding our acquisition progress and the funding I can provide to jointly invest in their production facilities.'

'All that went without a hitch?' checked Richard.

'Yes, without a hitch. I did think they might query some of my background but there was none of that. They're so keen. The one issue we thought they'd raise - why there were financial difficulties on my last visit, didn't come up. So we're all in the clear there.'

There was a heavy pause as the implications of what Colin said were recognised by both men. Good, thought Richard, we can put that behind us now.

'Then, we covered the science itself. They were very interested in this component of the discussions and excited to see previous test results. Of course, I was only able to give to them what you've provided to me, you know, older test data. Not enough information for them to tap into the intellectual property – but enough to show them that we're onto a good thing. They're waiting to receive from us the final test results proving the technology beyond any doubt, you know, the ones Gemstone should have already provided to us...' he left that hanging, expecting answers from Richard.

'What about their production plans and their investment in that, Colin?'

'Yup, there's good progress on that. Today, I saw evidence of all that. They have the experience and as well, investment ready for the type of production we require. They have planned facilities for expansion and are overly excited by this opportunity. They remain keen to be the only partner. In fact, they reiterated that they would pull out if there were other backers. This could be used to our advantage. Tomorrow we should get some papers signed from them, with detailed contractual commitments, but we need to share with them the latest test results,' then Colin paused, giving Richard another chance to talk about the latest study.

Richard could sense Colin hadn't finished his update.

'Go on,' he prompted.

'As well, there's a problem, Richard. The problem is, well, the way they want to conduct their business. It's evolving into something bigger than I'd anticipated. There are now links to the umm,' he lowered his voice even though he was in the privacy of his hotel room, 'links to the bloody secret service.'

Colin heard Richard's intake of breath.

'What?' Richard barked. 'What? They can't be serious. We can't have that!'

Richard was sitting up now, no longer in his relaxed pose. 'Look, Colin, we can't be associated in any way to that. We already know that there are implications here, but with those people involved, this could cause us real trouble down the line – not just there, but here. It's here I'm worried about Colin!'

'I know, I know,' Colin grimaced. God did he know it. Maybe he shouldn't have shared this with Richard – would he bail out? Surely not now, not with what they'd gone through and how close they were. The worst was over, this was supposed to be the easy bit. God he was annoyed.

'Bloody hell, Colin, what are they thinking of? Didn't you already tell them the deal was a business transaction only?'

'Yes, I did,' Colin sighed heavily. 'They blindfolded me Richard, to drive me to the meeting place,' he let that sink in.

Richard's mouth dropped open. He finished his G&T with a quick gulp and stood up to get another from the drinks cabinet. He wasn't happy.

'Colin, I need to think about this, ' he paused, they both knew they were too deep and too far along the plans to pull out now.

He continued, 'There was an interesting development here, as well.' He relayed the outcome of the meeting he'd just had with his VC Director.

'Gemstone isn't progressing in quite the way we thought it would, this final week,' Richard complained.

Colin digested the information. Project Gemstone was Richard's name for the full initiative, for the company he planned to buy outright and then work with the Chinese to deliver the post acquisition plan. After the acquisition the Chinese partners would productise the technology and make it saleable for the market. Given the secrecy of the project, Colin didn't know the actual name of the target company Richard was planning to acquire. In fact, he didn't know who was aware of the actual company name bar the Director of Richard's VC firm. Even Richard's secretary used the code name, Project Gemstone, at all times.

'Why is Gemstone delaying? And can't we get some indication of the recent test results? I don't know the guys there, Richard, but can you, you know, twist their arm a bit by saying you'll back out if they don't progress to plan? Aren't they desperate to take this stuff to market? And they must want the money?' Colin asked the obvious questions.

'Look it isn't that simple. These guys are different from our normal transaction – the normal companies I target. They need all kinds of assurances, and I think they are just slightly spooked. This is a big step they are taking. I'll ask my guys to put the pressure on, but we'll need to be careful how we do this.' Richard was normally so bullish but he knew this small company – and he was onto a winner – would take a bit of playing with to get to the finish line. His normal tactics would not work. Gemstone were concerned about ethics, not just money and that meant a whole different negotiation strategy was required.

Colin thought quickly to himself. He didn't have the evidence he needed for his meeting tomorrow because Gemstone was delaying. He needed time.

'Richard, I think I can buy some time. I can cancel tomorrow's session, on the back of the concerns I have with the 'secret service visitor' we had at today's meeting and insist that we conduct this as a business exchange only. This could buy you another day to secure the information we require from Gemstone. Can you do this? I can also threaten that we have other backers waiting on the sidelines, they should react to that too. What do you think?'

Richard liked his friend's fast thinking. It was where his mind had also been heading. 'Yes, do that.'

Tomorrow is Wednesday Richard mused. After that he had two days more and the weekend to get the job done. He needed it all tidy by early next week. The end of the month was fast approaching; and he never missed his own deadline. Richard twirled his glass in his hand, staring out over the Thames as Colin filled him in on the details of the day.

~ ~ ~ ~ ~ ~ ~ ~ ~ ~

Anjali smiled at Sara and Arun. They were both overflowing with excitement and had little crafts tucked under their arms. 'Hello darlings,' she said as they hugged her in turn. 'What have you got here?' The two chimed in, chattering away about their school crafts. Anjali was so involved in the conversations that she only just noticed Katherine collecting Maisy.

Anjali took her children's hands and moved towards Katherine. 'Hi Katherine, aren't their crafts great?'

Katherine turned round to see Anjali and gave her a wide grin, 'Yes, I'm afraid we were nowhere near as ingenious when I went to school!' The two women laughed and agreed how professional even child's play had become.

'Would you like to pop over for a cup of tea?' Anjali offered. Before Katherine could respond, Maisy had already accepted the invite.

'Yes, please, right Mummy?'

Katherine laughed a yes, and the two families turned to walk towards Anjali's home, pleased to be in each other's company.

They stopped in front of Anjali's house to open the gate. Although it was a fraction of the size of Katherine's, and despite its old world cottage structure, it was a most beautiful home and Anjali was proud of it. A cottage from around 1700, it had been perfect for her and James when they were first married, but with two children they'd decided to extend it. In fact, Katherine had offered to assist well before she'd become a sought-after designer. The two had created a space that was respectful of its heritage but also cleaner, brighter and easier for a modern family to live in. Katherine's mother had created a perfect cottage garden design for Anjali and as a housewarming present, arranged for her team to plant the garden. The result was delightful.

Katherine paused at the little gate in front of the cottage, and took in the thatched roof, the still flowering cottage garden, and the old apple tree already laden with early ripening apples. She smiled at Anjali.

'I just love it here, the house is simply beautiful and the garden is gorgeous, it feels like a secret garden hidden past your gate. Goodness, it's been weeks since we've been here.'

Anjali grinned with pride at Katherine's comments.

'Almost 3 months in fact,' she remembered because Katherine's mother had died about 6 weeks ago, and prior to that, she'd been away for four weeks with Arun and Sara on summer holiday to see family in India.

'Is it that long?' Katherine thought to herself how much had changed in that time. She knew change was inevitable and was happy to embrace it, but it was the unexpected change that always threw her.

They made their way into the kitchen, for a cup of tea and after school snacks for the children. Then, with tea mugs in hand, they sat in the back garden while the children played on the climbing frame.

'Katherine, how are things at the house now? Settling down?' asked Anjali. She was worried about being too inquisitive, but she was genuinely concerned for her friend.

Katherine took a deep breath. Anjali was a very close friend of hers. She'd married Thomas' best friend, James, two years prior to Katherine's marriage to Colin. While Colin was in London studying for his MBA, James and Anjali, Thomas and Katherine often socialised together. Even in recent years, she still frequently met up with the couple when Colin was away on business trips. He didn't much involve himself in his wife's and younger brother's set, and so, this suited both of them.

'Thomas popped over today and we went down to the river,' she looked cautiously at Anjali, 'to look over the area.'

Anjali's head twisted round.

'Really?'

'Yes, really.' She sighed, 'You know, Anjali, I've never been comfortable with the coroner's report. There seem to be some unanswered questions and so, we went to the river to look at – well – where my mother was found,' she had such difficulty referring to her mother's death.

'Heavens, okay. What do you mean, what kind of questions?'

Katherine had been so closed off from everyone for the last few weeks that it was odd now to share her feelings. But she ought to, she thought, it certainly made her feel better, and helped her to think.

'Anjali, they never found her other shoe. And, she has never ever had an accident down there at the river. She was like a ballerina stepping on those stones, she knew which ones were slippery, which ones to depend upon. And then, her towel was in the wrong place. Next, it was a Wednesday, and for the quick dip she normally took on a Wednesday, she was in the wrong place. Then, the tear in her shirt, could a rock really have done that? I'm so sorry but nothing is right yet, it all feels very wrong and implausible. The coroner seemed so sure, but I'm not so sure,' as she talked Katherine felt herself speaking more forcefully and checked that Anjali didn't think she was talking nonsense.

'Katherine, none of that sounds ridiculous to me. I'm the one who should be sorry. I had no idea that those questions were on your mind. I thought that the coroner's verdict had been accepted unanimously across the board: police, friends, family. Katherine, it all sounds quite unfinished. Who knows about this?'

Katherine breathed a sigh of relief. So her friend thought she was making sense, and Thomas too certainly seemed open to the fact that there may have been other considerations regarding her mother's death.

'Only Thomas - I spoke to him earlier today. You know he's back now from the States? In any case, he can see what I'm saying, but to be frank, he's worried that I'm holding out hope, when he thinks most likely it truly was an accident.' Her face was solemn.

'Thomas is being pragmatic as he always is, and probably just wanting you to be happy.' She laughed to try to lighten the mood. 'But you were very close to your mother. I often thought that, almost like twins despite the generational gap. If you sense something isn't right and have such specific examples as you do, then I think we should do something about it.'

Katherine smiled at her friend, and they agreed that tomorrow afternoon, Katherine would pick up the children, and Anjali would make her way to Katherine's house after work. Then, leaving the children with Edward, who loved having the children around him, they would head down to the river and take another look.

They talked through possible scenarios, but still none of them felt right to Katherine. They all seemed to link to a different variant of the original; an accident. And she felt somewhat dishonest. She hadn't shared everything with Anjali. The note, and the cotton fabric burning holes in her pockets, were two pieces of information not really yet pieces of evidence, that she needed to work through before she shared with anyone, even a well-intentioned and clever friend.

It was time to go.

'The tea was lovely, Anjali. I know you're busy with work and the children but it's been really helpful to talk through a few things.'

'Wonderful to see you Katherine. I was ready for a good visit too. We haven't seen much of you and Maisy recently, and in fact, I just finished off a major research piece, so my mind is ready for a new challenge! Hopefully my analyst's mind can help tomorrow afternoon.'

They waved goodbye and Katherine and Maisy headed back to school to pick up the car and drive home.

~ ~ ~ ~ ~ ~ ~ ~ ~ ~

Still on the phone, and with slightly dampened moods, Richard and Colin talked through the next steps regarding Gemstone. They covered several key points from the contracts and jointly reviewed the post-acquisition plans for production, identifying some gaps for the Chinese partners to clarify over the next two days.

'We'll get through this Colin, have a good rest with the hours you've got left,' it was late now in Shanghai.

Colin laughed dryly. 'Well, as agreed I'm cancelling the meeting for tomorrow so I should be able to get some shut eye well into the late morning.' They planned their next call most likely for Friday, or end of Colin's day Thursday, and hung up both determined that the next two days would be more successful.

Richard stared out across the Thames. The early evening sun was amber and in the distance the gold copper tips of leaves softly glowed fringing the streets along the Thames. He lowered his head and stared ironically at the view – there would be no gold on the horizon for him, unless his next steps were very careful and extremely considered.

~ ~ ~ ~ ~ ~ ~ ~ ~ ~

Katherine was eager to return home. She couldn't shake off her feeling of delayed start. She'd still not managed to go through her mother's papers and was keen to sort Maisy out with dinner and bedtime stories so she could close herself up in her mother's study and read through the papers.

She also wanted to reach out to her old family solicitors to set up a meeting as soon as possible.

The note in her pocket had tugged at her mind throughout the day, and she had a few more thoughts about its meaning, but she needed to check several things first. And the ripped piece of cotton hidden safely now in her pocket, that little piece of cloth she had spied floating in the autumn breeze, may just yet be a clue she didn't even know she needed, for a death only she was suspicious about.

~ ~ ~ ~ ~ ~ ~ ~ ~ ~

'Hey what's this?' Thomas asked Edward, when he took the small envelope from him.

'Read it when you get home,' was Edward's uncharacteristically secretive reply.

'Hey sure,' replied Thomas, 'Everything ok?' But Edward had already moved towards the kitchen saying he had some urgent tasks to tend to.

Thomas shoved the envelope into his jean pocket and left through the kitchen conservatory doors to head to his bike. Edward's secretive manner reminded him of the one thing that had been sitting so unwell in his thoughts for the last few weeks. Could Edward possibly know about his morning meeting with Katherine's mother on the day of....he turned to tightly grab his bike and pushed it firmly along the drive.

He was intrigued. Rather than cycle the full way home, Thomas parked his bike on the little lane, several miles long, between his home and Katherine's. He propped his bike against an old oak, and sat on the field with his back resting against the tree trunk. He relaxed there for some time, looking out over the soft, dried wheat fields, letting the still warm breeze blow gently past him. There had been so much change in such a small amount of time. Change that was unwelcome after years of comfortable relationships and happiness, despite Colin and his antics.

He squinted to beyond the tree line and worked through his thoughts. He was a successful doctor, with a profitable, growing business. He was an innovator in the field of fertility, well-recognised and sought after. His mind flashed back to Katherine's happiness, and the length he'd had to personally go, to afford her that happiness. He gritted his teeth and pressed his back hard against the oak tree, reflecting on the behaviour of his brother at that time.

Katherine's treatment had been a success and the outcome was a beautiful healthy child. Colin's reaction was disappointingly, reserved. But Thomas, Katherine and her Mother had been overjoyed. He grimaced then, with a guilty pain as he was reminded again of his recent meeting with Katherine's mother.

What was he doing? Her mother was right. It wasn't that it was constantly on his mind, but it seemed to be constantly on the mind of everyone else's. What was a successful Doctor like him doing single? Did he not want to marry and have his own family?

He knew what some people suspected. He sighed, because some people knew the truth and that was dangerous. Knowing the truth meant someone might act on it, and he couldn't risk that. That meeting with Katherine's mother, it wasn't what he thought it would be. So much was said.

He rubbed his eyes and ran his hands through his hair. What if. What if he'd reacted differently when he was confronted by her mother? He shuddered and a shadow etched over his face as he thought of the fatal accident. He was pulled from his thoughts when several acorns fell noisily around him on the back of a sudden brisk breeze.

And what of this note? He was in an ominous mood and reluctantly reached into his jeans for Edward's note.

~~~~~~~~~~

With the windows rolled down in the car, they could hear the crunch of the stone gravel as they pulled up to their home. Maisy was out in a flash, rushed up the stairs and stretched tall to ring the grand doorbell. Edward appeared moments later, just as Katherine joined Maisy at the top of the stairway.

'Hello ladies.' He thought how beautiful, happy and young they both looked. If only she could see them just now, why did she have to do what she did?

Letting go of his bitter thoughts, he spoke to Maisy. 'Hello there! How was school? Did you stop in the village on the way home? Come in, there's a lovely supper and pie waiting for you. The pie is your favourite...' he teased her to guess.

'Ooh, apple blackberry?' She asked.

'Of course,' and he opened the door widely so she could run in.

Katherine smiled at Edward, a loving smile; how wonderful to have him here still, with her and Maisy. But Edward didn't look at her, he was focused on Maisy and then glanced at the clock as he headed back into the house.

He isn't relaxed, thought Katherine. We'll catch up tonight, when he brings the tea. We can talk in mother's study and I'll surely need a break from the papers then. Her mobile beeped a text message and she grabbed a peak as she entered the stately house. Perfect, her family solicitors were able to meet her tomorrow. Finally she was picking up the pace. She grinned, excited at the prospect that tonight, she would be going through her mother's papers.

She had one other important task to do after Maisy was in bed and Edward wasn't around.

Chapter 9 - Revelations

'Hey Anjali, that supper smells delicious. How is it your dinners always smell nicer than mine?' James sauntered down the garden from the house to where Anjali was with the children.

They kissed hello while the children clambered down from the climbing frame and pulled at his sleeves for kisses. 'Nonsense, we all love your dinners. I didn't expect you back so soon. That's great, it's ready and I think we must all be hungry, right Sara, Arun?'

The children shouted yes, and were excited; they were chatty with news from school and the game that they were playing. Anjali felt so relaxed. She could see from James' face that the day had gone well, and of course, so had her own. The children were happy, and dinner was made. Her chest breathed in a huge sigh of contentment, and she thought, a glass of wine might be nice tonight.

'James, fancy a glass of wine with our pasta?' He nodded an appreciative yes, and they strolled hand in hand back up to the house with the children skipping ahead.

'Right, let's wash our hands and then talk about school over supper, ok?' Anjali guided the children and sorted the meal while James set the table.

Once seated, and with the children calmer and having run out of stories to tell, Anjali set in to review the day with her husband, 'So how was your meeting?'

James grinned instantly and took a deep breath.

'It was exceptional, actually. It went even better than I had planned. The new guys, suffice to say, are very keen to leverage what we've done and are respectful of the team. They've already thought through the investment the production side of the business will need – it was really enlightening to hear.'

James put his fork down, then quietly added, 'Entering this next stage of growth for my business, I was concerned about loss of control, and possible misuse of our work. Also, that these people wouldn't understand the full implication of what we've created. But I couldn't be more assured now, after this meeting, that this route is the right one.'

Grinning widely he continued, 'It has the potential, Anjali, to change energy challenges forever, you know?'

She was smiling, proud of her husband's accomplishments. She knew he was eager to share more, but couldn't.

'James, that's exciting. And you trust these people? You are sure they aren't planning to take it all away from you and the team? What about shared ownership, will you still have a say?'

'Yes, yes, it seems too good to be true. We are working on the ownership piece. It's complex because of the type of partner I'm talking to. It may not be about an acquisition, but rather more like access to financing. We have details still to finalise but it should all be sorted by the end of week.'

He nodded his head, 'So that's why I texted you earlier today, that Friday dinner for you and Richard should be fine.'

'Oh! I forgot about that. Ok, that's great, thanks, I can sort out the dinner for you,' she paused, 'James, I can't believe it's working out as you'd hoped. You and the team deserve it though. Maybe I'll get my husband back - less long hours perhaps?' She teased him and he laughed.

'And your day, all good?'

'Yes, I finished off that investment project I was working on, you know, the one I think has significant potential? The research is done, the last piece in my business case. Richard will love it. I'm presenting it to him tomorrow. He's indicated that he's very keen to move on this. He says he trusts my judgement, not just the numbers in my business cases,' she grinned at James.

'Yup, well, it's appropriate that you negotiated that salary increase last year. Pitiful what he was paying you compared to the men on the team. You should think about revisiting that now, Anjali, after you complete this piece. He's making a tidy sum off the back of you, and he knows it.'

She let out a short, wry laugh, 'I know, I know. Let's get this opportunity closed out and then I can raise it with him. You're right.'

Anjali wasn't keen to go back to the negotiating table with her boss. It had been tough last time around. She had felt disloyal, but her husband had been a huge driver and had insisted she should be valued and enumerated appropriately.

Of course, he was right. It wasn't fair. She was singularly important to Richard, she suspected sometimes more so than the senior men on the team. There was no reason why she shouldn't talk about a review this year. There were even more reasons why Richard should have taken the initiative and revised her package upwards already this year. She paused for a moment. Maybe in part that is what the dinner was about? Hmmm, maybe that's why he alluded to 'business of course' so she wouldn't suspect a pay rise? That was an interesting thought.

~ ~ ~ ~ ~ ~ ~ ~ ~ ~

Thomas surveyed the beauty of the autumn light and farm fields. He smoothed Edward's cream envelope and pulled out the heavy cream note paper. Ah, he had smudged part of the ink on the notepaper. It was written in calligraphy pen, and so easily smudged. He focused on the wording and then frowned. Is it so? He strained to read the smudged words but still despite their illegibility, the content of the overall note was obvious. Edward? The Edward he knew, or thought he knew, was becoming ever more authoritative. What did it imply?

He studied the contents again. Where did that put him, Thomas? What should he do next? As tempted as he was to return to the house to confront Edward, he knew he needed the evening to understand its implications. He stretched from his resting position and mounted his bike. His muscles flexed as he kicked into motion. He was lean and still powerful from his earlier, racing days, and quickly covered the miles back to his home.

~ ~ ~ ~ ~ ~ ~ ~ ~ ~

Richard was glum. His chauffeur had sensed his mood, and hadn't started the usual banter and breezy chats he normally had with his boss. A glum mood often led to a darker mood still; and the driver knew when to back off. He dropped Richard at his front door, then moved on to park the car. It was a beauty, a British racing red F-Type Jaguar that was the envy of many. But tonight, Richard didn't have eyes for his car, he was already striding determinedly towards his house. The front door automatically opened as he approached it, just like the gates to his property, both using the latest biometric and security technology.

Richard strode past the orchid display in the entranceway, freshly replaced that morning by the cleaner and headed straight for the kitchen. It was a massive expanse that was hardly a kitchen, but structured more like a huge reception area. The kitchen had hardware so outrageous that the fridge freezer was almost armoury - halfway between an industrial metal safe and an armoire.

It was a statement kitchen. Richard opened the fridge door and grabbed a champagne placed there by his staff yesterday. He popped open the bottle of 2006 Dom Perignon.

He'd decided to celebrate, in his own way, at the sudden twists Project Gemstone was throwing up. His glum mood had turned to an aggressive mood - a mood to race to the finish and push whatever aside to get there. With champagne in hand, he pulled a leather stool up to his kitchen bar and grinned. First though, he had an even more enjoyable job to do.

He reached for his mobile phone in his pocket and typed in a text. A text which he knew couldn't be misinterpreted this time. Yes, it was going to be a tough week, but with a fabulous ending. He grinned from ear to ear, finishing his glass and reaching to pour another.

~ ~ ~ ~ ~ ~ ~ ~ ~ ~

Katherine, Maisy and Edward sat down to their meal. Already, Maisy was hungry. It had been several hours since her snack at Anjali's and it was dinner time. She was in a giggly little girl mood, and Katherine was pleased her daughter was happy. She herself, felt lighter and this could only be a good thing. Edward, however, was still distracted, she could tell.

Katherine smiled at Maisy and asked her questions. In between, she studied Edward's face. What could he be so concerned about? Was it her mother still? Was he lonely? She knew how close he had been to her mother.

Since her father's death some thirty years ago, her mother had leaned more and more on Edward. They were very close and she had trusted him entirely. Katherine too was close; she had seen him as a surrogate Uncle. There were no other relatives and Edward was as close to a caring uncle as could be.

She reflected to herself, 'Just as I feel ready to pick up again after mother's death, Edward seems more troubled.'

Maisy had said something funny. Katherine laughed and Maisy's little face lit up, laughing with her mother. Katherine looked to Edward and tried to lift his spirits. 'Edward, wasn't that so funny?' She coaxed him to join in.

He looked at her and she took a deep breath in as his gaze met hers. His eyes weren't just sad they looked haunted.

'You are a very funny little girl,' he smiled weakly at Maisy.

'Thank you, I think I AM funny,' and this made Maisy laugh even more.

Edward pushed his chair back. 'Now, if I don't head upstairs and plan, I won't have the ingredients for your next favourite dessert, tomorrow, Maisy!'

'Pavlova!' She shrieked.

Despite his seriousness, he couldn't help but grin. 'Yes, my dear, pavlova. Now if you'll both excuse me, I'll collect these plates and head up to sort out the groceries for the rest of the week. Someone's got to feed the three of us!' He nodded at Katherine and began to tidy up quickly. Katherine reluctantly left him on his own. He was obviously not in a mood to talk.

'Let's head up to your room and do a bit of drawing. Then we'll draw a bath, and have a good story before bed. Ok?' Katherine took Maisy's hand to lead her upstairs.

'May we call Papa?'

'Papa is still on his business trip so we can't call him, but why don't we work on a new drawing so it can be finished before he returns?'

Colin disliked calls from Maisy when he was on business, especially China, due to the time difference. It was always confusing and a few times he had ended up having 'baby talk' at important corporate event. Katherine had reluctantly agreed that there were no 'child calls' while he was on business. Oddly enough, it didn't seem to bother Maisy too much.

'Yes, I have a new drawing to make, a special one,' she stated earnestly.

Up in Maisy's room, Katherine drew too. She didn't just play draw with Maisy, she drew properly. She had inherited her mother, grandmother and great-grandmother's artistic abilities and took great pleasure in her art. Charcoal sketching, watercolour and gouache, were her favourite but she also loved her traditional Chinese painting, known as guóhuà, which her grandmother had taught her. It was this latter method she adored the most. The same technique as calligraphy, it was essentially a Chinese brush with black ink or coloured pigments and she loved to mix guóhuà with romantic European landscape paintings.

It was important to her that Maisy continued the family artistic tradition, and Maisy had shown great interest and ability. There was so much family history linked to art. Katherine's great-grandfather had been posted to Shanghai in his twenties and his wife had gone with him. It was a sketchy time from what she understood, but they were honest in their dealings with the Chinese people. His wife took the opportunity to learn traditional painting and had revelled in its differences from the prominent European impressionist rage at the time. Katherine's mind was relaxed, as she focused on her sketch and remembered quiet painting sessions with her mother and grandmother. She looked over at Maisy and felt calmly content. Before she knew it, the hour had disappeared.

As usual, they kept their artwork secret from each other, until their painting session was up, or indeed if Maisy needed help.

'Darling, I'm just about to run your bath now – finish up your piece and I'll be back to have a look.' When Katherine returned, Maisy had her tongue to the corner of her mouth, concentrating on a final detail.

'There, Mummy, look,' and she put down her pencil and lifted the paper.

'Wow, Maisy, that's beautiful!' Katherine was truly appreciative. She loved her daughter's art and this sketch with some watercolour was no different.

'Shall I guess?'

'Yes please!'

'Ok, I can see a beautiful garden wall, roses rambling to the top, is that right so far?'

'Yes, and....?'

'...and a pretty door in the garden wall, like a secret door, slightly open with a little face peeking out, a...man's face?'

'Yes,' Maisy had her nose scrunched up and her lips pursed as she looked at the face, 'that is very good Mummy. And do you like the painting?'

'I love it, darling. The sketch is perfect. Are you planning to colour this in or are you done now?'

'I want to colour in the door, and colour in his hair.' She studied the drawing, frowned with distaste and said, 'His face isn't right. I'll fix that tomorrow. And I need to add a car and things like that.' She was very certain.

'Ok, I can't wait to see that tomorrow. Let's get you off to your bath and then to bed with a little story. You choose tonight, ok?'

'Ok!' And soon enough Maisy was in her bed, fast asleep.

~ ~ ~ ~ ~ ~ ~ ~ ~ ~

Anjali and James were sitting in the garden, enjoying the evening sun. It was cooler and they both had light jackets on, but the weather for an autumn evening was fabulous. The children were fast asleep and the couple talked about what they would do if James had more time for the family, and indeed, if Anjali could negotiate a higher salary. She laughed if she'd ever truly get the point across to her boss that she was only part time, and that three days was three days. They thought about travel, about buying and doing up another house, and sipped their wine companionably in the garden.

Anjali popped up the path and into the kitchen to sort out glasses of sparkling water. The Parmesan on their pasta had been salty and they were both thirsty.

As she neared the fridge she could hear her mobile bleep with a new text message. She found her phone by the toaster. It was another text from Richard.

She swiped to read the full message and shook her head to read it again. Her pulse raced suddenly and she turned her mobile completely off. What was this? She wouldn't think about this till tomorrow. In fact, it would be Wednesday, her only day of the week in the office.

She placed the sparkling water, two glasses, and with a quick decision the already opened bottle of wine onto a tray, and headed down the garden path, to her husband.

~ ~ ~ ~ ~ ~ ~ ~ ~ ~

Thomas was tired. The time difference was hitting him this time, and he needed sleep. He unlocked his front door and stretched as he entered his hallway. That was a fast bike ride and his muscles were tight. He kicked out the tension, shook his strong cycling thighs, and swung his arms down and around a few times. His arms bulked up with muscle as he lifted them for a big stretch. He kept up his cycling training and routine as best he could, despite the fact that he didn't have time to compete anymore. It kept his mind alive, and gave him quiet time to think through his research.

He often caught the women he met looking at him appreciatively and it always took him by surprise. James was convinced it wasn't because of his mind or family pedigree. 'It's your rippling muscles you muppet,' James would tease him, 'really, you could take your pick.'

But Thomas never did. He was competitive for sure, but not when it came to women. He always backed off when friends or business associates introduced him to women. He simply didn't have time or room for women in his life. He had thought about finding a partner, when James married Anjali, but soon realised with his increasing work commitments it would not be easy.

Plus there was the great time the four of them had together. Not so much recently, but the four of them used to get together often.

He frowned....a couple of years after James and Anjali married, Katherine and Colin married. He looked up to the ceiling and took a deep breath. Then almost as soon as he was married, Colin was off for two years, mainly staying in London for his MBA and travelling heavily with work commitments. The four of them were together often then, keeping Katherine company in the Cotswolds, and he had loved it, despite his concerns about his brother's behaviour in London.

He pulled his wallet from his back pocket, and then Edward's envelope from his other pocket. Both he placed on the hallway console table, and then he fingered the envelope. He stared absently at it, thinking.

His brother, to the contrary, had no concerns about his own behaviour. In fact, Colin seemed to hardly focus on his marriage at all. It irked Thomas tremendously. Katherine was besotted with Colin, but she never really knew him, Thomas thought.

He looked up at a beautiful painting in the hallway, a gift to him from Katherine's mother. She had photographed them as late teenagers, both back from a swim in the river, tanned, laughing, happy and obviously delighted with each other's company, oblivious to the person watching them. Katherine's mother had caught a perfect moment that had happened many times throughout their childhood and then had painted the photograph, almost real life, as a watercolour. She'd given her gift to Thomas when both he and Katherine had finished University.

He remembered that day well. He had cycled quickly over to Katherine's house, knowing she would be back from Uni, having just finished his exams himself. Edward had led him into the study. She was there with Katherine, both of them admiring the painting.

He didn't notice the painting, he was looking at Katherine. He almost couldn't speak. It had been a term since he'd seen her.. She was so beautiful; athletic, and her classical face was in profile as she studied the painting. She turned to look at him - but her gaze was different - shy and hesitant. He had felt the same, and instead of the normal embrace Katherine's mother had expected, there was an awkward silence.

She broke the mood, 'Congratulations Thomas, University is finished! I've no doubt that your grades will be excellent. Here is a small gift from me...' and she waved her hand towards the painting.

Katherine's mother was grinning, watching them both. Thomas turned to look where she was pointing.

'Oh! It's, it's a beautiful painting,' his voice was deep with emotion.

Recovering quickly he added, 'It reminds me of such good times, thank you,' and he embraced her.

'Mother you've painted us so well. Have we always looked that happy and carefree?'

'Yes my dear, you have when you've been together,' and she moved from the room to leave them alone.

But nothing had happened. The term apart had changed Katherine, or perhaps, both of them. The moment had passed and instead of divulging how much he'd missed her, Thomas could sense from Katherine's face that something was different. He cracked a few jokes to bridge the silence after her mother left, and challenged her to tennis. Just then, Colin walked in the room.

That was when Thomas first knew. Katherine blushed as Colin loudly stated, 'God you get more beautiful each time I see you Katherine,' his eyes were looking her over, assessing her, 'and more grown up.'

Katherine turned her head shyly from Colin, then looked back at him in a slightly coquettish pose. He grinned at her, his smile broadening, confident. Thomas felt punched in his stomach. Colin had never shown interest in Katherine – this was a bad sign.

And then years later, there was a marriage, a birth, and now, a death. He caught his breath in his throat as his mind raced back to recent events. His stomach contracted; that pit of guilt, again.

What if he had controlled events better? From the moment he'd met with Katherine's mother on that fateful morning before her accident, what if he'd acted differently? What if there had been another way? Another way to keep their happy lives, without, and he put his fist to his mouth, a death.

He pulled his eyes from the painting, took Edward's note from the envelope and headed to the kitchen. He was that tired and harrowed, he decided to forego supper. He'd have a quick juice from the fridge, shower, and go to bed. But not before he would muse over the note, one last time.

~ ~ ~ ~ ~ ~ ~ ~ ~ ~

Katherine slipped away from her daughter's room to the hallway. She looked at the family members hanging on the wall along the staircase. Such a family heritage, such rich characters, she knew all their stories.

She blinked, taken aback at her own negligence, and said out loud, 'Mother's portrait should be here!'

It dawned on her that her mother was now part of their story, and not so much actively part of her own, anymore. She made a mental note to add the portrait as another important job to do.

Now, before heading down to her mother's study, she had one important step to do.

She inadvertently put her hands on her two back pockets. She almost certainly knew what the fabric was, but had to verify her suspicions. She walked purposefully to her mother's room in the west wing. It was up on the third floor.

She held the thick balustrade with its ornate carving of oak leaves and acorns. She loved this stairwell as much as the grand entrance in the reception hall. The wood carvings were ancient and beautiful but it was the art on the stairway walls from the second to the third floor which captivated her.

Rather than portraits of ancestors adorning the walls, like on the lower stairway, here there was a flowing 17th century fresco winding to the third floor. It was a romantic image of the landscape, in fact her family's land, with the hills and fields, ancient trees, and wild animals of the estate. Her mother adored the fresco and had explained many times to Katherine why it wasn't just beautiful, but of historical importance.

An Italian painter had been brought over to paint the stairway. Typically, frescoes of the day were of hunting and shooting parties. But as her mother explained, their ancestor at the time, a Duke, insisted upon non-violent images of the land. Although he was a famous games hunter with many hunts organised on his property, he believed the stairway, like an upwards journey to heaven, should illustrate scenes of peace and contentment. And so, the house was noted for its more celestial frescoes, and in subsequent years many art historians were invited to the second floor staircase to study the fresco.

Katherine quietly pushed her mother's bedroom door open. She took a deep breath at the stunning room and grand views. The decor itself was sophisticated but it was the views that elevated one's eyes immediately from the bedroom to the terrace windows. The landscape was as stunning as in the study, but from a level two floors up. This gave anyone standing at the bedroom balcony, a great vantage point to view the full gardens surrounding the lime tree avenue and Orangery.

Her mother's scent was everywhere. Her soaps, her perfumes, and of course, her favourite fresh flowers, hydrangeas and roses, still arranged here weekly by Edward. Katherine walked slowly through the bedroom to the dressing room taking in her mother's belongings. Her eyes lingered on her mother's favourite items: a writing table, her bedside table and lamp from her own mother, and paintings made by Katherine and Maisy above her dressing table.

The dressing room itself was significant in size. It was organised well and Katherine loved to spend time here as a child. The majority of the dressing room held contemporary clothing; however her mother had two smaller cupboards which housed clothing from her mother and grandmother. Occasionally, her mother would don a dress from her grandmother, or a blouse from her mother. Although she would stand out from the crowd in the function she attended, she was always stylishly dressed even in clothing several decades old. Katherine smiled and remembered her mother saying, 'These items are historically important, and the pieces are simply timeless. Many of them are Parisian Haute Couture. They should be worn, albeit carefully, and certainly not shut away!' Too right, thought Katherine and she couldn't help but breathe out a small laugh at her mother's approach. Some of the more significant items her mother donated through the years to museums.

She moved towards the first of her mother's chest of drawers and headed straight to the top drawer – the very same she had been in, only four weeks ago. At that time, she'd had a hard time holding back the tears. It was the first time she'd been in her mother's room since her death. She had folded a beautifully embroidered white cotton shirt, freshly washed and smelling of warm autumn air. It was the man's shirt her mother often wore over her bathing suit on her daily walk down to the river.

It was also the soiled shirt the funeral director had given Katherine almost two weeks after the death, and a few days before the funeral. Remarkably, there had been no blood on the shirt. Only the earthen marks from where her mother had fallen. Without a thought, Katherine had returned home that day from the funeral director's office to wash the shirt by hand. Without any suspicions at the time, she had studied up close the significant tear in the cotton fabric.

It was then that Katherine became uneasy and unsure. The rip looked quite unlike something a slip on a rock might cause. She had gently placed the clean folded shirt in its spot and pushed the drawer close, staring at the drawer for some time, before turning away. That had been very hard, and not quite the closure Katherine had thought it might be. That terrible tear in the shirt didn't make sense. And it was this that had sowed the seed of her suspicions.

Today, she was feeling much stronger, and slowly pulled open the drawer.

'Uhh!' She gasped, open-mouthed. The shirt was gone.

'How…that…is odd,' Katherine didn't understand. She pulled from her pocket the ripped piece of cotton she had found earlier in the day by the river with Thomas.

It was small, but large enough to display a tiny section of intricate white embroidery, like that on her mother's shirt. There was nothing now she could compare it to.

She felt a sudden desire to leave; to leave the dressing room and her mother's room and to begin the long task of working through her mother's papers. Her small questions, her small investigations were not closing up the concerns she had, but rather, unravelling any reasonable logic that may have explained her mother's death. She pocketed the cotton again, closed the drawer and headed for the study.

She was looking forward to a good talk with Edward when he brought her evening tea.

Chapter 10 - Letters

Colin bolted upright. God, that lightness of head again. He hung his head a bit as he tried to remember where he was. Where? He opened his eyes and fixed his gaze on the first item that came to view - his desk bin in fact - and then he remembered.

What woke him? Ach, the dream was coming back to him, and he slowly fell back into it. Katherine was smiling at him, a smile like no other he had ever seen; close to the smiles of their early days, and simply radiant. Proud, happy, totally in love, trusting. But she was far away, she was....she was across some water, what WAS it? What water?

It came into focus, it was the river. The river was flowing, simply flowing as it always did. Katherine was there still smiling, but it was her mother he could hear. She was calling his name from somewhere behind Katherine and up, up higher, but from where? Her voice was taunting him, taunting him with what she knew and yet, it couldn't be true. She wasn't like that, taunting wasn't in her nature. And when he looked past Katherine and far up to find her mother, it was then that he understood. He saw her mother pointing at another figure, standing below her like a reaper, eager and satisfied. Colin panicked and looked back to Katherine.

Katherine couldn't see the figure, she couldn't hear her mother, and she was still, guilelessly, smiling at him.

Then he realised that Katherine's smile, that beautiful, devoted smile had been directed right past him, and shining its adoration not at Colin, but at his shadow behind him.

He turned to follow her gaze. His shadow transformed to an image not of himself but of another, standing tall and noble. A person he knew well.

Her mother shouted this time, for help. The reaper figure below her was reaching up to pull her down. Colin looked frantically between the disturbing scene, and Katherine, trying to warn her to help her mother. She was so close.

Katherine was unaware. She was focused on the figure behind Colin.

Colin turned around and shouted frantically at the figure. The figure disappeared and in his nightmare, Colin was relocated to the river, shoulder to shoulder with the reaper. He felt himself indistinguishable from the threatening figure; had he become the reaper?

Katherine's mother began to sob, he panicked and closed his eyes to the image, collapsing into darkness.

He heard a cry and thrashed out violently. It was long and deep, hopeless and sorrowful. He tried to make sense of the noise. Where did it come from? Then, he realised the guttural moan was his. He looked to Katherine for reassurance but she was gone. He moaned, again.

This time his moan woke him fully. He lay in bed, tense from the recollection of the dream.

He tensed further as he thought he heard a noise outside his door in the hotel corridor. He squeezed his eyes shut to rid himself of the dream and quietly moved from his bed. He stepped alongside his door, listening. There was a scuffling noise away from his door and then, the faint ping of the elevator.

He peeked through the hole in his door. There was nobody there. He decided not to open his door, but checked the double lock was on, and then went to the washroom. He took a moment to stare at his image. He was pale and shaken. Shaken like a martini, he grunted.

God, what a nightmare. He checked the time and returned to bed. It was only 3 a.m. and just an hour since he'd hung up with Richard. That awful dream, he didn't like it, nor the possible meaning of it. He growled angrily to himself; dreams have no meaning, right? He had a headache, that was real for sure, and he rested his head on the softest pillow he could find on the bed. He fell asleep, staring at his door with his head thumping, like a low deep drum beat.

~ ~ ~ ~ ~ ~ ~ ~ ~ ~

When Katherine entered her mother's study for the second time that day, she couldn't help but smile. It was a momentous task, to go through her mother's papers. But also, the room was so close to her mother, she felt again a calm presence. She needed a bit of comforting, after her discovery of the missing shirt from her mother's bedroom. She was looking forward to an evening alone, sifting through the papers and trying to connect the dots. She was also anticipating her talk with Edward about the shirt and any help he could provide regarding her mother's estate. She planned to broach the subject of his health too and check he was alright.

There were three things to tackle tonight: her mother's post which Colin had not yet gone through; documents she might need to have when the family solicitors met with her tomorrow, Wednesday morning; and anything that may help her better understand the note. Hmm, there was a lot to cover with Colin when he returned. Her mother had become more digital in the last six months, and she was sure Colin had all her mother's digital banking details and information on any investments or debts she may have left. Despite the fact that her mother had most items filed digitally, she hoped that some helpful information could be found in the study tonight. Certainly, the family solicitors could appraise her of her mother's banking and investment information tomorrow, so she could talk more knowledgeably with Colin when he returned.

Katherine settled down again, on the linen seat of the desk chair. She reached for the pile of letters and decided to sort them by type. They had stacked up over the last week or so, for sure.

There were letters from family and friends. There were business associate letters, the bank, solicitor letters, the funeral directors, the church, and several charities. She decided to work through the solicitor letters first.

Interestingly enough, they were still addressed to her mother, with 'care of' to Colin. She had signed legal documents giving her husband the right to deal with her mother's affairs. It was different now. She felt stronger, back to how she was before the death.

There were five letters from the family solicitors. Katherine read them from oldest to most recent. As she read through each, her heart picked up pace. Nearing the end, she paused to consider the implications.

She was in complete shock. Her mother had investments. In fact, she held several investments - enough to be referenced by the solicitors as an 'investment portfolio'.

Katherine shook her head. Was it possible? Didn't she know anything about her family? She had had no clue. Reading through this, there was no doubt that a portfolio existed. Whether her mother had invested and built the portfolio herself or whether she had inherited wasn't obvious, but what was now obvious was the scale of the investments. There was significant mention of charitable causes that her mother supported as well. The solicitor letters mentioned several holding companies with interests globally, although there was no detail as to what that meant. Katherine decided to ask the solicitors for further information tomorrow morning.

As exciting as this development was, it paled in light of the tone of the most recent letters. Katherine's eyes dilated as she re-read the information. The family solicitors had requested an urgent meeting due to 'movements within the portfolio and possible impact on the family and charitable causes'. The final letter, dated this week, had an ominous ring to it referencing an email and phone message, and stating that they had 'deep concerns' with 'recent financial activities' and 'lack of communication'. The letter ended with an urgent request to get in touch.

She found herself staring out the large windows at the evening darkness settling on the garden; thoughts racing through her head. What was happening? What were these financial implications? Were the investments in good shape or not and what was the nature of these 'movements'? And why were they a cause for concern? Was it the market and bad investments? Could it be so soon after her mother's death that whatever investments she had set up were already in a bad state?

She ran her fingers through her hair. Why didn't Colin respond to the family solicitors? Colin could be so hopeless, she thought. If he was caught up in his own affairs, he would never make the time to deal with this - especially if the portfolio seemed insignificant to him.

Katherine simply didn't have a clue. Her mother had kept the family finances away from her, letting Katherine focus on her own business and young family. Her mother had always intimated that there wasn't much family money left, that the old money was well and truly gone. She had more than once said that Katherine's corporate finance major could become a real asset to the family affairs, should there be a large enough portfolio one day. But what did that mean? Was this portfolio too small for her to have shared details with Katherine?

She was also disturbed because Colin, acting on her behalf must surely have been aware of the portfolio and had said nothing to her.

He had been very careful to ensure that she understood the house was hers, that her mother had already put this in trust due to inheritance tax, and that there was no debt. Not that this should have been a concern to Katherine.

Her online business was lucrative and her own company profits continued to grow. As well, Colin had always boasted about his company's success and his own family money. At the time of her mother's death, he'd said he would sort everything. Katherine had been in mourning and was grateful. She'd simply wanted to pull a cloak of comfort around herself: knowing the house was hers without crippling inheritance tax and that financially, her family situation was stable. That was all the reassurance she needed at the time. No need to sell the house, to move, to uproot. That was how she had felt.

She thought to herself, perhaps that's why Colin hadn't bothered her with the details. Or perhaps the details were bad news, and that was why he didn't divulge anything about this 'portfolio' while she was still mourning.

She returned to the papers with a furrowed brow. He'd been so secretive recently. The meetings with his friend, Richard, from his MBA days, had picked up in the last six months, with many long weeks spent in London and some associated business dealings in China. She had not seen Richard much, thank goodness, except for this autumn, when he began to visit Colin at the house again for 'urgent business matters'.

And then, he had been at the house twice in the weeks following her mother's death. Colin said he'd been involved in a joint business proposition and had also provided invaluable guidance since her mother's death. It could only have been a good thing, she was sure, but maybe there were problems with the investments, maybe it wasn't a profitable portfolio she had inherited, but costly problems. Despite her not liking Richard, maybe he'd been able to provide financial advice.

She wished the meeting tomorrow with the family solicitors had been yesterday. And then she would have known by now the family situation. She checked the letters over again, and went to the reception hall for her purse and mobile phone.

Returning to the room and checking over the papers she began to type an email to the solicitors. It was important that they knew she had 'woken up' and that they were prepared for her onslaught of questions tomorrow. Her email expressed thanks for taking the time to meet with her tomorrow, apologies that she'd been unable to meet with them despite their persistent request over the last few weeks and that she was hoping to have a complete review of the family interests at their meeting. This included a list of all investments and the state of each of these. She sent the message and then, tensed.

She froze with her mobile in her hand.

She could feel someone else in the room, staring at her. She turned to look and locked eyes with Edward.

He was watching her in an odd way, and then he stared too, at the papers spread around her.

'Ahem,' he cleared his throat and spoke in his calm, affectionate way, 'Miss Katherine, would you like your tea now?'

And the menacing feeling she had felt, just then when she locked eyes with him, dissipated. She wasn't sure whether she was relieved or whether she wanted to get to the bottom of what he'd been thinking. Was he unhappy or disapproving regarding the paperwork around her or, she remembered his sad, haunted looks over dinner, was it something else, maybe sorrow?

He did seem quite sad these days. Her worry about her mother's shirt seemed to fade. He surely had a reason for taking it, if indeed it was him.

'Yes, Edward, I could really do with a tea now. Would you care to join me? Perhaps a large pot for two and any biscuits you fancy. There are a few things I'd like to chat about that is, if you don't mind?' She looked at him again, smiling faintly, wishing him to stay with her.

'That's fine, I'll be back shortly,' he said in his comforting manner and left the room.

Katherine closed her eyes briefly and breathed in. Right, what could Edward tell her? She looked at the remaining pile of letters. He knew so much, he always did.

She was aware that her mother had carved out some estate matters for him to manage many years ago, and that these responsibilities had grown, so he certainly knew more about the estate than Katherine did. Perhaps he even knew about the investment portfolio.

She wondered about his sadness, could she help him with that, was he still mourning?

She questioned, too, whether she could tell him about the note, and the cotton. Could he decipher the note? Could she talk to him about parts of the note, without showing it to him or explaining the context? And the shirt - surely he would be the only other person to go into her mother's room? She folded the solicitor letters into a pile, and began to open the others, waiting for her tea and the conversation that would ensue.

~ ~ ~ ~ ~ ~ ~ ~ ~ ~

'I'm a bit chilly now, shall we go in?' Anjali asked her husband.

'Yes, good idea.'

They collected the tray and a few children's toys and headed up the garden path to the house.

Anjali continued their conversation from earlier, 'I'm hoping the demands on your time will slow down after this deal you're working on, James. It's been full on for you, and it would be nice to spend more time together with the children. You've worked hard for that. Could you negotiate a consultant-type role instead of completely hands-on?'

James grinned. 'I'm not sure I'm ready to be completely hands-off. But yes, with this option I'm pursuing, I should be able to keep control but also step back, and let the others step up to grow the business.'

Anjali could see his eyes were far away, focused on the meetings over the next few days and the complex negotiations involved.

'Ok, let's head up. You still have a few big days ahead of you, and I'm in the office with an early start,' she responded.

They companionably entered the house and closed out for the night, but not before Anjali turned her mobile on and had a final check of the text message that was niggling at the back of her mind. She pursed her lips at her discomfort. She felt an odd mixture of disapproval and anticipation. Would tomorrow be awkward? She put her concerns to the back of her mind, set her alarm for 5:30 and then settled to bed.

~ ~ ~ ~ ~ ~ ~ ~ ~ ~

Edward brought the tray of tea and biscuits and laid it down on her mother's desk.

'Let's sit down over there, shall we?' Katherine invited Edward to sit with her on her mother's large sofa, and to place the tea on the coffee table there. He picked up the tray stiffly and placed it as she had suggested, then sat himself, at one end of the sofa. She thought he looked uncomfortable, but why?

'Edward,' she began gently, 'you seemed so upset this evening. Is it about my Mother? I know it's all so recent...is there something I can help you with? And your health, is everything ok with you?'

He didn't move an inch, but stared at her, responding strongly, 'Miss Katherine, I'm fine. I appreciate your concern, but there's nothing you should be concerned about. Yes, I'm finding it difficult, I was close to your mother as you know, but I'm managing. It will just take time to heal the sorrow I feel. In fact, focusing on you and Maisy is a godsend so I apologise if I'm darkening your days in any way. I realise you've been unwell for several weeks, it is difficult isn't it?' He finished with a question.

'Well yes, Edward, and no, by no means are you 'darkening our days', quite the opposite. Is there something specific that has come up, since, well, since my mother's passing away, that you are worried about?' She paused to let him answer.

He sat quietly shaking his head and looking as if he was thinking through his response to that question. He was quiet for some time. Katherine tried a different angle.

'Maybe some of the financial aspects of our family estate? I know mother managed that, but you assisted, is that all in order?'

He looked at her obviously surprised. He collected himself, sat up straighter and relaxed his face.

'If you're ready to review the areas I've been responsible for over the last ten years which your mother entrusted me with, then I'll go over those with you. That should definitely happen, as it's important for you to know. You head up the family estate now, Katherine. However, I didn't think you were ready for such conversations, but I can see,' and he glanced at the papers on the desk and along the floor, 'that you're picking that up now? And taking the reins back from Colin who has sat in for you?' Ending with a question for her, again. He seemed very strained.

'Well, yes, I believe I am. I've been so wrapped in sorrow, Edward, I've had little space in my head to think about the bigger picture. Regarding my company, well I have dependable senior management in there, who can assist me. They've been doing a fabulous job these last few weeks. If they can continue in this capacity, then it should afford me time to look through and better understand the work my mother did and how she managed the full estate,' she was thinking as she was talking, like she often did with Edward and Thomas. It made sense, there was a path she could see herself taking, at least temporarily until she understood exactly what her mother did to manage the portfolio.

'We can cover this tomorrow, if you like,' he offered. Katherine thought on her feet. Tomorrow, Wednesday, she was with the solicitors for most of the day, then she had Anjali over, and later in the evening she would no doubt want time to deal with the outcome from the solicitors' meeting and to continue going through these letters. She decided to delay the financial session with Edward till Thursday, and it would give him more time as well, to get his papers ready.

'Edward, I would really like that, let's book some time together on Thursday, perhaps in the afternoon, and we can take that time to go through those affairs.'

'That's fine, Miss Katherine. Do you require any assistance here?'

She hesitated. No, she didn't want him going through the papers, but should she ask for help regarding the note, and what about the shirt? She grinned in a friendly manner and the words just came out.

'Well thank you so much Edward. I'm fine, actually, and enjoying the quiet time by myself going through mother's papers. If I've any questions, I'll check with you. Thank you.'

Something had arrested her from asking her questions; an inner feeling not to involve him at this point. Asking him about the shirt would surely raise his suspicions and she wanted the road clear to go through his pieces on Thursday. She knew something was still bothering him, and didn't want to weigh him down further with her own concerns. But why did he take the shirt? It must have been him.

'Ok, if you are sure....' he let his question hang, and she had to bite her lip to hold back from asking him about the shirt and whether he knew what the numbers '1190563 srt 409456' from the note meant.

Edward paused just a minute more, then smiled at her, bowed his head, said good night and left.

She stared after him, wondering if she had just lost a golden opportunity to solve her puzzles tonight. She worried that she had insulted him. He obviously knew something wasn't right.

At least he seemed in better health than he had at dinner.

~ ~ ~ ~ ~ ~ ~ ~ ~ ~

Edward calmly turned off the kitchen lights, checked the doors were locked in the house and walked slowly up the stairs to his room. He reached his door on the 3rd floor and unlocked it. His hands by now were shaking. He slipped in his room, closed the door, and leaned heavily against it, unable to catch his breath. His legs were extremely weak. He pushed harder against the door for support but felt himself falling; he cautiously slipped down the door and reached out for the floor.

He felt everything closing in on him, the walls and the ceiling, and momentarily everything was black. Then he saw her face smiling lovingly at him. He tried to hold onto that, to centre his fear, but horrifically a dark thick liquid began to ooze from the side of her head.

He groaned and turned onto the floor. The finances, her death....it was all too much again.

He covered his eyes in his curled up position on the floor, and knew to wait to recover his strength before he tried to stand up. He was so cold, his heart was pounding and his arm was sore. What had he become?

~ ~ ~ ~ ~ ~ ~ ~ ~ ~

Katherine finished off another pile of papers and headed up to bed. Only the hall and landing lights were on, and she knew Edward would have locked up the house. She checked in on Maisy, and then made her way to her own room. Although she hadn't been able to shake off her sadness since her mother's death, she felt she had a purpose now. She had to accept that her mother had died, but she didn't yet, have to accept *how* she had died.

It felt good, so good, to investigate the why and the how. She was getting there slowly, she only wanted the information to come more quickly. Tomorrow was the big day with the solicitors and she was sure to discover more then.

She quelled a sick feeling rising in her stomach as she thought that there was a possibility, based on the grave tone of the solicitor's most recent letters, that her mother's finances may actually be in serious debt. She needed to meet with the solicitors first but it may be that she'd have to meet with both Colin and Richard, if indeed he'd helped sort the finances. She grimaced, hopefully she wouldn't have to meet with Richard. A shudder went through her body. Yes, he was like Colin, with the same flashy characteristics, but Richard was several degrees worse. Richard was showy and well, sly. She didn't classify her husband as sly, he was too affable for that. But Richard, he was so smooth he merged into sly, and that was how she regarded him.

Before she had fully understood what he was like, Katherine had leaned on Richard some years back. Her husband had been full of praise for Richard and that had surely seemed a solid endorsement.

At the time, she'd been looking for some early investment for her young business. Given the growing surge of demand for her designs and products, her company required funding. Although her mother had insisted she would help set her up, Katherine was concerned that her mother had enough on her hands with keeping the estate afloat.

Colin too, had suggested there was money available that was 'hers as well, given we're married...' but he was vague. In any case, she didn't want his family money.

Richard seemed like a solid option. Not only had Colin endorsed Richard, but her good friend Anjali had begun to work with him. She had been ready to return to work after her children were born, and at a society event which Katherine's mother held annually at the family home, Anjali had been introduced to Richard.

The two had shared gossip about the City and some common characters they happened to realise they both knew. That introduction was the start of Anjali's return to work, and Richard agreed to offer her part-time employment. Anjali thought Richard was amazing at his job; and Katherine had been impressed that Richard realised how talented Anjali was.

With her husband touting Richard's success and Anjali enthusing about his business acumen and obvious respect for Katherine's business, Katherine had decided to accept Richard's offer of funding.

Katherine could sense her mother, however, held a reserved judgement of Richard. Perhaps because she thought he kept Colin in the City too much, when he should have been returning home to his young wife.

And so, Richard provided the initial financial backing. He was extremely slick, and she knew, well respected in the City. Katherine eventually realised how cunning he was. After a few years of investment, when Richard understood the full potential of her company, he became keen to invest further and increase his ownership to majority shareholder. Colin encouraged her to consider Richard's generous offer, but Katherine knew it was the last thing she wanted. She remembered well the conversations with her mother and Anjali.

'As much as I respect Richard's financial acumen, and he would surely grow your business tremendously, I'm not sure that's right for you, Katherine,' Anjali had sincerely shared her thoughts one evening when Katherine broached the subject.

'He usually takes control. By that I mean he puts his own people in the business to run it, and the owners well, they become,' she searched for the word, 'puppets really, for lack of a better word. Many of them don't mind that, but I think you will. And I suspect he won't really want to be a major shareholder. He'll get you to a point where he buys the business outright. That's how he works.'

Anjali had let that sink in then said, 'It was different when you were starting out. I didn't know then how he worked and also your business was quite small. You're in a different ballpark now. I'd pay his money back. He's had a tidy profit from you already. Get out, and do your own thing. You have an amazing design eye, and a phenomenal understanding of where the market is going.'

Katherine smiled at her friend's compliment but her eyes were focused.

'Yes, you're confirming what I've felt. And what do you think about my business plan without Richard's money? It's all in such a good place, and even after paying off Richard, there's enough profit to plough back into the business to build it further. Do you think the business plan stacks up as?'

'Yes, of course it does, and you didn't need me to check it over to know that! Go for it, Katherine,' and they had clinked their coffee mugs together.

It was the same with her mother.

'Yes, yes, and yes, Katherine. The company is healthy, you've got the energy, vision and drive, and definitely say thank you very much, but off you go, to Richard.'

Katherine had laughed at that.

Before she knew it, her mother had linked arms with her and was directing her towards a map in the hallway. It detailed the full family estate. She raised the subject of new headquarters which Katherine had included in her business plan. Her mother waved her hand at several areas on the map – a few buildings, old barns and cottages which Katherine could consider for conversions. Katherine could feel her heart pounding in her rib cage. She had squeezed her mother's arm with excitement. Of course, these buildings were perfect. The potential for her new headquarters felt tangible.

Shortly after, Katherine negotiated an early exit with Richard, and paid him a handsome return in order to do so. Richard had never quite accepted her decision and she knew, held a grudge against her ever since. He was like a player in a game believing he held all the best cards, and the right to win.

Since then, she was uncomfortable when he was around. She found he, leered at her? She was definitely uneasy when he was at the house.

To add to her consternation, Maisy as a young child didn't take to Richard. Without fail, whenever he visited she would cry. And so, Katherine had to request that Colin keep those infrequent visits from Richard to the evenings after Maisy was in bed. It also meant that on those occasions she could retire early and see less of Richard herself.

With Maisy starting school this autumn, she had acquiesced when Colin insisted that Richard be allowed to arrive on a few occasions after Maisy was at school. He claimed that he needed to see Richard more often now, due to a business venture. And so, occasionally Katherine would arrive home after dropping Maisy off at school, to see Richard's bright red flash car in the drive. The men worked in a far wing of the house, in Colin's home office, so she never normally ran into them. She'd had, however, the unfortunate experience of running into him twice, at home, since her mother's death. Richard's car was, as agreed, always gone by the time she left to pick up Maisy.

In her room, she prepared herself for bed, hoping that she would learn enough tomorrow to hold an informed conversation when Colin returned. She hoped also, she would not have to meet with both him and Richard. It was totally possible that Richard's presence at the house recently had nothing to do with the family finances and everything to do with this business deal in China.

She carefully took the note and cloth from her pockets and laid them down on her bedside table.

Thinking through what she'd discovered that day, she reached into the drawer of her table for the notepad set in its usual place. That notepad was a godsend, allowing her to quickly pen thoughts at bedtime. And that, she smiled, allowed her to sleep much more easily, having captured ideas racing in her mind, down on paper. She sighed contentedly as she added to her 'to do' list, 'mother's portrait'.

Then, she started a new list on the last page of the notepad. A hidden brainstorming list that included events surrounding her mother's death.

Chapter 11 - Visions

He was back at the river again. It flowed swiftly and swirled in a froth at the edge of the swimming hole. It was a clean froth, fresh and pure - so pure - that river was so damn pure. His heart was pumping and he saw her easily this time. Katherine's mother was calling to him, and waving a small paper in her hand.

'Colin, Colin, what can you mean? Colin dear, what does this mean,' again she was calling him, taunting him with the note in her hand. Was she taunting him? She was asking him for help, for clarity, but only he could see the clarity - she wasn't allowed. His hairs were up, up and stiff on the back of his neck. She shouted this time, fearfully, urgently.

'Colin! Ahh, help!' But despite her desperate urgent voice, everything was moving so slowly. She was waving that note, that bloody note, and asking for clarity. But she was waving so dramatically to gain his attention that her weight mass shifted. It shifted…shifted and…he could see her moving, slowly, the whole scene like molasses pouring from a jar. One foot slipped and with weight on the other, she tried to push back, but everything gave way, and tragedy as dark as treacle unfolded in front of him. The rocks waited and watched and the river opened its mouth wide to consume her body and throw it to the rocky riverside further below.

'Ahhh!'

She gasped but had no chance to react, she was already falling. He couldn't move, his eyes wide open with horror.

And then it was quiet. He stood still for another minute more, then walked towards her.

Her body was angled awkwardly along the river shore, with the water tugging at her body, gently rocking her. He stared at the body.

A siren pulsed in the distance. He was pulled back from the body and hypnotising water. He was jolted from a deep, and he knew, disturbed sleep. His mobile's alarm tune reverberated in his head, bouncing around forcefully and waking him up. He lay in bed, breathing heavily as the dream came back to mind.

'What in God's name? God, what am I dreaming?'

He was confused, and fearfully unsettled. He needed to get this business sorted and get out of the country. The whole thing was playing games with his mind.

He checked the time, and grunted, only a few hours sleep. He wanted to send some emails out, to let his Chinese partners know he wouldn't be coming today. That would gain him some much needed time, as agreed with Richard. But it would also serve to show them who was boss. He was calling the shots, not they, and they needed to know that. No more secret service. Or no deal. And the pace needed to pick up. He and Richard had targeted themselves to secure signatures on paper by the end of the week. That way they could begin the long process of commercialising the technology immediately. Advantages like this, never stayed advantages as time marched on, and they were aware of other companies creeping closer; other companies who would be after the same technology as they were. First out of the gate, didn't necessarily mean first across the finish line. But by God, he was going to do everything he could to make sure they were first at that finish line.

He fired the emails off and then ordered room service for breakfast later. There would be chaos at first when they read the emails, and he wanted a good hearty breakfast to face it.

He changed into his fitness clothes to head to the hotel gym. He couldn't face the chaotic traffic and pollution outside for his jog again today. Instead, the gym would be his exercise for the day. Pulling his door shut, he checked the lock was secure, then walked towards the elevator and pressed up.

The doors immediately opened. He was about to step in then couldn't help but take a step back.

That same man from the elevator last night, was standing there. Only this time, he was in workout clothes. He didn't look at Colin, but stared straight ahead.

'How odd, how very, very odd,' thought Colin, and he shifted uncomfortably as he stood in the elevator. The elevator pinged at the gym floor and opened. Colin checked in at the fitness and spa desk, giving his room number quietly, and then took his locker keys and towel and headed to the fitness room. He noticed the man didn't follow him, but instead sat in the lounge chairs in the spa reception with his towel, eyeing the pool.

'That's a bit of a coincidence,' Colin grumbled, then began his workout.

An hour later, and he was aching from a hard workout. Instead of showering at the spa, he decided to head back to his room, and shower there. Before he left the fitness and spa centre he noticed the guy in the same position, in the same lounger, not wet, and looking at his mobile phone.

'Maybe he's waiting for someone,' he thought.

Back at his room, he had a quick glance around, still feeling suspicious from the turndown service the previous night. He relaxed. His room was exactly as he'd left it. Before showering, because he couldn't resist the temptation, he checked his emails on his mobile.

'Ahh, all hell has broken loose,' he smiled craftily as he read through the panicked email responses from his Chinese partners.

Knock, knock. Two little wraps at his room door made him jump. Who could that be? His cloak of suspicion weighed heavily again upon his shoulders and he jumped up to look through his peephole.

'Room service, Sir,' said a young female voice.

'I'm seriously a bundle of nerves, of course it's room service,' he said gruffly to himself and ran his hand through his hair. He opened the door.

The young woman looked him straight in the eyes with a friendly smile and said cheerily, 'Good morning, your breakfast service. May I come in, and where would you like this, Sir?' She spoke in a heavy Chinese accent.

'Wonderful, just place it here please,' and Colin moved out of the way, holding the door so she could leave the large tray on his desk.

She placed the tray down then lifted the silver dome and presented his meal. It was simply fabulous - yes, he had ordered an English breakfast - but it included delicious additional surprises, a few dumplings, some fried Chinese cabbage with pork, and several vegetable bao buns still soft and steamy with heat. He thanked her and showed her to the door, signing off the breakfast service and adding a generous tip, despite the fact that the tip value was already calculated in the menu price.

'Enjoy the coffee, and thank you, Sir, for the tip,' she giggled slightly in return, flushed with the tip that he'd added.

'Oh, well thank you, nice breakfast,' he smiled back at her. She had exceptionally beautiful facial bones and a charming smile. He casually dropped his eyes down her body. He paused for a moment, considering, he did after all have the day to himself now…..but her face was slightly too confident for someone in service.

He took a breath and smiled at her, pausing for one minute more. She tilted her head and looked up at him, also anticipating his next move. He studied her face, smiled briefly and then wishing her a good day, closed the door.

The appeal of her face was on his mind, but his hunger refocused his attention. He turned to his breakfast and grinned at the amount of food. He settled contentedly in his seat, relishing both the food and the chaos he had created with just a few emails.

He read the email replies from his Chinese partners.

'Hah, so quick to appease when the glove is on the other hand,' he chuckled with his mouth full of egg. They had done such a quick turn around. He had underestimated how desperately keen they were to be the only investors, and to sign as quickly as possible with him before other investors were approached.

How easy was that? A few emails, a workout, breakfast, and the tables have turned already. They conceded to removing any links to government or secret service. They agreed to push forward with signing the final documents, and expressed great interest in the recent testing evidence he was providing imminently. They suggested that they reconvene the cancelled morning meetings to this afternoon.

'Ahh, well, I'll leave it till tomorrow. Let them sweat. This will give Richard time to secure the recent test results from Gemstone.'

He forwarded the emails to Richard with his comments saying he would pick up again with them tomorrow on Thursday. He also suggested that he and Richard should catch up on Friday.

Colin smiled. Sorted. He reached for another bao bun. He coughed for a moment, eating too quickly, and cleared his throat with juice.

There was sure to be entertainment Thursday evening, after a full day of negotiations. He shifted in anticipation in his seat. How delightful, he thought, and wiped his lips with the crisp napkin.

Then, just before he finished his breakfast, almost as an afterthought, he remembered to email Katherine. Best to let her know all is going well, and to give Maisy his love. His parental duties irked him at times, despite his relative fondness for his daughter. He quickly composed his email and closed off saying he would send another to her, later in the week after the negotiations were finished perhaps on Friday or Saturday.

'That's done,' he said out loud.

He took a large gulp of his coffee, a cafetière nearly finished now, and winced a bit. Too big a gulp. The coffee had a burnt flavour, deep with some top line of acidity. He cleared his throat again. He pulled his belly in. It was a taut belly. He was too vain to allow for any girth, but still he was full and needed to test the tightness of his stomach muscles, just in case.

'God, that was good. Delicious.' He stood and stretched for a moment. He checked the time – not bad for a Wednesday at 9:30 in the morning.

He opened his heavy hotel curtains to view the wide-awake city below him and yawned. A huge, contented yawn. Then he quickly grimaced as his full stomach stabbed at him again. The tumultuous events of the past few weeks flashed in front of him, woven as images alongside his recent dreams.

That jab, in his stomach, again. Not indigestion, he moaned to himself, just what I need. In a split moment he knew he simply needed to sleep. He'd had such little sleep the last few nights, and troubled sleep when he did manage to get some shut eye. Last night had been terrible. He definitely needed to lie down for a few hours. In any case, he had the day to himself.

The indigestion stabbed him mercilessly again, and as fatigue took over, images lay waiting at the fringes of his vision. He moved to his bed, apprehensive about returning to a fitful sleep, but desperately needing the rest.

He curled up, pulling his bed linen over him. That breakfast had made him heavy with sleep and the caffeine didn't seem to have made a difference. Another massive pain wrenched his stomach. He pressed his fist into his belly. God that was bad. He was tired, so tired. Did he need the loo? He contemplated that for a second only. The fatigue was unbelievable. Ahh, he moaned, this time his whole body shuddered with the stomach pain. He pressed his head into his pillow. What was in that coffee?

The fatigue overtook him. His clenched eyes relaxed and his fists loosened. Just like that, he fell away from the day and the complex life he lived. The images that haunted him faded to nothing and he finally, slept.

Chapter 12 - Anticipation

It was more chaotic than the average Wednesday. She knew why. James was off already, up early and out the door as planned. She was struggling to get the children in a place where they were ready to go, and she herself had fretted over her clothes for the day. Fretted over her clothes!? That was the reason why it was chaotic. Choosing her clothes was something she never worried about, and it annoyed her that it was making her late. Finally, with the children sorted, and her work papers and laptop packed to go, she popped the kids in the car to drop them off. Wednesday was the day she drove the kids to school. Literally a five minute drive, but necessary so that she could easily move on to work from there.

She dropped the children off, not seeing Katherine anywhere to double check the after school plan; and then drove to the village train station. From there it was a short forty minute train commute into London. On the other end, once in London it was a ten minute walk. All in all not bad for travel into the London office, one day a week.

The forty minutes on the train gave her just enough time to check over her executive summary and recommendations for Richard. Pleased with her work, she closed out her laptop. She stared out the window at the passing fields, then decided to look at the text once more. She shifted uncomfortably in her seat and squeezed her legs together.

'Switch of venue - Mandarin Oriental, Hyde Park. Still 8 PM. A lot to cover. Work till late. Room booked so bring overnight.'

The text was simple, the message, perhaps clear? Was she to become one of his inner group, where work dripped into leisure? She'd heard the stories and knew the opulence of the Mandarin Oriental, the fine dining and the rooms he held there. She sighed, it would be nice to do work over dinner, and then relax away from the children for a night. And she was shyly touched that he had invited her - they had only ever had the occasional work lunch on a Wednesday.

Although she was Richard's 'top man' as he put it, he never invited her to his late night meetings with the other top employees who were all men. These business meetings often slipped straight into the early hours of the morning, and blended seamlessly from work to play.

She knew there was a code: although the business was serious, the play too, was quite serious. Depending on the client, the entertainment could be pretty much anything. She turned a blind eye to all of this, not least because she didn't approve, but also because it'd never impacted her. She was able to influence Richard, and have a strong professional relationship with him, without any of the after-hours play that her colleagues took part in.

They all thrived on it. Most of them were not yet married, some of them were - but those relationships she thought, were on shaky grounds.

She wanted to ask Richard about this today, to check whether the work couldn't wait till Saturday, when she could do it from home. She wasn't certain what the 'great news' was about in his original text. She scrolled up to see it.

'Anjali great news, dinner at L'Esplanade this Fri. Late nite. Business of course.'

If it was all that urgent, and the work needed doing before Saturday, then she'd have to clear the time with James.

As the train pulled into London, she packed up and straightened her dress - her dress! She never wore dresses. Why the fuss this morning? She pursed her lips together, disapproving.

It took no time to walk the ten minutes to the office. The forecast was promising another beautiful soft autumn day, and she hummed to herself ignorant of her slim reflection in the impressive glass walls of the building. She glided through the automatic doors to the marble and steel-clad reception and scanned her pass at the desk.

~ ~ ~ ~ ~ ~ ~ ~ ~ ~

Thomas woke early. He'd had a fretful sleep, just terrible. His mind whirled through the night with thoughts about Edward's note, Katherine and Colin. He threw the bedsheets aside happy the night was over.

It was an important day. His clinic was booked with existing clients, however he had a consultation with a potential new client today with royal connections. He treated his patients in the same, professional capacity, regardless of their status. But clients with royal connections or fame always meant another level of security. He didn't know exactly who was visiting him, but it followed the pattern of other celebrities he'd treated in the past. There'd been an initial assessment with his secretary regarding confidentiality and the clinic's history, and of course an alibi name was used for the booking.

His heart quickened as he knew his other big agenda item for the day - stopping by Katherine's to see Edward. To see him and, he cleared his throat, to resolve the issue raised in Edward's note.

He left the house, locked the door and set off to cycle the distance to the train station which was on the main line into London. They had bike racks there; had put them up a few years ago, so it was ideal for him to fit in some decent exercise.

~ ~ ~ ~ ~ ~ ~ ~ ~ ~

Katherine's alarm went off. She'd had a most wonderful sleep and awoke totally refreshed.

She dressed quickly and popped the note and fabric into her pockets for later. She left her room to wake Maisy.

Her daughter was simply beautiful. Her curly brown hair was spread around her pillow and she was lying in the most awkward, stretched out, but obviously comfortable, position. I could never sleep like that, thought Katherine and quietly giggled at her daughter's ability to sleep in that position.

'Maisy dear, it's wake-up time.' Maisy's eyes opened in a flash. She focused on her mother and with a smile popped up and kissed her.

'Good morning, Mummy. Did you have a nice sleep?'

'Yes, dear I did and you?'

'Oh, yes, Mummy. Can I finish my drawing now?' She headed towards her artwork.

'May I, dear.'

'May I finish my drawing now?' She repeated smiling and giggling.

'Let's get ourselves sorted for school and see how much time is left. We may need to finish that off later. Today, Sara and Arun are coming home with you after school. They may not want to paint, but we can always finish it off before bed, don't you think?'

'Oh, I forgot, I'm soooo pleased Mummy to have our visitors!' And just like that Maisy was dissuaded from painting and encouraged to focus on getting ready for school. Katherine knew there was never time in the morning to play.

She helped Maisy to the bathroom and then into her school uniform. They headed downstairs holding hands, Maisy chatting about Sara and Arun.

Katherine was eager to see Edward this morning and hoped she hadn't insulted him the previous evening. His demeanour this morning would indicate if he was bothered with their conversation last night.

He was busy preparing meals for the day and finishing off the breakfast when they met him in the kitchen.

Katherine silently gasped – he looked terrible.

'Hello you two,' he tried to smile warmly at them, but it was a challenge too big.

'Hello Edward, breakfast looks yummy,' said Maisy and she popped onto her chair at the breakfast table.

'Good morning Edward, did you have an ok sleep last night?' She asked casually.

He stiffened somewhat and then continued, cautiously, 'Yes, my back was sore again, and my arm this time, not sure why, so it was an awkward sleep, but I'm fine, thank you.'

She smiled at him, poor Edward. He did suffer with a bad back, maybe that is why he looked so awful..

'Are you doing your back stretches? Anjali swears by them when she remembers to do the exercises!'

'Yes, she's spoken to me before about those. I haven't done them for the last few weeks,' the sentence hung in the air, 'but I should pick them up again, you're right.'

He smiled at her, and his eyes looked softer, calmer, than when he had first greeted them.

'I'm heading into town for a few things, then am planning to visit the office later today,' she smiled at him.

'Ah, they'll be pleased to see you. And it will do you good to be in the office again,' he nodded at Katherine.

With breakfast over, Maisy and Katherine sorted their bags for the day. Katherine slipped her note and fabric from her two pockets to an inner pocket of her tote bag.

She opened the heavy front door, and smiled, squinting her eyes against the strong autumn sun. Maisy ran down the grand stairs to the car and Katherine followed. She carefully tucked her daughter into the backseat, and did up her seatbelt. She hardly dared look at the top of the stairs, so it was a sideways glance only as she buckled in Maisy, but sure enough as always, there was Edward waving goodbye to them both. She sighed with relief and kissed Maisy.

The picture still wasn't perfect, her mother wasn't there with Edward, wishing them both a good day. But thankfully Edward was feeling well enough to wave goodbye. That was a good sign, she thought. She blew a few kisses to him as her car crunched along the Cotswold pebbles and they slowly left for Maisy's school.

~ ~ ~ ~ ~ ~ ~ ~ ~ ~

Richard was humming to himself, admiring his reflection and shaving.

His sleep had been simply amazing. His business plan for Gemstone, given the recent developments, had been refined to needlepoint perfection before bed last night. He'd read through several emails from Colin when he first woke and the news couldn't have been better. Colin had forwarded their response at 1:30 AM British time, while Richard was sleeping. The Chinese partners were bending and that was just what he needed. A bit more time.

And of course, today was Wednesday. A special day in the office for him, always.

He put on his favourite style of shirt. It had his monogram along the hem and on the two lower back panels of the shirt. He had received a gift once, from a girlfriend. He smiled arrogantly at the memory of her. She had monogrammed their two initials entwined along the hem of a Saville Row shirt. She hadn't lasted long, that was for sure, but he had loved the idea of his initials along his shirt hem.

And so he'd commissioned a new style, without her initials of course, and had chosen a delicate pattern to run along the hem with his own initials. The result he thought, was a personalised shirt with detail perhaps slightly feminine but, he didn't care. He loved the design. He preferred his white shirt for today, but remembered that he'd had to order a new one. His nose wrinkled at the reason why.

He considered his other option: today he would wear his pink one. With the cufflinks done on his pale rose shirt, he slipped on his tailored Italian suit - a light wool jacket and trouser suit in the deepest navy. He headed downstairs and checked his profile in the gold-framed mirror in the hallway. Straightening his tie a millimetre, he picked up his briefcase and left his home for the day, humming a tune.

He was still humming when his chauffeur opened his car door at the office an hour later. Traffic had been busy, but that had not dampened his mood. He loved Wednesdays; it would take a lot to change that. He strutted through the revolving glass doors, noting the brass detail had been polished that morning and waved to the receptionists who smiled admiringly, coyly at him, almost bowing their heads as he entered his own City building.

They released the security gate from their reception desk and he glided through, nodding a thanks to them. There was never the need to show his security pass. On the other side, his secretary was waiting by the elevators, having held one for him, ready for his arrival. He nodded good morning and headed into the elevator.

Today, the elevator wasn't going to the top floor, to his personal office and meeting rooms. Instead, she'd pressed the floor one level below. His secretary knew that Wednesday was the day he graced his presence on the floor beneath his; the floor where his top employees worked, and in fact, often played after hours. She knew that he took his time, chatting to his key players, spending personal time with each in their offices, checking on the status of business, clients, and indeed, their personal lives. But she also knew, as did they all, that he spent the longest time in one office in particular. An office that was only occupied on a Wednesday, the only day he did his 'back to the floor' executive round.

The elevator doors closed. His secretary began the morning drill presenting documents for him to sign. He couldn't stop himself from grinning. He felt a surge of excitement through his body – and his heart beat faster. There had been no answer to his message last night, so the message's intent must have been understood. He neatly licked his lips, they'd dried slightly, straightened his tie again, and powered out the doors when the elevator landed at its destination floor.

~ ~ ~ ~ ~ ~ ~ ~ ~ ~

Katherine dropped Maisy at school, but couldn't see Anjali anywhere. She assumed the after school plans they'd agreed yesterday were still on, and she'd be bringing Anjali's children back home with her and Maisy.

She hurried back to her car parked by the school. The solicitors were expecting her soon, and she didn't want to be late. She swung her large tote bag into the front seat. It was heavy today, with her laptop, the letters from the solicitors and a few other papers she planned to discuss with them.

Before heading off, she checked her mobile. An email from Colin had been there this morning when she woke, but with the rush to get out for the school run, she hadn't found the chance to read it.

She sighed. A typical note from Colin away on business. All very cursory - a casual update, a small mention of Maisy, and not to expect to hear from him till Friday or Saturday. Hmmm that could mean Saturday or Sunday, she knew from experience. She dropped her mobile back into her bag.

She carefully pulled out from her parking spot and headed towards the next major town where her solicitors' office was. The drive would be good she thought, a chance to review her plans for the meeting.

Out of the village, and on the motorway, she considered her meeting agenda. Satisfied she had all areas covered, her concern for Edward crept back. She reflected upon his lifetime of loyalty, the opportunities in life he declined to take, so that he could pick up his father's reins and continue working for Katherine's family. Katherine knew that his father had put Edward through University. He'd been a promising young

Maths graduate. Katherine's mother always talked proudly of how clever Edward was - the prizes he'd won as a student, the City employment offers he'd received after his graduation.

Although her mother was a bit vague about it she once intimated that Edward had begun his career in the City, but that he'd returned to the house after only a few years. Was it possible her mother had said that he didn't like the culture of the City firms? Katherine couldn't quite remember. In any case, way back then her mother would have been fresh out of University herself and possibly preoccupied with her own early career in art and garden design. And so she probably never knew the full details.

In Katherine's memory, Edward had always been a part of the house and her life, a special family member, like an Uncle.

'I never did know my father,' she said out loud in the car; a flicker of sadness flit through her mind. He'd died as a young man a few years after she was born.

Following Google maps she found her way to the solicitors. She had visited this place only a few times with her mother. She pulled up in front of the ancient, impressive building with its classical facade of arches in Cotswold stone. There was no trace of modern pollution. They must have cleaned these stones, she thought to herself. It was such a rich palette her designer's eye couldn't help but appreciate the golden ochre of the stone.

She had been instructed to pull up outside the front door so the doorman could assist her with parking. True to instructions, within a few seconds the doorman stepped down from the entranceway and opened her door. She smiled and thanked him as she emerged from her car and gave him the keys.

'These are safe with me,' the well-dressed gentleman assured her.

She confidently hopped up the steps with long strides, her tote bag in hand. At the front door another doorman stood waiting for her, holding the door open.

She felt calm and completely at home. She loved classical architecture and grand buildings, and the history and continuity that they represented.

'Refined elegance,' she said quietly in awe as she entered the reception. She took a deep breath - this building compelled one to feel protected and impressed. It exuded wealth, privilege and prestige. She knew she was fortunate, but the question as to whether she was *still* fortunate, depended on the outcome of the meeting she was about to have.

Her eyes followed the arches in reception upwards to the ceiling and she inhaled again; she'd forgotten the beauty of the small eight-sided cupola high up in the entranceway. It was simply magnificent. Blue skies and cherubs floated around symbols of trust, loyalty, prosperity and time. The coat of arms of the family who built the building, was placed throughout the artwork. They'd been prominent aristocrats and scholars. She remembered reading about the family in the reception book when she'd first visited with her mother.

Not only was she comfortable in her surroundings, but she was looking forward to the meeting.

Katherine loved business meetings, especially where the agenda was finance. A collection of people making decisions that impacted the success and future of a business fascinated her. She loved nothing more than looking at the facts, listening to the evidence and then making a final decision. She had been successful with her online lifestyle company, not just because of her design nous but because of her business head. Her degree had come in handy, all those years ago, and she knew how to run a business.

Today felt no different. She was acutely aware that by stepping into her mother's shoes, she would soon quite possibly be sitting at the helm of yet another business: the family investment portfolio. But how much time would that take, and in fact, was the portfolio so damaged that there were very little funds left to manage? She didn't know what she'd inherited – a major problem or perhaps a minor asset?

She heard a clipped walk. It was someone with heels, on a schedule. She turned her head to see an older woman, slim, exquisitely dressed with demure heels. She was moving quickly towards her.

'Hello Miss Katherine, welcome back,' she smiled engagingly at Katherine, 'we are so pleased to see you. Follow me this way.' She nodded at the receptionist and waved a security pass. The receptionist buzzed them through.

Katherine was pleased to see the firm's most senior secretary. Her mother had been close to her, and they did at times socialise. She was aware that her mother had both trusted and admired her – she was as intelligent and savvy as the men, but being a traditional solicitor's firm, her place was always seen as, secretarial. Her mother did say once, that much of the detailed work was done by her, given her years of experience. The firm partners were completely dependent upon her.

'How are you, Miss Katherine and how is Maisy? It was all very busy at the funeral, there was little time to talk.' She asked in a careful and caring manner and Katherine replied that although it was difficult, they were slowly all coming to terms with her mother's death. Then, the conversation turned to business.

'It's been some time since we've seen you. I know the partners are keen to spend the morning going through the affairs with you. Although they won't mention this, they were relieved to receive your recent invitation to meet, ' she smiled in a conspiratorial way.

'There is much to discuss and they've been eager to review the documents and affairs with you. Your husband has not been very contactable, and although initially he was very interested in the affairs, after only a few meetings, he didn't engage any further with us,' she pursed her lips, the concern apparent.

'He also heavily discouraged us from contacting you, given the situation,' she looked at Katherine with some sadness.

'There's a significant amount of business that cannot be left for more than a few weeks, and we've flagged some perturbing movement,' she glanced quickly at Katherine, '...in any case, the partners will cover this with you.'

At this, she opened and then waved Katherine through an intricately carved oak door. She followed behind and announced, 'Miss Katherine, gentlemen.'

There were three older gentlemen in heavy conversation, leaning towards each other over the conference table. With the announcement of her arrival, they politely stood up and came forward to shake her hand. The solicitor closest to her bumped his briefcase by mistake as he stood up. His papers were pushed to the edge of the table.

A single creamy, thick slip of paper, with dark calligraphic writing on it floated to the ground.

It caught Katherine's attention. The solicitor quickly bent down to pick it up and slipped it under another document in his briefcase.

'Welcome Miss Katherine,' he said and her eyes met his. He looked to his colleagues who also welcomed her, and her eyes took in her surroundings.

The room was designed to impress. She had not yet been in this room, and marvelled at its architecture and detail. It was unashamedly classical. The plasterwork was intricate and most obviously by master craftsmen from an earlier age, perhaps the mid 1600's, and the stucco ceiling was a pale blue, with gold and white throughout. The men had been seated around a large, heavy oak table itself delicately carved with oak leaves and acorns. In fact from where she was standing, she could just make out that the massive central base of the table was a rather romantic interpretation of an ancient oak trunk.

She gracefully extended her hand towards the men.

'How wonderful to see you all, thank you for taking the time to meet with me, and so last minute,' she smiled at them and shook hands.

She was comfortable in a room of men. Even in her world of design, which often had a decent representation of women, her business meetings were almost always with men. She had learned how to deal with arrogance, or indeed, suspicion: clever women and most notably, clever and kind women were not seen as a recipe for success.

She wasn't sure if it was being a woman, or being gracious and considerate that threw off the business men she met, but it didn't matter in the end. She was successful, hugely successful in her own right. She had learned to read the signs; and how to best deal with men who didn't rate her because she wasn't a man. Most men were like most women she met and treated business associate professionally regardless of gender. But sometimes the older generation of men, or particular individuals took a long time to take her seriously.

It wasn't like that today, despite their obvious age. For today's meeting, the person in charge was her. She could read that from their faces and their demeanour. She assumed that her family paid a hefty bill to this firm, but they had also been a rock to her mother. She wasn't at all interested in replacing them. She was hoping to tap into their knowledge and experience and together they could sketch a plan so that she could, at least for the time being, smoothly transition any 'portfolio' work from her mother to herself.

On the table were documents, plenty of documents, file folders and several laptops. There was also a large media screen, in this room of classical art and craftsmanship, that was placed perfectly between two stone pillars. The wide screen had a presentation title slide on it – her family surname and the date – so she presumed they would walk her through a presentation. At the top left was their logo – a solid oak tree romantically etched.

They offered her drinks and she asked for tea. She took her seat, and the secretary served her a china teacup and saucer with a teapot of English breakfast tea.

'I leave you in good hands,' she said to Katherine and smiled at her as she turned to go. She couldn't help but look twice at Katherine's face. Her expression was calm and firmly determined.

The secretary hid a satisfactory grin, and murmured under her breath as she left, 'Just like her mother but with one huge advantage – her finance background...'

And she knew just in whose good hands she had left who.

Chapter 13 - Clarity

Thomas arrived at his clinic near Hayley street where a cacophony of fertility clinics had sprung up over the years. Some were discreet, but most shouted their success at the potential clients, with huge claims on windows, on websites and on images of smiling parents with the most angelic looking babies.

His was on a quiet side street. There was no advertising, no branded banners, just a gold plated sign with the street number, and the name of his clinic. His office stood back from the street. There was an established yew hedge between his property and the two properties on either side. Both yew hedges were clipped to head-height perfection and had bordered this plot for two centuries or more.

There was a sturdy, matt black iron fence along the sidewalk, separating the large front garden from the passers-by. The iron gate was also painted black and permanently open, a welcome first view of his office for his clients. The sizeable front garden was perfectly designed and balanced on either side of the front path. The small gardens off the path, were stocked with roses, lavender, and several curved benches. The benches were a faded oak with deep inviting seats, their curved backs ornately carved with roses.

In later years, just behind the sidewalk fencing, to afford some privacy to those who might want to use the front garden, a row of olive trees had been added. These olives were neat standards, running the full length of the fence. Sitting primly below them, was an old clipped box hedge. It reached halfway up the trunks of the olives.

When James first selected this property to accommodate the success of his clinic, he thought both the building and garden were perfect. His clinic had become known for its discretion and caring service - and the private garden was the first view his clients had of his clinic. It was ideal, he had thought at the time, and as he headed up the pathway to the front door, he was pleased that one could smell the rose and lavender perfumes.

He didn't linger in the garden as it was a full schedule today. He was early and wanted to get on top of the work before his clients arrived.

His receptionist grinned a genuinely pleased smile when she saw him. 'Hello! It's so wonderful to have you back. I thought those Americans wouldn't let you return,' she teased him.

'It's great to be back, and what a lovely reception you're sitting in,' he was referring to the fresh bouquet on the reception desk and the new armchairs and sofas in the reception area. They had ordered new furniture sometime ago, and it had obviously arrived, finally.

'Yes, and not a day too soon,' she replied, 'you have special visitors later today,' she referred to a couple he was seeing that day, and although their identities were still secret, the pre-vetting that had taken place linked them to the British royal family in some capacity.

He smiled at her and moved towards his office, down the hall. He paused, picking up a different smell, and then noticed the new glow of colour from the walls.

'Do I detect a slight smell of fresh paint?' He looked back at her.

'Indeed, we asked Katherine for her advice....her favourite Farrow & Ball Old White. Do you like it? I hope the paint smell isn't too strong!'

'No in fact, there's hardly a smell. And yes, I really like it, and recognise it, Katherine does love her favourites. It's amazing that a grey green can glow - looks good with the new furniture,' he nodded approvingly and noted to say something to Katherine when he was at her home later that evening to meet Edward.

He pushed open the door to his large office, and sat down to prepare for his day. First he turned on his laptop, then pulled papers from his backpack. As he did so, a small creamy piece of thick paper fluttered to the ground. He stiffened.

Edward's note. He picked it up, and put it back into his backpack, not even giving it a cursory glance. His day was fully packed, and he would deal with that, later. But the peace he had felt on arriving at his office, was replaced with a cold, empty feeling in his stomach. As a Doctor, one renown for his empathy as much as his success, it was amazing what he'd been capable of in the last few weeks. There'd been a cry for help from someone he loved and for the first time in his life he had done something unforgivable.

~ ~ ~ ~ ~ ~ ~ ~ ~ ~

James was relaxed. He was with his five colleagues, enjoying a coffee and talking over the progress of the previous day. They planned out what was left to cover, concessions they were willing to make, items that they couldn't move on. Overall they were pleased with their progress and excited about the next steps.

'Can't wait to see this plan kick off, once we agree to the final details and sign all the documents,' said one of the more senior colleagues. 'Shall we go through this one more time before the negotiating team from yesterday show up later this morning?'

'Actually, unfortunately I can't,' James replied cautiously. He had to step out and attend a separate meeting at a pub restaurant in a neighbouring village. He frowned a bit when he thought about this pub meeting. Important business associates wanted to meet with him today to talk about the future of the business. They had been his sole investors two years ago when he needed funding for further research and development. As a result, they owned minority shares in his business. He was compelled to keep them on side, till the negotiations this week were completed.

It wasn't that he thought the negotiations would fail; if all progressed well and he signed this week with the new business partners, then he could offer to buy the shares back from his original investors, giving them a good return on their investment. On the other hand, if the negotiations did fail this week, then there was always the real option that these original business associates would step up to provide the money he needed. The problem was that they wanted to step up now – but he had concerns about them which they hadn't yet addressed – specifically around the security of his technology. And until he was sure of his technology staying in the country, he simply couldn't progress with these business associates. They also wanted to own his company outright and that didn't sit well with him.

The good news, however, was that security of his technology was top of the agenda for the option he was currently negotiating, and company ownership wasn't even on the cards.

However, James didn't like dishonesty in business, and a face to face meeting seemed appropriate with his original investors. He didn't want his team distracted with other offers of investment, and so, he carefully crafted a story to suit.

'I'm off now and will be gone for a few hours. Anjali is in London today, and I need to be at the school for a few hours for parent/child activities. Timing isn't good, but Anjali couldn't take the time off,' he said to the team around the table.

'Can you work through these final pieces and then brief me when I get back, just before the negotiating team arrives? I shouldn't be gone for more than a few hours, so there should be time for an internal, thirty minute prep before our guests are here, ok?'

The men nodded and turned to review the content again. James took a deep breath as he left the room. The drive was about half an hour to the pub restaurant, they would most likely have an early lunch, then he had a private matter to see to after the meeting was over. He dictated the pub name to his navigation app and set off.

~ ~ ~ ~ ~ ~ ~ ~ ~ ~

Edward waved good-bye to Maisy and Katherine. She was right, he wasn't feeling so well this morning. But it wasn't his back.

His head drooped sadly, and his eyes were solemn as his mind wandered off. All that support he'd given to her and her daughter, why hadn't she listened to him? Did it have to end the way it did?

He was alone today. With Katherine off for most of the day, he wondered when Thomas would stop by. He was sure Thomas would want to see him today, after reading the note. He had Anjali's children after school as well, and then Anjali herself once she finished work would be over to visit Katherine. He planned to make a large dinner, it felt like there could be a decent-sized get together for the meal tonight. Perhaps the children first for a high tea, and then the adults later for dinner.

He made his way to the kitchen to finish his cup of tea, and plan the evening meal. He picked up his mobile and was pleased to see an email from yesterday's visitor. The gentleman wrote that there'd been a most interesting development and he'd know more by the end of the day. Did Edward want to meet tomorrow, Thursday?

Thursday. He would be several hours, if not easily half a day with Katherine. He was sure she would want to go through the estate details, and she'd be surprised at what that entailed. It might be tricky to fit the two in together. She had said the afternoon, so the morning could fit conveniently.

He replied to the email, suggesting Thursday morning, at his visitor's office this time, not the house. He certainly didn't want Katherine running into his visitor. Then, he had a look at several websites he tracked, checking the status of particular items, before he returned to his kitchen duties.

~ ~ ~ ~ ~ ~ ~ ~ ~ ~

Anjali was verifying some final stats on her presentation. She'd bundled the business case in paper form, but knew that nine times out of ten, Richard would just use her presentation to make a decision. He hardly ever read her full digital version of her business case in google docs and just as rarely read a hard copy. But it was traditional to present a full business case this way, and so she continued as it had always been done.

She was standing up leaning over her desk and checking her data, when she heard her door open. No knock, just the door, and then Richard was there. As she turned she caught him looking at her legs and lower dress when she was bending over. She instantly blushed – he never saw her in a dress.

'Why, hello Richard, how are you?' She asked carefully. She knew his moods could be up or down. Generally they were very up with her, but she had learned not to second guess his temperament.

'Hello Anjali, I'm absolutely fine, thank you! Looking forward to your presentation this morning,' he grinned at her, a full-on grin she thought, almost like a school boy, teasing her.

'When will you be ready?'

'As soon as,' he smiled invitingly. 'Why don't you come with me now?' Presentations were normally done in the privacy of his executive room on the same top floor as his office.

She collected her document and laptop and when they were in the quiet of the elevator she turned to him, 'Richard, Friday evening, what's the work you'd like us to cover? I'm not sure how late I can to stay. Is it work that can only be done on Friday? I could always pore over the detail during the weekend from home,' she sighed inwardly. The objective was to control work better, not for work to control her further.

'Ahh, I thought you might ask me about that. Yes, I'm planning to close out some work on Friday. I need some documents reviewed and signed off by then, and the work may take till very early hours Saturday morning. The people on the other side of this deal, never accept weekends as a reason to delay. So I'm afraid we'll need to work through till late,' he glanced at her, measuring her reaction. There was none.

He pushed on. 'I never ask you to do these late nights, and it's a one off, Anjali. This is a very important deal, and I need you on the final numbers reviewing the terms with me.' There was a slight moment of silence with no response from her.

'Of course, you can take Monday off, that's not up for discussion,' he finished with a flourish, pleased that he'd thought of that offer.

Anjali didn't want this to become a habit. She didn't mind being left out by his late work nights with other colleagues because she'd always preferred being at home with her husband and children.

She thought, this sounds really important to Richard. Plus, she felt devious even thinking this, if she could get the work done late Friday then perhaps - perhaps she could manage a lie in at the hotel on Saturday morning. She'd had so many late nights working on her business case, and interrupted sleeps with the children. A lie-in, at a sumptuous hotel, wasn't such a bad deal. But, it was important that James was comfortable with the plans. She looked up at him.

'I wanted to check with you how important this job is. And I can see that it really needs doing. However, I'll pass it by James first before I confirm, if that's ok. He has a lot of work on this week and the children have swimming lessons on a Saturday morning which he'll need to do.'

Richard didn't twitch a muscle. It seemed to have worked, his game was on. And oddly, oddly enough, she still didn't seem to realise his full intentions. The whole situation was delightful, and his anticipation so great that he felt again that surge of power. He moved closer to her as she turned to face the elevator doors, with his hand just centimetres from her waist. She smelled so clean, there was a faint scent of, was it roses? He leaned closer and felt himself gently lulled by her scent. And her innocence was so sweet. His eyes closed in on the back of her neck, to a vulnerable soft spot of skin at the nape. Bending towards her, his lips almost brushed her hairline just as the doors opened. She stepped forward.

Richard's head fell forward behind her, a motion like he was nodding to sleep. He instantly blinked and pulled back. She noticed his pause and turned around to look at him quizzically. Collecting his demeanour he breathed in and stood to his full height. 'Yes, of course, check with James, and let him know how important this one-off meeting is, will you?'

That was close, he thought. Keep it calm.

Anjali smiled at him, 'Will do,' she said and the two walked down the hall to the Executive meeting room.

'I have a good feeling about your presentation. Once this Friday deal of mine is sorted, we can focus in on your new business opportunity come Monday, er Tuesday. Your ventures never seem to fail, Anjali,' he repressed a delighted sigh, she was gloriously beautiful and intelligent.

She gave him a confident but curious smile. He was trying.....too hard, something was up, but she couldn't quite put her finger on it. She knew he was a difficult one to trust. His employee turnover rate was relatively high bar his favourites - but even then some seemed to simply leave the firm, without any explanation. Fortunately, she'd always got on with him. She swept her concerns aside. It didn't matter just now, because she was about to present her work to him, and was almost certain it would be one of their best ventures yet.

~ ~ ~ ~ ~ ~ ~ ~ ~ ~

Thomas was calm. He treated all his patients the same: wealthy, private clients or referred through the NHS; black or white; Christians or Muslims. To him they were all the same – a community of people desperate to have children, who simply couldn't. They came to him often as a last resort, and were usually in a state of persistent melancholy, with relationships almost torn apart.

His secretary called to say the next patients had arrived. He had their information in front of him, but it was sparse given the confidentiality of the case, and the fact that their real names had not yet been provided.

He stood up from his desk and walked to the door, opening it just as the couple approached. He blinked with surprise and only just kept himself from gaping as his body pulled back to assess them properly. He immediately refrained from raising his eyebrows and despite his normal, calm demeanour was astonished to feel himself react to their celebrity. He didn't realise his potential clients would be such important royals. His immediate reaction was to how beautiful the wife was, even more so than the photos in the papers. The husband, although young like his wife, had a commanding but measured air about him.

'Welcome to my clinic, please follow me this way,' they smiled nervously and he led them through the door.

As they settled themselves in the chairs, his secretary came through, leaving a fresh cafetière of coffee and brewed pot of English Breakfast tea. She left after doing what seemed to be a short curtsy. He held back a chuckle, as it looked so bizarre here, in his office.

He'd been briefed on the formalities by his secretary, but wasn't comfortable with this. Within the walls of his clinic, they would need to be on equal terms and comfortable with each other. He required all of his clients to trust him, and so, he began the session cautiously.

'I hope you're both well, and welcome you to the clinic,' he smiled warmly at both of them. 'I realise this may not be the correct protocol, however, my assistant did impress upon your secretary prior to this consultation that here, at our clinic we are best to treat each other as trusted partners. We like to use first names, and that seems to work really, very well indeed,' he paused to allow them to react. There were smiles and nods only.

'What's discussed in our clinic, and any activities linked to the clinic and a client's treatment, remain completely confidential. The clinic couldn't function if we didn't both practice confidentiality. I ask that you are also confidential regarding your treatment, or other people you may see in this clinic,' he smiled in a friendly manner. 'Apologies for being upfront about our protocol and courtesies, but we do have many people coming through our door, including those known in the media, and we hope that this makes sense to you both?'

'Yes, of course,' the husband immediately responded in a deep yet clipped voice.

His wife spoke softly, 'We're pleased that confidentiality is so critical to this clinic. We accept your stipulations and thank you again, for seeing us.' She held her head at a slight tilt and fidgeted with her sleeves.

He carefully studied them - so young and so much pressure on them to have children. They would feel a pressure not many of his clients would ever know. He could tell that they were not yet at the state of no return. Some of his clients had tried so many times unsuccessfully that the shadows behind their eyes betrayed a sad longing.

'Good, and now, although I've read through your notes, I must admit at this point, they've been rather short in detail,' he waved his hands over the documents on his desk.

'Ah, yes,' the young man coughed into his fist and with a straight back leaned towards Thomas. 'That would be our secretary. He thought it necessary that we meet in person before all details were shared with you.' His wife held her head shyly and nodded in agreement as she looked at Thomas apologetically.

'That's fine. I understand. How about then, if you each talk me through why you have come to see me, and I can study your notes later when they are sent,' he respectfully waved his hand to encourage the young lady to speak first and then leaned back in his chair, letting them take control. He was relieved that they would be like any other client; he had a method of working successfully with his patients and already he felt they could relax with him. That was key.

~ ~ ~ ~ ~ ~ ~ ~ ~ ~

'Alright, shall we start?' Katherine asked the men around the table.

The gentleman who had introduced himself as the eldest partner replied. 'Yes, of course. We read through your agenda and have prepared our information. We'll walk you through the presentation and take any questions you might have.'

He drew in a breath, pressed his tie to his stomach and brought up the next slide.

'The diagrams and tables on this one pager, summarise the portfolio status.'

Katherine's head stretched forward as she squinted at the screen.

'What?' Escaped from her mouth. And then she gasped.

She covered her hand with her mouth, trying to contain her shock. They looked at each other and gave her a moment.

'Are you alright?' he asked.

She nodded her head and noticed her hands were very cold. She warmed them on her teacup and sat forward to listen. How could this be?

'Please, continue,' she replied.

~ ~ ~ ~ ~ ~ ~ ~ ~ ~

Richard stretched back in his chair as Anjali came to her final slide. Her presentation had been completely engaging. In fact, he rather thought that she was adorable. It occurred to him that she could probably sell her vision and ventures as easily as him she was so personable and knowledgeable. Only, it was his company, and his place to do that.

She was right, her business opportunity was perfect. Her research, recommendations, vision for where it could go was unchallengeable. It could be as strategic as the Gemstone opportunity. He leaned back in his chair to admire her further. In fact, Gemstone was also one of hers, a tip-off she'd given him early days. He tensed his stomach muscles. Yup, she was clever, for sure and unlike the others on the team, modest.

And God she was good looking. Her dress pulled tight in all the right places. One would never have known that she'd had two children. Her arms were elegant as she pointed to her slides, and her legs, well, the dress wasn't quite as revealing as he would have liked. But he knew, he could tell her pins were slim and firm.

'And that, is that. Final recommendation.' She grinned proudly at her slide and turned towards him, waiting for his reaction. She was slightly flushed.

He wanted her to relax, he wanted more of her time, and he couldn't wait till Friday.

'Anjali, that is brilliant. You are brilliant.' He moved towards her and taking advantage of the mood, gave her a congratulatory embrace. Trying to keep it professional he awkwardly thumped her back - as he did with the guys - he didn't want her spooked.

But he couldn't help himself. Her body was so close, and after one pat of her back, his arms automatic closed around her waist and pulled her to his torso. When there was no immediate resistance he moved his head back to look into her eyes.

Her head was sideways to his shoulder, so he couldn't see her. But he could feel something. Something familiar, that he had known many many times, but not with her.

It was always the same, but he thought it would be slow to happen with her.

It wasn't. He could feel her melting and his pulse began to race.

He jerked himself back to reality and stepped away from her. Not now, not too soon, it all had to be professional until Friday night – or Friday might never happen.

He cleared his throat and apologised.

'Anjali, I'm so sorry about that. I was taken away with excitement. I would normally jump up and give the guys a big clap on the back, when we sense a good deal, but given, well given that such a clap would probably knock the breath out of you, I couldn't help but give you a proper embrace! Bravo, Anjali, amazing work!'

Before she could respond he changed the subject. 'We need to celebrate! It's lunchtime, so let's catch a quick one down by St Paul's. Ramsay has some great jazz on at midday and the weather is beautiful.'

She smiled quizzically at him. She was relieved that he'd explained his little performance, and grateful as well, that he could see the potential of her business case. She felt a little weak at the knees, knowing how big this opportunity was, and the deal they could land. But also, she was weak from the embrace. It had knocked her sideways for sure, and caught her completely off-guard. She'd had no time to steel herself against such an invasion of her space; and no time to plan her response.

She could appreciate his beauty, but she would never have been attracted to his perfect looks and showy ways, even were she single. She wasn't attracted to him, which made it all the more odd that she had not recoiled immediately at his closeness. She put it down to the mood in the room, and didn't plan to worry about it anymore.

In any case, there was absolutely no way he was coming on to her. She wasn't his type.

'Lunch would be wonderful. I'm actually famished,' she realised how empty her stomach was.

He smiled at her, then called his secretary to book a table for their working lunch. Perfect, he thought, game on.

~ ~ ~ ~ ~ ~ ~ ~ ~ ~

The solicitors looked at Katherine with surprise, 'Were you not aware?' They spoke at the same time.

She swallowed slowly to calm her voice and shook her head, 'No. I had no idea.' Her mind was racing. How could her mother have a portfolio like this, and never discuss it with her? She sat straighter still, ready to take notes on her iPad.

The solicitor presenting gave her a gentle smile then returned to the presentation. 'Alright, let's work through this,' his tone was serious.

He provided a broad overview of the family portfolio, the different categories of investment and the status of major accounts. The top line spreadsheets colour coded risk, profitability and length of term. Katherine instinctively chose to listen till the end of the presentation. Her shock was obtrusive, she lacked ability to process properly. It took them sometime to work through the material.

'That's it for the overview. Have you any queries at this point, or should we focus on two areas of particular interest: the charities your mother was involved with and the real estate category?'

'I think it's best if you continue,' she replied quietly.

They divulged such unbelievable information. Her mother had been involved in many charities around the world. They explained that she had personal notes on each charity, in the case that something happened to her. She wanted Katherine to understand the importance of each charity and why she'd chosen that particular organisation. She had clearly planned for her daughter to inherit this one day.

Katherine was spell-bound. Her mother's background to her choice of charities was captivating. It wasn't what Katherine had expected today. She still couldn't believe what she was hearing. And her mother had the foresight to document this knowing one day Katherine would take over, and she might not be there to handover! Why, how could her mother hide all of this? It was overwhelming.

'Let's dive into the real estate now,' another solicitor attracted her attention as he took up the reins of the presentation.

'This is one of the larger investment categories. The real estate portfolio is truly global,' and he worked his way through the information glancing at Katherine's bewildered and slightly pale face every now and then. They were responsible for all geographies bar the UK, which was Edward's domain. They covered the scope of Edward's involvement and were hesitant to provide more information on that piece. He managed the family's UK property, estate and investments.

The gentleman who had picked up the fallen note turned to her and clearly said, 'We strongly recommend that you meet with Edward at your earliest convenience to discuss the UK portfolio and, other matters he may want to cover with you.' The latter part of his sentence was expressed in an odd way.

Katherine nodded in agreement but was puzzled with his tone.

The first gentleman picked up. 'You're surprised and you do look pale, Miss Katherine. Did your mother not intimate at all about the family portfolio? Do you have any questions at this point?'

'Am I?' She didn't doubt it. Her hands were still cold. 'No, she didn't breath a word of this. I don't understand. The portfolio is substantial – and the profit is, well, extraordinary and hard to believe. Am I understanding that correctly?'

'Yes, it is considerable. One of our larger portfolios actually, Miss Katherine.'

They provided Katherine with a list of next steps she should consider, given the value of her inheritance, demands of some of the accounts and changing markets over the last few weeks.

'We worked with Colin, as you requested, but the engagement was not as well, cooperative as we had hoped.' They cautiously covered their recent dealings with Colin, given he was the family member responsible for the accounts based on Katherine's request.

'And now,' the solicitor looked at the other two uncomfortably then looked carefully at Katherine, 'we don't want to alarm you unnecessarily, but we need to bring the following to your attention. It's a concern of ours,' the elderly solicitor stated. He drew her attention to another slide on the screen.

'There has been recent liquidation and transfer of money from these investments to external accounts. In other words, very strong performing investments have been cashed in – without our involvement – and the money transferred outside of your portfolio to 3rd party accounts.' The solicitor was grave. 'These transfers could only have been executed by someone with access to the accounts, and at this point, Colin is the only person, other than ourselves, who could do this. Our last contact with Colin, was at a meeting we held here, with him and his business colleague, Richard. Since then, and while these transfers have happened, it has been impossible to reach him.'

Katherine sat, angry and speechless. She was in shock; she didn't speak because she didn't trust her voice. She realised the silence was uncomfortable for the gentlemen, but she wasn't ready yet to speak. She stood up and poured herself some cold sparkling water from the cut glass carafe it was chilled in. The ice cubes tumbled into her glass and the sound was loud in a room that sat still, waiting politely for her response.

She took a deep breath.

'Well, may I first say, thank you for a most comprehensive overview. I can see that much work was put into this. The structure of the presentation grouping the investments into key categories, and the summary status of each has been very helpful and appreciated. The charity activities are inspiring and I'd like to thank you for assisting my mother with all of this.' She paused for a moment, checking her emotion.

'I'm, of course, deeply shocked. I can't describe my reaction any other way and will just be candid with you. There was some indication last night, when I read through your letters that my mother was managing an extensive portfolio but as you now know, I've never been privy to this information.'

She paused to ensure that they'd digested what she said, then continued, 'I'm shocked for three reasons. Firstly, I cannot believe the wealth my family holds. My mother always led me to believe that we were an older family, of aristocratic background, but of little remaining wealth. I often thought that when I was younger we were living off the proceeds of my mother's successful career. And I had always hoped the house could still be ours for the next few generations. I never imagined that the state of the family investments was as extensive or profitable as it is. And of course, this responsibility now falls on my shoulders, to maintain and grow, if I can,' and she smiled at them shaking her head displaying her disbelief still.

'The second reason I'm shocked is that almost the moment I discovered from your letters that investments of some sort existed, I also was alerted to the fact that you had concerns about these. And so, my immediate thought was that mother had investments that had 'gone sour' and were money pits so to speak!

'However, based on what you've just covered in your summary I can say that I'm now more concerned about the activities of my husband regarding these investments, rather than my Mother's ill judgement,' her brow was furrowed and her eyes looked hard. In response, the gentlemen nodded to each other, and to her.

'Mother had managed everything perfectly well through yourselves up to the day she died. Why did Colin not engage continuously with you, given the fabulous guidance you have provided to my mother? Such solid guidance is evidenced in her respect for your firm and your long-standing work for my family, but also, in the highly profitable status of these investments. I don't understand why my husband involved his friend, Richard in the final session with you, and not meet with you since? I find this all very disturbing.' She couldn't help but frown with distaste at the thought of Richard becoming involved in her own family affairs.

What is happening? Her head was rammed with questions. Colin is my husband, and I thought he respected and adored my mother. Why would he mess with her well-performing investments? What would transpire in the next few days as she confronted him on his return from China? Angered and sad she turned away for a moment from the men.

The solicitors were watching her, one looked about to speak.

Before he had a chance, she whispered solemnly, 'The liquidation of some of the investments, and transfer of that cash to other third party accounts, and the amount of money we are talking about,' she took a deep breath and spoke more loudly now, 'I can only assume this was for diversification into other reasonable investments?' But she wasn't as certain as she sounded.

'We don't know,' one of the men responded.

She was on the same page as them, then. The concern they had felt, and now unburdened on her, was palpable. Colin had full access to all the accounts. In her earliest days of mourning when she couldn't think properly and because she was sole inheritor, she had signed a power of attorney giving her husband full financial power. She had asked the solicitors to bring her husband up to speed on anything that needed doing.

Colin had reassured her that he'd take care of anything urgent. So much had been dark after her mother's death and she had been so very tired; her husband's interest in the family financial affairs and his involvement was a godsend at the time.

And so, she had given power of attorney to her husband. A husband who upon reflection, she realised, had shown no grief at the death of her mother, nor indeed lack of energy as she herself had experienced. Colin had had boundless energy then, she reflected back, organising all, and still holding his business meetings with Richard. Deep inside she recognised that at the time she was coiling away from him; that his lack of grief in the days following her mother's death firmed her against him.

She vaguely remembered the funeral, with a singular moment most clear in her mind: she'd caught Colin looking around smugly at the mourners. She had flinched at his expression and then noticed that he was focusing on someone. He had caught Edward watching them closely. At that moment, he possessively moved to grab her hand. Spontaneously, she recoiled from him. His overture had felt repugnant. What was he trying to prove to Edward? She'd already known then, that something couldn't have been right.

Someone coughed. She was courteously brought back to the present.

She took a moment to collect herself and smiled at the solicitors. 'Leave it with me, I'll be speaking to Colin in the next day or so, and he'll be back from China this weekend.' She gave them a confident look that she didn't feel. She didn't want to think further about her husband just now.

'Third, although I'm not shocked to learn about Edward's involvement in the family affairs, I am interested in the information you've provided regarding Edward.'

At this, one of the men shifted in his seat and looked around the table at his colleagues. It was the same partner who had picked up the fallen note when she had first entered.

'Thank you for clarifying his responsibilities versus yours. I was unaware that Edward managed the whole of mother's UK portfolio including the estate. In fact, I'm meeting Edward tomorrow afternoon to specifically discuss the areas he managed.'

They talked about the next steps for a little while longer, but she was ready to go, and wanted time to herself, to think.

She moved as to pack up, and the men stood up from their chairs to shake her hand. One of the men locked eyes with her, the same who had picked up the cream notepaper. He had been sitting beside her and he impulsively leaned forward to place his hand gently on her shoulder when they stood up.

He remarked softly, 'I was very close professionally to your mother, and I know it is much to absorb, but you will be fine, whether it is us who assist you, or another firm. It's important you know that.'

Katherine smiled at him. 'I understand that, thank you, I won't be changing firms anytime soon.'

There was no question that she was satisfied with the firm, but she was angry about Colin's actions and what seemed like Richard's involvement in the family business. The secretary was already waiting at the door for her. Katherine collected her belongings and turned to leave.

'Miss Katherine,' it was the same man. His face was sad but serious.

'When there are large sums of money like this, people do - uncharacteristic things. People behave in ways that one sometimes couldn't imagine. We need you to be aware of this and consider who you share this information with.' He was looking intently at her.

'Thank you. I appreciate your concern and I understand,' she just managed to catch herself from biting her lip as she left the room. Didn't that sound a little bit like 'trust no one' from her mother's note?

Chapter 14 - Lunch

The session had gone well. Thomas felt he could help this couple, but they needed space now to decide if they wanted his help.

There was a knock on his office door. He excused himself and opened it. A man and a woman stood outside, and the man said they were there to collect the couple. Thomas smiled and confirmed that the session had finished on time.

The couple joined them at the door, and meaningful expressions were exchanged between the four of them. The woman asked if they were ready to go and they nodded, thanking Thomas for his time. He felt a real warmth towards the two fo them.

The woman talked into an earpiece, and checking the hallway, left with the couple through the back door of the building. The gentleman held back and approached Thomas.

'I'm wondering whether you could afford time to lunch with me for a few hours today?'

Thomas was taken back. 'Why, thank you for the offer. Let me just, let me just check this, with today's appointments.'

He was busy today, that he knew, but clients did sometimes cancel at the last minute. His consultations were also booked hours apart so that he could complete more detailed notes on each patient or follow up on their results.

He headed down the hallway to his secretary and explained the situation. She indicated silently that he had a 1.5 hour lunch slot just now, and that she had given him 1.5 hours after that, for follow up planning he may have needed to do regarding the couple he had just seen. Thomas smiled at his secretary and nodded to her. He returned to the gentleman.

'Thank you, that should fit in very well indeed, Mr....' And he reached out a confident hand to shake the gentleman's.

'Ah, yes, the name is Quinn, Mr Quinn. I'm the private secretary to the couple,' and he shook Thomas' hand.

'If you don't mind, I've already reserved a table in a French restaurant I frequent that is close to St Paul's. It's discrete and we will be at a table where we can talk.'

They agreed to catch a taxi, and Thomas was surprised at how laid back and friendly the private secretary was. He was intrigued about the lunch, and had a hunch that this gentleman might indeed look for updates much as Katherine's mother had, during Katherine's treatment. Although, he never did update her mother with progress; he always encouraged her to talk directly with Katherine.

He caught his breath as his mind wandered to his last meeting with her, and his plan to catch Edward later that evening. He pushed those problems from his mind and turned to his lunch partner in the taxi, as he was saying something very interesting.

'They would like to engage your services, however it may not be as straightforward as you think. I'm sure you have many celebrities and titled clients, but this couple as you may now realise, is titled like no other. And with that comes not just formality, but procedures that we will need to follow. I'd like to talk you through all that over our meal.'

'As well,' and he turned his head from the window to looking directly at Thomas, 'I'd like some clarity on the type of treatment the couple may have to undertake and any side effects of this, length of time, etc.' His voice was clipped, professional, and very educated.

'That's fine, we can walk through general information over lunch. However, until we run some tests and I have several consultations with the couple, I'll not know which treatment is right for their personal care. But, I can provide a decent overview of the types of treatments we have had the most success with.' Mr Quinn bowed his head and acquiesced at that.

'Here we are,' Mr Quinn indicated as the taxi slowed down and he began to pay the taxi driver.

'Let me,' offered Thomas but Quinn had already paid, and was opening the door.

As Thomas stepped out into the still quite warm autumn sun, he squinted and looked around at the street and buildings. He'd been here before, in this area, a few years ago. St Paul's Cathedral was around the corner.

He dug deep on his memory trying to place the situation, who, what, why was he here? And then something caught his sight. He did a double take.

Walking on the other side of the street were Anjali and Richard. His initial reaction was to flag them over, he was so pleased to see Anjali. Richard, he wasn't very keen on, but he was a good friend of his brother's and he knew that Anjali respected Richard as a boss.

He raised his hand and just stopped short of calling out to Anjali because he noticed at that instant, something not quite right. His hand froze in mid-air.

They were walking very close together. Anjali was walking straight and laughing, smiling, occasionally bumping into Richard. He was leaning too close to her, she couldn't help but bump into him. He was leaning towards her face and was inches from her cheek and mouth. Yes, there was traffic and he knew Anjali had a quiet voice so it was plausible that Richard had to walk close to hear her. But this was oddly, too close. They weren't in a club with music banging in the background.

It was evident that Anjali was telling a story that made them both laugh. She looked young and happy, Thomas thought. Richard was smiling, attentive, and focused on her face. But what panicked Thomas wasn't just how close their faces were, but the position of Richard's left hand.

Anjali was walking to his left, and he was leaning inwards towards her. But his left hand, which perhaps could have stretched protectively across her shoulders, wasn't in that acceptable position. Instead, his arm was stretched down across her back, with his hand resting below her lower left back. Squinting again, he was disgusted to see that Richard's hand was hanging over her lower left buttock, but not touching it. Just there, possessively and certainly, suggestively.

He couldn't quite believe it. He was watching them walk away and it was certain that Richard had his hand very close to touching her bottom. She wouldn't have felt anything and most certainly wasn't aware what it looked like from behind.

They had passed by so quickly, but Thomas' face still had time to go red. He was angry. That was his best friend's wife. And Anjali seemed completely clueless to the situation. Richard almost certainly hadn't touched her bottom, but it didn't matter, he should never have had his hand in that vicinity.

He didn't trust Richard and his intentions. He knew that when Richard liked a woman, he either saw her as a sister (arm would have been stretched across Anjali's shoulders) or as a potential lover (arm would no doubt be on her 'ravishing arse', language that Thomas had heard Richard use).

Mr Quinn was waiting for him on the sidewalk in front of the French restaurant. 'Are you alright?' he asked Thomas.

'Ah, yes, apologies, I thought I saw people I knew, but I was wrong,' he shook his head to indicate his mistake, but also in disbelief at what he had witnessed.

'After you,' indicated Mr Quinn pointing to the open door.

Thomas smiled thank you and stepped into the restaurant. It would surely be an interesting lunch, but he couldn't shake the image of Richard's arm, wrapped so closely around Anjali, and the position of his territorial hand.

~ ~ ~ ~ ~ ~ ~ ~ ~ ~

James was settling into the pub meeting with his business associates. The venue was beautiful. A country gastro-pub which, confirmed by the accolades in the reception area, was Michelin-starred. James knew he didn't really have time for this session in his diary, what with the current negotiations going on, but he was pleased to see his old business associates. They were always positive and supportive, and had repeated again when they shook hands hello that they were still very keen to 'get in on the act fully now, to help his energy technology reach its potential'.

The meeting began on solid terms, catching up on each other's personal lives and the mood was jovial as they ordered. But within 15 minutes of the meeting, the business associate pressed his tie to his chest, pulled himself up to the full length of his torso, and spreading his hands on the table, palms down, began to explain the reason why they had requested the meeting.

'James, I need to be clear here. We want to buy your company outright and then swiftly roll out production. As you know, we'll pay you handsomely and although we require full ownership we are completely open to giving you total reign to run the business as you like.

'Look, this is my job. We are in a tight place now. I work for a venture capital firm and it is our business to find new ventures. We have been courting E2E for some time and are looking for full ownership. Our funding supported you in the last couple of years to grow your research and development. Now, on the cusp of our two year anniversary, we couldn't be more complimentary. We don't want to influence you to sell to the highest bidder as most VC's do to secure a big payback, we, your partners for two years, actually want to buy your business.

'You know us! What could be better? And look, James, we either want to be fully in, or unfortunately, fully out. At twenty percent stake, which is what we have right now, well, that's just not good enough anymore for the portfolio.'

James could detect that his business associate was talking honestly. The man looked uncomfortable, and evidently didn't want to discuss his pressures too openly. He paused to let James reply, but James waved the gentleman on, waiting for the punchline.

'If we can't sign the deal till early next week, because you need to think it through, then I'm under pressure to provide evidence to my board. Evidence that your delay isn't because of lack of results and questions about of your technology. We need more up to date evidence, James. Evidence that your technology works - it doesn't need to be all your intellectual property, but evidence that the recent tests you've done have full, positive, results.'

He looked directly, intently into James' eyes. Their business relationship was a good one, and he didn't want to break now, with James.

'As well as that evidence,' and he held James' gaze to continue to his next point, 'if you cannot sign papers to sell to us this week, and don't forget, all that documentation is in order and ready to pick up from where we left off, then we need a letter of intent from you. A letter of intent that describes your intention, soon, to sell.'

He paused to stress his next point.

'Otherwise, James, I'll have to strike you off our target list.' He let that sink in then added, 'Unfortunately, James, if that happens, we won't be swooping back in again like a white knight to provide the funding we know you need. We'll have moved to the next company interested in our backing.'

James studied the men around the table. They all looked so earnest, and were obviously keen to grow his business. James could understand the situation - but during the previous negotiations they had not provided the one thing that he had asked for - a written commitment that the technology of his company would not fall into the wrong hands.

James' decision was simple. He was ultra conservative by nature, careful and considered in his actions. He couldn't risk losing this offer of purchase because he might need them if the other negotiations later today didn't conclude successfully by the end of week. But equally, he didn't want to be pressured to expose all of his test results. What if the results were shared with a competing or malevolent party - and for the latter he was thinking of bad characters from other countries who would love to get their hands on his technology.

James was firm in his reply.

'Alright, I understand the situation. We can't do anything this week, we are at a critical point with our research and finalising the full impact on the energy market. I can, however, provide some initial findings from this research, and the projected impact it may have on the energy market,' he paused.

'However I'm also waiting on your written assurance that should you acquire the company, that my technology will not fall into the hands of bad characters.'

His business associate held his gaze that bit longer and responded slowly.

'Of course, you're referring to the government's national security bill protecting certain UK sectors - like energy - from foreign investment without first having been heavily scrutinised by the government. I understand your concern and that isn't a problem here, we're working on having written confirmation in time for the transfer of ownership.' He paused keeping his eyes locked on James.

James relaxed and nodded. 'The sooner the better - I can't move without that lined up. I don't want any time wasted in negotiating the sale of my company, if this needs to be quite rightly, scrutinised by the government.'

The business associate moved slightly as if he were uncomfortable. 'Right, you don't need to worry about that - we'll get you the confirmation that it's all above board. I'll check what the hold up is with the legal team,' his voice was conciliatory.

James wasn't finished. 'And when you refer to 'giving me full reign', the terms should include scenarios and conditions for both parties. Without ownership I don't want to be caught in a situation where I can't do what is right for the company.'

'Ah yes, of course, we can revisit that in the terms. In any case, we've trusted you to run the company for two years and look how successful you've been. We wouldn't look to change that model,' he replied. Having dealt with that issue he moved to his other point. 'James, what about the letter of intent to sell to us?' The challenge to James was clear.

'Yes, I can sign a letter of intent to sell. I can't agree to sell to you at this point, but I can indicate an intent to sell the business in the short term,' James was firm.

'James, that sounds like you might be considering several suitors....?' He let the challenge hang in the air.

James smiled and shrugged his shoulders, 'You know we are being courted all the time. When we get to that stage and it could be tomorrow, it could be in two weeks, you must be aware that you might be up against others?' He was sure that the business associate realised other suitors could be involved.

The associate chuckled and slapped his hand on the table gently. 'I think you're in the wrong business James. You should be in mergers and acquisitions, you'd be well-positioned there! Alright James, a few things, we need up to date evidence of the technical performance as quickly as possible, for my main board. We need that done for today.'

He tapped one finger on the table, then tapped a second one.

'We also require today, your letter of intent to sell in the short term. As you are aware, I'm under pressure to have this all sorted as soon as possible – and the deadline is next week.'

Then, he banged his full hand on the table.

'Right, I'll also check with the legal team for our statement confirming there aren't any 'bad characters' lurking in the background,' he paused to smile at James as if sharing in a joke.

'Look, it's been a good lunch but I've got to get back now - lots of pressure back at the office.'' He nodded at his colleagues around the table, and they all stood and shook hands with James.

As James pulled out of the Gastro-pub and reflected on the early lunch, he thought it had been a balanced outcome. He would need to get back to them immediately with evidence – evidence that wouldn't jeopardise the secrecy of his energy technology. He also had to pen a letter of intent he was comfortable with, and that they would accept. In any case, he needed their legal team to get back to him on the security of his technology under the terms of their deal. Truth is, none of this would matter if his current negotiations completed this week, but it was always wise to have a back up. He simply needed more funding, there was a lot going on.

He drove carefully through the country lanes. He was early, it was only just after lunch and he would have time to do what they requested back at the office, before picking up the other negotiations. His timing was perfect because he was also early enough to attend to a private matter. He'd arranged to meet someone around noon or just after.

He turned his car into a small lane, and headed in the direction of Katherine's house.

~ ~ ~ ~ ~ ~ ~ ~ ~ ~

Edward knew he would need a good part of the day to prepare for Katherine tomorrow. He wanted everything just so, such that Katherine could easily get up to speed and clearly make decisions he needed her to make.

It was important that he didn't burden her or cause her any alarm. And there was enough to be alarmed about, if one looked at the detail. He thought about the meeting he'd had with his visitor yesterday and the information they had exchanged; the note he had given his visitor with a long list of points. He pursed his lips, and there was the matter of Thomas, and the note he'd given Thomas. If she looked just that bit further, the veneer cracked everywhere.

He had skipped lunch today, there was simply too much to do, plus he was expecting yet another visitor very soon, for a half hour only. Then, he could get back to preparing for his session with Katherine.

Chapter 15 - Wealth

Having left the meeting with her solicitors Katherine was en route to her office; a converted barn on the family estate that housed the team and served as corporate headquarters. She couldn't stop the thoughts racing through her head. So much had changed over the course of the last few hours.

What inconsiderate game was Colin playing? Was he pilfering the family money, or re-investing it in his own way? Regardless, it was unacceptable.

Despite the spread of investments, until she understood what Colin was doing, she wasn't sure that her newly-inherited wealth was safe. She knew many families where the wealth simply disappeared with bad management, or because individuals had cashed in on the money, and she was concerned that her mother had entrusted her, and yet already there were problems.

After her mother died, in her heavy state of sorrow Katherine had begun to worry about many things. Her company was stretched at the seams, and this was despite a slow growth plan where she had tried to strategically manage the company's expansion. Her mother's death jolted her confidence and made her question the health of her business. What if the business was to collapse under the pressure? What about all her employees, her suppliers, her clients – and her family? The life she had known and built, and which seemed so solid and dependable, felt much less secure and stable since her mother's death.

And then she had also worried about the family affairs. What if her mother had not planned appropriately, and significant inheritance tax would consume the family? What if the home her family had lived in for hundreds of years, was to be taken from them? Colin had at least assured her that would not be a problem, she thought ironically. And then there were the letters she had read from the solicitors, urgently asking for meetings to cover the investment portfolio. She had in the last 24 hours, assumed the worst.

She sighed. Today, anything but a normal Wednesday, she had learned that the family estate was vast and still intact but under threat and eroding, it seemed, in the last several weeks.

She glanced in the rear view mirror and spoke out loud.

'I can't possibly hold down two jobs this demanding. The family portfolio and my own business. No wonder mother had pulled back from her garden writing, events and appearances. And here I was thinking she was retiring!'

She let out another sigh and could see now what had happened. No doubt as the portfolio and her interest in investments and charities grew, her mother had taken on a full-time job managing that. No wonder she was so busy, no wonder she offered to invest in my business, thought Katherine.

'Why did I know so little about my mother? Why didn't she talk to me about this? I thought we were so close!' She spoke vehemently and then coughed nervously as she remembered the sober events leading up to this discovery. The river, the morning swim, the death of her mother.

She held back a sob, there were still plenty of things to worry about. Was her mother's death really an accident? And now that she knew how wealthy her mother was, she wondered who else knew.

Edward. Edward would have had a strong picture of her wealth, and she exhaled slowly - already she wasn't in a 'good place' with Edward. He had taken her mother's shirt which made her, well, in fact, she was suspicious of his actions. And his mood swings - he was definitely not the Edward she had known, since her mother's death.

She'd had a neat understanding of Edward's life, in fact she realised that it was, unfairly, defined in her mind as an extension of her and her mother's life. But now, she needed to redefine the Edward she knew. As she did her own mother. What was he capable of? Was that why he had taken her mother's shirt. Did he take the shirt to hide something?

And of course, Colin knew. But he would have only known about her mother's vast wealth after her death. She sighed heavily as her heart quickened pace. Why didn't Colin tell her about this? And why did he pull away from the family solicitors who had guided her mother so well?

'Why in heaven's name did he move all that money?' Katherine spoke out again loudly this time through her teeth. Where did he move it to? What were those '3rd party accounts' and what was then done with the money? She tried to relax her muscles.

And there was of course, one other person who might have known how wealthy Katherine's mother was. Someone who was very close to them both.

Katherine had been aware that for some time her mother had invited Thomas for private tea and conversation. There was a period when they were together often, and it certainly would have dovetailed with three events: from what she learned today it would have been when her mother was looking to expand the family portfolio into smaller, riskier businesses; it was also when Thomas was looking for initial investment to grow his already successful clinic; and lastly, it was when Katherine and Colin were heavily involved with Thomas' clinic to become pregnancy. But at the time, Katherine had not paid much attention to the tea meetings between Thomas and her mother.

Was it possible her mother had invested in Thomas' clinic? She had vaguely assumed her mother was keeping in touch with Thomas and the treatment progress. That was very much like her mother, quietly in the background checking everything was ticking properly. To be truthful, she was never certain that Thomas shared much with her mother anyway, he was so stern about client privacy, even when it was family. In any case, Katherine kept her mother up to date on the treatment and the eventual pregnancy itself.

Sometime after her difficult period of treatment and after Maisy was born, Katherine was aware in the distant background, that the tea invites had slowly become few and far between. Was it because the treatment had worked, or because her mother had perhaps invested in the clinic and the private meetings, on business terms, were only necessary very infrequently.

Her mother had loved Thomas as a son; they all knew that, even Colin. Thomas and Katherine had been inseparable, and her mother supported Thomas when his own parents were absent on diplomatic visits, or absent because they were simply too focused on Colin, the eldest.

So it was possible that Thomas knew; that he was aware of some family wealth, if her mother had offered to invest. It was also highly plausible that her mother had invested in his clinic, it fit her portfolio perfectly.

Tapping her hand on the steering wheel, she literally gasped aloud, 'Of course, I could find out. That should be easy enough to check tomorrow, before my session with Edward. Perfect,' she was forming a plan in her mind.

She couldn't be suspicious of Thomas. It was impossible that he had anything to do with her mother's death but then, she would have never imagined her mother had such a - well - such a double life to put it mildly. And the solicitor did state how people can behave oddly when money was at stake - where did that put Thomas, if he did know? He had said to her in recent months that he was thinking through how to accommodate surging patient demand.

She also couldn't believe her husband would be so disingenuous and in fact, duplicitous with her, his own wife. She'd come to know her husband better over the years, and had learned that he could be somewhat shady with his business dealings. Well he certainly didn't conduct business the way she did. But withholding this information from her, and the transfer of monies, that was unimaginable. In her books, it ranked as unforgivable.

Before she knew it, the entrance drive to the barn loomed to the far right. She was here! She took a deep breath, she'd been away too long. She knew though, that it was bittersweet - it would most likely be sometime before she could properly return to run her business.

~ ~ ~ ~ ~ ~ ~ ~ ~ ~

The lunch had gone well.

Thomas reflected; he had another royal couple now about to be treated by his clinic. It was an accolade others might capitalise on. However, as their private secretary had stated, these were royals at a different level. He understood, but he wasn't one to be sidetracked by titles or celebrity.

He had got on well with the private secretary - who himself was relatively new to the job. They were both very keen for the treatment to succeed, and to remain highly confidential from prying public eyes.

Thomas had cabbed it on his own, back to the office. He had two client appointments left, then he would not stay late. He was determined to return in time to see Edward. Edward often retired to his top rooms early evening, after serving

Katherine her evening tea. He needed to catch Edward before that. His stomach curled as he thought how the conversation might go, and then, what then? He frowned - what did Edward know?

~~~~~~~~~~

She tingled all over - it was the effect of champagne midday, despite the fact she'd only had 1 glass. She could drink wine or sparkling in the evening, but drinking midday wasn't a common activity for her. Everything seemed to be stimulated. Her brain was buzzing, her senses seemed heightened, everything was touch and light sensitive. Richard had covered so much ground over lunch - asking her key questions about her investment opportunity and respectfully listening to her viewpoint and evidence. She was elated. To have spent so many months researching, pulling together the business plan and now to visualise the success of this venture with Richard, over lunch, over champagne, with his obvious stamp of approval...well she was feeling triumphant.

She looked around to take in the atmosphere. Jazz played in the background. Professionals everywhere were talking, laughing, plates softly clattering, glasses clinking, candle flames flickering even in daylight, her skin, tingling.

She had given all this up years ago, to focus on the children. A waiter saw her looking around the restaurant and checked whether she needed service. Ahh, she smiled at him, shook her head no, and then dipped her head as she rubbed the side of her neck contentedly.

All through lunch, Richard had looked at her intently, leaning close to listen to her responses. Although the ambience was muted and sophisticated, the combination of jazz and people's laughing and talking, made it difficult to make herself heard. And so, he had moved round the table to be beside her, rather than across the table. The waitress had kindly moved his setting to accommodate this.

She knew he was leaning on her every word, so significant was this opportunity and investment. It was no small amount of finance she had recommended - or rather, requested. Overall, the lunch had been wonderful, thought Anjali. Her boss had been so attentive, and encouraging, but as always, on the ball - keen to pull out the details and check what he instinctively knew to ask.

With their coffees finished, he turned to her and smiled.

'That's amazing work, Anjali. Pretty water-tight, and in more detail than I could have expected. The sooner this other business is off the table, the sooner we can initiate this piece of yours. Let's make sure Friday happens, ok?'

She nodded, caught up in the moment. And then she remembered she had to check with James.

'I'm expecting papers on the current negotiations to come through by Friday evening. Then Friday we can hold another working meal together - this time at the Mandarin Oriental. It's perfect for confidential discussions. Given it's the final revision of the contract, it'll be a lot more intense than today. In fact, your point of view, given that you have not been involved to date, will be invaluable.'

He stood up and pulled back her chair.

It had been a great working session, and if she could get through Friday, then next week would be very exciting. She looked at him.

He had not moved. He was still standing there, close by, watching her. He stepped forward and she took a short, quick, intake of breath. She thought he was about to kiss her cheek.

He reached out to grasp her shoulder and he gave it a squeeze.

She breathed out. What had just run across her mind?

'No big embrace like earlier,' he joked sheepishly, 'but no less the thanks. You've done great work today, why don't you head home and text me later about Friday?'

She breathed out, 'Are you sure?'

'Yes, very sure, get back home to your kids - you might not see them Saturday morning!' He gave her a cheeky smile and she nodded in response.

'Ok, I'll text you later to confirm Friday. Thanks for seeing the potential here,' she replied and with that they left the restaurant together. He hailed a taxi for her and she left in the direction of the tube station. He waved goodbye and felt like clicking his heels as he turned to walk back to the office.

~ ~ ~ ~ ~ ~ ~ ~ ~ ~

James was pleased with the first half of the day.

He had managed to meet his old business associates, slip in the personal meeting he'd planned just after lunch, and return to the office in good time.

He was feeling extremely productive for a mid-week Wednesday. He parked and walked with a contented gait to the office. They were such a tiny operation, they didn't pay anyone to man reception. That suited him fine anyway, with the confidential nature of his recent meetings. He knocked on the boardroom door, then entered. His colleagues looked up surprised. They were focused on the documents they were preparing. They broke into grins and all began to talk at once.

They had progressed a lot in the time that he was gone and were clear that the contract could be completed this week. James rubbed his chin and thought it was best now, to bring them up to speed on the wider picture, especially as they seemed so close with these current negotiations.

'That's great work. Let's go over it in about half an hour. We'll still have plenty of time for any final edits I might have before they arrive this afternoon. In the meantime I've something I'd like to share with you.'

They grinned wryly. James often surprised them with a positive development or sometimes, a challenging curveball. They were curious.

'You know we've had several companies recently interested in our business. And two serious finance options have come through. My focus and number one priority has been the opportunity we are working on right now. This is the right step forward, and appropriate for the value and future impact of our business.' He paused to let that sink in. It was important that they understood all this work on the current proposal, and the intense negotiations this week were the priority.

'However, our old friends are still keen to acquire us. They claim to have everything lined up: the post-acquisition production plans; the distribution model; the pricing. Although we are negotiating with the right finance deal at this time, I didn't want to put all our bread in one basket.'

'Really, James? You didn't want to put all your bread in one basket? You're not kidding?!' Joked one of the guys. They all knew how cautious James was.

'Ok, so you know me well. But you can see where I'm coming from. We haven't yet signed with our new finance partner and there are only two more days of discussions left this week. We are running to the line on this. And because we haven't 100% agreed on everything, I'd really rather not lose this other investment opportunity. And so, I met our current investors this morning,' he looked a bit sheepish.

'The business associates are still keen to acquire us out right. They're absolutely not the preferred option, but I don't think we can afford to lose them at this point. They can wait till early next week for a final answer, but are looking for two documents now: a letter of intent to sell; and the latest evidence of our tech's successful performance in recent tests we've done. Regarding the latter they want assurance of the transformational impact it will have on the energy market. I can pull together the letter of intent, but for the tech – I thought we could repurpose something we had prepared for this afternoon? Would that work?'

They agreed which content could be repurposed, and yet, still protect their confidential IP. Within half an hour James was able to send an email to his solicitor with both attachments. He urgently asked his solicitor to review both documents and respond as soon as possible with any changes.

With that, he settled down to review the most recent changes his team had made earlier, to the longstanding proposal and contract. There wasn't much to change.

'Version 29, and almost tidied up. I never thought we would get to the end! This is very good. Just a few small edits, ' and he talked them through his changes. James was very pleased; it was highly probable they could get through this by Friday.

The visitors were early. James welcomed them in reception and led them to the boardroom. As they sat down, he brought them up to speed.

'The team has done much work this morning reviewing and responding to the amendments we received from you last night. We believe we have a revised version which will suit all parties, and can move us to the final stage. We addressed each of the comments in your document and I'd like you to note that we are able to comply with the National Security and Infrastructure Bill which the Government has introduced. We've put strong safeguards within the wording of our contract that will support the short and long term objectives of that review.'

Both parties around the table nodded in agreement and in recognition of the importance of those safeguards. The visitors were keen to review the E2E changes and move to contract signature stage. Friday was looming close for them, and they had to report up.

They turned to their laptops to work through the google document. They were positive about the day. James knew it would most likely take the next two days for the final contract to be ready, but they had made significant steps already. Very soon, his dream and that of his team, would be realised. The weight on his shoulders, of which nobody knew, slowly began to lift.

~~~~~~~~~~

Katherine's car pulled up to the barn door entranceway. She sighed so contentedly. The Great Barn was an extraordinary structure. It had been a ruin on the Estate when she chose it. On its last legs, it was a tumbledown half-structure with four still standing gables and a few Cotswold stone walls that were built of coarse rubble.

There was also a lovely midstrey which she had repurposed as the office entrance. This was a projected gable porch at the front of the building. Two great doors stood inside the porch. Fortunately, the midstrey had hung over and protected the ancient doors for centuries. She had been delighted that they could be restored, made airtight, and returned to their rightful place.

The porch still carried the remains of ancient, cusped roses carved into the wood. English Heritage had confirmed that the great barn was clearly of the medieval period and created by monastic craftsmen. It was in keeping with an older church in the village, and remnants from an older part of Katherine's family house. The pitched sweeping roof with gables had been renovated and new windows put in the original openings. The result was a grand barn of ancient and modern design, with beautifully exposed beams and a lightness of atmosphere inside due to the impressive windows.

By the time Katherine had parked her car and emerged from the driver's seat, a welcome congregation was standing before the barn doors. The excitement at seeing their CEO was palpable.

She was taken aback by the emotion of the moment. Her two board members were grinning widely – visibly pleased at her appearance. One stepped forward to take her heavy tote bag, while the other guided her into reception. Colleagues were gathered around her, asking how she was and trying to entice her to see the latest collections. There were smiles everywhere; the mood was celebratory and there was much chatter after weeks of her absence. Katherine learned in her meeting later that her colleagues were very worried about her and the future of the company, due to her absence following the death of her mother.

She realised that she'd left it too long. If she were to step back from this, and step into her mother's shoes for the short term; then even for that short period she would need to provide clear direction to her employees, and especially to the board.

There was a real buzz in the Great Barn, despite its huge space. Most of next year's collection was spread out on tables, hung from stone walls, or arranged as 'themed rooms'. Today, they were preparing products for a photo shoot and there was excitement among the teams.

Outside, by the detached Granary barn and terrace, they had already begun to shoot some of next summer's collection.

The light was so bright for autumn, they had decided to take advantage of the summer-like weather. They led her through the Great Barn to the back door exit. She passed colleagues at their Macs, or at tables working mood boards, or in huddles trying out the products. She had a comment for many of them: asking about a child; making a recommendation about a web page design; asking someone about the safety of a particular product; commenting on the feel of a fabric; repositioning a product display slightly. They all grinned at her, always pleased to hear her comments and relieved that their head designer was back.

Outside by the Granary, the photo shoot was progressing well, bar one problem. The luxury outdoor table and chair collection had arrived but the table top had a mark on it, caused by transport. They were trying to touch it up but the result wasn't good.

'Hi Katherine!' One of the senior buyers waved her over.

'Look at this,' and she pointed to the mark.

'What a shame,' Katherine rubbed it. 'What have you tried? And did you check the shipping process?'

'Yes for sure, won't happen for the customers when it hits the catalogue. But for our shoot....' the senior buyer waved her hands despondently.

Katherine nodded with understanding and rubbed the mark again.

'Hey, give me a moment,' and she mysteriously left for the Great Barn. Inside, she picked up a pair of scissors and a new product she had spied passing through. It was huge glass trifle bowl on a raised stand. She thanked her colleagues for letting her take the items and grinned at them. She teasingly snipped the scissors in the air and said, 'Just borrowing this bowl for a short while!'

Back outside, a few of the team were chatting around the table. She placed the trifle bowl over the mark.

'Hang on,' she smiled to the buyer.

Katherine walked around behind the Granary, to an area she and her mother had always loved, just to the far side of the terrace. The sweep of hydrangeas that grew along the border of the terrace was breathtaking. The hydrangeas were a magnificent blend of mauve and light pink, white and cream, and the palest of baby green. They were in their perfect autumn prime. She clipped a huge selection of hydrangea heads with short stems. On her return to the table she placed the flower heads in a circular fashion around the base of the raised trifle bowl and then arranged even more hydrangeas inside the bowl. It was lovely. She adored hydrangeas just as much as her mother had. She stood back to check the proportions.

The team around were laughing, saying she was up to her old tricks. For her, a bowl of flowers, any kind of bowl and any kind of flower, would always lift a room – even, obviously – an outside room. They were teasing her whether the table would sell, or requests for floral arrangements instead! She was laughing with them, and they were happy – pleased that the problem was solved and contented that she was amongst them again.

As she laughed, her eyes scanned the group and her two board members exchanged meaningful looks with her. It was time for their meeting. She nodded towards the Great Barn. It was time to focus on the serious matters at hand.

She wished the team luck with the shoot, commented on the beauty of the set up and quality of products, and then the trio walked towards the board room in the Great Barn.

She had about two hours, maximum, she calculated, before Maisy's pick up. She had to squeeze a loaded agenda into a very short time with her two directors. She sighed, she could do it, had to do it in fact, and she picked up the pace of her walk.

Chapter 16 - Accident

Anjali was on the return train home. The glass of champagne she'd enjoyed had worn off, but it did nothing to dampen the effervescence of her mood. She texted James about Friday's change to check he was alright with that and whether he could take the kids to swimming on Saturday morning. She also texted Katherine to say she was early and would pick up the kids today, saving Katherine a trip, and would bring them to Katherine's house.

After this, she quickly opened her laptop and brain dumped a number of things that she wanted to follow up on, given the string of questions Richard had asked earlier. No issues, just dotting the i's and crossing the t's. In a flash the forty minutes on the train whizzed by, and before she knew it she was in her car on her way to the school. What a great day she'd had. She was looking forward to sharing the news with Katherine. She sobered somewhat as she thought also that the plan later was to help Katherine at the river. Anjali's brain drifted from work as she mulled over what Katherine had shared with her yesterday. It didn't sit well with her. There were quite a few open questions, and she hoped their river search later today would be fruitful.

~~~~~~~~~~

James checked the time, and saw the text from Anjali. He decided it was easiest to catch up with her at home regarding the weekend.

He looked at the team around the table. They'd made such good progress. He suggested that they stop for the day given they'd agreed on the changes in the documents. Tomorrow both sets of senior solicitors would iron out the final wording with them. There was electricity in the air, despite the heavy content, and they were hyped with the prospect of a closure the next day. If not, it was certain that all would be done by Friday.

When his visitors had left, James returned to the boardroom and shook hands and clapped his team on their backs. They were in a celebratory mood, but they agreed to wait till Friday before celebrating. Not that their celebrations were affairs that needed major lie-ins the next day. In fact, they were a pretty boring bunch. But it was important that they kept their eye on the ball and had the bottom line signed before they considered the deal done.

James had still not heard back from his solicitor regarding the two documents the other business associates were demanding, so he sent a follow up text and prepared to head home. If his solicitor didn't reply he'd give him a ring from the car.

In all, it was a very good day. The documents were in a great place for Friday, and he'd managed to fit in that small, personal task at lunchtime. A task that made all the difference in his decision to progress with his chosen finance option.

~~~~~~~~~~

Katherine checked her text message. It was from Anjali. She would be back at a decent hour. That's great, she'd be early and sounds like her day went well, she thought. She texted a reply: 'Yes, please pick up kids that would be v helpful. Am at the office and will stay a bit later now, thank you. Edward knows kids are together after school. C u at home.'

Then she returned to her discussions with the Directors. She was already a good way through the plan she'd formulated so that her senior directors could manage in her absence for a few months. A bit more time with them to agree the final plan, would be perfect.

~~~~~~~~~~

Richard couldn't believe his luck. He'd scored twice today: getting Anjali to relax and spend more time with him; and finding another large investment opportunity. God, she was good. He'd taken a risky move - getting closer to her prior to Friday - but it made him feel so young, so virile. He was sure she would stay at the hotel Friday night, and he broke into a smile, he also knew how sweet she became with Champagne.

He couldn't wipe the grin off his face. Better yet, she didn't have a clue. He could make her so happy. And wealthy, of course. And her children. He smiled ruefully as he thought of her husband.

He was sure Anjali could discard James easily. Once Richard made it clear how untruthful James had been to her, and once he revealed the financial and professional state James would be left in shortly, he was confident she'd quickly leave him. He'd be sure to evidence that James' professional conduct is in question, and by comparison Anjali would realise how solid he, Richard had always been.

He returned to the office to review her new business case. Although his priority was Gemstone, he was impatient to close that out and move onto this new opportunity. It could be so fruitful, how could others have not seen it? But that was her secret. Anjali was able to see businesses from another angle; pick up low value companies and identify their potential. And they were always such unassuming opportunities. She had a point of view he didn't often come across, in fact, a way of working he didn't often witness. Less aggressive, less bullish, less focused on obvious winners....she was in it for the nobility of an honest investment in an underdog, so to speak....and not in it for a quick win, or bragging rights. And she was loyal that's for sure: loyal to keeping his money clean and spending it carefully; loyal to him, and loyal to her ethics. She would never recommend a company where she distrusted the management.

He thought about it – her approach was, well, virtuous. And he didn't think that because he fancied her. He wondered why the other senior advisors he had on the team weren't like her.

As he entered reception, a whole group of those very guys were loudly laughing and guffawing at a joke someone had said. They were on their way out for a mid-afternoon beer. The weather was good, business was good, and they could talk about deals over a drink. They were athletic and smart. He had personally chosen the best from Oxford and Cambridge. Most of them were sports captains and their university results were unsurprisingly brilliant.

Richard looked at them and his mind was eclipsed by a sudden realisation: their brilliant minds all worked the same way. For the first time he recognised the aggressiveness in their walk, the vainness in their posture, and the arrogance in their speech. He realised too, how they took advantage of others' weaknesses, and their possibly unethical efforts to secure the 'best and quickest' deal. In fact all of these were the very qualities he valued in himself.

And then, just like that, he knew why Anjali was so successful. The reason why no one else put those unique opportunities on the table was because they all thought and worked the same way. They were a set of men with the same background. Anjali was his only female on the team, *and* he grinned wryly, even though her skin was as white as the cocaine his team sniffed on weekends, she was his only black person in a senior position. There was Indian in her. He had known it, but he hadn't thought about it. He hadn't realised the effect it had and could have on his business.

His mind burned with ideas. Once he had Anjali where he wanted, starting immediately, he would put her in charge of a new practice. A practice for ethical investment both in means of working methods, and target acquisitions. Sustainability, climate, underprivileged peoples....a perfect start. She could build up her portfolio of under appreciated companies with super assets and potential. And she could build her team of high-minded, effective thinkers, and bring more women into his business. Who knows? Maybe even minority ethnic groups as well - maybe they could bring a different, prosperous spin to his business. He nodded absently at the blokes in reception as he thought of a nobler, more ethical future for his business. There was certainly money in it!

He headed to the elevator, snapping his fingers to a tune inside his head and smiled magnanimously at his secretary waiting for him. Almost imperceptibly she raised her eyebrows in confusion and smiled nervously back at him.

~ ~ ~ ~ ~ ~ ~ ~ ~ ~

Anjali smiled fondly at the three children as she walked them to the car. They were so happy, so care-free, and excited to have high tea together. Anjali herself was eager to catch up with Katherine after such a positive day at the office.

The manor's carriage drive was breathtaking. The height and row of purple beech trees always left visitors in awe. Their burgundy leaves flitted in the autumn breeze and the lawns below were mowed to perfection. Anjali smiled, rolling down her window to breath in the fresh scent of cut grass. She always loved the feeling she had when driving slowly up this private road - it left one anticipating the fabulous home and grounds beyond.

And before one was ready for the carriage drive to end - there it was, Katherine's family home. The soft Cotswold coloured manor was palatial, sitting proudly at the very top of the long carriage drive. The structure was soft-honey coloured but today it seemed to reflect the golden leaved plants surrounding it and the orange-hued autumn light.

She parked at the top of the drive, and all four of them quickly popped out of the car. Anjali could smell crisp autumn leaves everywhere. The water from the fountain at the centre of the drive had a lovely, musical trickling sound. She noticed a pile to the far right of the garden wall. A gardener was mid-chore, raking the leaves. As his rake crunched the leaves, the smell rose high on the breeze.

'Children - can you smell that autumn scent. Here,' and she picked up a few stray leaves, crunched them in her fists, took a deep breath of the leaves and then opened her hands for the children to smell. They were delighted with the game.

'Ooh,' squealed Maisy. 'Let's play with the leaves!' And the children buried their faces in the fresh leaves as they crushed their own.

The gardener was watching them with a smile. He waved at Anjali.

'Hello Anjali! Let them jump in my pile of leaves, nothing hard under there,' the gardener suggested in a gruff voice that seemed at odds with the playfulness of his words.

'Wonderful, thank you, Sam!' she replied. She had thought of it herself, but would never have ruined the gardener's work.

'Children - look what Sam has done here, and he's said we can jump into the leaf pile!'

Maisy broke into a happy grin, 'Sam is my buddy!'

'Yes! What a nice buddy. Shall I show you how to do it?'

There were shrieks of joy at the prospect of jumping into the leaf pile - and especially at seeing Anjali do this.

Anjali wasted no time and strode up to the pile. She measured her distance stepping backwards and in a flash ran up to the pile and somersaulted into the centre. Poof!

Her head emerged with leaves absolutely everywhere:; leaves in her hair, down her neck, on her light autumn coat. The children were trying to clamber on top of her, and the tall leaf pile was slowly melting away in all the excitement and movement. But she could hear Sam chuckling loudly as he came closer to the scene. 'That was a great jump! Any more jumps?' he asked the troupe.

Pretty soon it was chaos. Children, leaves, screeches of laughter, it didn't take long before Edward swung open the fortress-like front door.

'Hey - what's going on here?' When he saw the delightful sight, a wide grin broke out across his face.

'Edward,' shouted Maisy, 'join us!'

Edward elegantly descended the stone steps and met them by the leaves.

'Hey,' said Sam, 'let me just sweep this up again into a proper pile and maybe Edward will do a trick for us?'

'Well, I could give it a try,' smiled Edward. He felt himself loosening up, relaxing in this scene of care-free childhood excitement.

'Yeah, yahoo,' the children were shouting and giggling.

Anjali witnessed a sight she could never have imagined. Tall, refined, somewhat stiff, straight-backed Edward moved away from the leaf pile and then ran at it, with quite a speed. Once there, he jumped forward, as one could imagine a cliff jumper - arms out straight and momentarily suspended before the fall. He was tall, so the moment seemed to last - that second of hanging. But the landing was soft and the leaves fluttered up around him, and settled to cover him again as he lay there. No fancy flip but it was simply hysterical.

The children were giggling and Anjali was clapping. She and Sam were laughing together. 'Edward, that was terrific!' Anjali cheered.

But Edward didn't move.

Anjali and Sam exchanged looks and Sam moved closer. 'Edward, you alright?'

There was nothing but for a muffled noise.

Sam rushed forward towards his head and moved a small pile of leaves. 'Edward, is something wrong?'

Edward struggled to say something to Sam - it wasn't clear, but it was enough for them to understand there was a problem.

'He's struggling to move. It's his arm and chest.'

Sam stood up and whispered behind his hands so the kids couldn't see, 'He's in pain.'

Sam and Anjali quickly established that Edward wasn't in a good place. He couldn't move and was in deep pain - and they were frightened to move him.

She whispered to Sam, 'I'll call 999 straight away – don't move Edward, and make sure he has space to breath in those leaves.'

She ran back to her handbag and pulled out her mobile to dial 999. Sam had cleared space for Edward's face and was telling the children that Edward was just resting, and to stay out of the leaf pile.

'Now, Edward's an older gentleman and a big jump like that can be tiring. Let's let him rest a moment, eh children? Why don't you play hide and seek in the bushes over there?'

The children raced off to where he was pointing.

999 answered immediately. Based on the medics' response, it could be serious. She was told to make sure he remained lying down and rested, to keep him warm, check his pulse, and get him to talk if she could every once in a while. They would be there within ten minutes.

She pulled a small blanket from the car and approached Sam and Edward.

'How is he?'

Sam shook his head, 'Not too good.'

'They'll be here in 10 minutes.'

Sam looked at his watch.

'Edward, can you hear me?' Anjali asked gently as she moved close to his ear.

Muffled sound.

'Ok, I can't understand you but the main thing is that you are awake. We're putting a blanket on you to keep you warm, and I'd like you to listen to me and answer – even grunts are fine. The ambulance should be here in ten minutes and in the meantime they'd like you to stay awake and stay rested. I know you are in pain, but can you rest in that position?'

He grunted very faintly.

'I can't tell if that is a yes or no, let me get closer and if it's a yes, and you can rest in that position, then grunt. If it is a no, because it is too painful, then say nothing'. She moved closer and again, there was a very faint grunt.

'Good, we'll keep you in the position you're in then. I'll also need to check your pulse periodically. Fortunately, that's easy enough given your arms are stretched out - like Superman,' she joked to lighten the mood. But there was no grunt.

Sam laid the blanket over Edward, while she checked his pulse. She didn't know a lot about pulses, but his was pulsing fast. She counted 120 beats per minute.

She asked Sam to get her handbag so she could check pulse rates on her mobile. Over 100 would be considered fast. Ages fifty to seventy, and a heart attack could quicken the heart beat but also slow it....she had to stop worrying.

It might be that his ribs were broken - but it was such a soft landing...she tried to stay calm. They simply had to sit tight and do as instructed until the ambulance came.

'Sam, can you stay with Edward while I sort the children out for something to eat in the house, away from here? I'll also give Katherine a call, ok?'

'No problem, Anjali,' he replied.

Anjali collected the children and thought the situation was the last thing this family needed just now. She knew how special Edward was to Katherine.

They settled themselves in the kitchen. Edward had prepared a lovely selection of finger foods for the children - all healthy, all delightfully delicious she was sure. But she wasn't in the mood to taste them with the children. As they went to wash their hands she laid out some plates and napkins.

'Maisy, may I ask that you help your guests to whatever they may like?'

Maisy proudly took up the role of hostess, like she had seen her mother and grandmother do, and the fright of a few minutes earlier disappeared given the importance of her new role, and the yummy food in front of her.

Anjali walked to the far end of the kitchen, in the light of the bright conservatory, and called Katherine's number. There was no answer. She tried again, and this time left a voice message. She also texted Katherine: 'Edward isn't well. He's conscious but has chest and arm pain. He jumped into a pile of leaves playing with the children and me. An ambulance should be here in five minutes. I have the kids in the house. Sam is with Edward. Call me.'

She then texted a message to her husband. She could see the children were behaving well, and slipped out of the kitchen conservatory to the front hall. She stepped outside to check on Edward and Sam.

Sam waved to her and gave her a 'so-so' signal with his hand. She ran down the steps and then slowed to a walk as she approached the two men.

Sam slowly got up from his position close to Edward's face, and walked towards her. 'He's still awake but I think his pain is getting worse. I asked him to grunt if he felt worse pain, and he did. He seems to be fading.'

Anjali checked the time. It was 7 minutes since she called 999. She decided to call again.

She pulled her mobile from her pocket and called. After going through the screening questions again, and giving her location, they put her on hold. The lady who then picked up told her the ambulance should be there in the next two minutes - it was en route and close. Thanking her, Anjali hung up and informed Sam. She moved close to Edward.

'Edward, the ambulance should be here in a minute.'

Just then they heard the sirens in the distance.

'Sam are you good to talk to the medics, or do you want to swap places with me, and stay with the children in the kitchen? I think it's better if they stay away from the scene.'

Sam agreed and chose to entertain the children in the kitchen. He kneeled down and whispered to Edward.

'Edward, stay strong. The medics are here now. Anjali will stay with you, ok? I'm going in to take care of the children in the kitchen. Listen to what they tell you to do, alright?' He was obviously fond of his old friend. Both their families went way back in the history of the estate.

Sam patted Anjali's back, and despite his age, and creaking bones from years of gardening, jogged to the house to join the children.

~ ~ ~ ~ ~ ~ ~ ~ ~ ~

James was just about to leave the meeting room when he heard a text bleep on his mobile: it was his solicitor. He grinned and called him.

The solicitor had created the letter of intent to sell without stating who to; and had also read through the abridged document describing recent, positive test results for their technology. There were a few items he needed clarification on. James discussed the content and they agreed on the final wording.

He asked his solicitor to send the two documents immediately to the business associate he'd met at lunch, and to copy him in on the message.

The office was quiet now and James whistled a tune as he settled in his car. He was thinking about tomorrow. His phone bleeped and absentmindedly he reached for it before he started the car. It was Anjali - and there was a situation with Edward. Oh, God, he thought and he quickly decided to drive straight to Katherine's to help out, if he could.

~ ~ ~ ~ ~ ~ ~ ~ ~ ~

Thomas had tidied up his work. Not such a typical Wednesday, he thought to himself - and the day wasn't over yet. He pursed his lips determinedly. He'd managed to finish at a decent hour and knew he would surely make it to talk to Edward later that day. He swung his backpack over his shoulders and wishing his colleagues a good evening he left for the train.

~ ~ ~ ~ ~ ~ ~ ~ ~ ~

Within two minutes, the ambulance was racing its way up the carriage drive with flashing lights. It was a world away from the calm Anjali had felt when she drove up well less than an hour ago. Thankfully, although the siren could be heard on distant roads, it had been turned off as it neared the estate.

The medics jumped out of the ambulance, introduced themselves and asked their names, moving swiftly towards the patient. They questioned Anjali for the details. Anjali was factual, and calm.

They explained the test they were doing, an electrocardiogram or ECG, to determine if the symptoms were due to a heart attack. One of them spoke to Edward, while the other put small sticky patches on his arms and legs. They carefully checked him and moved him into what they called, 'the recovery position'. The medic put some patches on Edward's chest after loosening his collar.

They waited for his ECG results. The head medic wasted no time explaining them.

'Edward, we think you are alright but would like to take you to the hospital.'

She turned to Anjali, and said, 'Based on the specific changes seen on the ECG, we believe Edward may be experiencing a heart attack. This isn't a cardiac arrest but it's still serious. We'll be taking him to A&E. We suggest you accompany us in your car, can that be done?'

'Yes, of course,' she replied. Anjali felt tears come to her eyes. Poor Edward, he'd been through so much. She should never have jumped in those leaves and encouraged everyone to have fun. She wiped the tears from her eyes and walked to

Edward to explain she was following in her car. It wasn't obvious if he understood.

She warned the medics that she quickly needed to check in on the children first. With that, she left them shifting Edward onto the stretcher.

She made immediate arrangements with Sam, then told the children that she was bringing Edward to the doctors for a check up. She didn't want them to see the ambulance so distracted them to keep them inside, and didn't dare kiss them goodbye. She returned swiftly to the scene and got into her car. The ambulance was almost ready to go.

She grabbed her mobile and texted Katherine: 'Possible heart attack. Ambulance taking Edward to A&E. I'm following in car. Sam with children.' She turned off her mobile phone service that diverted calls whilst she was in the car, so she could take Katherine's call and charged the mobile so she had enough juice to us it in the hospital.

The ambulance slowly turned around at the top of the grand drive, and Anjali carefully followed. They were off.

~ ~ ~ ~ ~ ~ ~ ~ ~ ~

Katherine had her windows halfway open to catch the warm breeze. The sun was on her arm and she felt like her normal self - confident, busy and excited with work and a lot on the go. But still her life felt very different: her mother wasn't here; she had significant financial and personal issues to discuss with her husband; she had a family estate to oversee; and she had an investment portfolio to manage with many charities that depended on the financial stability of that portfolio. A financial stability which was possibly at risk due to the activities of her husband.

Regarding her own business, today had been an excellent day. The senior team had run it well in her absence, and there was a plan in place now for the next few months so that she could focus on her family's financial affairs. As well, the fondness her employees felt for her, and the delight she had felt among them had raised her spirits. It gave her additional energy and ambition to find answers to the questions she had about her mother's death. She was looking forward to the next piece of the puzzle: her meeting with Edward tomorrow afternoon.

She heard the siren way before she could see the ambulance lights. Sirens always made her nervous; she was keen to move out of the way when she heard them, but often couldn't tell in which direction the ambulance was coming. Fortunately, she didn't hear sirens out here much, although her heart skipped a beat with the fearful thought that it might be Maisy.

She slowed down and could see the lights ahead of her but through the forest on a road much further up the hill. She could only just make out the lights as they passed by her on the upper road, going in the opposite direction as her. She found herself then automatically speeding up, to see where it might have come from. There was still a nagging doubt that it could be Maisy, but she forced herself to slow down, back to the speed limit. In a little while she couldn't hear the siren anymore and her mind returned to all she had recently learned.

She thought through the family portfolio and the categories of investment. It was the real estate category that felt the most tangible to her. Real estate was property, something she could relate to, and she'd been gobsmacked to learn that some of the property were family homes spread right across the world. The solicitors were careful to impart that her mother, in fact, leased a good number of these historical houses to private individuals for a tidy profit. But she also leased the majority of them for nominal fees to various social charities - orphanages, independent schools, communities for social care and outreach. They stressed the importance of this setup to her mother. They were also clear that some of the estates were leased at a fair price to friends and distant relatives.

She smiled, remembering that as a young child her mother and grandmother would bring her to holiday in beautiful villas and estates across Europe, parts of North America, India, China and Southeast Asia. There were other places too, but these were the ones she remembered. She had never thought about it. As a child and teenager she'd been told that the homes they stayed in belonged to old family friends or distant relations. As an adult she never questioned that. Why would she, when her mother occasionally reminded her that they were not wealthy, despite their beautiful family home in England.

Katherine shook her head. She just didn't comprehend why her mother had led her to believe that there was very little money. She was reminded of a conversation with Colin just before they were married. She had mentioned to him that it would not be a match regarding family fortunes. He'd turned sharply at her and growled slightly, 'What makes you say that?'

She'd been surprised at his reaction. 'It's just what Mother has said to me on occasion.'

'What does she say?' Colin's voice strained to be casual.

'Well, that we don't have the family money everyone thinks we do!' she replied, worried that it would cause problems.

She saw him visibly relax. His eyebrows raised, he laughed arrogantly, and said, 'Ah, right your family fortune. Well, let's not worry about that now, alright?' He had sauntered over to her, and kissed her cheek. She'd found that slightly condescending but occasionally he did that kind of thing. She chose sometime ago to overlook these lapses. No one was perfect. She put her annoyance to the back of her mind and smiled at him, relieved that he wasn't surprised. She thought for certain that he and Thomas had known about the family.

But today she'd discovered another story: that those homes actually belonged to her family, and now belong to her! The people were tenants, sometimes old family friends who rented the homes for a significant period of time; sometimes the tenants were business individuals who rented the estate for farming, or vineyards, or indeed to host weddings and special events. The solicitors had explained that in all cases, contractually, there was a clause that her family could visit at pre-arranged times and stay to holiday or for business reasons. The latter was to check in on the running of the estate, the tenant's business or the charitable organisation. Her mind goggled at the craziness of it all.

'I can't believe it!' She said out loud, feeling simultaneously stunned and exhilarated.

She sobered. Why didn't her mother want her knowing? Was it linked to Colin? Was she wary of trusting information with her and Colin? Was she suspicious of Colin - worried that he might act in the way he had acted, since her death? She dwelled on that....thinking through, trying desperately to remember if her mother had given her any signs, had mentioned any threats to the wealth? But, she just couldn't pinpoint anything, and couldn't get over the fact that her mother had been so very secretive.

'Maybe it was to keep me on my toes, and encourage me to hit University and then strike out on my own. Being born into money could be demotivating,' she talked aloud to herself in the car, trying to justify her mother's approach.

The entrance to the family estate was just up ahead. She turned into the carriage drive and sighed contentedly. She would solve this, and now she was meeting Anjali. Hopefully, Anjali's fabulous brain could help her to piece together the evidence. Tonight, she was planning to share everything with her. She had decided that if there was one person she could trust, who could really get her teeth into the evidence, it would be Anjali.

She pulled into the drive and noticed immediately that Anjali's car wasn't there.

'Oh my heavens!' She gasped. 'Did I get it wrong? Maybe I was supposed to pick up the kids, not Anjali!'

She jumped out of the car and sprinted up the stairs. The door wasn't locked, so someone must be home.

She pushed the door open and as she did so, could hear peals of laughter – children's laughter. She relaxed and giggled herself. They were so adorable, and such good friends, perhaps Anjali had popped out. Edward could be a fabulous clown for children. Just then, her phone bleeped twice. There were two messages; the phone had registered that she was no longer driving. She always had the 'do not disturb while driving' feature switched on in her mobile settings.

She dropped her purse on the table, rooted for the mobile and shouted out, 'Hello Maisy, hello children!'

Mobile in hand she headed to the kitchen. There was so much commotion! She shook her head smiling at them. Oddly Sam was there, not Edward. They were laughing at a napkin on his head, but Sam wasn't laughing. He was solemn, staring intently at her.

His look made her swallow, and she instantly glanced at her phone while the children jumped up to show her what they'd done with their napkins. She could see the initial content of each text and panicked.

It was evident he wanted to say something, but not in front of the children.

'Children, you are so funny! Wow! What sterling work, those napkins are funny flowers and hats. Can you make me one? I'm just going to chat with Sam to check what you've eaten while you make some new ones,' and she left them giggling as she and Sam moved to the conservatory end of the kitchen.

'Miss Katherine, it's Edward, he collapsed,' and he told her in his straightforward way, the events of the late afternoon. Katherine shook her head grimly, her hand to her mouth.

'Are you ok to watch the children while I join Anjali?' She asked.

'Yes, of course, not a problem Miss Katherine.'

She knew that Edward would have organised dessert for the children. She could see already that Sam or Anjali had found his finger sandwiches for the children's tea. She moved swiftly to the pantry and pulled open a door which revealed a marble table top with several types of cupcakes and fruit on little plates.

'Sam, you can give the children these, and then they have a favourite programme early evening. Not while they eat, but after. Maisy can set the television up in the movie room. Are you sure you can stay? I'm not sure how long I'll be, but Anjali can return....' she trailed off.

'Miss Katherine, it's not a problem. Reminds me of my own grandchildren, these young ones and I miss them a whole lot. Stay as long as you need, same with Anjali,' he smiled affably and waved her off.

Katherine kissed Maisy and the two other children goodbye. There were no complaints, their eyes were on the platters of small cakes which Sam was bringing towards them.

She left the house, her heart picking up speed as she focused next on getting to the hospital. She was deeply worried about Edward. He'd been unwell, no doubt emotionally unwell, but physically he had not looked good.

Perhaps the death had been too tolling on him. Thomas always stressed how much the mind can affect the body and she wondered if this was the case here with Edward.

As her car picked up pace down the carriage drive, she saw another car turn onto the drive from the road. It was James!

They pulled alongside each other and rolled down windows. In a matter of minutes they had agreed a plan. James would stay with the children to relieve Sam and manage their bedtime. Anjali could stay with Katherine as long as she needed at the hospital.

They also agreed that James would text and call Thomas. He was very close to Edward and they knew he would be hit badly by this. They decided too, that Thomas should contact his brother, Colin to tell him the news.

Katherine was relieved that James didn't ask why she preferred not to be the one to call her husband. The fact was, she simply wasn't in the mood to talk with her husband just yet.

James waved Katherine goodbye and reminded her to drive slowly. 'We don't need a third accident,' he said.

'Don't I know it,' she replied grimly.

Then, under her breath as the window slid back up, she murmured, 'Only, the first wasn't an accident.'

Chapter 17 - Sorted

Standing in his grand office, he swirled the liquid in the cut glass tumbler and stared below, looking out over the Thames and London. His smile was broad. He was feeling gracious after his intimate lunch. He'd actually asked his secretary how she was when he was back in the office. And despite the distracting thoughts in his head since lunch, he'd still managed to progress work in the afternoon.

Any minute now, he was expecting a call from his VC Director. He could feel in his bones that Gemstone went well today. He didn't expect to hear from Colin till tomorrow or Friday because he'd successfully delayed his meetings with the Chinese team. In any case, Colin's email from this morning was already a successful outcome.

His mobile rang. He remained standing. 'Hello?'

The conversation lasted for sometime and in that period, Richard asked many questions, but his manner was light. He was pleased, the Gemstone session had gone well earlier in the day and the pieces were lining up. Not as fast as he would have liked. He would have preferred the deal to be done yesterday given the time pressures, but all the same, progress was being made.

'Send those documents over to me asap then. I've got someone who will be very interested in that....' he dictated. He slowly moved towards his desk and laptop, playing with his drink. He sat down elegantly in his leather chair and checked for the email.

'Got it, just a sec.' He clicked eagerly on the email his Director had forwarded to him and read the two attachments, zooming in on specific details. A grin slowly grew on his face. 'Perfect, just what we need. What's the timing on these now?' He paused to hear the reply.

'Ok, so we think Friday could still be a go? Or should we count on Monday?' The person on the other end of the line confirmed what Richard wanted to hear.

'Good, keep pushing the pace.'

He hung up. It was just the information he needed. Colin needed in fact.

He sent a text to Colin to alert him about the email. Then, he forwarded the email to Colin with some instructions about the attachments. They were just what the Chinese business partners needed about Gemstone.

He decided to leave the office, and in the privacy of his home, review the documents which Anjali had left with him. This was an exciting new opportunity and with Gemstone just about over, his mind was ready for the next game.

~ ~ ~ ~ ~ ~ ~ ~ ~ ~

James pulled up in the drive and parked to the right of the large fountain, prominent at the top of the carriage drive. He breathed in the crisp air and hurried up the large steps to the front door. He pushed an ancient bell - a brass button in a brass plate - and could faintly hear the deep ring inside. Within a few seconds, an older man appeared at the door.

'Hello, Sam. How are you?' The shook hands.

'Come in! Anjali is with Edward at the hospital. He's been taken badly and the ambulance took him to A&E. Katherine's on her way,' his eyes were sad.

'Yes, I met Katherine on the drive. I'm here now and can stay with the children till the ladies return. Let's head in. You can go home and I'll get the kids ready for bed later.'

'Thank you James, if that's no problem for you,' and Sam led James through the open door to where the children were. Sam kissed them hello but they were occupied by the characters on the large plasma. They didn't even much notice Sam say goodbye.

James settled down by the kids. He texted Thomas with the update, asking him to ring as soon as he could. He knew Thomas was often in evening sessions with his clients at the clinic and didn't want to disturb him with a phone call. He then checked the time. The children would need to go to bed in about an hour's time.

~ ~ ~ ~ ~ ~ ~ ~ ~ ~ ~

His mobile bleeped. It was startlingly loud. In the darkness of the early hours two pairs of eyes stared at the mobile. One pair made its way to the mobile and read the first few words of the message. There was a moment's hesitation, and the person reached back for something and pulled an object forward to touch the mobile. Then, she read the full message and grinned at her cleverness. It was a touch-screen lock and it wasn't her mobile, but that didn't mean she couldn't unlock it.

She swiftly brought the mobile to the other person who was busy doing some work on a pc and showed him the text message. Then she clicked on the phone's gmail app. It didn't take a moment. The two grinned as they realised what they had. It was the evidence that they had been waiting for in order to progress with the deal. But their business partner had been playing games with them.

She scrolled down the email, and her eyes widened as she turned to look at her colleague. The email had been forwarded from the original solicitor in the UK, and there were some key names copied in that email. It didn't matter that the company name was still confidential in the documents they already had, because it was there, plainly in the email, who the key person and the company was.

She whispered something to her colleague. He smiled and licked his lips. She pointed to the pc. He shook his head and indicated that he was still searching. She urged him to move faster and then nudged her head in the direction of the bed. He looked at her knowingly then returned to his search.

Their business here was almost finished.

~~~~~~~~~~

'I can't believe this,' Katherine was only just managing to hold back tears whilst driving.

She was definitely still raw from her mother's death and Edward's accident had shaken her.

'He has definitely been unwell, why didn't I suggest that he go away for a break?' Katherine knew why. Because his presence had helped her with her own grief.

She found parking at the hospital, and managed to figure out the hospital wing where Anjali was. She walked quickly along a large corridor with many waiting rooms off it and strained to spot Anjali.

'Hey, Katherine,' Anjali gently touched Katherine's shoulder. Katherine turned around quickly.

'Anjali!'

They hugged tightly.

'How did it happen, what state is he in, is it bad?'

'Let's sit down here, I'll explain. I managed to get us both a coffee,' replied Anjali.

'Ah, perfect,' Katherine smiled a thanks to her and wrapped her hands around the paper cup. They sat with their heads close together and Anjali quietly talked Katherine through the events of the late afternoon and early evening.

The hospital had done tests and were busy stabilising Edward. It was definitely a heart attack. They talked some more about Edward and his grief, and the possible impact on his health. Katherine knew that Thomas would be texting Colin, but she finally decided to also send a text.

'Contact me urgently please. Edward in hospital.'

She frowned as she felt again, anger at her husband. There was nothing else that could be done now, but to wait for Edward's test results which hopefully would come back shortly.

'Anjali, since we're waiting here, why don't I fill you in on a few things? There's more I'd like to tell you about Edward, about my mother's death, and about the family. Now's as good a time as any, given we are simply waiting, and can't do anything else.'

'Yes, go ahead,' and Anjali took another sip of her coffee, knowing her own news could wait. She was very keen to hear what Katherine was about to tell her.

'As I mentioned the other night, I've never been happy with the 'death by accident' conclusion. Several things make me uncomfortable: first, Mother would never slip on a rock; second, there was a rip in her shirt that did not look like a rock caused it; third, her towel wasn't in the right place being upstream from where she always left it; fourth, they only ever found one shoe and fifth, based on the evidence they found, my mother was about 500 meters upstream from where she normally took her quick swim on a Wednesday,' she paused to take a sip.

'I was bothered about all of that.' She looked straight at Anjali. 'Then, I found a note.'

Anjali's eyes grew larger as she registered this new bit of information.

'...which I'll show you in a minute, in the secret drawer of my mother's desk. It's concerning, especially when I tell you what I found out at the solicitors today. More on that in a minute.

'Yesterday, when Thomas and I were scouring the river and banks, I found a piece of ripped cotton at the river, floating from somewhere on the back of a large breeze. It was from my mother's shirt - same style, with embroidery - and I had seen that same sized rip, or gash call it what you will, on her shirt when I washed it, then put it away. But when I returned later to check the piece of cotton against her shirt, the shirt was gone.

'Only Edward would do that! Why would he do that? And his moods have been very odd,' she paused for a moment to allow Anjali to comment.

Anjali was staring intently at her, and motioned for her to continue. She liked to hear all the facts, and stopping someone mid-flow wasn't very conducive for fact-collecting.

'Well, I saw the solicitors today. My mother left the family estate in exceptionally good order. I'm ashamed to say...' she paused and checked with Anjali, '... all of this is confidential...'

Anjali gave Katherine a solemn nod.

'Of course, but why are you ashamed?'

'... because my heavens, Anjali, there's so much wealth. It's mind-boggling!'

She was shaking her head, still in disbelief, and Anjali had a puzzled look on her face.

'I thought you told me you were old money and the estate was eating a hole in your mother's finances, despite her fabulous career,' Anjali whispered so no one could hear.

'Yes, that's right. That's what my mother always told me. At times I even worried that profit from my own business would not be enough to run the estate, once Mother retired.'

'Didn't you offer to help with the running costs of the estate? I seem to remember your mother wouldn't hear of it and it annoyed you to no end!'

'Yes, I did! The annual bills are shocking. But maybe that's why she didn't want me to contribute – she actually had the money! What worries me is that I didn't know my mother was actively managing the family portfolio. In fact, her garden designing was only a tiny fraction of the work she did. She had a pretty much full-time job actively working the investment portfolio and managing the charity investments. Our solicitors provided guidance all these years. I simply didn't know we had such vast wealth! But I'm worried, Anjali.

'One of the solicitor's parting comments to me today, was to beware. That people do odd things when that much money is involved. And so, did anyone else know? Is this linked to my mother's death? And why didn't she tell me and Colin?'

She paused, and took a deep breath before explaining the suspicious behaviour of her husband.

'Look, Colin has been untruthful to me. He was aware of this wealth after Mother's death and never told me. Even in my concerned state about the family house, he only ever clarified that the house was still ours....but he never mentioned all that other wealth. In my grief I gave him access to whole portfolio. And that access had rights. Rights to take money out...'

She swallowed, and steadied herself for the next piece.

Anjali sat stock still. She felt a stiffness moving up her spine and her eyes were riveted on Katherine's face. She intuitively knew what Katherine was about to say.

'Huge tranches of money were transferred from one of the investment accounts into third party accounts, Anjali,' she whispered and swallowed again to clear her throat.

'Colin did this, the solicitors were clear about this, and I trust them. Not only that, but Richard, well... his daytime visits to our house increased this autumn, since Maisy started school, but they were still only occasional visits. Thinking back, he visited twice after my mother's death supposedly helping Colin with some big business deal....but I found out today at the solicitors that he was also in the last meeting Colin had with them.'

Anjali's eyes couldn't be larger, she was very worried for Katherine. And she was puzzled. What was Richard doing, involved in all this?

'I'm speechless, is this all true?'

Katherine nodded her head and frowned sadly.

'Hey, look, thank goodness you didn't tell me that the family estate was in a bad place, and that all the money had been transferred out. So that's a good thing, right?'

She was trying to focus Katherine on the positives so that her mind would relax - she needed Katherine to answer a lot of questions.

'I've some questions about the transfers but let's just park that for a minute. Where did you find the piece of cotton, and what does the note say?'

'The cotton was very close to.....well, where the police found my mother's body. I have it on me. The note is here,' and Katherine reached into her tote bag.

'What do you think?' She opened it up for Anjali to read. 'I don't recognise the handwriting of this note except the words in capitals at the end. That sentence is definitely my mother's handwriting.'

Eco friendly as you asked. Rock solid.

1190563 srt 409456

No more niceties now, we are proceeding

By end of play today. There can be NO DELAY.

Remember NDA and trust no one.

TRUST NO ONE

Anjali scanned it over, and then immediately said, 'Heavens! That last line is dramatic!'

She looked at Katherine, opening her eyes expressively, then re-read the note.

'Well, the numbers are pretty easy. I would say that was an account number and sort code. Given what you just said about the money transfers it may be that my mind is focused on that, but I probably would have thought this anyway.'

'Of course, that makes perfect sense!'

Anjali smiled absently to Katherine as she continued, 'It sounds like your mother must have signed a non-disclosure agreement, this 'NDA', so she obviously knows this person and must have met and talked about this before. If the numbers do relate to an account, then this sounds like a confidential business transfer. And if what you say about your mother is correct, her involvement in the family portfolio and investments.....then, I would say this is a reminder that she needed to transfer money to that listed account by the end of the day.'

Katherine's eyes were wide, fixated on Anjali's face and her interpretation.

Anjali paused as she considered her next words.

'The note is threatening as well. The reference to not being 'nice' anymore, perhaps that means polite and slow-moving? The capital letters of, 'NO DELAY', and the reminder of the binding confidentiality and not to trust others, this person is sounding desperate and keen to ensure she doesn't renege on the secret, and be tempted to tell someone else,' she looked at Katherine, 'perhaps even you, or Colin.'

Katherine's mouth was slightly open, she couldn't believe how quickly Anjali interpreted the note. 'Anjali, I think you must be right, anything else?'

'Well, let's think. Is your mother into ecological investments? Did the solicitors mention that? And why the 'rock solid'? Is the author confirming that the investment, despite being ecologically sound, is also a sure bet? The writing is odd too - calligraphy? Who sends a note in calligraphy these days?'

Katherine felt her eyesight dim, she dropped her head down, and closed her eyes for a moment.

'Edward writes in calligraphy all the time,' she said quietly, then slowly looked up at Anjali. 'I forgot to mention, he played a significant part in the investment portfolio, assisting my mother. Both he and the solicitors mentioned it to me. I'm supposed to be meeting him tomorrow afternoon to review the state of the affairs he is responsible for.'

'Ah, mmm,' Anjali could see that Katherine was visibly troubled. She was suspicious of Edward.

'Katherine, let's not jump to conclusions. Let's just think through the pieces we know.'

'Yes, ok, you're right. Regarding the ecological investments, I can check with the solicitors whether Mother had any of these and if so, whether there was any movement of monies.'

She made a mental note to add that query to the growing list of questions she had for the solicitors. Her mind whizzed through them: ecological investments; any transfers to the account number in the note; any investments in Thomas' clinic, although that wasn't ecological, was it?

'Did you also say you had the piece of cotton?'

'Yes, here it is,' and Katherine pulled the cotton fabric from her tote bag. Anjali smoothed it out on her lap. It had a trace of some intricate white embroidery on it, and was from a high quality, thick cotton white shirt. There was no blood.

Katherine watched Anjali study the piece of fabric and then spoke out loud. 'So, we know my mother was being threatened by the tone of this note. And that the author of this note was known to mother and wasn't a particularly nice person. So, why would Edward have written this note, when he saw her every day?'

Anjali nodded in agreement.

'You know Anjali, I've wondered whether Thomas knew of my mother's vast wealth, and whether he asked for investment in his clinic.'

Anjali gasped inwards and looked sharply at Katherine.

'What are you saying Katherine – that you suspect Thomas of foul play?'

Katherine felt so guilty.

'No, not really, but Anjali, at this moment you really are the only person I trust. Once I realised how wealthy my mother was, it dawned on me how important that note was. Someone was desperate for her money, and probably knew about her wealth. And there were not very many people close to my mother. I just need to check investments she made in the run up to her death, and if any, the owners of those accounts.'

Anjali squinted at Katherine. She's beginning to suspect her close friends. That's not good, she thought.

'I've considered the timings too, Anjali. I know this note wasn't in my mother's drawer the night before her death. I was with her then, and saw the drawer open – it didn't have this note in it. I'm sure about that. I found the note yesterday, partially tucked under scissors in the drawer. If the note had been there that Tuesday night, my mother would have been much more cautious when she opened the drawer in front of me. Anyway, I would have easily seen it. Given the contents, she also wouldn't have been so calm while we were chatting.

'We both retired to our rooms from her study that Tuesday evening. So she must have put it in her drawer the Wednesday morning of her death. No one else knows about her secret drawer or how to get into it, not even Edward. I'm certain. It was my grandmother's and mother's secret, and now...' she smiled at Anjali, '...yours too.'

Anjali raised her eyebrows, and smiled gently. 'There's so much interesting history in your family, Katherine. And now, perhaps secrets?'

'Yes, it's true. But there have always been secrets. My grandmother told of confidential letters she used to hide in that drawer, during the war,' she paused only for a second as she debated divulging the other secret space in the room, among the bookshelves. She decided not to, not yet anyway.

'Our post arrives in the morning, which is before my mother's swim. She either already had the note that morning, or it arrived by post. Then she must have put it in her desk drawer before she left for her swim. My mother died that Wednesday morning sometime. The urgent timeline of 'end of play today' referenced in the note must have been the Wednesday that she died.'

'Or, she could have had the note for a few days and only put it in her desk drawer on Wednesday morning,' Anjali suggested.

'I don't think so, Anjali. My mother didn't seem in any way frazzled on Tuesday evening when I was with her. She was relaxed, if a bit tired. Surely if she'd already been aware of this note I would have noticed some change in her demeanour,' she paused.

'There seem to be too many possibilities!' She shrugged her shoulders earnestly and looked at Anjali.

They sat quietly for a moment.

'Of course, someone could have hand-delivered the note on Wednesday morning,' added Katherine.

'Mmmm, true. Quite fancy embroidery on this fabric,' Anjali remarked as she handed it back to Katherine.

'Yes, I'm sure it's from my mother's shirt if only I could compare it,' she replied. 'I'm desperate to get back to the accounts and history of transfers. It worries me dreadfully that Colin was moving money around, without my approval or at least, checking in with the solicitors. I'd really like to understand that....' she looked at Anjali and decided to expand further.

'Unfortunately, Anjali, Colin's family estate is not in a good place.'

'Oh, no! That complicates things, Katherine.'

'Yes, it does. It's upsetting. I almost told Thomas yesterday at the river. He surely won't be aware because of Colin's casual bravado that everything is always just perfect.'

'Are you sure about this?'

'Well, I think you know this, but Colin, as the eldest, inherited almost everything and manages it himself. I don't know how bad the estate position is, but I overheard him talking to Richard about this, a month or so ago. It didn't sound dreadful, but Colin wasn't happy. Perhaps my husband would use my money to help his own business affairs - thinking we are all one family....?'

Anjali frowned at her. 'That sounds like you're making excuses for him, Katherine. It's your money, and it's not his right to access it without your approval.'

'Maybe not, Anjali. In fairness he did offer to invest in my business early on with his own family money. At that time he had said his money is our money...'

Why was she trying to excuse her husband? Who was she trying to fool? She realised Anjali was certainly not falling for it. As well, despite having only heard part of the conversation Richard and Colin were having, it was still obvious that Colin had struggled with family money issues for many years. In fact, she wryly thought, maybe it even pre-dated their own wedding. Maybe that's why Colin was so agitated when she'd mentioned she had no family money way back then, when they were getting married. She grimaced. It was all so, ugly.

She looked at Anjali. She was still frowning and shaking her head.

Anjali wasn't keen on Colin. Although he and Richard were tight, and Anjali respected Richard, she'd always had her reservations about Colin. She thought Colin didn't appreciate Katherine, and wasn't home enough for their little girl, who had taken so long for them to conceive.

Anjali squeezed Katherine's shoulder. 'We'll get to the bottom of this,' she smiled confidently at her.

'Yes, I'm determined to solve this. Thanks for your input, you've really helped, ' and she put the note and piece of cotton back in her tote bag.

~ ~ ~ ~ ~ ~ ~ ~ ~ ~

His eyes were intent on the screen. Suddenly he motioned wildly to his colleague who was scanning documents with her mobile. She moved quickly beside him and looked at the document he was pointing to on the laptop.

It was titled, 'p@sswords'.

She laughed silently but contemptuously. How stupid. How typical. She put her hand on his shoulder and smiled at him. They would need those passwords back at headquarters, for their 10 AM meeting with their boss. That was the last piece of information they needed. She checked her mobile – it was so early – 10 AM was a long way off. There was certainly enough time to assess all the documents back at headquarters.

A mobile bleeped again. It was neither of theirs.

Their eyes moved from the screen to the mobile. She quickly grabbed the phone and walked towards the bed. Again, she unlocked the mobile using the same trick as last time. She flipped to messages to read the text and shook her head.

They were definitely urgently trying to contact him. And that made the situation more difficult.

She conferred with her colleague and they quickly made a decision. They closed the laptop and briefcase, and pocketed their mobiles. She nodded then nudged her head in the direction of the bed. Her colleague reached under his jacket.

Their business here was almost finished. And they didn't need their business partner anymore.

~ ~ ~ ~ ~ ~ ~ ~ ~ ~

'Anjali?' A doctor in a white coat entered the room and called out her name.

Both Katherine and Anjali stood. Anjali explained who Katherine was. The doctor smiled at Katherine and showed them down the hallway to a small office.

The news was good. Edward was stabilised, it was a heart attack, but fortunately there had been minimal damage. He was asleep and needed his rest. The doctor suggested they return the next day, Thursday afternoon during visiting hours. They thanked him and made their way towards the car park.

'Why don't you and James stay over tonight, so that we don't disrupt the children. Surely James has put them to bed by now. Perhaps we can talk this over a bit more, back at the house, and you can tell me about your day?' Katherine didn't feel like being alone tonight. Not just that, but they'd been so focused on her own family and Edward that there'd been no time for Anjali's update.

'Of course, that's a great idea,' replied Anjali. 'I'll text James with the update on Edward, and that we'll stay at yours tonight.'

With the plan agreed, they both made their way back to Katherine's house in their own cars. For Katherine the drive back home was a swift one; she kept turning scenarios over and over in her mind. Anjali of course must be right about Thomas - how could she suspect him? The portfolio session with Edward would need to wait, but that made the situation more difficult. She felt guilty for thinking this way while Edward was in hospital but what did he know? What was the state of the accounts he managed, and why did he take the shirt?

Chapter 18 – Get Together

Thomas was pumped for sure. He was cycling at a speed he hadn't reached for some time. He was eager to get to Katherine's house. He swerved onto the carriage drive and nearly lost balance on the pebbles. Knowing his speed would be thwarted by the Cotswold gravel, he swung off his bike and pushed it up towards the house, through the beech tree avenue. He was breathing heavily. It felt good, he'd been due a decent workout.

Katherine's car wasn't in the drive. Oddly enough, James' car was. 'Hey great,' he said out loud.

He stood his bike against the garden wall and sprinted up the steps. Rather than ring, he knocked, knowing that Maisy would most likely be asleep at this hour. Nothing happened, so he turned the handle and sure enough, the door opened. Hmm, not locked?

He made his way down the entrance hall to the kitchen. Nobody was there. He heard low noise further down the hallway and walked towards the lounge where the television was. There was James, absorbed in the news.

'Hey, is this the type of care Katherine and Anjali leave their children in, when they go out? With the door wide open?' He teased James, figuring the ladies had stepped out for the evening.

'Ahh, my God, Thomas, what a fright - and more so, what a fright now that I see you! Put your muscles away. Do you need to flaunt them in your Lycra in such an established house?' Thomas laughed but James quickly sobered and changed the subject.

'It's not good Thomas. I assume you received my texts?'

'No. 4G has been pretty bad around the back roads.'

'I keep forgetting about the spotty coverage. It's Edward. He's been taken to A&E. They've told Anjali and Katherine it's a heart attack.'

Thomas' face fell, and he placed his backpack on the floor.

'What? How? What happened?' He felt a surge of concern. Despite Edward's very recent behaviour, he was extremely fond of Edward. How could he be in hospital, so soon after the death of Katherine's mother?

James told him what he knew and the two stood in silence for a short while; Thomas acutely aware that he may have contributed to Edward's stress. Edward would surely have anticipated that Thomas would drop by tonight to discuss the note he'd given Thomas.

Had a combination of Edward's stress and the physical act of diving into the leaves caused his heart attack? Thomas ran his hand through his hair. Was it possible that he was in part responsible for Edward's accident, like he was for another? That pain, in his stomach again.

Thomas pulled out his mobile and saw the texts from James. He messaged his brother, aware of the time difference: 'Colin, call me. Edward in hospital. Heart attack. Katherine will need support. Can you return asap?'

Colin would be asleep but he'd read it first thing in the morning.

The reality dawned on Thomas. So Edward was unwell, very unwell. The conversation wasn't going to happen today; and most likely, not for sometime.

'Hey, are you ok?' James checked. Thomas had been too quiet.

'Yeah, just thinking. Hey, when are the women expected back?' He shook his head. He felt he needed to see Katherine and make sure she was ok.

'Anjali called a short while ago. They were planning to leave then, as there wasn't anything else they could do.'

They discussed the events of the evening some more, and then talked about work. James explained that he was close to signing a new deal for his green energy tech and Thomas shared some funny stories from his recent seminar circuit in the US. Although they were close, Thomas didn't mention his new clients. He also didn't say anything about seeing Anjali and Richard in London earlier that day. He despised gossip and drama and had thought about this on his cycle ride home. He'd already decided not to say anything; it seemed arcane and ludicrous. He knew Richard. Anjali had been working with Richard for sometime now. If he fancied her, he would have made a move many moons ago.

And so, the two talked companionably, pleased to be in each other's company, and waiting for the women to return.

~ ~ ~ ~ ~ ~ ~ ~ ~ ~

The two cars parked outside the house. They emerged from their cars and slowly made their way to the front door. They were tired and famished. Katherine unlocked the door and they walked down the long hallway to check the kitchen. It was empty.

Then, they could hear some chatting further down the hallway. 'Sam is still here?' Anjali asked Katherine.

The two hurried forward down the corridor. Turning into the lounge, they saw James and Thomas.

'Well, what a surprise!' Katherine laughed. Thomas got up from the settee and she found herself heading straight towards him. His embrace was just what she needed. She felt his strong body against her. He was in his cycling gear and he still smelled of fresh autumn air.

'How is Edward?' He pulled back to look down at her.

'He's been stabilised. Thank heavens,' she took a step back and said hello to James. James and Anjali had embraced as well, but were now settling into chairs.

Anjali studied the other two without being obvious. How could Katherine suspect Thomas? They were sister and brother-in-law and it was apparent how much the two adored each other. She realised just how muddled Katherine must be with all her questions....muddled enough to suspect Thomas!

Katherine squinted at Thomas while he moved to greet Anjali.

He turned then, to catch her intense gaze, and did a double-take, 'Are you ok, Katherine?'

'Just wondering what brought you around this evening - had you heard the news about Edward?'

He hesitated, and wished he hadn't, but her question had caught him off-guard. He couldn't say that he was here to meet Edward about the note.

'In fact, to check up on you after yesterday.' He was careful not to say much more as he didn't know what she had divulged to the others.

'And no, James had texted me but,' and he looked apologetically at James, 'I didn't pick the message up. Signal isn't always great on the country lanes as you know.'

His hesitation bothered Katherine. Maybe he's worried about saying too much; perhaps revealing information she had told him in confidence yesterday. Or maybe there's another reason....it did suddenly occur to her that Thomas also knew where her mother's clothes were. As young children they used to play in her dressing room.

Thomas checked his mobile. 'I texted Colin when James told me the news. But I can see there's no response. It's very late over there, he probably doesn't get his alerts late at night.' The four of them looked at each other, not sure if Colin would have actually responded even if he was awake. He wasn't one for sympathy. James broke the silence.

'I realise that a serious occasion has brought us all here tonight, but - you know - it's great with the four of us together again. It's been a long time! Do you mind if I change the subject from Edward and ask Anjali how her day was?' James looked at the others.

'Yes, great idea. Let's hear your update!' Katherine settled back into the settee beside Thomas who was nodding in agreement.

'Well,' Anjali sighed, finally relaxing after the odd turn of events. 'It was a pretty amazing day. In a nutshell, Richard loves the business case, totally supports it. He has one more investment to finalise this week but next week his desk should be clear and we can kick off the initiative!'

They all congratulated her and simultaneously asked questions. Katherine realised her stomach was rumbling more loudly now.

'Hey, let's get some food sorted, and a bottle of wine and we can relax and hear the details. Does that sound good?'

No convincing was needed. They all moved to the kitchen. Katherine opened the fridge and just as she'd suspected, Edward had prepared a tray of antipasto and large bowl of pasta. He must have thought she and Anjali would want dinner after the children.

She frowned and thought about Edward. He was so considerate of everyone else. She took out the antipasto, and selected Edward's fresh baguette from the pantry, then reheated the pasta. In no time at all, they were at the kitchen bar enjoying dinner together.

'And he was pretty astute, asking the questions I thought he would, and more. Everything lined up. He totally understood my approach and the potential here.'

Her husband had a knowing look on his face. His eyebrows were arched and he was nodding his head.

'And so Anjali, you'll get some of this potential new revenue upfront this time, right? Richard should give you a stonking big bonus for finding such a fantastic business opportunity for him.'

She laughed. 'You're only ever interested in the financial gains, James.'

'No, that's not true. You need to fight to get recognised for your work. He should really be giving you a bonus for the find, and then a percentage of the profits. And a salary increase,' he said quite seriously. He knew how well his wife should be paid.

Katherine nodded earnestly in agreement.

'It may seem rude to ask for the financial reward, Anjali, but it's true. I'm sure the guys at that level wouldn't think twice to push for an increase.'

Anjali sighed. 'Look you're all right. Anyway, my initiative should kick off next week. Not Monday because I hope to have the day off.'

James looked at her quizzically; he wasn't aware of her plans.

'Well, in fact, he's asked me to close out some other work on Friday so that we can start on my piece Tuesday. I'll take Monday off given the Friday demands. This does mean an all-nighter on Friday, James.'

'Ah, is that what your text was about?' James queried.

Thomas was suddenly brightly alert. His look went from Anjali to James.

'We have to review the final papers which won't be with us until the end of the day Friday and they need to be turned around by Saturday morning. We're meeting at the Mandarin Oriental for a working dinner. It will be late from what I understand. But the company has hotel rooms already booked for late business meetings. They often run over. Will that work for you James? Can you bring the kids to swimming on Saturday morning?'

James shifted uncomfortably.

'All the more reason for a package review, Anjali. I thought you were looking to reduce your hours. You work three days officially but on Thursday and Friday, and evenings your nose is still in your research and business cases. Are you sure you want to set a precedence?'

'Maybe the 'Friday night situation' is a good opportunity for Anjali to broach the subject of a package review next week?' Katherine suggested.

She knew how Anjali shied away from those conversations unlike her colleagues who, as she understood from Anjali, aggressively challenged their remuneration all the time, and expected handsome pay packages and bonuses.

'The thought did occur to me too,' Anjali agreed.

Thomas butted in. 'Ah, ahem,' he cleared his throat. It was unusually dry. 'Like James mentioned, are you sure staying late wouldn't set a precedence? He's booked rooms? That seems a bit over the top. Is that normal?'

Anjali looked at him trying to understand his line of questioning.

'Yes, it's normal. The other seniors on the team hold late night meetings and stay at the hotel frequently. I've never had to do an 'all nighter' as they call them. But I won't be setting a precedence. I already covered this with him today. Richard's said it's a complete 'one off' and to be honest, he's never asked me to assist this way before,' she stated.

Thomas didn't respond. He had such a sense of foreboding. He just couldn't shake it. Richard was a rat, and he simply didn't trust him. But Anjali was fond of her boss, and he figured, knew him well enough and had worked with him long enough, that she wasn't worried.

'I was thinking of taking the team out on Friday, after we - fingers crossed - close our finance deal. But, look, it's not a problem, that can wait till next week. You should be good for Friday,' James smiled at Anjali.

'You're closing a deal?' Katherine queried.

James paused before answering. The opportunity was so close to being complete, and he'd already chatted to Thomas about it, he decided to bring Katherine into the picture.

'Yes, it's a big thing, and has taken some time. We've found a financing option to enable us to grow our business, package our IP and productise this new, ecological way of producing energy. We're buzzed! It can change climate discussions as we know them.'

Katherine smiled - she couldn't help but be proud of her friend's dedication and innovative work. She didn't know the details of course, but she knew the background of his research and understood the significance this could have on greenhouse gas emissions and on the energy market. James had been talking for years about the national and global changes that would have to happen regarding energy.

'This option is the best of both worlds regarding ownership and production capability. I can't go into it much at this point - a few days makes all the difference - but next week it will most likely get some coverage.' he was brimming with excitement. He looked at Anjali. She nodded at him with a large smile.

'Well, congratulations, James,' and Thomas raised a glass. They all joined in congratulating both James and Anjali.

The conversation flowed - from work to the children to the mild weather. Despite Edward's state, and the recent death of Katherine's mother, they managed to relax. Thomas was the first to break the conversation of the evening when Katherine offered to top up his glass of wine.

'Hey,' he said softly, 'it's ok. I still have to cycle home you know,' and he smiled at her. He was so relaxed. It would be great to stay but he needed to push his body that final ride home.

Katherine suggested that Anjali and James retire to the first floor. There was always a bed prepared there, with fresh towels and bathrobes. They offered to tidy up first and began to put the food away. Katherine turned to Thomas.

'Thomas, are you sure you can't stay?'

'No, thanks, I've got to get back. I came on my bike so it won't take long.'

He said goodbye to the others and Katherine walked with him to the front door.

'I didn't even notice your bike when I came up the drive,' Katherine smiled. 'Are you sure you're ok about Edward? I know how close you two are.'

'Yes, I'm fine,' he lied.

'Would you like to visit him at the hospital with me tomorrow, if he can take visitors?' Her eyes were soft and sad.

Thomas felt he was disappearing into her eyes and loosing his resolve to leave. With a sharp intake of breath, he looked away.

'I'll check my clinic schedule tomorrow and maybe you could let me know when Edward is allowed to have visitors. Ok? We can keep each other posted.'

She smiled, relieved at his reply. As they always did, she reached up to kiss him on both cheeks to say goodbye. But at the second cheek, she found herself linger. She was leaning against him lightly and suddenly realise how tired she was. She relaxed her weight against him for a few seconds more. It felt so good.

Thomas instinctively wrapped his arms around her.

He felt himself wanting to stay to care for her tonight, but when did he not want to care for her? Tonight, it felt different though.

He pulled her closer and rested his chin on her hair. He felt her relax further, and then, he did the unthinkable. He couldn't help it. He kissed her hair ever so gently. There was no reaction. Either she didn't feel it, or she didn't mind it. His eyes were wide open and he felt the blood race through his veins. His pulse quickened and he felt himself automatically pull her tighter into his torso, his muscles tensing.

There was a sudden laugh, down the long hallway from the kitchen, and he froze. He slowly drew apart from her, his pulse pounding in his stomach. He was a mix of emotions - irritated with himself, guilty, and unfortunately, exuberant with his pulse still racing. He kept his eyes averted as he moved towards the door.

'Thanks Katherine, we'll talk tomorrow,' and he opened the door. Desperate to leave on a normal tone, his mind scrambled to say something unrelated to what had just happened.

He remarked, 'I like your choice of paint at my clinic.' He flinched. That was so obviously too random but he didn't wait to hear her reply and left, jogging down the steps. A huge gust of wind swept through the hall as Katherine moved quickly to hold the heavy door.

She gasped to catch her breath and shouted to him as he swiftly took the stairs.

'Thank you!' For what she wasn't sure but she felt strangely both calm and alive. Her pulse was beating quickly.

'Take care on your bike!' But her words were whipped away in the wind. Without looking at her, he raised his arm to say goodbye then pushed his bike toward the dark avenue of beeches. She watched him disappear in the night, then fighting against the wind pulled the heavy door closed.

He reached the lane and mounted his bike. It was a short cycle home but he sprinted it through the lanes. Thoughts raced through his mind just as quickly. He was reacting more strongly to Katherine's presence now, especially when she was close, and that would have to change. He was annoyed.

He'd been strong for so long. What had chipped away at his bloody stoicism?

What about poor Edward. Should he visit Edward when he was sure it might upset him? When should he broach the contents of the note with him or should he wait for Edward to mention it himself? It all had to be addressed at some point.

With a welcome pause in the wind, he took a deep breath. He felt again that warmth of Katherine's body. It was amazing. He felt the energy surge through his body and pushed for the final mile home. She'd felt so close. He couldn't shake the pleasure he'd felt. He cycled harder in the hope biking pain might sort him out.

Thoughts flashed through him. What if Colin never came back? He shook his head as he cycled up the final steep bank. How could he imagine such a thing?

Chapter 19 - Transfers

It was a delightful Thursday morning. The kids had been beside themselves to discover in the morning that James and Anjali had also stayed the night. With all this excitement the children didn't even ask about Edward. James had left early to shower and change at home before heading to his full day of contract review with the solicitors. Anjali took the children to school,

With everyone gone, and time to herself, Katherine headed straight for her handbag hanging in the hallway. Somehow, last night, she'd forgotten the important pieces of evidence in there, and was determined to keep them close today. She half expected them to be gone.

They weren't. The note and piece of fabric were both where she had left them. She popped them into large buttoned pockets of her shacket. She was eager to pick up where she'd left off yesterday. She took her mug of tea - in the main it was Edward who used tea pots and tea cups - and headed to her mother's study.

The sun was shining through and the familiar smells of the study set her up to focus. She planned to review the notes and files from the solicitors, and connect with them so that they could answer her new questions. Plus, she had a request for them - one that they would be pleased to fulfil she was sure - as it had been a recommended next step from their session yesterday.

She'd sent them an email yesterday evening, requesting about two hours with them this morning. And sure enough, when she checked her emails over her first tea this morning, they had confirmed that one of the partners would cancel his morning meetings and take her call. So that was sorted.

First though, she was calling the hospital, then updating Thomas, and finally contacting Colin. It was unacceptable that he had not yet called her. It must surely be late afternoon his time at this point, so he'd had more than enough time to respond.

'Hello, would you put me through to ward 11?' She asked the hospital receptionist. She was put through.

'Hello,' a voice said.

'Hello, I'm calling about one of your patients. Would you be able to provide an update on his condition and whether he'll be up to receiving visitors later this afternoon?'

'We'll try to help, although it depends upon whether the consultant has reached the patient. Your name please, and the patient's?' Katherine provided the information, and explained she was a family friend, then waited as she was put on hold. It wasn't long before an update came.

'Yes, ok, let's see here. He had a bit of a restless night. The consultant though, has not yet seen him. Can you call back at around eleven and we'll advise whether he's strong enough to see patients this afternoon. It's worth saying, we can't give out private patient information to friends, so I'll need to check with the consultant what we can share about his condition.'

'Ah, I'm his only family actually, and he lives with us. Thank you very much for your help, I'll call back at eleven then. Good-bye,' Katherine absently bit her lip. Poor Edward, was he still in pain or at risk? She hung up, then rang Thomas' number.

'Hello,' the sound of his calm, deep voice mellowed her immediately.

'Hi Thomas. Did you sleep well? It's Katherine.'

'Of course I know it's you, Katherine,' his velvety voice teased her gently. She found herself blushing. She was full of mixed emotions. Last night's goodbye had left her questioning her reaction. It had all felt a little too good. Yet she still, possibly suspected him in her mother's death? She swallowed. How could she?

He continued, 'Yes, I slept well, did you and the others?'

She couldn't shake the shyness from her voice. The truth was, her dreams were odd last night but that something she absolutely wasn't going to discuss with Thomas.

'Yes, all of us did. It was a bit chaotic this morning, but the children went off with Anjali to school in good spirits. Thomas, I still don't know about the hospital visits and Edward's condition. The consultant had not yet seen him this morning. I won't have an update until around eleven or so. Is that ok?'

'That's fine. I've had a look and the schedule is pretty full today, so I might be better visiting tomorrow, if you're seeing him today,' he replied.

'Ok, I'll check when I call,' she paused before she asked the next question.

'Thomas, did you hear back from Colin? I haven't,' her voice was deadpan, trying to hold back the anger she felt.

'No, I haven't. I hate to say this, Katherine, but my brother wasn't the fondest of Edward and you know him – he isn't one for sympathy.' He let that hang a minute. 'But he should have contacted one of us, it's not right.'

Katherine was nodding her head. 'Yes, I agree. I'm calling his hotel now, thanks Thomas, I'll keep you posted.'

Sitting at her mother's desk, she checked her emails and texts again to ensure she hadn't missed a message from Colin. Nothing.

She sighed angrily. He didn't have to be so audacious in his response – even silence could be rude. Didn't he know that? He didn't care much for Edward, but the rest of them did and he should show some care. She searched out the hotel booking confirmation from Colin's secretary, and then rang the hotel. After two rings, a receptionist answered.

Katherine checked that he was still at the hotel. Yes, reception confirmed that he was still checked in.

She asked to be connected to his room.

'Madame, I would do so, but I can see here that housekeeping put a note on his record that the 'do not disturb' sign was on his door during their Wednesday morning round yesterday and indeed, was still there this morning. Typically that also means our guests do not want to be disturbed by phone.'

'I'm his wife and it's urgent. May you kindly put me through or I'd like to speak to the manager.' Katherine was not one to complain but she was angry now with her husband. Why ever did he have the 'do not disturb' sign on his door two days straight? Perhaps he was taking conference calls from his room.

The receptionist reluctantly put the call through. Katherine sat up further, straightening her back and crossing her legs. She decided to keep the conversation to Edward. They would discuss the financial situation when he was home. She pursed her lips tighter; he would surely have a good story, but this time it would need to be a credible story because she wasn't ready for him to push her concerns aside. For now, she was focused on convincing him to return home immediately. She wasn't planning to do much talking, and she surely wasn't about to tell him about a decision she would take later today with the family solicitors. Better to do what she knew was right and face his reaction later, then try to appeal to his common sense prior. The phone rang and he picked up.

~ ~ ~ ~ ~ ~ ~ ~ ~ ~

Thomas had not expected to hear from Katherine so soon.

He'd woken up early, feeling tormented. It'd been a fitful sleep with dreams that didn't seem to make sense. He had showered and dressed and worked in his home office to review some of his clinical research, and particular client cases.

And then she had called. After they hung up, he made himself another strong coffee. He didn't say it on the call, but felt sure he shouldn't see Edward today. He didn't want to upset him in hospital, and was pretty sure his secret was safe while he was recuperating.

He eased himself back down in his office chair, coffee in hand. Thank God he was working from home today, he could not have cycled far. His stomach was experiencing those cramps again. He'd never had health issues. The cramps were recent, and he was sure, linked to events over the last six weeks. He wasn't the type to be easily stressed – maybe this was a symptom of internalising his guilt.

~ ~ ~ ~ ~ ~ ~ ~ ~ ~

The click Katherine had heard on the phone, wasn't Colin. It was the answer machine. Disappointed, she left a voice message. 'Colin, please call me when you get this message. We've been trying to reach you. Edward had a heart attack and is in hospital. Can you cut your business trip early and return home as soon as possible?'

She then sent him an email, another text, and left him a voice mail on his mobile. She could do no more at this time. There was a niggle in her mind. She could check if Richard had heard from him, but she preferred to do that only as a last resort. Colin would surely reply to her. Maybe he was out and didn't want housekeeping in his room if he had confidential papers in there, hence the sign on his door.

Despite Colin's behaviour, and Edward's condition, Katherine looked forward to the day. There was much to do with the solicitors, but also with Anjali.

She and Anjali had agreed last night that they'd meet at lunch and search the river area again, given yesterday's plans were superseded by Edward's accident. Katherine wanted to return to the spot where she'd found the cloth to scout out if anything else was there.

She also hoped to do a hospital visit afterwards. Anjali had offered to collect the children if Katherine was detained at the hospital. She'd invited Katherine for dinner, but Katherine wanted to spend some quiet time with Maisy tonight.

Katherine looked through more documentation and prepared for her meeting with the solicitors. At 9:30 she clicked through the Zoom meeting invite from the solicitor.

'Why, hello, Miss Katherine,' greeted her solicitor. He was already on the virtual meeting.

'Hello – how are you?'

'I'm fine thanks but more importantly how are you?'

She realised that a lot had happened since yesterday – and of course, they knew Edward.

'I'm afraid I have some bad news. We're all fine, but Edward is in the hospital. He had a heart attack yesterday.'

The partner was evidently shocked.

'Heavens, how is he, and when did this happen?'

'Yesterday late afternoon. He was stabilised yesterday, but I've yet to get an update on his condition today. I've called the hospital but the consultant hadn't seen him yet so they'll provide an update later today.'

'That's really bad news. Poor Edward. Can you keep us posted on his condition?'

'Yes, of course.'

'Thank you. It's worth thinking about the portfolio component Edward manages, Katherine, if he is unwell for some time. Let's talk about that in a few days, once we understand his recovery process.'

'Of course, that makes sense. I'll keep you posted.'

'Well, shall we begin?' He cleared the way for her to start.

'Yes, and thank you again, for your time. I've been through the documents, and there's still much for me to review, but I already have some key questions I'm hoping you can assist with.'

'Fire ahead,' he replied.

'Good, ok, is it best if I first list them out and then you decide in which order to tackle them?'

'Yes, perfect.'

'Here we go, then: First, I couldn't see this in the accounts' activities but has any money in the last six weeks gone into the following account: 1190563 sort code 409456, and if so, how much.

'Second, how can we find out what type of account that is? Would it be an investment linked to green or sustainable initiatives? And did my mother invest in these types of companies - ecological ones? I have the list of her investment categories here which you provided, but that isn't listed as a category.

'Third, did my mother invest in a specific fertility clinic? I can provide the full name to you, but don't have account information.

'Next, the recent liquidation and transfer of monies....can you advise what accounts those went to? Types of accounts, who owns them, location? And exactly how much went to each account. I'm wondering, in fact, whether one of the accounts is the number I just provided,' she paused for a moment.

'Shall I stop there? I have a few more requests....'

The solicitor quickly replied that it wasn't a problem and asked her to continue.

'Is it possible to have a breakdown of mother's investment activities across the portfolio in the four weeks prior to her death, and the six weeks since her death. I think that would help.'

She smiled at the solicitor on her laptop screen.

'There's one more thing. I've reviewed the firm's recommendations and I'd like to action one of them straight away. Before we work through my requests, talk me through how I revoke access rights from my husband,' she thought her voice would be shaky when she said this, but it wasn't. It came through loud and clear - as most certainly did the underlying message.

'Well, there's a lot there, Miss Katherine. Beginning with your last point: as you are the only inheritor of the family wealth, bar an account for Maisy, then you have the right to control access to all parts of the family portfolio. We can change the passwords now to all the accounts but it will take a bit of time, perhaps half an hour.'

'As well, you gave Colin power of attorney right after your mother's death - you may want to revoke that,' he replied.

Without a moment's hesitation she replied.

'Let's do it.'

'Ok, good, let's see then...' and he began to sift through some papers on his desk. He put on his glasses and squinted at his screen, then he lifted his desk phone and buzzed the secretary in.

Within seconds she was at his door. Katherine smiled at her laptop, greeting the secretary. She could see the room easily given the video conferencing facilities the solicitor had in his room. There must have been several cameras. The secretary looked as professional today as she had the previous day. Katherine couldn't help but notice the neatly tailored suit that appeared to be camel-hair, perfect for the autumn day, and her upswept hairdo. Stately, grey hair, thought Katherine, in a lovely chignon.

'Yes, how may I help?' asked the secretary, and she looked up at the large monitor on the wall and smiled when she saw Katherine there.

'Hello, Miss Katherine, how are you today?'

'Fine thank you. I've managed to digest most of what was shared with me yesterday at the meeting.'

'Aha! I knew you'd have no problem talking our language. It was such a pleasure having you with us yesterday,' the secretary laughed warmly and smiled at Katherine.

'Katherine has several areas she'd like us to investigate. Could you join us to assist with some of the items?'

'Yes, of course,' and the secretary sat down at the table, looking up still at the large monitor.

'Right, I'll share my screen so that you can both see what we have here. Can you see that, Katherine, on your end?'

'Yes, perfect, thank you.'

The solicitor set out the next steps that needed taking. He brought up the dashboard of the accounts.

The secretary gasped.

'Oh Lord!' The solicitor exclaimed. 'That alert message on the dashboard...there was another major transfer in the early hours of this morning. Let me see. Yes, very early in fact, at about 2:15 AM. Interestingly enough, exactly the same as the other three transfers, £3 million,' the solicitor had a grim look on his face as he studied the data on the screen.

'Oh my God,' Katherine's stomach lurched. She knew in the scheme of things that wasn't a lot of money given the vast wealth in the portfolio, but it WAS a huge sum of money - a sum she never thought she would have in cash, never mind ever take out of her own business.

'Can we change the passwords now, so that no more transfers can be made?' Panicked Katherine.

'Yes, we'll work in priority order and you can reset your passwords. In the meantime...' the partner looked at his secretary and then back at Katherine, '...as you mentioned earlier, I believe you should revoke the power of attorney immediately.'

'Yes, my thoughts exactly,' she replied.

'Right, we'll sort that out with you right now.'

The secretary arched her eyebrows and nodded. 'Leave that with me, I'll be back for your signature shortly. We can accept an electronic signature, so no need to come in.'

'Thank you,' Katherine's mind was racing.

2:15 AM today – the coincidence was blatantly obvious – that would be today, Thursday, 10:15 AM Shanghai time where her husband was. She was almost blind with anger. Ok, she swallowed, let's stay focused and sort out the power of attorney so no further money could be taken.

Where had this money gone, as well as the other transfers? How could he do this? She blinked hard to focus: she was so angry. Was she right to think this last transfer was Colin also?

The solicitor called her attention back to the matters at hand, as he began to work through her list of questions. There was a knock on the door, and one of the other solicitors entered. She could see it was the same gentleman who had been at such pains to ensure she understood how money – significant sums of money – often resulted in odd behaviour.

'Ah, apologies, I didn't realise you were on a conference call,' he stated and turned to leave.

'No, that's fine, it's Miss Katherine actually, on the screen,' his partner replied.

He peered more carefully at the large monitor.

'Ah, hello Miss Katherine. Good to connect with you again today,' he paused for a moment considering something then continued. 'Not wishing to disturb the meeting, but, would you happen to know if Edward is at the house?'

His question stunned her. She was so focused on the task at hand, she had to take a moment to answer his simple question. That's odd. Didn't they say to her yesterday that the accounts which Edward managed on behalf of her mother were quite separate to the family portfolio they had covered with her? Why would the firm need to know if Edward was around?

'Good morning, and actually, no. I mentioned at the start of the meeting this morning that Edward is poorly. He's in hospital and had a heart attack yesterday.'

'Oh my good Lord, that's why.'

'Oh no, my heavens!'

Katherine wasn't certain who said what first - the partner who had just entered the room, or the secretary. The secretary had her hand over her mouth.

The solicitor asked, 'How is he, where is he?'

Katherine very quickly gave them a summary but was interrupted by the solicitor holding the meeting.

'Look, there's nothing we can do just now for Edward, but we have to sort these accounts for Miss Katherine.'

He turned to his partner. 'We've had another transfer, exactly £3m at 2:15 early this morning.'

'What?'

'Yes. We need to check all the accounts for any irregularities and work through the password process. Katherine has asked us to ensure Colin can no longer access the portfolio and also, to revoke the power of attorney she had given him.'

'I'll join you. Let's see how quickly we can get through this,' and he deftly opened his laptop and sat beside the secretary at the table.

Katherine felt like they were in a race, who knew when the next amount would be removed from the accounts. She couldn't stop the nagging thought in the back of her mind - why did the partner ask where Edward was, and why did he say 'that's why'?

She remembered too, that he'd been uncomfortable when she'd mentioned Edward...and oh heavens...he was the one with the creamy note that had fallen from the table! A note with calligraphy handwriting - of course, it was possible... Edward's writing?....she was so confused and so quick to be suspicious. That had only been yesterday, at her first meeting with the family solicitors. Already so much seemed to have happened since then.

'Miss Katherine, did you catch that, what we need you to do next?' She shook her head and put her concerns to the back of her mind. She asked the solicitor to repeat, and then prepared to focus on the huge task at hand.

'I should text Colin first so he knows that he will no longer have power of attorney.' She searched for her mobile in her handbag.

'Miss Katherine, maybe you should hold off on that, and tell him in person. There's nothing he can do now and it's probably best to discuss when there's a solicitor in the room with both of you,' the secretary gently suggested.

'Ah, yes, of course,' Katherine replied firmly. Of course, she thought sadly to herself as she dropped her mobile back into her handbag. It will have to be that way now.

Chapter 20 - Confidentiality

Richard checked his messages. Nothing from Colin. He thought for sure there would be some sort of congratulations. Those documents that he'd sent yesterday evening, the early test results and confirmation of Gemstone's plan to sell, were like gold to Colin. He needed those for his side of the bargain and must have presented them to the Chinese partners today.

Given he hadn't yet heard from Colin he figured he wouldn't now hear from him until late Colin's evening, most likely after his dinner. Hmmm, or perhaps depending upon Colin's dinner entertainment, he smiled deliciously, he might not hear from him till the morning.

Right then. He decided to call Colin first thing tomorrow, Friday morning, if there was no word. That would be Friday mid afternoon in Shanghai. Colin would surely by then have all his papers lined up including the detailed contractual commitments from the Chinese - which they promised after seeing the test results.

Richard was working from home today. And that was good. He'd slept like a baby last night, and thought he'd lounge in his bed for a bit longer. There was no hurry to get up. Today he wanted to clear his desk and think strategically about the business and about his plans for Anjali's unit; whether he should set up another offshoot business, like the venture capitalist firm he had created for his riskier business investments, or whether he should keep the unit within his existing business.

There was a lot to think about, a lot of great stuff to think about for the future. He tapped his fingertips on his lips and smiled salaciously. Yes, lots to think about, indeed, especially his Friday night plans.

~ ~ ~ ~ ~ ~ ~ ~ ~ ~

'Now that the passwords are changed, let's go through your original questions,' the solicitor said. 'We'll check if any money went into the account you mentioned.'

'What was the account number?' queried the partner who had asked about Edward. His voice sounded too casual. The partner recited the number Katherine had mentioned earlier and Katherine could see on the shared screen that he was running a query across the accounts. 'No, nothing to that account and sort code combination, Miss Katherine.'

Katherine didn't know if she was relieved or disappointed. In any case, her mother had not succumbed to the threat in the note. But maybe THAT was why she'd had an 'accident'.

'Miss Katherine, are you alright if we deal with the second question? It was whether your mother invested in eco-friendly, green or sustainable companies and you had queried why there was no such category of investment in our overview.'

'Yes, that's correct.'

'I can answer that one straight away,' answered the partner who'd been interested in Edward. Katherine could easily see him in the room and she studied his face while he replied.

'Yes, in the last few years your mother became more and more interested in businesses that were ethically and ecologically sound. She was interested in renewable energies, ethically strong scientific breakthroughs, and businesses that helped developing nations, the list goes on. We didn't have a specific category because such investment types appear in most of the portfolio.'

'Oh, I see,' Katherine replied. Her stomach tightened at the mention of 'ethically strong scientific breakthroughs'. Thomas' clinic would qualify for that.

She said slowly, 'I was also specifically interested if my mother had invested in the following fertility clinic,' and she provided the full name of his clinic on Harley Street.

Again, the new query was run against the accounts, and again, nothing returned.

'Hmmm, nothing against that company name but of course, there could be another investment vehicle set up to fund it. I have to say, there would be something in the notes if we were involved, and I'm not aware of your mother having any other investments other than those Edward was responsible for.' Katherine wasn't sure how Thomas would have organised his funding, but she couldn't imagine it would be that complex. She relaxed slightly.

'Ok, for your last two questions: what happened on the account the four weeks prior to your mother's death and the past circa six weeks after her death. Where did the money that was recently liquidated and then transferred to third party accounts go to? What can we tell you about the third party accounts. Let's have a look at all this.'

Katherine watched him run numerous queries on his shared screen. He noted her interest. 'If you like, we could set you up with the dashboard so you can easily monitor the accounts?'

'Perfect, that would be excellent,' she replied.

'Ok, this is what we have: Prior to your mother's death, there were the standard ups and downs in the portfolio - but no trading, bar a small green energy company in the UK. I can remember that. In the weeks after, there were three significant movements. Funds from a long-standing solid account were sold for a total of £12 million sterling. Of this cash, a total of £9 million was moved out from this account. For your interest, the funds in this account were profitable. They were solid long-term investments so there's no obvious reason why they should have been sold. And of course, no indication why the cash would then be transferred out of the portfolio. Three equal tranches of £3 million were transferred to three separate 3rd party accounts '

Over his reading glasses, he looked at her face on the screen, to confirm she was following.

'I see,' she nodded.

'Then each tranche was dealt with separately. The first third went to an account in the Cayman Islands. The second most likely went to China as we can see from the transfer charge and currency exchange for RMB. And the third went to an account in Panama. Then, this morning's,' and he paused while he checked a few things, 'well, well, interestingly enough, this morning's transfer went to the same account in China.'

He sat back in his seat, took off his glasses and looked at his colleague and secretary, 'I don't feel comfortable with this.'

The other solicitor nodded and sighed heavily looking at the secretary.

She replied, 'Nor do I. No one can access the accounts now, except us and Miss Katherine. Prior to that it was Colin and whoever Colin may have shared the information with. Miss Katherine I take it that you didn't share information yesterday after our session?'

'No, I didn't. But I do have another question...'

'Yes?'

'Did Richard know the password information – was that part of the discussion the day he met with you?'

'No,' both partners responded instantly.

'That is confidential information that was shared only with Colin, given his power of attorney. And so we would never have shared that with another person,' the partner running the meeting answered.

The secretary quickly added, 'It doesn't mean, however, that Colin didn't share that information.' She looked pointedly at Katherine and her comment hung in the air.

'I see,' Katherine replied.

The secretary smiled encouragingly at Katherine. 'We'll get to the bottom of this. In the meantime, I've sent you the power of attorney letter through digital document signing. You should have the request now. Could you follow that and let us know when you're done? We'll hold on as it shouldn't take a moment.'

Katherine shook her head slightly and closed her eyes. What a mess. She looked back into the monitor and smiled at the secretary.

'Yes, I've got it. Let's do that now.'

Chapter 21 – Cotton Again

Katherine made herself a strong coffee. She didn't often drink coffee and when she did it was milky and frothy. Today it was so strong she winced after her first sip. She needed a super-strong coffee.

After her work with the solicitors was done she called the hospital. The news was alright, but not as she had hoped. The consultant had visited Edward. They unfortunately, couldn't share the details with her, but they could tell her that he was unable to take visitors today. He was stable but weak, and needed to rest. He was, they told her, in and out of sleep and on strong medication.

She explained her relationship to Edward again, but it didn't result in further details. Katherine realised she had to be content with that information. The duty nurse advised her to call back in the evening.

She tried Thomas on his mobile but he didn't pick up. She left a message and texted so he knew Edward couldn't take visitors today.

The wonderful aroma of the coffee filled her kitchen. She put her mobile down and breathed the earthy scent of the coffee beans. She looked at her coffee machine and her mind wandered. It had been a gift from Colin. Of course, it was over the top, and she had said he'd spent too much at the time. But heavens, she had come to love the coffee it made. It was a Jura, a heavy-duty looking, barista-style piece of machinery and simply too expensive for a home-made coffee machine. However, it did make two of the most delicious latte macchiato. She sighed.

'Why couldn't life be back to where it was when I last had one of these lovely little coffees?' She dipped her finger in the froth and licked the creamy topping. After two sips of the bitter coffee her mind refocused.

She couldn't help it: accusations were flying around in her head. Why did he have to spend so lavishly? Why could he not have been more careful with his money? He was like that in everything he did. And yes, she thought, I too, spend money. And then she surveyed her beautiful kitchen and conservatory.

But this was all paid for. She had been paid handsomely in her corporate finance role and having received several bonuses - used them for her kitchen makeover. That was all before her business kicked off.

What about Colin? Had Colin overstretched himself - spending when there was no money?

The doorbell rang.

Katherine looked at the old kitchen clock and smiled,. Always perfect with timekeeping, Anjali was spot on the hour.

Katherine jumped up and answered the door.

'Hello, fancy seeing you again so soon!'

'Hi. Mmm, I smell something amazing.'

'Our favourite coffee, and one just made for you!' Katherine smiled, pleased that her friend liked her coffee, and handed her the glass mug.

Anjali took a sip and licked the froth off her lips. 'Oh heavens, that's wonderful.'

'Well, come on through into the conservatory, I've got some stuff to tell you that isn't so wonderful....you'll need that coffee!'

'More news, I'm still digesting what you told me yesterday,' Anjali replied. She then continued, 'Katherine, I haven't mentioned anything to James but you know how close we are. Is it safe to tell him about your concerns, or more like, your suspicions and my heavens – your family wealth?'

Katherine thought that over and sighed.

'I think so, Anjali. He's so close to Thomas though, I worry that he may approach Thomas himself....and I worry what one of them might say to Colin when he returns. Do you mind if we keep it between us until I have a chance to talk to Colin when he's back from China? It should be this Saturday or Sunday – although I'm expecting him to cut it all short, so hopefully Saturday at the latest. I'd also like to speak to Edward and to be frank, I need to be more honest with Thomas soon, too. Is that ok?'

'Of course, that makes perfect sense. My head will be stuck in my work, and James right now is very preoccupied with his company and the finance deal he is closing out this week.'

'Thanks, Anjali.'

They sat in matching light grey-green chairs that were perfectly positioned to take in the full sweep of the East side of the garden. Anjali could see the tennis courts in the distance. Two of the large french conservatory doors were open and the house seemed to blend seamlessly with the outside. The Cotswold cream terrace stretched in a stately manner around the full conservatory, curving alongside the East wing of the house as well, and branched into a pathway to the courts.

Anjali admired the view. There were cosy seating areas on the terrace, arranged with grey wicker sofas and glass topped wicker tables. Herbs and mini hostas were displayed in small cream pottery planters on each table. Large, antique water troughs with elegant olive tree standards created atmospheric 'rooms' along the terrace. Bright red flowering geraniums spilled out of faded stoneware pots along the full edge of the terrace.

'Would you prefer a seat outside?'

'Oh, no, we're fine here. I'm just admiring your beautiful terrace,' she smiled. 'Your home is gorgeous, Katherine. I love coming here. It simply,' she paused to express the mood, 'calms me. It feels luxurious but serene. A little bit like a bubble of calm if you know what I mean.'

'Well, thank you, yes, homes should be comforting places and for me that's definitely calmer palettes. It's so individual. But when you say serene...serene beauty perhaps, but not serene peace, at least not recently...' Katherine prepared to drop the bombshell. 'Anjali, another amount of money was transferred from my mother's account at 2:15 this morning,' she let that sit for a moment.

'What?'

'Yes, and it's an odd time to do a business transaction. But,' she paused and checked if Anjali had already registered this, 'that is about 10:15 AM in Shanghai.'

'Colin!?'

'Yes, well, we don't know. The solicitors and I immediately stopped his ability to access the accounts this morning. I was in a panic to be frank. We had a conference call to go over some of my questions, and they saw the alert on the dashboard. It is a large amount of cash. I can't understand it,' she emphasised her frustration.

'That's terrible! And you're sure it is Colin, could it be a rogue hacker?'

'No, it's not possible. In the meeting yesterday they went through all of their security measures. And the process to change passwords this morning was complex. It could be though, that Colin told someone else the information...'

'He wouldn't do that, would he?'

Katherine shrugged. She looked pretty upset.

'What else did you find out today, with the solicitors?'

'Well, here we go: the note from my mother's drawer mentions an account number, remember your suggestion? The solicitors told me today that no money has been transferred to that sort code and account number. Nothing. As well, my mother didn't invest in Thomas' clinic, at least not that we can easily identify. She *was* interested in small businesses though, that focused on scientific breakthroughs and had ethical or ecological maybe green angles to them...'

'...like James' business,' interjected Anjali.

'Yes, and these types of investment were spread widely across all the categories of her portfolio. There were no fishy transactions at any point in the four weeks before or the six weeks after her death, bar these three - now four - recent transactions since her death. She did make one single investment in the four weeks prior to her death, in a green energy company, as you say, like James' company, but that was aligned to the type of investment she would normally make and the solicitors were aware of that one.'

They looked at each other, thinking this through.

'Anjali, I'm concerned now that since my mother didn't make any transfers to the account that was referenced in the note - maybe that IS why she had her 'accident'. It's plausible, isn't it? The note was rather threatening, perhaps they wanted her money, by 'end of play today'!'

'Yes, it's possible,' Anjali's voice was grave. They were both quiet for a moment, contemplating what that meant.

'Right let's get a top up of our coffees, pop them in travel mugs and head down to the river, is that alright with you?'

'Yes, of course.'

The two women headed with purpose to the kitchen. Anjali put her arm around Katherine's shoulder and smiled at her.

'We'll sort this.'

Katherine sighed. She wasn't certain Colin could be sorted but she hoped at least, that the river would provide more clues about her mother's death.

~ ~ ~ ~ ~ ~ ~ ~ ~ ~

'How is he, Miss Katherine?' piped a voice from behind a collection of lemon trees in large stone pots.

'Oh, my heavens, Sam, what a fright you gave me! I'm so happy to see you. I looked for you this morning, early, but couldn't find you. He's better. But I'll call back later this evening to get an update. He can't take visitors today as he's on heavy medication and as I understand, in and out of sleep. But, he's definitely better, they aren't worried about his condition anymore.'

'Thank heavens for that,' Sam replied. 'I won't be disturbing you anymore, just now. Thank you, Miss Katherine.'

Katherine smiled. She adored Sam. He'd been with her family as long as she could remember and was always so caring about the family. He was a perfectionist with the garden.

'I'll keep you posted, Sam,' she replied and waved a small goodbye as she and Anjali continued down towards the river.

'Let's take this path, away from the swimming hole,' said Katherine. She directed Anjali further up the river, to where she had discovered the ripped piece of cotton.

They walked in silence. Eventually, Katherine pointed to a section of the river. 'Here we are,' she paused, 'this is where my mother's body was found. They think she slipped on that rock,' she pointed to a large mossy rock, 'and hit her head. The river moved her body about five meters downstream to here.'

Anjali shuddered. It's so peaceful here, like nothing terrible could ever happen. But her mind was alert. If her friend had suspicions, well, she had to have them too.

'Over here,' she pointed to a place about a meter from the large rock, 'is where I found the cotton. It seemed to be blowing from the oak, but who knows.'

They both looked around, inquisitively.

'I'll have a look over here,' said Anjali as she moved slightly upstream, towards the large rock where the slip had supposedly happened.

'Ok, I'll back up for a wider view and think through where the cotton could have possibly floated from.'

Anjali moved amongst the woodland flowers and river bank plants, moving them aside to look under the foliage. She checked behind rocks that could have been stepping stones, and into the cool clear water. There was so much to look at, so many opportunities for tiny pieces of evidence to be found.

Katherine stood back. She took a deep breath and thought hard about the direction of the drifting cotton when she spotted it. Most likely it came from the right bank where the oak was. She studied the bank and couldn't see anything odd. Again, another breeze and her eyes travelled upwards to the smaller waving oak branches; they were artistic in their movement and fluttered their golden leaves. Her eyes froze on the branches.

The branches hung directly above the rock and stretched from the oak trunk anchored at the far end of the riverside. From the rock to the oak the riverside was many meters wide, sandy, pebbly and dotted with large stones. The rocks stopped at the steep bank to the meadow and it was there that ferns and some thorny bushes grew around the trunk of the oak tree.

The tree itself was part of the bank; and several large, solid roots had been exposed over the many, perhaps hundreds of years it had grown there. They were weathered and twisted and certainly housed small animals given the holes and tunnels burrowed around the roots. It was a massive old oak with a girth she thought, of at least six metres and its branches were tree-sized themselves. The trunk was partially hollowed with cavities and the branches lay in many directions. They reached towards the meadow and stretched along the bank both ways.

Elegantly, and effortlessly, a single huge branch stretched out towards the river and hung directly above the rock. Clusters of leaves on smaller branches created a golden, hanging canopy. It was already thinning despite the warm autumn weather.

Katherine squinted her eyes and zoomed in on what had alarmed her. There were two smaller branches that were broken and suspended at an awkward angle. She could see that this may have not been noticeable even a few weeks ago. Now however, with the leaves dropping and the broken branches swaying and lifting in the breeze, she could clearly make out the two broken branches.

'Anjali, I'm just going to climb this tree to check something,' she shouted to her friend.

She skirted around the back of the oak, up the bank onto the level of the meadow. From here, she navigated her way around the thorny branches of a large bush.

'Evil!' She couldn't help chuckling at the challenge the bush gave her. It was deadly and could easily have ripped her skin and clothing. She found a clear space behind the bush where she was able to climb onto the low branch spread out towards the meadow. She stretched her leg up over the branch and twisted her body around it, pulling her weight on top and resting her torso flat along it. She lay her cheek on the rough bark and caught her breath. Her breathing slowed as her fingers automatically traced the deep fissures and ridges. The texture was comforting and familiar. How many times had she run her hand over tree bark; each type of tree so distinctive. She remembered a childhood game. With her eyes closed, her mother would take her hand and run it over several small pieces of bark. The challenge was to guess which tree. She rarely got it wrong. She smiled and and sat up.

Katherine looked around to contemplate her next move. Balancing herself with the main trunk, she slowly stood up on the branch. She rested her foot on a stumpy section of the central trunk and grabbing strong branches from above firmly shifted her weight to her foot. She stepped to another stump, and then was able to reach the next major branch. It was the large one that arched over the river. Carefully, still holding on to higher branches, she pulled her body towards it then gently manoeuvred herself to a sitting position. She paused for a moment. Given she was no longer on the meadow side, but the river side of the tree, there was already a significant drop to the ground. Sitting astride the thick branch, she contemplated the distance to the broken branches. Basically, the whole of the riverside would need to be traversed at the height of the branch, and the branch was only stretching higher.

She slowly and confidently shuffled her body up towards the two broken branches. It was slow going.

She'd been an avid tree climber as a child and her mother had delighted in showing her how to safely climb trees. She'd often join Katherine explaining precautions to take and how to best attack a tree climb. Oaks were always one of the easiest; if you could reach their lower branches, it was pretty well home-free from there.

She arrived about a meter away from the two broken branches. Without meaning to, she looked down. The spot was precisely over the large rock, a dizzyingly far drop below the branch she was sitting on. She quickly focused on the two branches again, squinting to rid herself of the dizziness she felt.

What? She squeezed her eyes shut to clear her vision.

What was that in the branches? She swallowed to calm her pulse, and peered through the dappled sun to the spot in the branches.

She licked her dry lips and squinted harder. What was that? She inched her body up the trunk to get closer.

There, caught on the tree bark, flitting gently in the wind but well secured, was a piece of cotton. A small piece, looking slightly ravelled, but defiantly clinging to the bark. It was pure white, certainly a familiar piece of cotton. But the cotton wasn't the only item caught there.

She gasped, a low throttle sound.

Hidden, but slightly exposed and secure in the branches and thick leaves remaining, was an object. And it wasn't a piece of cotton.

Chapter 22 - Brainstorming

Katherine cried out and focused on the main branch again to collect herself. She suddenly felt dizzy, dizzy and light headed. She knew it wasn't the height, it was because she had discovered something incredible.

'Anjali!?' She shouted for her friend, not believing what she saw.

'Yes?' Anjali replied from far away in a slight panic, alarmed at her friend's tone of voice. She tried to locate the voice looking skyward.

'I'm up here, above you, in fact far above you.'

'Oh my God, Katherine what are you doing there, and so high up?' Anjali's voice was shrill - she didn't want another accident and couldn't believe how high up Katherine was.

'Anjali, I think I found something.'

'What? Up there?'

'Yes.'

Katherine's voice was ominous. Anjali shouted out.

'First, are you sure you're safe up there?'

'Yes, you know how I love climbing trees. But that's not important. Anjali, there's another piece of cotton up here. Like the one I showed you yesterday. It's stuck on the bark. And...'

'And what?'

'And there's something else!'

'What else!?'

'A shoe!'

She shouted the word with emotion and the anguish in her voice was washed away by the burbling of the river.

'What?'

'It's my mother's shoe, Anjali. My mother's shoe is here!'

'Ohh! No!'

'Yes! There are two broken branches, angled downwards, just here above the rock. Oh my God Anjali, my mother must have been up in this tree! She must have fallen and her shoe was pulled off, her shirt ripped.' Her eyes were darting around the branches for more clues. 'Oh no, Anjali, how horrible...' and she moaned softly as the reality of the accident dawned on her.

'Oh, Katherine....' Anjali's voice trailed off as she looked at the height of the tree down to the slippery heavy rock below. She sucked her breath in through her teeth.

'Oh no. What are you saying Katherine?'

But she knew what Katherine was saying, she just didn't want to imagine it.

'I think she was up here. She climbed up here, it's not that hard, even at her age. But for some reason she fell. I'm sure this is the same cotton as her shirt. And this is definitely her shoe. No one could have thrown it up here, it's way too high. And of course, the cotton could not have been thrown. She fell, breaking the two small branches on the way. She hit the rock, and she *did* hit her head. She did slide into the river...' her voice grew softer.

'...and she *did* have an accident,' Katherine finished her own sentence. Anjali could hardly hear her.

'Katherine, would you mind getting down from the tree. You're making me nervous. We can talk about the scenarios down here. Are you ok to get down?'

'Should I take the piece of cotton? What about the shoe? I think I should leave them in case...'

'Please don't stretch any further to get the cloth or the shoe. Yes, leave them in case. If what you're saying is true, the police may want to see them both in situ,' she didn't say it, but the piece of cloth and shoe up in the tree would just confirm their verdict: that it was an accident. A verdict that up until now Katherine had been resistant to accept.

Katherine slowly backed down the tree, descending in an even more considered manner than when she climbed up. If her mother could slip, so could she.

Anjali met her at the bottom of the tree. As soon as Katherine was on the ground, she pulled her close for a tight hug. They stayed like that for a few minutes. 'Shall we sit down?' Suggested Anjali. Katherine nodded. Her legs were shaking now. She slowly sat and rested her head in her hands. She felt heavy and couldn't stop trembling. She was cold.

What a death, she thought to herself, what a terrible terrible death. Was Mother in pain, did she lie awake for awhile, what went through her head as she fell? Did she try to grab those small branches? What a way to...

Anjali put her arms around her friend and hugged her. Normally so level-headed, she found herself beginning to quietly sob. The thought of how her friend's mother died was too horrific, and she cried also for her friend who was so painfully sad. What a tragic, tragic story.

Their silence was broken by a flock of geese. Katherine looked up to spot their A-formation move elegantly by.

She became very still. Apparently a sight like this, was a sign of good luck. Suddenly, her mind was as focused as the A formation above. She knew instinctively, that her mother's death couldn't have been a simple accident, despite the evidence of a fall. Something wasn't right.

She drew comfort from the fact that she felt closer to understanding her mother's death, but she knew it wasn't a complete understanding yet. She lifted her head and looked at Anjali. 'Are you ok?'

'Yes, yes, silly me crying but, you're not in tears, are you in shock?'

Katherine smiled gently. 'Yes and no. But I do know this much: I still don't believe this was an accident.'

Anjali leaned backwards to look at her friend in a better light. What more evidence did she need?

'No, I don't,' Katherine could see the look of surprise in her friend's expression. 'She didn't climb trees for fun anymore, Anjali. In fact she often sighed when I would join Maisy, explaining that she couldn't climb anymore because of her hip.' She paused for a moment.

'I'm quite certain she would only climb if she felt she had to.'

'As if to escape?' Anjali's eyes were wide.

'Yes, exactly. She was trying to hide or to look for something from high up, or perhaps, she was desperate to get away from something – or someone,' Katherine explained her intuition.

Anjali sighed heavily. 'Katherine, should we go to the police?'

'I don't know. I think they will still believe it was an accident. This will be just more proof.'

'Yes, my thoughts exactly.'

'Actually, all of this has drained my energy. I hate to admit it, as it seems so mundane just now, but I'm famished. Shall we head back up to the house and have the lunch I promised you when we were having breakfast this morning?'

Anjali forced a smile, 'I'm ashamed to say, I'm hungry too! What a good idea, let's head to the house.'

They stood up and linked arms. As they moved on to the riverside path Katherine looked back at the solid oak. It was grand and it was constant – she and her mother had always loved oaks. So her mother had sought refuge in an oak...

She tried to locate the piece of cotton and shoe from where she was standing. But she couldn't. No wonder the police couldn't find the evidence. They were just small objects, in a tree that spanned hundreds of years and innocently hung over a riverbank in a picturesque and peaceful scene.

~~~~~~~~~~~

The morning had moved swiftly. James and the two teams around the table were in a jovial mood. Yes, it had been a serious and focused morning but it had been positive, with no issues arising. So far, Thursday's agenda was progressing at a fast pace.

'How about we break for lunch now,' James addressed the people around the conference table. 'At this rate we should be through our agenda by five or six today.'

They agreed and broke for a working lunch. Before he joined the others at the far end of the room for a bite to eat, James walked to the large windows in his meeting room.

He looked out over the fields and shook his head.

It was sinking in. He was thinking of his years of work, of all his concerns, of his steadfast endeavours to stay on top, his efforts to keep his small group of colleagues onboard and commitment to paying them handsomely for their intellect and loyalty. He stood there staring, his musings uninterrupted.

Hopefully tomorrow, Friday, at the end of a long week, all of his concerns would be written away, with one single signature. All of his revenue obstacles and funding challenges, all of his cost issues, his sleepless nights, the secrecy, it would be a clean slate. He smiled, noticed his stomach grumble and turned to join the others. Almost done.

~ ~ ~ ~ ~ ~ ~ ~ ~ ~

'Yes, I'm aware of the implications, yes, Mr Quinn did explain that to me,' Thomas completed the call with a chuckle. 'Yes, that's fine, thank you, let's book those.'

He hung up. His secretary was very keen that they accommodate his newest client and manipulated the diary somewhat to fit in a set of sessions. He didn't treat any client different from any other, regardless of their station in life, and wouldn't move other client sessions. He'd managed to arrange a block of sessions, mainly by eating into his private life. Fact is, he didn't mind. The couple needed help and he was happy to accommodate several late night sessions.

He'd had a busy morning and was tired now, having been up so early. His stomach at least, was in a better place. He thought to have a light lunch and afterwards, planned to cycle to Katherine's. Some client results he was waiting for would not be returned from the lab until late evening, so it was best to head back after lunch and sort out a personal task he'd originally planned for the evening. He'd decided finally, that they needed to talk. He was sure in any case, that Edward would be expecting him.

~ ~ ~ ~ ~ ~ ~ ~ ~ ~

Richard found himself staring at his mobile. He wasn't easily distracted but today, his mind kept thinking about tomorrow. Friday. He grinned. He buzzed his domestic staff for some food.

His eyes, then, returned to his mobile. He wanted to text her. He wanted to tease her, and test her reaction, but he didn't dare. He had her in a perfect place. He just needed to know that James had approved her stay on Friday night. Had he or perhaps had there been an argument between them? Did James not approve? Richard smiled, ah, there was a lot he wouldn't approve of, if only he knew. He decided to wait until the end of the day before texting her. After all, she didn't work Thursdays or Fridays.

~ ~ ~ ~ ~ ~ ~ ~ ~ ~

'That was a fabulous lunch.'
'Edward's five bean salad, and his homemade ciabatta,' replied Katherine sadly.
'You're calling back this evening to see how he is?'
'Yes, hopefully he can take visitors tomorrow. It would be very odd if he couldn't,' Katherine remarked. She added, 'I wish I knew where he put that shirt.'
'But, you don't know for certain it was him.'
'I. know, you're right,' her mind darted to the other people it could be - Thomas or Colin - and then her mind was back to the scene of the accident. 'I think I should return and get that piece of cotton in the tree, Anjali, to be certain it matches my mother's shirt, when it shows up. And of course, to collect the shoe, too.'
'So you don't think we should leave the evidence there, for the police?'
'It's been whirling around my head during lunch. I need to be sure the fabric is from my mother's shirt and.....I'm worried that someone else may very well be interested in evidence and do the same thing we did - look for any evidence in the tree, such as the shoe. Wouldn't you agree?'
Anjali nodded slowly. 'Right, just don't do it on your own. Can you wait till tomorrow, I can come back and go down to the river with you, ok?'

'Yes, ok, it can wait,' she looked impatient but smiled at Anjali.

'Thank you so much for helping me. I certainly feel closer to knowing the truth now,' her face was still pained. 'You know, I'm angry with Colin. I just can't understand why there's been no news from him. If I still don't hear anything by tonight or first thing in the morning, I'll have to ask Richard.'

'Hey Katherine, he's not that bad. Would you like me to ask him?'

'Oh no, no-no, that's ok. I can contact him Friday morning if I have to.'

'Oh, heavens, oh!'

Katherine looked at her friend who was searching around in her handbag.

'I forgot to tell Richard that I'm ok for Friday. I totally forgot with everything else going on.'

'That's unlike you. I'll clean up - take your time.'

Anjali found her mobile and read the message again. They'd talked about it at lunch yesterday. It was almost a day she'd left it without responding. He wouldn't be happy about that.

'Switch of venue - Mandarin Oriental, Hyde Park. Still 8 PM. A lot to cover. Work till late. Room booked so bring overnight.'

She typed a simple reply: 'All good. See you Friday at the Mandarin Oriental. Will need to leave early Saturday.'

It was important to tell him that she couldn't continue the work on Saturday morning. She was a mother and had to return home. Work could pick up again on Tuesday, if she really could take Monday off. If for some reason, they didn't finish everything Friday and it was urgent she could continue Saturday but it would have to be from home, not the Mandarin Oriental.

She dropped her mobile in her handbag and focused on Katherine again.

'All sorted. Are we agreed then, that I'll pop by tomorrow at the same time, and we can collect the cotton and shoe from the tree?'

'Yes, thank you so much, that would be great.'

They walked to the front door and Anjali offered to bring lunch tomorrow as she jogged down the outside stairs to her car. Katherine thanked her then watched her friend turn around in the drive. She waved goodbye as the car disappeared down the beach avenue. She stated at nothing for a moment, then slowly closed the solid door.

Inside, she leaned her back against the door and took a deep breath in.

Then, like she hadn't a moment to spare, she ran deftly upstairs to her bedroom, pulled open the drawer of her night table and removed her notepad. She ripped out the page with the list she'd written Tuesday evening.

She jogged down to the kitchen, boiled some water and prepared a pot of tea. She put the tea pot, cup and saucer, linen napkin, small sugar pot and creamer with milk on a large whitewashed wooden tray. Exactly as Edward would do. She lifted the tray and walked through her kitchen conservatory and out the wide French doors to the warm sunlight. She continued past the seating areas along the terrace until she reached the study. With only a cursory look back at the house, she headed down the lime tree avenue. Her gait was purposeful and she slowed only when she reached the Orangery at the end of the trees. She emerged and closed her eyes for a moment. Even in the autumn sun the glare from the Orangery windows was bright. There were so many windows, even the lead laced through wasn't enough to dilute the bright reflection of the sun.

She opened her eyes and squinted through the sunshine as she balanced her tray to the Orangery door. She needed thinking and writing space.

It opened easily. Sam left the Orangery unlocked during the day. Inside, she laid the tray down on the Oval Table. She sat on one of her comfortable chairs, poured the tea and calmly took a sip.

She was going to attack this in an organised fashion. There were pieces of evidence all over the place, and some were coming together. She re-read her list, then grabbed a clean sheet of paper and began to summarise what she knew.

1. Note:

A. Mother had received a threatening note at some point, possibly Tuesday but most likely Wednesday morning.

B. Could have arrived in Tuesday's post, Wednesday's post or hand-delivered. But if Tuesday, why wasn't the note in her drawer late Tuesday night? I did not see it in the drawer Tues eve when we were in her study together.

And as I mentioned to Anjali at hospital, Mother was not in an agitated state Tues eve before bed.

C. Mother had definitely read it before her death because it was in her desk drawer. She must have put it in there at some point before her swim on Wednesday.

D. She did not act on the note; the account activity confirmed that. The note said that the transaction must happen by end of play.

E. If mother's death is suspicious, this means that whoever wrote it was pressuring her to act by the end of a particular day. But what day was it? Was it the end of Tuesday and by Wednesday morning she had passed the deadline - and that was the day she died. Or was the day actually the Wednesday - and she really did die of an accident - and never had the opportunity to execute the transaction later on Wednesday?

F. The note was written in calligraphy - Edward often writes calligraphic style with his pen from his father.

G. Mother wrote on the note: 'TRUST NO ONE'. Was she making a point that she was to trust nobody - not even the author of the note? Was it possibly a message to me, thinking I might find the note in the drawer, and she could warn me?

Katherine paused there. She gazed out to the lavender walk down to the river. She couldn't believe she was thinking this, but with Colin's suspicious activities she *was* thinking it. She shuddered and couldn't stop herself speaking out loud.

'Could my husband have been the one? Could he have left the note somewhere for mother to pick up, even though he was in the house? Then followed her down to the river to influence my mother but he ended up threatening her?'

She stood up from her chair and paced a bit then walked to some citrus trees close to her table, to crush and smell their leaves.

The orange zing was refreshing and comforting.

'If he needed the money, which he evidently did, then maybe he always had the intention to deal with Mother if she didn't play by his game.'

She stood very still contemplating this, breathing in her citrus-scented fingers. It was simply not possible. The life she had known was under threat. What about when Colin returned home? Maybe she didn't want him to? Maybe the financial questions she had were inferior to questions about her mother's death. Should she share her concerns with the police?

'*How* can I think this way about Colin?' She asked herself again. She shook her head and returned to her Oval Table to write.

2. Wealth:

A. There is no doubt that mother was an extremely well-heeled person.

B. Who could know? Edward and Thomas. Colin and Richard would have known most likely after my mother's death. But did Colin know before that?

C. Since Mother's death, and since I have shared power of attorney with Colin, three amounts of several million pounds were transferred out of the account. This account was a solid long-standing family account. The investments were converted to cash and most of the money was then sent to third party accounts: one to China, one to Bahamas and one to Panama. Total £9m!

D. Bahamas and Panama are known for their off-shore funds. Criminals and wealthy individuals use them for laundering money, evading taxes and hiding shady business transfers.

E. This morning another tranche was transferred to China. Same account. Total again was £3m. That is now the full £12m from the investment that was liquidated to cash. ALL of that has been transferred out of mother's portfolio.

F. Richard was helping Colin with the portfolio, as he was in the solicitor's last meeting with Colin.

G. My husband didn't tell me about my inherited wealth.

H. Nor about the transfers.

I. Prior to her death, my mother did invest in an energy-friendly company. It wasn't the account in the note. But in any case, she had many types of investments like this, across all categories of her investments.

J. She did not invest in Thomas' fertility clinic, or at least that wasn't obvious.

3. Shirt and Shoe

A. I found two pieces of mother's shirt at the scene of the 'accident'.

B. One close to the ground (floating) and the other, high up on the oak tree. Still to collect fabric in the tree - am convinced it's mother's. The cotton fabric I have has embroidery on it like mother's shirt, as does the one in the tree.

C. In the oak tree there were two broken tree branches, smaller ones, directly above the rock where mother apparently hit her head. If she fell from the tree and grabbed branches or was tangled in the branches, this could much better explain the rips in her shirt - from the broken branches - rather than rips from the rock which is what the police claimed.

D. My mother did not slip on the rock and have an 'accident'. She climbed the tree. But she never climbed these days because of her hip. So she climbed for a reason. To see something far away, to get away from someone - reason unknown.

E. Her missing shoe was in the tree, tangled in the broken branches. Her shoe most definitely became dislodged as she fell.

F. Both small pieces of fabric could have come from the tree.

G. I need mother's shirt to compare the fabrics.

H. I put the cleaned ripped shirt in mother's drawer 4 weeks ago at the time of funeral. It had embroidery on it. The shirt was gone this week when I checked mother's drawer.

I. I suspect Edward hid the shirt. Is he guilty?
J. But Thomas could also know where the shirt was.
K. And of course, presumably so could Colin, or at least he could easily access the shirt.

She studied her thoughts listed under the Shirt and Shoe, and said out loud.

'I need to get my hands on both the shirt and the 2nd piece of cotton. This will prove she was in the tree. Why would someone hide the shirt? Could it be Edward? What does he know – and perhaps did he need money from mother also, if he had financial troubles? The solicitors didn't know the status of the financial matters Edward was managing on behalf of my mother, and suggested I talk directly to Edward. What about Thomas – did Thomas take the shirt at some point? Or Colin? To hide evidence?'

She poured herself more tea.

4. Wednesday Morning, Mother's Death:

A. I was at work Wednesday morning – had left early for the Great Barn – about 7:00 AM. Colin drove Maisy to school and then worked from home Wednesday.
B. Edward was at home Wednesday.
C. Colin had to pick Maisy up at school later in the morning as she was ill.
D. Thomas popped by Wednesday morning before Colin returned with Maisy. He had a coffee with my mother. He said later that she wasn't in her normal mood. What does that mean? Does Thomas know something else?

She put her pen down. Quite some time had passed and the afternoon was moving in.

She walked over to the pinboard close to the Oval Table and fingered some of the fabrics she had put there, a day before her mother's death. She'd been looking at new ideas for the business and had been coordinating different palettes for next season's conservatory range.

She looked at the fabrics wistfully. How simple life was then. And good. She did often pause to appreciate her life and the people around her. She often reflected with her Mother and Thomas how fortunate they were with their health and careers, but she realised now that she took the safety of her life, family, friends and colleagues for granted. One didn't often think of safety and security. Murder seemed on a distant shore, but that is what she was considering here.

'Hey, how are you?'

Startled, she jumped at an unexpected voice and turned around quickly.

'Katherine, I'm sorry, I didn't mean to frighten you!'

Thomas took several long strides and put his hands on her shoulders. 'Are you alright?'

She leaned forward and on that cue he pulled her close for comfort. She could smell his woody soap, feel his solid body and his hand gently rubbing her back. She took a moment to re-focus. Then, she steeled herself and pulled away. Why was he here? She was becoming so suspicious.

She looked carefully at him, about to speak, then saw the expression on his face.

Thomas' eyes were focused - but not on her. He was looking at her Oval table, at the list, just beside them.

She backed away, realising what he must have seen.

'Thomas, how was the clinic now that you're back from the States?'

She tried to catch his eyes and steer the conversation away from any questions he might ask about her list on the table.

He slowly moved his eyes to look into hers.

'I think we need to talk,' he said firmly.

He motioned her to follow him to the sofa. He sat and waited for her to join him.

Oh no, she thought, what did he manage to read? She needed time to think. She was so suspicious of everyone, the whole situation was too unreal. To be suspicious of Thomas was pretty low - betrayal of a trusted friend - far more trusted than her husband had recently been.

She was certain Thomas had been able to read most of what was on the table.

Moving cautiously to join him, she sat on the far side of the sofa. She looked at him for some reassurance.

But his expression was far from comforting.

Chapter 23 - Secrets Shared

The mobile bleeped. His head snapped back towards his mobile as if it was connected with an elastic band.

It was from her. Fabulous.

And the text was simple....tomorrow, Friday night, was on.

He stood up and stretched. Why had he ever worried? Didn't he always get what he wanted? He grinned ear to ear and sauntered over to a large mirror to check his reflection. He still hadn't heard from Colin, but he was far less bothered about that now. Now that he knew Anjali would be with him tomorrow night.

In any case, he still planned to contact Colin tomorrow morning if he still hadn't received the reciprocal documents he was expecting tonight. The Chinese had said they would provide detailed contractual commitments, after they saw the latest test results and they were usually good to their word.

All was fine, all moving like clockwork. He nibbled at the food his housekeeper had brought earlier, and rang for service. A good glass of wine was certainly in order.

~ ~ ~ ~ ~ ~ ~ ~ ~ ~

Her eyes were fixated on his. He was staring out at the garden with a far-away look in his eyes. The way he had spoken, she knew he wanted to say something first, so she waited.

He turned his gaze to look at her. She tried not to react, but couldn't help it. She kept her mouth closed, but took a long breath in through her nose. His eyes; they were the familiar calm grey-green that denoted his intelligence but today there was a new emotion. It was unmistakably sorrow.

How beautiful his eyes are, thought Katherine to herself, and how odd that she had never really noticed how handsome a man he was. Here was Thomas, her childhood friend so obviously saddened about something he was planning to say, and she notices how beautiful his eyes are. She blinked the thought away and prepared herself for what he was about to say.

'I can't even express my shock at what's written here. I have so many questions, Katherine!'

He paused. She felt a chasm grow between them.

'First, Katherine, there are things I need to say to you - important things. I've not said them because I've been worried that the life you lead, well, it'll be greatly impacted by what I'm about to tell you. I didn't want to change your life or Maisy's and to be frank, the life we all have together.' His voice wavered with his last line.

She kept her hands folded on her lap and didn't move, her eyes riveted on his.

'Your mother and I had an argument, the morning of her death.'

Katherine's hands tensed She looked down for a moment then returned her gaze, locked into his.

'It was a terrible argument. I've never argued with your mother, I respect her far too much, but she was asking me to do something I didn't agree with. And I realised then that although I'm fiercely loyal to your mother,' he looked away and frowned before finishing, 'I'm more loyal to you.'

'I'm going to tell you what she told me. Believe me Katherine, I didn't want to tell you this. However, I can see that you need to know; not least because you're suspicious of me,' he waved his hand towards her list on the table, 'but also because it will answer your questions about.....about your mother's death. There's no sense continuing as we are then, so I'll tell you.'

He waited to see if she would say anything, but she couldn't. She couldn't move or talk, she simply wanted to hear what he was about to say.

'We were close. Your mother and I were always close, but then when you were being treated by my clinic, your mother and I had frequent meetings. She always wanted to know how you were progressing, how she could help....and so we became confidants in a way. Of course, I could only tell her about my research work and conferences - your personal progress I always kept confidential - and I encouraged her to speak to you.

'Your mother became interested in my clinical work, and asked my opinion on other small clinics like mine that did the same type of innovation - in their own field of work. She was interested in my point of view about their relevance, the difference they might make to science and also their financial viability in the face of changing markets.

'She was keen to invest in my clinic, but to be truthful, I didn't think it was a good idea. I'd always understood that there wasn't a lot of money in your family - aristocratic family but little wealth and all that - so I never really thought she was serious.

'And although we didn't have so many sessions together after Maisy's birth, we still remained very close. I think it was because of this closeness, and my relationship to Colin, that she told me the following, on the morning of her death.'

Katherine's spine tightened at the mention of her death. She realised she was clenching her teeth, and forced her mouth to relax.

'We met at about 10:45 that morning. She had pre-arranged this session earlier in the week. The conversation didn't last very long. I'm sorry I have to tell you this, Katherine, but she told me that Colin was in financial difficulty. You understand your mother was talking about my family estate, that the estate was in great difficulty, and he was struggling with his business as well.'

Katherine's brain registered - so Thomas knew about that, and her own suspicions were true, but it sounded like the financial strains were worse than she had thought. Is this it, is it possible that this is the only revelation from Thomas? She began to relax slightly.

'And that he had asked for some financial help but she didn't know whether to support him or let his business and family estate collapse. He was part of her family now, she said. She worried about the impact on you, Maisy and me.

'She revealed something else too; that he was becoming 'aggressive' in his assertions that she assist him financially. She mentioned something about confidentiality and a threatening note which she thought was from him, but she couldn't be certain.'

Katherine's eyes widened, her head dropped a bit in shock as she stared at him.

'She was worried – worried that whatever money she gave him would be for naught, that he'd invest it unwisely or spend it lavishly and worried also about the influence Richard was having over Colin...'

He looked down at his hands.

'Katherine, are you ok if I continue? There's more but it isn't good.'

'I'm fine, go on,' she answered immediately. She couldn't take her eyes from his face.

He registered the effect his conversation was having on her, but ploughed on. He took a deep breath and looked at a section of old brick on the floor.

'Your mother said as well, that she was quite certain Colin was having an affair.'

He couldn't look her in the eye, and his throat was parched. Suddenly his voice he was forceful, and the words came out in a stream of anger and frustration.

'She asked me to talk to my brother - about the affair, about the family money, about the aggression. She asked me to talk to you - about all of the same things. She felt that I had a unique relationship with you both, and would be best placed to talk things over with the two of you. She had very strong views - that you should leave Colin, that she would not support him, and that he would need to leave the family and deal with his own doings. She was ready to take those steps to free you and the family from Colin's reckless activities but she wanted me to orchestrate the conversations. To pave the way.'

He pushed up from the sofa and paced a few steps, then turned around to face Katherine.

He didn't dare divulge that Katherine's mother had also suggested that he tell Katherine about his own feelings. That was the one topic he knew he couldn't share with Katherine, not now anyway, and possibly never.

'But I didn't agree. I couldn't believe that Colin would cheat on you. I know he was a lech before he married you, but I was certain he was loyal after. I still don't think he would do that, he wouldn't dare,' his eyes were dark with anger.

'And our family money, well, Colin's money in fact. I'm certain your mother couldn't have heard correctly. He's so financially astute that there's no way the full family estate could be dragged under like that. Perhaps a single investment went sour? I felt that your mother couldn't give me enough proof. I also couldn't comprehend where her money would come from, how it was even possible she could assist him financially. I thought that her family finances were under duress - based on what you and I have always known.

'I asked for evidence of his cheating and of the financial loss Colin seemed to have incurred. Your mother did provide some examples but they were overheard conversations. Conversations with Richard, of all people!'

He rubbed his head and ran his fingers through his hair, as if to clear the memory from his mind.

'She mentioned an odd text she happened to see on Colin's mobile when he put it down close to her once recently....not enough proof for me to present this to you as evidence of an affair...'

He walked absently to the armchair opposite and sat down.

'In the end, I agreed to confront my brother. But she was very insistent that I should talk to you about Colin. She felt it would be better for the two of us to speak than for her to become too involved. Colin is after all, my brother, she said. Unfortunately, I couldn't agree to this.' He stood up again and paced.

'Your mother was quite agitated that I wouldn't speak to you until I knew more. She had funny ideas in her head about the affair, and thought I should tell you immediately. I'm afraid we exchanged stern words. I left her, Katherine, in a state of agitation. I've never actually seen your mother like that. Her calmness, her serenity which I've associated with her all these years – were gone. It was as if she saw the happiness of your life disappearing, and she just wanted the whole thing to be dealt with quickly...'

He walked towards Katherine on the sofa and then crouched down in front of her.

'Katherine, I don't know if you've registered all that I've just said, but I left your mother in a state of extreme agitation. It was Wednesday morning, the Wednesday of the accident.'

He looked down at her lap then stared hard at her, his mouth set forlornly.

'I think I caused her death, Katherine. I believe she went swimming in that state of mind, and slipped and fell, to her death. She was asking for help, and I didn't help her. All those years your mother helped me, and I didn't help her. I just....I just needed more evidence until I knew for certain. I think that's me, in my nature, as a doctor. But in the end,' he paused a moment to prepare himself for the vocalised confession again, 'I think I was the cause of your mother's death.'

He felt cold, but that cramped, knotted stomach pain of guilt and grief was gone. He stood up.

'I'll go now, and give you time to think...' his sentence hung in the air, as he turned to leave.

Katherine shook her head and stood.

A strong urge to embrace him, overcame her. She closed her eyes, and resisted.

Instead, she reached for his large hands and just held them, standing arm's length away.

'No, Thomas, just stay a moment. Please. It's a relief that you've told me all this, really.'

Did he hear her correctly? He felt his shoulders relax, and his legs were oddly weak. She had an unfamiliar expression on her face – he couldn't make it out.

She quickly turned her face away and tugged him towards the Oval Table. He knew that she didn't want him to read her expression. What was she feeling?

'Let's get you some tea. I know I need a refill.'

She was matter of fact. Like nothing had happened.

'Thank you, tea would be nice.' But it came out gruff, deep and puzzled.

She pulled a large heavy oak chair out for him and then went to the armoire to collect another teacup and saucer. 'Strong, milk and no sugar. Here you are.'

He squinted at her. He was ready to leave and to be frank, to move beyond his brother's world and his brother's wife. It was time. He knew it. But - she seemed transformed. How is it that what he told her, didn't have the impact he thought it would?

Katherine topped up her own teacup and sat down. She spread her hands out on the table around the list she had started.

'Before we get to this list that you saw, I just want to say that I'm so relieved you told me all that.'

'Yes, relieved,' she repeated when he looked sharply at her.

'You didn't cause the death of my mother. Of that I'm sure.'

His eyes were glued to her face, unbelieving but closely listening.

'Yes, I'll explain more in a moment.'

He took a sip of his tea, willing himself to remain calm, and to believe her.

'I suspected there were financial troubles. I overheard a conversation between Colin and Richard. Given what I overheard then, there was no doubt a money issue existed. I almost told you down by the river on Tuesday, but then didn't, for various reasons. I had no idea how bad it was – if what Mother told you is true. But I didn't know about an affair Colin might be having.'

Shrugging her shoulders sadly, she put her tea cup down and rubbed her eyes.

'It doesn't surprise me, and in a way, relieves me. I had come to assume that such a situation would happen at some point. If it's happened already, then that's all the more reason to do what I need to.'

She paused and looked outside at the garden.

'What you've just said, worries me too. The note my mother mentioned to you, and the aggressive behaviour. Maybe Colin was in such a terrible state that he was willing to go to any means to secure his future? Thomas, I know you had a quick glance at these but read them through properly and tell me what you think.' She pushed the brainstorming lists towards him.

Thomas took the papers and leaned back in the chair. He read her notes carefully. His face was serious, and brows furrowed when he finished. He shook his head at her.

'Katherine, this, this doesn't look good.' He was surprised at the details on her list and her train of thought. How could she be so suspicious? He looked at the notes again. What was this about these vast sums of money? And it was unbelievable that Katherine had found her mother's shoe in the tree. This note on Katherine's list must be the one her mother had mentioned to him.

Although shocked at the information, he was also experiencing a slight elation. All the guilt, and fear he'd felt over the last few weeks was simply gone. In its place was a determination to solve the mystery Katherine so aptly described in her notes.

'Of course, I can strike you off the list now,' she said with a very small, sad laugh.

'It's ok,' he replied gruffly, 'I thought I was the cause.'

'No, my mother would never slip and fall into the river, no matter how angry she was. No, she was being pursued, I'm certain. Someone else caused her accident. She was trying to hide or get away.' Katherine was firm. Her voice was firm, her mind 100% definite.

'By climbing the tree?'

'Yes, that's what I think.'

He nodded his head slowly, still absorbing the information. He had more questions.

'Katherine, these sums you have noted here – these are significant amounts of money. What does this mean? That your mother was actually a wealthy individual? Are you sure about this? I thought there were issues with the family finances – wasn't that right? Isn't that what your mother always lead us to believe?'

'Yes, same. I thought exactly as you. But that wasn't actually the case. My mother's family wealth still existed. But, Thomas, let's keep that for another conversation. Rest assured, she most definitely could have assisted Colin. For some reason, I suspect he knew.'

He looked at her. Right, we can talk about her family wealth another time - she seems so sure of this, and she knows her stuff, he thought. He moved to his next question.

'So reading this then, are you saying that Colin or Edward caused her death? What note are you referring to here?' He pointed to the list 'A'.

Katherine pulled the smoothed note from her shacket pocket. She handed it over to him, and watched him read.

'Lord, that is threatening. So that's the note your mother must have been referring to when she spoke to me. Certainly fits the bill. You say here, on your list, that she never did the transfer?'

'No, she didn't. And to your earlier query, yes, all I have right now are Colin and Edward. Colin has so many more motives but Edward....'

'I don't think Edward should be on the list,' he said. 'Yes, he was there for certain, on Wednesday morning. I know that, because I know he overheard our conversation. Katherine, I have something to show you now,' and he pulled from his short's pocket, his note from Edward.

Katherine opened it up to read it, her eyes visibly widened; another note written in calligraphy!

Dear Thomas, I would like to talk to you soon. I'm aware that you had an argument with Katherine's mother on the morning of her death. It was only the 3 of us in the house. Colin had left to pick up Maisy from to school that morning because she was ill. After the argument I thought you left in the direction of your home. I walked to your house after the incident to talk about this, but you weren't there. I've left it too long, We must discuss this. I have many questions. Yours, Edward.

She looked quizzically at Thomas.

'I wasn't home because I headed off to the clinic after the disagreement with your mother. When I read Edward's note which he handed to me in your garden on Tuesday this week, I was fearful that he'd challenge me about the argument. That he'd insinuate I could have contributed to the death by putting your mother in such an agitated mood that she couldn't help but have an accident down by the river. And I wasn't ready to hear that because I already felt guilty. '

He paused to emphasise his next point.

'Edward couldn't have had a hand in your mother's death. I'm sure he suspected my involvement or he would not have wanted to raise such a personal matter with me. In any case, he was most likely at my house, when the accident happened. He walked and I just think that places him too far away from the scene of the accident.

'Katherine, as well, Edward is independently wealthy. He offered some time ago to invest in my clinic. Given the clinic's success and direction of travel, and how supportive Edward was to me when I was younger, I thought to include him in the success of the business. It seemed the right thing to do. And I would never have accepted investment from your mother. As you know I thought she had significant financial challenges keeping the estate afloat. Although your mother isn't invested in my clinic, Edward is.'

Katherine's initial response was relief – relief that Edward couldn't possibly have done this. But as her smile grew in response to Thomas' information, almost immediately a fearful doubt began to build.

'But Thomas, why would Edward take the shirt? It must have been him. What if he was the one who is implicated in my mother's death? What if he was trying to make out like you were the guilty one? Then he would be off the hook. Maybe he used Estate money to invest in your clinic. Maybe it wasn't his money. Maybe he needed money and wrote the note – why else in calligraphy? That isn't Colin's style. But it is Edward's!'

She stood up and paced.

'Katherine, I can't imagine Edward would do that. He loved your mother, you think he would have threatened her? To access more money? And why that day, of all days? It just doesn't make sense. I know Colin is my brother, and I shouldn't be saying this, but he has many more motives.'

She turned away to think harder, and noticed the clock on the wall.

'Oh! It's pick up time shortly! I need to get Maisy. Are you ok here, would you like to stay?'

She still had so much to talk about: the fabric in her pocket, the two new findings at the river, her family wealth. He must wonder how she now knows that her mother was in fact, a wealthy woman.

'Would you like me to stay?' He asked her. His heart thumped. *Would she like him to stay?*

It was an odd question. She could begin to feel that things had already changed between them. She heard the tone in his voice and wasn't ready for what it implied.

'Thank you Thomas, for dropping by. It's great we spoke. But, I need time alone with Maisy tonight. Can you call me if you hear from Colin? I'll do the same, and if not, we'll talk first thing in the morning, ok?'

'Ok, you go ahead I'll take the tea back. You'll be late,' he replied.

She moved quickly. She ripped her brainstorming notes from the pad on the Oval Table, and hesitated before she picked up Thomas' note from Edward.

'Do you mind if I keep this?'

'No, of course, keep it all together, that's fine.'

She rushed from the Orangery, giving him a quick smile goodbye and he, with the tray of tea, watched her turn and run back to the house up through the lavender path.

Chapter 24 - Testing

Katherine and Maisy finished dinner. It had been a late start to their meal. Katherine had purchased a few items from the corner store after picking up Maisy, and together they had made their pasta dish.

Maisy was surprisingly ok without Edward. Katherine was puzzled, but to Maisy helping Mummy cook was a big adventure. And as long as Katherine told her Edward was resting in hospital, Maisy was alright with that.

They tidied up and giggled about some washing up soap that flew onto Maisy's hair. Then, they headed to Maisy's room for their evening ritual: artwork, bath, then bedtime reading.

Maisy continued to work on the drawing she had started earlier. Katherine found herself sketching a landscape. Before they knew it, it was time for Maisy's bath.

Lots of giggles and splashes took Katherine's mind off the recent events. When bath time was done, she wrapped Maisy in a large towel and brought her back to the bedroom to dry her hair. Maisy chose her nightgown for the evening then scrambled onto her bed. Katherine tucked her in and settling herself beside her daughter began to read a favourite bedtime story. The familiarity of their nighttime ritual was calming. It was almost possible to think everything was normal.

She kissed Maisy goodnight.

'Mummy?'

'Yes, darling?' Katherine was surprised Maisy wasn't drifting quickly to sleep, she had been so tired.

'Do you like my drawing?'

Katherine walked to the painting area of the room, and appraised the drawing. It had progressed significantly since the last time she saw it. Now there was a bright red car in the magnificent drive, to the right of a face peeking from the garden wall.

'What a fabulous red car,' remarked Katherine. But when she turned to look at her daughter, she saw a little girl almost already asleep.

'Fancy racing car...' Maisy murmured. Her brow was furrowed, and then, it just relaxed. Her hair had drifted across the pillow and her lashes looked long on her cheeks. She had just fallen into her little girl's sleep, with lips very gently curved at the edges. Katherine sighed and smiled. She tiptoed out of the room and gently pulled her daughter's door to halfway closed.

She stood for a minute outside the door. How fortunate she was to have Maisy in her life. Without Thomas, Maisy would not be here. And then she thought about Thomas this afternoon.

Thank heavens he had been honest with her. It made a huge difference in so many ways. She knew now he was the same Thomas: honest, caring, dependable. But she felt differently about him and her situation.

It was surely, because of Colin. She realised that Colin, with all of his perfections, was the most imperfect of the two. She couldn't even begin to wonder about his affair. She simply didn't have the energy and didn't care. It actually made her life easier; easier to make decisions she should have made a long time ago.

Surprisingly, it was Thomas who she couldn't shake out of her mind. He thought he'd left her mother in such a state that she later slipped on the rock and died. How terrible for him, all this time. He should have said something and she was perplexed he hadn't. And to have argued with her mother – for that to have been the last exchange between the two of them...

She whispered out loud. 'Why didn't Mother talk to me directly? I would have listened to her. Why Thomas?'

Maisy moved in her bed.

Katherine peered in the room to check Maisy was alright then headed to her own room. She decided to read in bed and turn her light out early; she couldn't believe how tired she was.

She opened her nightside table and put her expanding collection inside: her mother's note; Edward's note to Thomas; the piece of fabric and as well, her long list she had made in the Orangery. Tomorrow, she'd have to find a place for these that was a little more secure.

Whilst she prepared for bed, thoughts raced through her mind: Colin, and his financial problems; his supposed affair; Thomas and his guilt; Edward and was he really so wealthy? Why did her mother insist that Thomas should be the one to talk to her, why couldn't her mother have spoken to her directly? She could understand that she insisted he talk to his own brother, but why to her as well?

What had her mother done after Thomas left? Changed for her swim immediately? Did she confront Colin herself in the end, after he returned from dropping off Maisy...did he even return before she left for her swim? Why would she confront Colin even if she had the chance, as Thomas agreed to speak to him, and that is what she wanted.

Katherine fell asleep dreaming she was on a branch. The branch was swinging and a comforting, warm wind blew. It was gentle, so gentle, and she was swinging contentedly.

She heard a voice and turned.

A face appeared. It was familiar, it was so familiar but, different. And it was threatening. It was coming too close. She moved to escape, and then....she grabbed at anything she could, but there was nothing, nothing to hold onto for balance. She was suddenly free-falling.

She looked below, reaching out to break her fall. But there was only a cool, clean river. She screamed.

~ ~ ~ ~ ~ ~ ~ ~ ~ ~

His alarm went off at 6 AM. Thomas woke instantly and looked around, confused for a moment, he'd been in such a deep sleep. It had been weeks, just over a month in fact, that he hadn't been able to sleep well. He rubbed his eyes and ran his hand through his hair. He didn't even remember falling asleep – but he must have easily slept ten hours. Ten hours straight through. He dropped his head back onto his pillow and stared at the ceiling. He was already beginning to feel better. He should have spoken to Katherine earlier. He realised his guilt at having such cross words with Katherine's mother had played with his mind and stretched his imagination to thinking he was the cause of her accident. He could focus now on helping Katherine better understand the exact events surrounding her mother's death.

~ ~ ~ ~ ~ ~ ~ ~ ~ ~

It was early but all his gear was on and already he was exercising. He felt his energy pulsing. He was throbbing all over. Yes, it was the weights, but more than that, his heart had been racing when he woke this morning.

Friday.

His anticipation of the day pumped him with adrenaline. For such a calm guy, he was thrilled that another individual, a sensual female, could arouse him so much. He was surprised at the weights he could pull today – man, did he feel powerful. He grunted through his teeth as he eased some weights down.

He wasn't planning to communicate with anyone today. He wanted to lay low so that the day played out just as he'd planned. There was one important call to make and an email to send and then, he could just take it easy.

~ ~ ~ ~ ~ ~ ~ ~ ~ ~

James was already in his office. He was early. Friday, the day his negotiations would conclude; he simply couldn't wait till the day was done.

The burden would then be off his chest. He could plan ahead then, and get on with what needed doing. And he'd be on his way to achieving his vision, and well, yes, the wealth that that would imply. The stresses were slowly easing out of him, things he had kept so quiet wouldn't matter so much anymore.

~ ~ ~ ~ ~ ~ ~ ~ ~ ~

Katherine woke and immediately sat up to listen. She'd heard a noise. She quietly slipped out of bed and walked to Maisy's room. Peeking inside, she jumped slightly as her daughter shouted, 'Go away!' She saw that Maisy was still asleep. It was a dream and not a very pleasant one from the sound of it. She remembered her own, frightful dream last night and shuddered from both the memory and the early morning cold. Katherine rubbed the back of her hand softly on her daughter's cheek to comfort her and Maisy sighed, cuddling further into her duvet. Katherine waited there for a few minutes then returned to her own room.

She decided to dress despite the early morning hour and to get the day started. Today, she hoped to see Edward. She also had her husband to deal with. If she couldn't reach him, she'd have to contact Richard. She grimaced. Anjali was coming over today as well...there was a lot to sort out.

She needed time in the day too to consider her options and whether now may be the right time to involve the police....but she'd think that through later.

Downstairs in the kitchen she prepared a frothy coffee and called the hospital. They put her through to the ward almost instantly.

'He's still in intensive care but you can visit today, early afternoon. The consultant had asked for some tests to be done first thing this morning.'

'What tests?' She was alarmed.

'Could you repeat your name please, we need to check our system.'

Katherine repeated her relationship and hoped they'd be forthcoming. This particular nurse was empathetic and continued to chat.

'The tests were to check what was in his body – whether anything had caused his heart attack. Some test results have already come through, and he had traces of medication in his blood which could have caused a reaction. We are now doing a few more samples,' was the answer.

'What do you mean?'

'Well did he take prescription medication, or was he given drugs or medication on the day, that he wouldn't normally take?'

Before Katherine could respond the nurse continued.

'We see that you completed a form for us on Wednesday including information about his GP. Do you know if he took any prescriptions?' Katherine replied that she didn't know, but that he wouldn't share that with her anyway.

'I understand. We won't have all the results until later today. Probably the end of the day.'

Katherine hung up. What did that mean – 'or was he given drugs or medication'? She was puzzled – it was so bizarre, here she is suspecting Edward and now the hospital is querying whether someone may have given Edward medication that caused a heart attack?

She quickly checked her mobile for texts and emails, but there was nothing, absolutely nothing from Colin. She found that odd and rude, there was no disputing that. Sighing, she pursed her lips. She'd have to talk to Richard today. But not before trying Colin one more time. She texted and emailed her husband again.

She decided to WhatsApp him on his mobile. It rang out, with no response. She rang his mobile directly. His usual voicemail came on.

It irked her that he wasn't responsive. Where was he? What was he doing? She called the hotel. This time she had the room number – but again, his room phone rang out and clicked onto voicemail. There was no answer.

She checked the time, mid-afternoon his time in Shanghai. Was he in meetings? It was not a good enough excuse. He could still respond.

She jogged upstairs to Maisy and woke her daughter for school. She reminded her it was Friday, nearly the weekend. Together they had a small breakfast and then prepared to leave.

Just as she locked the door, her mobile rang out. She quickly fished it out of her purse. It was sure to be Colin.

It wasn't. It was Thomas. She needed a quiet moment without Maisy around to talk to Thomas, so she left it, and clicked open the car door for Maisy to climb into. With both of them buckled in, she turned the motor on, and eased her car slowly out of the drive. With Maisy chatting non-stop on the way, it took no time to arrive at school. Maisy was desperate to get out and run ahead having spotted her friends.

Anjali and Katherine waved to each other across the playground. They came together as they lined their children up.

'How did you sleep last night? And any news on Edward?' Asked Anjali.

'They're doing tests on Edward,' she thought to tell Anjali more when they met later. 'And I didn't sleep so well,' she made a face to indicate it didn't matter. 'I'll fill you in later today. Thomas came to visit yesterday - it cleared a lot up - but also left me with a few unanswered questions. See you later, same time?'

'Yes, of course. I'll bring lunch today, ok?'

'That would be lovely, thank you. I'm really looking forward to the two of us heading back down to the river to collect...' Katherine caught herself at the last minute from saying, 'the shoe and cotton fabric'. She didn't want the children asking questions, nor risk anyone else overhearing them.

Anjali nodded knowingly at her. The two kissed their children goodbye and headed to their homes.

~ ~ ~ ~ ~ ~ ~ ~ ~ ~

Anjali enjoyed the short return walk to her cottage, and let her mind wander. She was sorting dinner today so that James didn't need to worry about that later tonight. She smiled - they shared the workload at home normally - but over the last few years with his work ramping up, it had been hard to share. As she had been working part-time only it seemed fair that she did more of the housework and child sorting.

She was hopeful that with this deal he was signing today, he'd have more time to spend with the family. The kids were getting older and holidays together would become more important. It had been really challenging for James to accommodate holidays over the last few years.

Her smile faded as she reflected. He had taken a lot on, and she knew he was burdened by some of the extra work demands over recent years. He wasn't able to share those issues, as he explained, because of the nature of his work. Anjali was willing to accept that but she was aware that he was sometimes, especially over the last year, affected by the workload and pressures. Whether the pressures were technical, scientific, competitive, or of a financial nature she didn't actually know.

He certainly never seemed solely interested in the pursuit of money. She was quite certain that her husband was much more interested in something more noble: in this new form of energy that would change the way people lived. And he was definitely a people-person. He thought about his team often. James ensured they were remunerated generously, and that he provided balanced recognition for their work.

Anjali unlocked her front door and glanced back appreciatively at her front garden. It was an almost purist version of a traditional cottage garden with a mix of useful edible plants and colourful, old-fashioned favourites. The few remaining tall blue and pale pink spires of hollyhocks sat just behind bright clumps of orange and yellow chrysanthemums. The dahlias were a personal favourite of Anjali's even at this time of year. They provided a muted collection of oranges and ambers and soft autumnal colours of peach and apricot. Anjali's extended family in India prided themselves on their dahlias, and Anjali was just as competitive with her own mother here in England. Their shared dahlia collection was the envy of many friends.

The honeysuckle still flowered prolifically and wound along her fence up into her apple tree. Lavender bushes, ornamental cabbages, and rosemary lined the pathway which in some places was only just visible beneath overflowing pinks and campanulas now well past their best. At the back of the border were her artichokes, bay, a few late flowers from dozens of deep blue delphiniums, sweet pea runners and sunflowers which the children had planted.

In her moment's reflection admiring her garden, the scent of a rose unexpectedly drifted on the autumn breeze. She looked to where the scent came from and enticed, walked to her late flowering rose, Generous Gardener. She breathed in deeply the delicious musky scent of its beautifully formed pale pink flowers blazing a trail up her cottage wall. One rose was partially broken at the stem, and she twisted it off, sniffing it appreciatively as she entered her house.

She loved her home and wondered if today would change anything. Was James selling his company or was he securing additional investment? And after tonight, she could more confidently approach Richard for a remuneration review.

The two put together would perhaps mean a larger house and garden?

That would be great, with the children getting older, they needed more space now than the cottage could provide. She hummed happily with thoughts of the future, and then turned her mind to the evening ahead.

She was pleased that Richard had sought her out from the men on the team for this piece of work, but puzzled that he couldn't give her any information in advance to prepare. She had to wait until this evening, when he received the final documents, before she could help. She was eager to assist Richard and close this mystery deal out so they could start on her new opportunity next week.

She sorted the dinner, tidied the kitchen and headed up to her room to pack her work items and overnight bag.

'Lord!' she caught her reflection in the mirror.

'I'm thinking again about what I should wear. Twice in one week! Now that's not like me.'

Determined to be swift in her outfit decision, she pulled a pale beige cashmere sweater dress from her closet, which Katherine had bought for her birthday last year. It was something she would never buy, or think she could afford – but she absolutely adored it. She had worn it once, when she and James went out for dinner much earlier this year, but aside from that they hadn't been out together again for dinner, and she had so little other occasions to wear it.

Pulling it out of her cupboard to pack, Anjali touched the soft fabric. It was such a luxurious cashmere. She knew which heels she would wear. There weren't many to choose from and only one suited the work evening. Then, she packed her clothing for Saturday: jeans with a simple t-shirt and sweater. She added her work items. There wasn't much paper to pack, most of it was on her laptop, and she packed that as well. Given she had no work to prepare for tonight, and it was her day off, she planned not to log on to work today.

She smiled and sighed. The Mandarin Oriental. That will be nice. And she closed the door to her room.

~ ~ ~ ~ ~ ~ ~ ~ ~ ~

Katherine parked her car by the fountain in her driveway. The trip home from Maisy's school had given her some time to think. She jogged up the grand stairway. At the front door the faint ringing of the hallway phone was tantalisingly perceptible. She fumbled with the front door lock, trying to move quickly to catch the caller.

In a second, she was through the door and picked up the phone at what felt like the very last ring. She was sure it was Colin.

'Hello?' She answered.

'Hello, is that Miss Katherine?' The voice queried.

So it wasn't Colin. It wasn't Thomas. She recognised the voice, but only just.

'Yes, who is speaking please?'

'Hello Miss Katherine, it's your solicitors here, we are calling to ask how Edward is, and how you and the child are doing?'

Ahh, she recognised the voice. It was the solicitor who had asked about Edward at her meeting yesterday morning. The one who had the cream notepaper in his briefcase with notes written in calligraphy.

'Why, thank you for calling to check, that is very kind. Unfortunately I didn't visit him yesterday, he was unable to take visitors,' she explained.

'Ah, I see,' there was a pause.

'And today they are doing more tests, although he should be able to receive visitors in the afternoon,' she added.

'Tests?'

'Yes, I queried that as well. They are running tests, to um,' she wondered if she should share the information.

'Yes...?' he prompted her to continue.

'To check if perhaps he'd taken a prescription or something that might cause a heart attack,' she stated.

'Really? Edward? He's so careful, and healthy for his age...' was the surprised reply.

'Yes. Well, they also mentioned the possibility that someone may have given him something, to cause the heart attack.'

There was a small but audible gasp at the other end of the line.

Katherine paused.

'Miss Katherine, I think I should come to see you, as soon as possible.'

She was perplexed, what now? Was this to do with Edward's health? How well did he know Edward? Or was it more to do with the finances?

'May I ask if there has been another issue with the portfolio, or whether this is about Edward?' She inquired politely.

'Yes, ah, both in fact. I'd prefer to talk in person and I have something to show you as well.'

It was obvious that he was reluctant to provide further information on the phone, and wanted to see her.

'I'm free until about 11...' she replied.

'Perfect, I shall collect my items and leave very shortly. Thank you,' and he hung up.

Chapter 25 - Unexpected Visitor

She was intrigued - what could he know?

She dug in her handbag for her mobile whilst heading to the kitchen for a cup of tea. She rang Thomas to return his missed call from earlier. Two rings and the phone was answered.

'Hello?'

'Hi, Thomas,' Katherine felt slightly shy again. How odd she thought.

'Hey, Katherine, how are you?'

'I'm fine, thank you. I was driving Maisy to school earlier and missed your call. I'm home now. Is everything ok? Did you hear from Colin?' She was so hopeful that he had been calling earlier with news.

'No, no news from Colin,' there was a heavy pause on the line, 'I'm better too. Talking to you yesterday was obviously therapy, I had a great sleep!' He allowed himself a small chuckle.

Katherine let out a relieved laugh, this was going to be ok.

'Guess you haven't heard from Colin either? I was also calling earlier about Edward.'

Katherine's face became serious.

'No, nothing from Colin. I sent him an email and a text this morning and called his hotel room plus mobile. I'm giving him a final chance to respond before I text Richard later today. I don't like reaching out to Richard. Colin is my husband,' she paused, 'I should at least know where he is!'

She broke off, expecting a comment but there was none. She knew how he felt about Colin's odd behaviour and his involvement with Richard.

'The news about Edward is a bit mixed. He can take visitors later today so that's good. He's still in intensive care though. And they are taking tests, have been taking tests, actually.'

She took a deep breath. 'They asked me if he took anything or had a prescription, or in fact, if someone gave him something that might have caused the heart attack.'

'What? Really? That's odd, Edward wasn't keen on pills. He thought himself far too healthy for that. And who would give him something, did the doctor say what they meant?'

'I think they're referring to medication, no details were provided. I don't believe he took any prescriptions either. Thomas, I know you don't want to hear this, but what if he did cause my mother's death? What if he couldn't deal with the guilt of that and did take something?' She held her breath, waiting for his answer.

'Katherine, no, I simply can't imagine that of Edward.'

'The alternative is that someone else caused my mother's death and may also have tried to deal with Edward. Maybe Edward knew something.'

'Look Katherine, this is getting complicated. Maybe he just had a heart attack jumping into a pile of leaves at his age,' she could hear Thomas' frustration over the phone.

'Yes, maybe,' she bit her lip as her mind raced with thoughts.

'One of the solicitors is coming around this morning. He knew Edward very well, and had called to check how he was. When I told him about the tests, he insisted he visit me today to talk about Edward, not just the finances. That wasn't his intention when he first called. I'm sure the news about the tests changed his plans for the day.'

'Hmmm, that's odd. Would you like me with you, when he visits?'

'It's ok, Thomas, I know Fridays can be crazy for you at the clinic. I'll be fine. And I'll let you know what he says. Are you planning to visit Edward with me later?'

'Yes, I'd really like that, when do you plan to go?'

'I'll probably head to the hospital after lunch, before I collect Maisy. Anjali is popping over for lunch again today. I'm guessing the solicitor will be gone by then.'

'I'll need to check that time with my secretary. I'm sure that I can move a few things around.'

'Ok, I'll talk to you after lunch as I'm leaving. We can meet there.' They said goodbye.

Katherine made herself a fresh coffee. Too much coffee for a tea drinker, she reflected. She thought she'd log onto the portfolio and the tool the solicitors had given her access to, in order to familiarise herself with the investments. Now was a perfect time to have a look at the portfolio and plan how to pick up from her mother's amazing work.

She brought her coffee into her mother's study and opened her laptop there.

Her eyes swept across the room and the view beyond the elegant french doors. It was the perfect place to pick up her mother's work, different from the Orangery, more grounded, which is where her brain needed to be looking at these figures.

She checked the balances. There had been no transfers since yesterday morning. She sighed with relief.

The solicitors had suggested a follow up session at their offices next week to focus on the charities. They had files of information to walk her through, and she had agreed that a personal handover from them would be appropriate, given the sensitivity of some of the charities.

And so now, should she start with understanding the real estate? She was hugely keen to discover the full scale of the property portfolio.

She also took a personal interest in the investments her mother had made across the science vertical - small, innovative research companies. Thomas mentioned that her interest in these may have stemmed from her involvement with Thomas' clinic. As well, her mother had always loved to hear the work that James was involved in. Katherine was keen to understand where her mother had invested into green energy and technology - maybe that would help to solve the elusive contents of the note.

She thought to start with the last investment her mother had made, a small research company, not unlike James'. Then she would dive into the real estate portfolio. The latter would be even more tangible if she could find the properties in google maps. She smiled as she thought again about the 'holidays' her mother and grandmother would take her on. Holidays for her, and she shook her head with some pride in her mother's secrecy, but work trips for her mother to check in on the family properties across the globe.

She would love to pick up that same holidaying tradition with Maisy as they discovered these locations together. But this time it would be different. She already had thought about this, and hoped to prepare Maisy for what one day, fingers crossed, she'd inherit.

As well, she had already considered that the two of them may need to get away for a short while if the situation became difficult with Colin. She flinched as her mind flicked back from holidays to reality. A deep sinking feeling came over her. She shook her head and looked at her screen and some papers in front of her. Focus on the next positive step, she thought. She picked up a letter that she'd opened from her mother's desk the other day, and researched the property. It was in Italy, Puglia in fact. A good place to start she smiled.

The doorbell rang. That was quick, she thought.

She answered the door, and the solicitor stood there looking haggard. She couldn't believe the difference in his face from two days ago, and from the video call yesterday. He looked unwell; he had obviously rushed to drive here. He was sweating slightly and seemed quite unlike the calm gentleman solicitor she had met with on Wednesday. He was nervous, and sighed in relief when he saw her face.

'Thank heavens you answered the door.'

That's strange she thought but replied in a welcoming manner, 'Hello, come in, are you alright? It's warm today, isn't it? Shall I make you a coffee or tea or perhaps something cold?'

She opened the door wide to let him in. He looked around furtively and replied.

'A tea, yes, that would be perfect. And somewhere private where we can talk.'

His secretive, slightly frightened demeanour didn't set her at ease. He was uncomfortable, that was for certain.

'Yes, of course, let's make your tea then we can sit in mother's study and close the door for complete confidence,'

She was truly intrigued but there was a niggle. Why did he want to be in a private room? She had found his behaviour different from the other solicitors, and odd to begin with. Was it wise to sit in a closed room with him?

She made the tea and tried small talk but it didn't work. She also tried to encourage him to share what he'd come to divulge, but that didn't work either. His nervousness was infectious and Katherine became quite concerned. At least Thomas knew about the solicitor's visit if there was trouble.

And of course, Anjali was coming for lunch. Katherine glanced at the kitchen clock. She should be here in a few hours to help collect the shoe and cotton fabric. A few hours. She cast a sidelong look at the solicitor and saw that he was still sweating. It was cool in the kitchen, so it wasn't the temperature. He was preparing for something unpleasant - of that she was sure.

She asked him to step in front of her as she guided him down the hallway to her mother's study. Once in, she suggested he sit on one of the furthest chairs, away from both the French doors and the study door - so she could theoretically access either if need be. She placed down their tray of tea, watching him all the while, and then returned to close the study door.

It clicked shut. She turned around to face him, and her jaw dropped.

Chapter 26 - Solicitor's Surprise

Thomas was in the office for several client sessions. His last one was at 11:00. The afternoon had been booked out for clinical research and to catch up with some of his research analysts. However, after his call with Katherine, his secretary helped to re-organised the schedule to pick up his work on Saturday and check in with his analysts Monday.

With a clear diary this afternoon, he could meet Katherine at the hospital and visit Edward. He was eager to see him and talk to the consultant.

There was a possibility that the consultant would share information with him - professional to professional - despite the fact that he had no family relationship with Edward. He cleared his desk, and prepared for his next couple's session. He smiled, this couple was near the end of their treatment and the signs were all very positive. He put his concerns for Edward and Katherine to the back of his mind and focused on his clients.

~~~~~~~~~~

Richard wondered what game Colin was playing at. The last time Colin had left it so long to communicate, had been several months ago and he had been 'caught up' with an 'intoxicating woman', Colin's words exactly.

Why the bloody hell didn't Colin just drop him a line? It wasn't that Richard was worried about Colin's side of the bargain - he had proved himself loyal to the game in a way that surpassed Richard's original expectations. It was surprising how far Colin would be willing to go to reach the end game.

No, it wasn't that he didn't trust Colin. But it was a matter of courtesy. He should have dropped a line to Richard. And he needed those Chinese documents, time was closing in on him.

He opened his laptop and picked up, again, the last email from Colin. He checked: it was on Wednesday at 1:30 AM British time. That would be around Wednesday, 9:30 AM in Shanghai. It was now Friday morning and there were no updates. He responded again to that email, putting **Urgent** in the subject line.

He typed his email impatiently: 'Look Colin, this is great news. These assurances are just the ticket. I assume you received and read through the information I sent regarding Gemstone's recent test results on Wednesday? Did you share this evidence with your Chinese partners? If so, where are the detailed contractual commitments they promised? I need these documents now from your Chinese counterparts - for

18:00 my time - I've got resource committed to spend the evening combing through these.

'I get it that you are probably otherwise engaged, but we need these documents. Don't forget the timings on this, the original time frame is running out. We'll lose the upper hand if we don't get this completed before then. Call me immediately if there are issues.'

He checked that his email expressed the urgency of the situation then decided to add more: 'Colin, if I don't hear back by 18:00 my time today, I'll call the hotel and demand they check in on you. Wouldn't want to disturb you in the early hours of your morning. Am sure you'll be busy with other matters.'

He smiled wryly but he was still extremely annoyed with Colin. Colin's only two weaknesses were women, good-looking women, and luxury, a little bit of luxury, always. And they both sometimes got in the way of business.

He grinned, he could deal with these weaknesses, especially now that Colin's net worth was astronomically higher since his mother-in-law's death. He grimaced as if he had tasted something sour. In fact, he corrected himself, it was his *wife's* net worth, but it was just as good as Colin's....

He called the Mandarin Oriental in London and asked them to place his favourite Champagne and two glasses in both his room and the room he had reserved for Anjali. He checked that their best flower bouquet would be on the centre table of her room with smaller arrangements throughout the suite as well. They assured him all was in hand.

He also requested that Champagne be served immediately upon their arrival for dinner. And he checked that the intimate corner spot he had reserved was still held for him.

'Of course, sir,' they replied. It was the only answer he expected.

~ ~ ~ ~ ~ ~ ~ ~ ~ ~

The pairs of eyes were the same, but the location was different. The light was bright, a few naked light bulbs – bright and clinical – and the walls were grey. There were other people in the room.

The situation was definitely heating up. They checked again the texts, emails, and voicemails over the last 2 days. It was Friday, they'd have to decide on a response today.

The boss smiled with satisfaction and spoke with authority to the team. His message was clear. We've taken what we can, and have the information we need. Let's think about how we keep them at bay while we cover the scent of our trail.

The team nodded in respect and bent their heads close together quietly talking through the next steps.

~ ~ ~ ~ ~ ~ ~ ~ ~ ~

Katherine's pupils were dilated – what was he doing?

The solicitor had hopped up from the sofa and was waving a paper in his hand with gusto.

'This note, I have come to talk to you about this note,' he was obviously distraught.

'Would you like to pass me the note, so that I can see it?' She was sure it was the same cream notepaper she had spotted fluttering to the floor at his office.

'Yes, of course, I apologise that I'm so, so nervous. But I'm worried, and your call this morning confirmed some suspicions I've had.'

He walked towards her with the note and explained the context, before passing it to her.

'Two days ago Edward and I had a meeting here, at your house. He'd booked the meeting sometime ago and had intimated on the phone that he had some important business to discuss. Business about your mother.'

Katherine's eyes narrowed as she tried to determine what surprise was in store for her. What terrible things could he possibly tell her? Were her suspicions about Edward correct? Could she trust this man?

'When we met, Edward produced this document. It's his note, in his writing. On the document you'll see dates, times against those dates, and observations.'

He took a deep breath and his large stomach seemed to reach his neck as he held his breath for a moment.

'These observations are his timeline of events and activities of key individuals, people he didn't know whether to trust or not.'

He looked at her, to see if she understood. She didn't.

'You see, Miss Katherine, Edward was convinced, and must still be, that your mother's accident….wasn't an accident. He's convinced that it was foul play of the worst kind. And he documented his evidence, or links to the death, in order to understand the timeline and sequence of events.'

'Oh my God,' Katherine stepped back. She felt faint. This is it, the confirmation she was looking for - someone else who also suspected. She quietly turned around to sit on the sofa.

'Are you alright, Miss Katherine? I'm so sorry to be the one to break the news to you, I apologise,' his face was etched with concern and he passed the notepaper to her.

She swallowed a few times and absent-mindedly rubbed the smooth creamy paper. He deftly moved to pick her tea up and gently sat near her, holding it for her. She smiled a thanks at him, and took her tea, sipping it slowly.

'Please, carry on, tell me what you know.'

'Yes, of course. He came to me because he believed he could trust the family solicitors. He knew your mother had held us in the highest esteem,' he struggled to keep the pride out of his voice. He obviously wanted to impress upon her the seriousness of the situation and why Edward had trusted him enough to share this information.

'As I said, he had concerns about some key individuals. He didn't want to unnecessarily upset you and was very worried about your health given your grief,' he nodded at her to check she understood Edward's motives.

She nodded back.

'And so, he was collecting his observations and his evidence until he was certain, and then he planned to share this with you and with the police. In the first instance, he was always, always concerned with your well-being and Maisy's, and then with the health of the estate.

'He was afraid that, during your grief, the estate would be exposed to possible fraudulent activity. And he was aware also, that your mother had been threatened,' he locked eyes with her. 'Ah yes, it was unfortunately so.'

'When I was here, he went through this note with me in detail, and so I pass it now to you, to read. During our session, and in the strictest of confidence, he covered the sections of the family estate he managed, to demonstrate how financially profitable these are. And I can tell you, he has done some fine, fine work. Your mother's interests under his stewardship have most certainly flourished. He managed your mother's UK interests with honesty and efficiency. The profits have been excellent.

'I might also add that he had his own separate, personal investments which have been highly profitable over the years. He absolutely kept these strictly separate to your mother's affairs he managed. We sometimes met to discuss the markets. He has a brilliant financial mind. And it was because of this that your mother asked him to take over the management of her UK estate and UK interests quite some years ago. She trusted him completely.'

He paused to reflect. Katherine was still digesting the information and thought he had more to say. But when she saw he was thinking to himself, she began to read the note.

He quickly placed his hand on her arm to stop her for a moment more.

'In that session, I required him to sign a letter of confidentiality. He requested private financial information, and in order for me to do this, I had to verify some of the family accounts. This means that it was necessary to divulge the existence of these accounts, and thus the reason for the letter of confidentiality.'

She nodded at him again. 'I understand, I'd like to read the note now,' she was desperate to compare Edward's evidence to hers.

'Yes, of course, please,' he replied and sat back, smoothing his thick grey hair back into place.

She flattened the note on her lap and began to read.

Chapter 27 – Great Minds

It took her a few full minutes to digest the information. She scanned through it the first time, and then slowed down to read it again. She wanted to be sure to understand what Edward was saying.

She tried to summarise the information in her head.

He had overheard a conversation between Richard and Colin, after the death of her mother. And it seemed from the notes that during this conversation there were two accounts mentioned. He must have surely checked these with the solicitor?

Edward had also heard raised voices between Thomas and Katherine's mother on the morning of her mother's death. He didn't suspect Thomas of foul play, but wanted to understand why the argument had happened.

The greatest revelation of all, was that Edward was deeply suspicious of Colin, and was concerned about Richard's influence.

She pointed to the note. 'Did he ask you about these two accounts?'

He peered over her arm, 'Yes, indeed he did.'

'And what did you find?'

'Well, there was one where we found no match. Nothing, absolutely nothing.'

He continued. 'You may remember that four tranches of money have been transferred out of the family estate, since the death. These transfers were not to this account,' he pointed to one in particular. 'Both you and Edward asked about particular accounts,' he took a deep breath, 'and no money, not even the fourth transfer yesterday morning, was moved to either this account I'm pointing to, or the one you queried us about earlier.'

'What about this other account number here, which Edward says was mentioned between Colin and Richard? I seem to recognise it.'

'This is the concerning part. Yes, you will recognise it. This is the existing family account that was highly profitable and then was liquidated recently. All the investments in that account were converted to cash, as you know. It was from this account that the four tranches of money were then transferred to accounts in the Bahamas, Panama and China.'

She stared at him. He looked at her, waiting for her queries, eager to help.

'So perhaps that isn't so surprising, given we believe Colin was the only one who had access to the accounts,' she added quietly. 'Sadly, I gave my husband the right to access the accounts...'. She left the sentence unfinished.

'Yes, agreed. However, we have sorted that now, and yes, we all do what we think is best, even in grief. I confirmed to

Edward on Wednesday that this family account - a highly profitable investment - was the account Colin and Richard were discussing, and has since been, for lack of a better word, plundered. In the knowledge of this, our requests to Colin to meet, became more urgent. But as you know, we've had no response.'

She asked for a moment, looking at the notes again and then stated the obvious.

'Richard must have been in the house if Edward overheard their conversation, do you know?'

'Yes, it wasn't a, shall we say, virtual meeting, he was at the house, because on that date we met with them both. It was our third and last meeting with your husband.'

'You had already met Colin twice before that, in the few days after my mother's death?'

'Yes, my dear, you were very grieved and as I recall, quite bedridden. Colin was most keen to meet with us, as we were with him. You can understand that. The death was foremost in our minds, as were our sympathies with your family, but your family estate is significant in value and we would have been remiss in our duties to not just you, but your mother if we had not met with Colin as soon as we could. We reached out to you, but Colin asked us to deal with him. And of course, you had given him the power of attorney,' he added to ensure she understood.

'Yes, I understand the situation.' She nodded at him.

'There is more on the back,' he pointed to the flip side. She couldn't believe she had missed that and quickly turned the note over.

<<a word here not legible>>:

1. Innocent?

2. Six weeks before her death J visits house. I find out later (point 4) that K's mother had asked to meet with him. She had questions about green energy and wanted him to help her with some market research.

3. Five weeks before her death, they meet. J is here for several hours. They talk about the green energy sector and also about J's company. She tells me this (point 4) but I don't know details of conversation.

4. Two weeks before her death at one of our Tuesday portfolio reviews, she confirms to me that she was looking to invest in a green energy company in the UK. She says that James needs funding for his business. But she left it at that. I didn't press her further. It's at this time she tells me about points 2 and 3.

5. Did she invest? What company?

6. Monday, week of her death. J visits again - K's mother's invitation.

7. Next day, Tuesday, day before her accident, she tells me at our Tuesday portfolio review that she had hopes to invest in his business. I don't know whether J knew her intentions and whether she had discussed this with J in point 6.

8. She said she had some information potentially about J's green energy market that she had shared with him. K's mother felt it was necessary to share this with J but he was very agitated when he left. And she hadn't been certain about the accuracy of her information. She was herself, unhappy with this exchange.

9. K's mother also mentions that she's looking to invest with C in a UK company and would cover the details with me by end of the week. She tells me she delayed sharing this with me, because I wouldn't be supportive. She must

not invest with C, but I couldn't persuade her to rethink this investment. We exchanged heated words. It was very troubling. This was Tuesday.

10. She also left me with impression that she was being pushed into a corner regarding her investment plans in green energy. 'They' were lobbying her aggressively. Not just this, but 'they' were getting aggressive and she felt it was serious. Make or break. K's mother was uncomfortable. No details. Who was pushing her? Who were 'they'? Was it J or C or hopefully another party? I should have been more calm, maybe then she would have divulged more. She was upset with our raised voices - and she would not provide details to me.

11. Wed mid-morning C has to return to school to pick up Maisy. While he is out, T visits in AM. Argues with K's mother. T leaves upset. C still not back yet. I walk to T's house hoping to catch him there. He isn't in. And I'm not at home when river accident occurs.

12. At funeral, J and I talked about the events surrounding her death and the weather. He said he was in office the whole day, and didn't realise it was warm enough to swim.

13. In fact, J wasn't in office on day of murder, nor at home. A mentions this when she visits K on day after funeral. A tells K that J was out on business that day.

14. J has no alibi?

She felt like someone had knocked her in the stomach. She looked at the solicitor to ask a question to which she already knew the answer.

'What about this word that isn't legible at the top of the list? Why did Edward smudge that out? And I'm not sure I understand who we are talking about here,' she didn't trust herself to say what was becoming apparent.

'Ah, he didn't smudge that. That must have been me,' he answered sheepishly as he realised the word was rubbed out. 'Apologies, I didn't notice that. Afraid I was holding the note too tightly.' She thought about how much he had been sweating when he arrived at her door.

'It says, 'James.'

Her hand flew to her mouth. She felt sick to her stomach. He confirmed what she'd suspected. How was that possible?! The solicitor was watching her closely. 'James' could only be one person....

'James? And 'A' is Anjali? 'C' is Colin and of course, 'K' is myself. Did, did he mean our James?'

He nodded in response.

'No, it can't be possible! Did my mother invest in James' business? Did Edward ask you this?'

'Yes, Edward asked me this. And no, I couldn't find any evidence. She did make an investment in an energy fund, as my partner mentioned to you yesterday. But I couldn't find a reference to E2E, James' business.'

She swallowed, ok, so that meant he was in the clear, right....thoughts were racing through her head.

'I was concerned enough after the session with Edward to speak to my partners about this. We decided not to alert you as there was no hard evidence, and at this point, Edward was only collecting his evidence.'

That hit home, exactly the position she had been in.

'It doesn't mean James couldn't have been involved in your mother's death. It doesn't mean that these other people who were 'pressuring her' didn't get to her money. For instance the energy fund she invested in, could have been indirect funding for James' business, through another investment vehicle,' he added.

So, James wasn't in the clear.

'As our secretary aptly said as well yesterday during the call, we don't know who Colin shared the account information with. He may or may not have given that information to Richard. Knowing him, he most likely didn't. But he may have. And he may have given the information to someone else.

'Or indeed, if Richard was taken into his confidence, Richard may have given the information to someone else. Again, I can't imagine it. Access to that kind of money...

'It's evident, however, that there was an urgency to Colin's business dealings, otherwise he wouldn't have made the transfers so soon. At some point, you would come out of your grief and get wise to the activities on the account. Certainly he must have known we, the partners, would query these transactions. He evidently wasn't worried.'

Katherine took a deep breath. It was a lot to take in. How had she missed James' visits to the house? She must have been at work those days. She reflected. The one thing Edward didn't have on his list of observations, was that Colin's family estate was in deep trouble. Perhaps that was why he was moving so quickly with the transfers. Was Richard helping Colin with his money issues? She struggled to set the blame solely at her husband's feet.

She couldn't swallow properly. What about James and....Anjali? What did she know? She couldn't possibly have known about James visiting her mother. She would have said. But, if it were possible that James had a hand in her mother's death, then could Anjali know? She shook her head. Anjali wouldn't have been so shocked at all the information Katherine had been sharing with her.

She looked down at the note. There were three other things. He touches on Thomas' argument with her mother. He does't mention the lost shoe. But the shirt, it was on Edward's list also.

'I know about the argument between Thomas and my mother and so this doesn't worry me. But, he thought the shirt provided some evidence?'

'Yes, he said that he thought it was evidence of a struggle. He didn't believe a rock scrape could have caused that. I understood from the way he spoke, that he had your mother's shirt in his possession. He felt that was a key piece of evidence, and wanted it somewhere safe.'

And so, they were back at the shirt. So he did have it. He does have it....where is it? She knew what she would need to do the minute the solicitor left.

'Did he say where the shirt is?'

'No, I'm afraid not. And I didn't think to ask.'

'That's fine and, thank you, thank you so much for this,' she was absorbing the information, her brain was racing ahead but she was still stunned at the same time. Like she was moving very slowly in time and couldn't get where she wanted to fast enough.

'I decided to bring this all to your attention when we spoke this morning.'

'And why is that?'

'Well, if someone 'gave' medication to Edward – were they trying to poison him? If so, then most probably he was on to the right person. And they might try to get to you!'

He looked around the room. 'Would you like me to go to the police with you? Are you safe here? Is your husband back soon?'

She was staring at him. What did he just say? She was trying to register the urgency in his voice and his deep concern. What was he concluding – that someone was trying to kill Edward to protect themselves. That meant one of the people on the list: Colin, James, possibly Richard was a murderer, or indeed, whoever else was threatening her mother? She realised she had also been indirectly charging someone with murder, but it seemed so real now.

She shuddered.

'You think I may also be a target? But hardly anyone knows I'm suspicious....' she trailed off.

'Who knows?' He challenged her and his eyes focused closely on her.

'Thomas, Anjali, that's it.'

'Hmmm,' he swallowed and looked at her twice before saying the obvious, 'and Anjali is the wife of James, correct?'

'Correct,' she closed her eyes. Oh my God, what is going on.

'Is Colin back yet, from China?'

'No, due back any day now, most likely Sunday, but it could be today. He isn't responding to my or Thomas' messages.'

'Thomas?'

'Yes,' she replied, 'he's been texting Colin about Edward. And he is James' best friend.' Why did she say that? She had already decided Thomas was in the clear, and so had Edward. It didn't matter that he was James' close friend. And what if Colin turned up?

She so desperately wanted to see Edward now.

'Should we take this to the police?' He asked her again.

'No, no, I need to digest this. I just need a bit more time to think things through.' She was desperate now, to collect the shoe and fabric from the oak, and find her mother's shirt.

He looked at her with concern. 'If that is what you wish at this point. But text me if Colin shows up.' He was obviously not comfortable with her decision.

She cast her eyes downward, feeling guilty that she wasn't sharing everything with him.

'Please take care of yourself, and please, would you mind calling our firm by the end of the day. It's important you check in on us daily. I trust Edward's judgement – he's a good man – and until the doctors know what may have caused his heart attack, I think you need to be careful, for yourself and for your daughter.'

Her eyes flew to a portrait of Maisy in the room. Could Maisy be in danger as well?

'Katherine,' he asked for her attention as her eyes had watered over looking at the portrait.

'Yes?' She squinted at him to focus.

'There's a lot at stake here. There's a lot of money, and as I've said, people you think you know, can behave in ways that you could never imagine, even criminal. We deal in these kinds of family estates and I've seen this happen on numerous occasions. If you're worried about your safety at any time, call the police, call us.' His voice and eyes were serious.

He stood up, much more calm and confident now. He had delivered his news and had laid a framework for caution.

'Would you like to keep the note?'

She deliberated. It would be safer with the solicitor, for certain. But she wanted to study it further.

'Do you mind if I keep it?'

'Not at all, keep it safe. And keep yourself safe.'

Katherine led him to the front hallway. They shook hands, and he departed, warning her again. She watched him leave then carefully locked the door. She read Edward's note again, then carefully pushed it deep into her back pocket. She wasn't taking any chances with the note, or with home security.

She walked quickly to the conservatory doors in the kitchen and locked them. With the weather as kind as it had been, the doors had been left open in the daytime. But now, she didn't want just anyone strolling in. She sat in the calm surroundings of her conservatory and her mind strayed for some time as she thought through the information shared with her.

A small tap tap on the lower left conservatory window jolted her out of her thoughts. It was a small robin tapping at the window. She smiled. She didn't know why, but they did that. She'd been sitting in the same position for awhile and stood to stretch. Time to get going.

She headed upstairs to her bedroom. Opening her bedside table, she gently laid Edwards information from the solicitor in the drawer on top of the other evidence. She noticed a window in her room that she normally left slightly open for fresh air and sighed. That needed closing too.

Then, she moved to Maisy's room to close a small window she kept open a fraction on child lock. She was fiddling to close it when she heard the doorbell ring.

She jumped. 'Oh, no.' It was Anjali. Katherine had forgotten Anjali's planned visit. The time had just flown.

She truly didn't know how she would react. She certainly couldn't share the information from this morning. And she didn't know how she felt about retrieving the piece of cloth and shoe from the tree with Anjali by her side. She swallowed. Oh, God, how was she going to do this? She also wanted to search for her mother's shirt now, but again she couldn't do this in Anjali's presence, just in case.

She jogged down the stairs, steadied herself and answered the door.

'Hello.'

'Hi Katherine - what a lovely day again!!' Anjali exclaimed. She was so cheery and her face flushed with the autumn air. She entered the hallway bringing lightness with her.

Katherine just stood. She was quiet, weighing up her options, but it was apparent what she needed to do.

'Anjali, thanks for coming! I'm so very sorry. The office called 2 minutes ago. I've just come off the call and an urgent matter has come up. They need me there immediately. I tried to sort it out but I have to be there in person, I'm so sorry, you've come all this way!'

Anjali's eyes arched in surprise and her face looked concerned.

'Is everything ok, I mean is it really bad?'

Katherine looked at her and shook her head.

'Oh no, no-no, not like that. It isn't good, shall I put it that way, but it's not a world disaster. We'll get over it...'

'Are you sure? Is that more important than collecting the cotton? I guess you can always do that tomorrow, or would you like me to collect the cotton?'

'Oh, no, Anjali, the cotton and shoe can wait. I'm just sorry to waste your time.'

And she was sorry. She was sorry about everything; distrusting their friendship; suspecting James; and her family's ridiculous wealth and the problems it seemed to cause.

'Hey, no problem, Katherine. It's ok,' she replied softly and stepped back towards the front door.

'Here, have this,' and she thrust the basket that was in her hand at Katherine.

'It's lunch. I made your baguette especially as you like it!' she grinned and smiled mischievously at Katherine. 'Make sure you eat it, you're getting thinner each day!'

As she moved down the stairs to her car, Katherine looked sadly after her.

Anjali started her car and shouted goodbye.

'Katherine, call me tomorrow afternoon if you need any help. I'm collecting my two kids this afternoon, then James will be back. Remember, he has the kids tonight. I'm meeting Richard for the Friday all nighter!' She rolled her eyes and laughed lightly, shrugging her shoulders. She waved goodbye, and her car slowly crunched towards the avenue of beeches.

Katherine stood, waving goodbye. A complete shudder raced throughout her body. She was cold. And yes, she was hungry, but....she looked down at the baguette and polished apple in the basket....she wasn't going to eat this meal, lovingly prepared, just in case.

Ridiculous. She returned inside and locked the door.

She picked up a sweater from the front hallway and rummaged in her handbag for her mobile. No news from Colin. She checked the hour and was relieved - she still had time of course to get her next job done before leaving to see Edward.

Should she call Thomas? If both she and Edward believed Thomas to be a friend, and Thomas' own story corroborated with Edward's note, then she must trust someone.

She rang on her mobile. It was answered immediately.

'Hello Katherine.'

'Hi, Thomas, can you talk now?'

'Yes, it's fine, I'm alone.'

Should she tell him now, all the news, or wait? There was too much to be done before the hospital visit, she would tell him later.

'I'm planning to be at the hospital at about 13:15, would you like to join me?'

'Yes, for sure. I've rearranged my schedule so I can easily meet you there.'

'Ok, perfect, see you then,' she wanted to say something else, perhaps how much she appreciated his being there, but it seemed so disingenuous, so she let her speech hang.

He waited. Nothing. 'Ok, see you then,' he replied and hung up. He stared at his mobile for a few seconds, then returned to his work.

She also, looked at her mobile for a moment, then shook her head. She would tell him more later. On to her next job. She grabbed a small canvas bag she had prepared earlier, dropped her mobile in it and rushed outside. She was in a hurry, and jogged down to the river's swimming hole. There, she briskly followed the river path to the site where her mother had hit her head on the rock. It took about 5 minutes of fast walking and she questioned again, why her mother would be all the way here, up river on a Wednesday morning; a day of the week when she normally enjoyed only a quick dip.

She looked far up into the oak branches. She couldn't see the cotton or the shoe.

The leaves must be hiding them, but her heart still pounded.

She looked around, checking she was the only person there, and moved quickly to the trunk of the oak and around the back by the meadow for an easier climb.

She double checked. It was only her, she was completely alone.

She carefully climbed onto the large branch and moved herself along. As with the first time, she made her way slowly to the spot where the two broken branches hung.

Once there, she paused. There was the cotton fabric just as she'd left it. The shoe, as if stuck in a death trap, was still hanging there. She sighed with relief. It was easy to imagine that they would be gone, it was all becoming so bizarre. A real plot, a real murder. Her mother's life....

She froze. There was a sound below. She heard a noise like a movement in the long grass behind the oak. Or was it closer to the river? She tried to see through the brown and green foliage without moving, but it was impossible to see anything that far down. She waited several minutes with her heart pounding but didn't hear it again. She took a deep breath, and then moved the last metre or so, inching closer to the fabric.

Ok, she was there, close enough to get it.

She wasted no time, and reached into the canvas bag slung across her body. She pulled out her mobile and took several photos of the two items, then each individually as close ups. She popped her mobile back in her bag and moved slightly closer still to the fabric and shoe.

'Gently, gently,' she softly soothed herself and tried to steady her hand.

Taking a shallow breath, she pulled out new cleaning gloves from the bag and put them on. She had thought about this, and didn't want to contaminate anything.

The cotton was simple to tug off and she placed it safely in a clean plastic bag, then pushed it into the canvas one.

The shoe was more difficult. She found herself struggling to reach it. She shifted her weight a bit and tried to stretch closer.

'Difficult, ah, just too difficult,' she moaned quietly and clinging to the branch like a sloth she slowly inched closer.

'Perfect, come here, you shoe.' She straightened her back and then leaned far forwards.

Her fingers tantalisingly touched the shoe but she couldn't grab it.

How did her mother get her leg out there? She looked around quizzically to determine her mother's position hoping it might help her to reach the shoe.

'Ah, God,' she suddenly felt sick. Her head had moved too quickly.

Darkness ebbed at the sides of her eyes, playing with her sight and there was the real possibility of fainting. She lowered her head flat alongside the branch and pressed her body tightly agains the bark.

In a moment, her dizziness faded and she could feel her sight return, even with her eyes closed the stars at the edges of her vision disappeared. Slowly, she thought, slowly does it.

She stayed in position for a moment more, then opened her eyes.

'Eek, that was close.' She had clear vision now and chanced a look down. It was a far way down. Focusing her eyes back on the pattern of the bark, she shuffled just a bit closer to the shoe, still flat against the branch.

Hesitantly, she straightened her back and stretched forward again.

She had it! Jiggling the shoe slowly, she could feel it dismantle.

And then it was loose. She held it still in her hand for a moment as a shudder went down her back. She felt death. The success of securing the shoe was lost on her, as she automatically replayed the horror of the scene and the fatal role the shoe itself must have played.

A strong breeze snapped her back to the moment, and she gripped the the bark tighter with her free hand. She squeezed her hold on the shoe more firmly and then made her move.

Deftly, she pulled the shoe towards her in one continuous move and hoped it wouldn't snag on a small branch.

It was clear!

She couldn't look at it, not there at that height, given what it represented. Feeling still a bit queasy she gently dropped it in another plastic bag and placed it in the canvas one as well. She breathed a deep sigh of relief and glanced back down along the branch.

'Ok, just need to return now.'

She tried to relax her jaw and body, but she was tense and the near blackout she had had a moment earlier worried her. She gently moved her bag, still slung sideways on her body, around to her back and then clung to the branch. Pacing her return downwards, she kept her eyes on the bark, well away from the ground below. The breeze was picking up.

What was that? She was midway down the tree. She paused till the leaves hung still for a moment. Then, she heard the noise again. Definitely the noise came from the meadow near the oak trunk. She turned slowly, almost too frightened to look, and between branches, saw a movement in the long grass.

Someone was there.

Her body shivered and she swallowed despite a parched throat. She clung tightly, feeling strength from the oak and lipped her dry lips. How long could she wait there? The whole situation frightened her. Was she being pursued, as surely as her mother had been?

Chapter 28 - Doctor Talk

His mobile rang. He wasn't expecting a call at this time. It was the director from his investment firm that was involved with Gemstone.

'Yes, hello,' he answered.

He listened, nodding for a few minutes and then he shrugged.

'Look, I'm not that worried at this point, it can wait till next week. The most important piece is what bloody Colin has not yet provided. Your piece can't happen till we get this through anyway. God, he's annoying,' he confided to his director.

Richard repeated that Colin needed to send the papers by this evening. Then, he had a work evening lined up to do some final due diligence on the documents. He would then send the documents off to the director, as soon as he had finished with them - most likely early Saturday morning.

They hung up, both on tenterhooks.

Richard checked his emails again. He was getting restless, he pinged off another email and text to Colin. This time, his message was short. Colin had to act, or else.

~ ~ ~ ~ ~ ~ ~ ~ ~ ~

Katherine was nervous but she couldn't stop herself looking again. She squinted to see better. Who was there? She lay low in the tree hoping that she couldn't be seen.

And then she saw a figure.

A person stepped out. It was Sam.

He was looking around, and looking bewildered. Should she say anything, should she attract his attention? She felt exposed, and didn't feel safe. But it was Sam, who like Edward, had treated her with kindness since she was a young child. She thought to wait first, and see what he was doing.

'Miss Katherine, are you alright?' He spoke out loud. He looked around again, and moved quickly to the river's edge.

Ah, he must have seen her hurrying to the river. He looks scared. Perhaps he's worried for her.

She didn't want to shock him by shouting from so high up in the tree, so she rustled a thin branch. He looked up from the river and around him.

Gently she said, 'Sam, hi Sam.'

He struggled to identify the location of her greeting.

'Miss Katherine, where are you?'

More loudly this time she replied, 'Sam, hey, I'm up here, in the oak tree.'

He stretched his neck back, and putting his hand over his eyes peered far up into the tree.

'By God, Miss Katherine, what are you doing there?' He sounded worried.

'It's ok, Sam, I'm just coming down.'

'Take care, Miss Katherine, go very slowly.'

She shuffled down carefully without mishap, and slid off the last branch onto the meadow. Her legs were shaking, she didn't realise how nervous she was.

Sam made his way to see her.

'Miss Katherine, why were you up there?' Her ways never ceased to amuse or amaze him. He thought she was impulsive and intelligent all at the same time. And so it didn't surprise him to see her in such an odd place.

'Hi Sam, I was just looking over the area. You know, I just felt I had to see the spot of mother's accident from high up.' There was a catch in her throat.

'Hmmm, I understand Miss Katherine, you do what you need to do. It will all be fine.' He looked at her sadly, as if to say, they all missed her mother.

'I need to head off now in any case to see Edward, would you like to join me?'

'Ach, no thanks. I've got so much work on, Edward will understand. You give my greetings to him for me, won't you?'

They had begun to walk back to the house. Katherine had stopped shaking and took strong strides alongside his.

'Yes, I will, for sure.'

She waved goodbye at the Orangery. He picked up the wheelbarrow he'd left there, and giving her a friendly smile he began to whistle as he turned out of sight beyond the Orangery.

'Well, at least something's normal around here,' she smiled, watching after him for a moment. A church bell chimed in the distance, and remembering her time constraints she jogged up to the house. The first stop was her bedroom. She collected the contents from her bedside table then headed downstairs to her mother's study.

Closing the study door quietly behind her, Katherine bent her neck back and loosened her shoulders to shake out the tension she felt. Then, she walked purposefully to the bookshelves behind her mother's desk.

The bookshelves ran from floor to ceiling, across the full width of the wall. Katherine placed her hand at a particular row of shelves chest-height in front of her.

Resting her hand on a thick volume that stuck out only slightly, but certainly not noticeably from the other books on the shelf, she took a quick breath and looked behind.

Reassured that no one was staring through the french doors she pulled the volume out a third of the way, and waited only a second to hear an almost inaudible, 'click'.

Like magic the first four books on the shelf shoulder-height in front of her, silently slid behind the next four books to the right. That whole section of books was fake, and in fact a panel split in two. The moving panel in front of her settled neatly behind the other section of 'books'.

Open, in front of her, was a private compartment that only she and her mother knew about.

She moved with no delay. Placing her mother's shoe in the far corner, she added the note from her mother's desk, her own brainstorming list, and the first piece of cotton she had found blowing in the breeze. She laid Edward's notes: the one to Thomas and the much longer one to the solicitor, inside the compartment. Lastly, she placed the new piece of cotton fabric from the oak tree.

She eyed her evidence, noting that nothing was in the way of the panel. She felt content now. Everything was together in one safe place.

On the shelf chest-height, she pushed the volume back in to line up with the other books on the shelf. The panel above immediately repositioned itself and looked once again, like a normal bookshelf.

Katherine couldn't help but smile satisfactorily. Leaving the study, she returned her canvas tote onto the hook in the hallway, and dropped her mobile into her handbag.

To the hospital now. She had the cotton, and the shoe, thank heavens. Tonight, when Maisy was in bed, she would look for her mother's shirt. Maybe Edward could tell her today where it is....should she ask?

~ ~ ~ ~ ~ ~ ~ ~ ~ ~

Thomas waited for Katherine in the hospital's reception. She must be running late, he thought. She wasn't normally late, and his calm mind began playing games. The more he wondered where she was, the more uncomfortable he became. Where *was* she?

He stood up and paced for a few minutes, He knew he should have accompanied her when the solicitor visited. Maybe she and Anjali lost track of time. He was just about to ring Katherine when he spotted her walking from the car park.

He grinned, of course she was safe.

They met at the reception sliding doors and had a brief hug.

'Sorry I'm late. I hate being late, it's just that the traffic was bad.'

'Traffic problems,' he gave her a teasing grin. She laughed and looped her hand into his arm, as they often did and together they entered the hospital.

'Do you know where we need to go?'

'Yes. I checked while I was waiting. This way.'

The hospital was a maze of corridors, but they found the ward. The nurse at the desk welcomed them and confirmed Edward's location. She pointed to a room down the hallway, with glass doors fronting it.

'You can visit and talk with him. But he is delicate just now, so please keep the visit short,' she smiled kindly.

They moved together to his room. Katherine looked through the glass and held back a gasp. He looked so unwell. His eyes were closed and his face was turned away from the glass wall, but she could tell by the colour of his skin that he gravely ill.

Thomas gently pushed the door open, and motioned for her to step through. Edward didn't register.

She moved cautiously to his bedside, where his head was resting and pulled a chair closer to sit by him. Thomas stood at the foot of the bed, watching them both.

She softly spoke Edward's name. His head shifted slightly and he slowly opened his eyes to focus on her. He smiled faintly.

'Edward, hi,' and she put her hand on his shoulder.

'It's Katherine and Thomas. We're here at the hospital to visit.'

He shifted and moved his head to try to spot Thomas. Thomas moved closer into his view, by Katherine.

'It's ok Edward, you can sleep, you don't need to talk...' Katherine tried to comfort him.

His head moved back to the direction of her voice, and he opened his mouth, then licked his bottom lip very slowly. His lips were dry and he was hooked up to a few tubes.

He raised his fingers off the bed, then dropped them again. She decided to hold his hand and he closed one of his fingers weakly around hers – he had so little strength.

She sat there for a while.

'Our solicitors and Sam have asked after you and hope you feel better soon.'

He opened his lips to say something again but couldn't. It was evident he wanted to speak, but couldn't get his voice working.

'Edward, it's ok, please don't worry. I can see you're trying to say something. Everything is fine. I've met with the solicitors, and Thomas is here, we've spoken and I know about the accounts, and the finances. We're addressing this. And we know there's something not right going on, but we're safe, you're not to worry.'

As she spoke his finger tensed on hers, and despite his fatigue he managed to purse his lips.

'Please, can you relax your finger, to let me know you understand? I don't want you worrying, and I knew that you would be....I had to tell you now that I know about the finances so that you wouldn't worry. Can you relax your finger, can you do that now?'

His finger remained tense on hers, and she could see his pursed lips turn into a frown. Oh, no, she thought, why did I bring this all up. Maybe he had forgotten, what does he want to say?

She turned around, looking at Thomas and whispered, 'I've agitated him.'

Thomas came closer to Edward.

'Hey Edward, it's alright, you know? We can see that you are concerned. And you can't tell us what's bothering you. I'll tell you what, I'll stay with Katherine, at her house, until you get out of hospital, does that make things better?'

Katherine's heart suddenly beat quickly and loudly it seemed, in her ribcage. She wasn't sure how she would react with Thomas staying at her home. She held her breath waiting for Edward's response and couldn't believe it when his finger relaxed. She turned to look in amazement at Thomas.

'Edward's finger just relaxed,' and then she turned to look back at Edward and noticed his frown lift at the corners - he was grinning, she was sure.

'Edward, ok, that's sorted then. Thomas will stay with me and Maisy. But you also need to get better. This is the first day we've been allowed to visit, so you're heading in the right direction.'

His smile became a bit stronger although lopsided. His breathing was already more laboured in the short time they were there. They sat quietly with him and talked about old times and the house, while he watched them. After fifteen minutes or so, his eyes began to slowly close.

Thomas nodded at her, motioning to Edward.

'Edward, I think we may lat you rest now. The nurse has told us to keep the visit short. One of us will visit tomorrow, ok?'

He raised his fingers from the bed. Thomas leaned forward to check it was goodbye from Edward and not a request to stay. But Edward had already closed his eyes again. 'Rest Edward, everything will be fine.'

Katherine bent down and kissed his cheek.

In the hallway, they didn't look at each other straight away. They were both overcome by Edward's condition, and the fact that Thomas would be at her home possibly for a few days, hung between them. She walked to the nurse and asked her about the test results.

'Well, I'm afraid we can't share that information with you,' and then she looked Thomas over.

Thomas stepped towards the nurse, rested his arms casually on the high counter and asked when the consultant would arrive.

Katherine did a double-take, registering his engaging manner, his warm smile and deep and authoritative voice.

The nurse was lifted from her mood.

'Just a moment, sir,' she said with a beautiful smile. Katherine looked from the nurse to Thomas and sensed something. His face was straight. No visible reaction. But Katherine could feel the nurse react to his presence and the smile he had given her.

She was young and quite attractive. The nurse came around from the back of the desk and checked that Thomas was still looking at her. He was. She walked by them, and gave another smile to Thomas as she passed. He grinned charmingly at her.

Katherine couldn't believe what she had just witnessed. Was his smile that great? It couldn't have been his professional, authoritative voice – she surely wasn't reacting to that.

Katherine stole another glance at Thomas. He was a very good looking man. He had removed his sweater in Edward's room and his t-shirt showed off the strength of his arms and torso. Thomas caught her looking at him, and he raised his eyebrows at her. She averted her eyes.

In a minute or so, the nurse returned with a young male doctor. He headed directly to Thomas and Katherine, and the nurse introduced the consultant.

He asked them who they were. Katherine mentioned the family relationship, that she was at the hospital Wednesday, had been on the phone Thursday and earlier today, and was waiting for test results.

The doctor seemed hesitant to share confidential information.

Before Katherine could respond, Thomas stepped in. He explained Katherine's relationship in more detail, that she was as close as next to kin as one could get, given the circumstances, and his own, long relationship with the patient. Then he introduced himself with his title and reference to his clinic.

The young doctor listened, and at the mention of his clinic, cocked his head and broke into a grin. 'Hey, I read your research, I hope to specialise in fertility eventually but am doing my foundation and working here just now.'

Thomas and he spoke very briefly about the clinic, and then Thomas asked about Edward's condition, and the status of the tests.

The young doctor ushered them away from the desk to talk privately.

'Right, the nurse will need you to sign a few papers, regarding next of kin. Edward is definitely in a better state than he was, but still very weak. He's on intravenous, which can be normal for a heart attack. His heart has stabilised and there are no other complications. His other functions are working well.

'Regarding the tests, it's routine to check what's in the blood. We found a solid amount of drug that's nothing more than you would find in-over-the counter prescriptions. And perhaps he had one too many doses on the day, forgot he had already taken a pill, we see that sort of thing happen all the time. It isn't conclusive in the file whether he takes prescriptions - is that correct?'

'As mentioned on the phone this morning, I'm not aware of Edward taking prescriptions but he wouldn't normally share that information.' Katherine explained.

Thomas nodded in agreement.

'Ah, right. Well, he had no deficiencies in his blood. He actually has a clean bill of health except for that heart attack.

Was It possible that he was under duress, and that he took medication for that?' he looked at them.

'Yes, that's possible,' Thomas answered. 'His lifelong employer died a few weeks ago, and I think he is taking it very hard. Plus, an old timer like him, jumping in a bunch of leaves, probably wasn't a very good idea. Maybe that in itself caused his heart attack.'

'Hmmm, yes,' someone had just called for the Doctor's attention.

'Are you alright here? I must see my next patient, but any questions, just seek me out and I'll see if I can help,' he smiled his goodbye.

They thanked him. Thomas then casually strode back to the desk to thank the nurse. He gave her his perfect smile and she grinned back, blushing slightly.

Katherine waved a thank you to the nurse and turned her head to hide her smile as she walked towards the exit.

Thomas took only a second to catch up with her, taking long legged strides. 'Hey, feel better now?' He asked her.

She looked up sideways at him, and said, 'Yes, much, thank you. And I can see you haven't lost any of your people skills!'

He laughed.

'He looked pretty bad, Thomas.'

'Yes, he did,' he looked down at her sobering, and carefully added, 'the doctor knows what he's talking about. Edward is over the worst now, he'll be fine. He just needs to recover.'

'Do you think he took one too many prescribed pills, or do you worry there's something more sinister at play here? I'm not sure the doctor's information was conclusive one way or the other. And Edward was definitely worried about me and Maisy.'

'I'm still not sure. I think if he felt his life had been at risk he would have communicated that somehow. I agree - he seems worried about the two of you.'

She nodded, then changed the subject.

'So you're our bodyguard then, till Edward gets out,' she poked his arm.

'Yes, that is, if you don't mind,' he let the sentence hang.

She paused, and despite her slight discomfort earlier, her response came easily.

'No, I don't mind Thomas. It'll be really nice to have you close by in the house.'

He waited, she had more to say.

'In fact, I've been thinking about when Colin returns. It might be a good idea to have you at the house for a bit. Or maybe Maisy and I move out for a while until some of this is settled.'

She bit her lip. Why did Colin have to do all of this? And what was he up to that she had no clue about? She almost didn't want to find out; it would probably be unbearable.

He stopped and turned to her, face on. 'Are you saying what I think you are?'

'Yes, Thomas. Mother said it and I believe it. He's most likely having an affair. He's done something devious with my mother's money - mine and his daughter's money now. He didn't say anything to me about the family portfolio. And well, I can hardly say it, but we all think he could be responsible for my mother's death. I just can't bear to think of that. So yes, I'll have to leave him, Thomas.' There were no dramatics, there was no need. She was simply being factual.

He put his arm around her shoulders, 'Ok, let's get you home. You know you and Maisy can stay at mine, anytime,' he gave her a small squeeze on the shoulder. Her shoulders are so small, he thought, and his arm lingered there.

'Thanks Thomas. I really appreciate that. Maisy would love a long sleepover at yours at some point. I'll need to seek advise about moving Colin out of the family house, so we aren't away too long.'

It was agreed that Katherine would collect Maisy, and Thomas would head to her home, and wait for her there. She gave him the keys as he'd arrive first to check the house. He would collect his clothes later in the day. Before departing, they both checked mobiles to see if Colin had responded. Nothing.

On her drive to Maisy's school several scenarios raced through her mind. Her thoughts seemed tangled. However, amongst all the noise in her head, loud and clear was the throbbing concern about what the next steps meant with Colin. None of the options were good.

Maisy was so very happy when her mother picked her up. She was happier still when Katherine explained that Thomas would be sleeping over for a few days.

Once home, Maisy rushed through the front door, excited to see her uncle waiting for them there. He almost staggered backwards from the exuberant hug she gave him – like she was reunited with a long lost friend.

'Hey, my favourite little lady – how are you?'

'Very fine thank you! Let's go play!'

'For sure,' he said. 'That sounds great.'

He smiled at Katherine, his arm being pulled by Maisy back down the stairs to the drive, and whispered to her as he passed by, 'I've checked the house and it's completely safe. I'll whizz over to my house later for my clothes and work stuff.'

Thomas scooped up Maisy and headed towards the door in the garden wall.

'After that you can come inside for some dinner, Maisy,' Katherine shouted after the two of them.

She took a deep breath and smiled, watching them walk through the garden door. Hmm, the garden door to the property was open. But then, Sam tended to leave the gate unlocked or open when he was working close by. She supposed it was safe.

Maisy began to giggle uncontrollably as her uncle tossed her in the air and she couldn't help but laugh herself. As she returned through her front door, the happiness she felt, disappeared. She was worried about what she'd find out over the next few days. Who had been involved in her mother's death? Colin? James? Richard? She still had to tell Thomas about James. She shivered, uncharacteristically locked the front door, then went to the kitchen to prepare supper.

~ ~ ~ ~ ~ ~ ~ ~ ~ ~ ~

Anjali was expecting James back soon. She had her bag packed, with laptop, work papers, and sleepover bag. She cast her mind back to when she'd last had an evening away from the family. She laughed – she hadn't been alone for an evening since she was married.

She looked at the Mandarin Oriental hotel on her iPad, and couldn't help but smile. A Friday night on her own without being disturbed in the middle of the night by the children... now, that would be nice. She'd miss them of course, and James, but knew that he didn't mind. He'd attended a few evenings away over the years with his team to work intensively on particular 'research'. She relaxed. It should be a great work night and she was looking forward to the deal Richard wanted her to review. What could it be?

Chapter 29 - Deals Done

James surveyed the people around the table. He smiled proudly, with an air of relief.

'Thank you all for your time.'

He looked at his business associates. 'It simply would not have been possible without you. Helping us navigate around the maze of funding available to us, and how best to structure that, has been incredible. And it has helped us to deal with some difficult issues.'

He pushed his document towards the middle of the table.

'Investment deal, done!'

There was a great cheer then they shook hands and clapped each other on the back. Everyone was grinning.

He grabbed a glass of sparkling water. 'To green energy!'

They held up their glasses and cheered.

'To green energy!'

~ ~ ~ ~ ~ ~ ~ ~ ~ ~

Richard felt his muscles in his stomach all afternoon. They were hard, and taught. He was so eager for the evening to come. But he was also in a parallel universe. What the hell was Colin playing at?

~ ~ ~ ~ ~ ~ ~ ~ ~ ~

James left his office in high spirits. So much now he could put behind him. It took no time to drive home, his mind charged with the success of the day and thinking through next steps.

He drew the car up outside the house, and could hear the children in the back garden. He made his way through the cottage and popped down into the garden, 'Hello!' He said in his usual cheery greeting. As planned he was early so that Anjali could head off to the train station.

The children ran to hug their father. Anjali smiled at him; he looked so refreshed and visibly relaxed. She was sure he was going to say the deal was done.

'We signed the papers today!'

'Ah, I thought so! Fabulous news, James, that's so exciting!' She kissed him congratulations and the children could feel the excitement in the air.

'Have you sold everything, who's the acquirer, do you still have ownership?'

'Whoa that's a load of questions! Yes, I still have ownership and the financing is sorted. I'm not sure it's the type of deal you're imagining, but given you need to get off, I'll go over all of it tomorrow when you're back.'

Her face changed from a proud smile, to a small frown, 'You really should be celebrating with the team tonight...'

'Don't be silly. We're all tired, and I'm sure it will be an early bed for every one of us. It's been pretty intensive, and in any case....'

'In any case....?' she queried.

'There may be some final items to sort out next week, but I'll tell you about it tomorrow,' he replied.

'Ah, secrets!' She smiled in her response.

Her train was due soon, so she kissed her husband and children goodbye and headed off to the station.

'Say hello to Richard,' shouted her husband after her, as she waved from her open car window, 'and tell him I'm expecting you to get a pay pack upgrade after this evening!' He was laughing.

She was laughing too, she was so pleased that her husband was relaxed and had successfully closed his deal. Maybe tomorrow night, when the kids were in bed, he could finally tell her all about his green technology, it had been so secretive! She was excited to hear what his business plans were and she was very interested to know who the new partners were.

The train arrived on time, and she found her seat. Sipping a take-away tea, she settled onto the train, thinking through her tube connection to the Mandarin Oriental at the other end. And then, her brain began to work on overdrive - how much did James sell his business for? Who were his partners? How much authority will he have, as that was so important to him?

There were so many questions she had for him....but they would have to wait, till tomorrow.

~~~~~~~~~~

The team was tired. It was very late, in fact, very early Saturday morning.

There had been discussions, many discussions over the last two days as the emails, voicemail messages and texts arrived. There was however, one very urgent email that had popped up earlier in the day and required immediate, mitigating action before 2AM.

It was late and finally, there was group consensus: a decision with an agreed approach. The person at the laptop, on precise orders, attached the final version of a lengthy document to a very simple-worded email and sent it.

The person in charge of the mobile phone, within moments of the email, sent a text message. Again, there was much discussion. Because of the late hour, a few tempers flared. Despite the involved discussion, they were all agreed, this would buy them more time. They certainly didn't want anyone alarming the hotel.

The boss picked his teeth and clicking his tongue on the roof of his mouth hissed, 'I would say, case closed, yes?' And he left the room telling his team to tidy up the remaining loose ends with the time they had gained.

~~~~~~~~~~

'I'll be back,' waved Thomas as his car left down the grand drive. Katherine and Maisy waved goodbye.

'Ok, Maisy, let's head up to do some artwork. Wasn't it fun having Thomas for dinner?'

'Yes, he was so happy playing with us. Mummy, he liked your dinner,' she said emphatically. Katherine grinned.

In Maisy's bedroom, the two settled down to sketch and colour. Katherine noticed that Maisy had picked up her same drawing – the one she had been working on for most of the week.

'Do you like that drawing, Maisy?'

'Yes, I think so, Mummy,' she replied. The two began to work in silence, each focused on their artwork, and respecting each other's concentration.

In what seemed a very short time, the doorbell rang. Maisy jumped up, 'Oh, it's Thomas!'

'Yes, I think it is....why don't you finish your picture Maisy, and I'll let him in, ok?'

'Ok.'

Katherine made her way to the front door, down the beautiful staircase. The family portraits seemed to be following her with their eyes. She hurried past them and said under her breath, 'We'll sort this.'

She did feel very close to solving her mother's death. And she had two people she could be sure of now – Edward and Thomas. Right now, she was simply pleased that Thomas was staying. The house was very large without Edward around. Going forward, if she could help it, Colin would not be in the house for very much longer.

She peeped through the window to the side of the door and saw Thomas' profile. She quickly let him in.

'Hello, Thomas.'

'Hello,' he smiled at her. He bent down then, and kissed her carefully on her cheek.

'Evening.'

The colour rose in her cheeks, and she laughed inwardly. My God, she was no better than that poor nurse, slave to his smile.

'Come on in, Maisy is waiting for you.'

'Ah, Maisy, and no one else?' Again, that smile. He had always been such a terrible tease.

She bowed her head and couldn't meet his eyes. Sternly she replied, 'Why of course, it's much safer having you here.'

She had to get this back on track - why were they so - funny with each other? It was surely the circumstances. The whole situation of the last six weeks was emotionally charged for both of them.

'Follow me, your niece is waiting patiently!'

They made their way upstairs. At Maisy's door he was welcomed with a screech of excitement.

'Hi Uncle Thomas! Look at my drawing!'

He sauntered closer, and had a good look. Katherine noticed him frowning.

'Hey Maisy - do you know this person, and the car?'

'No,' she replied.

'No? You don't?'

'Do you like my drawing?' she asked him again, not answering his question.

'Yes, very much so, Maisy. I'm not much of an artist myself, like your mother is,' he smiled at Katherine, 'but I can tell that your drawing is, well it's very detailed, and grown up for a person your age.'

Maisy giggled. 'But I am grown up! I'm in kindergarten!'

'Ok, Maisy, bath then bedtime,' said Katherine.

'Thomas, please make yourself at home, downstairs. I'll be with you in about an hour, is that alright?'

'Of course,' he turned to Maisy. 'So, little lady, this means goodnight. Would you like a big hug goodnight from Uncle Thomas?'

'Yes, and a kiss please!' she replied.

Thomas gave Maisy a hug and kiss on both cheeks.

'Can you stay with me for awhile, Uncle Thomas?' Maisy asked. He caught Katherine's eye and she nodded to the door.

'I'll tell you what Maisy. Let me get settled in your big house tonight and tomorrow I can read to you in bed, ok?' Maisy was very pleased with that arrangement and let go of his hand. Katharine watched him leave with mixed emotions. In all of Maisy's life, Colin had never been a natural when it came to hugs and kisses with his daughter; and he had never properly cared to comment on her drawings.

~~~~~~~~~~

Fresh from the shower, he surveyed the luxury of his surroundings. Ah, the Mandarin Oriental. He loved the rooms, the decor, the service. And this room particularly was like a second home to him. They kept this room for him, waiting, until he popped in for an evening. For many years, he was most certainly not alone in the room. But, recently of course, he hadn't entertained female guests here.

He took a deep breath and smelled the delightful scent of the flower bouquets placed throughout. They were everywhere – the central table, console table, side tables, en-suite, dressing room, windowsills. Some were delicate arrangements, others depending on their position, were grander works of art. He smiled, he had asked for the same touches in the other company room that was being occupied tonight.

Strutting over to a gilded mirror, he looked at himself while towelling dry. The shower had been fantastic, as it always was. There was soft golden lighting everywhere in the room and he really thought – as he admired his reflection – that his body shone like an Adonis. He studied his athletic form, and the muscles that still defined him. He had to work out more these days, and watch his food, but he knew he was in great shape.

He went to the dressing room, running his hands through his boyish hair, and looked for his toiletries case. He spotted the leather bag and reached for the salon hair gel.

Did he hear his phone bleep? He suddenly frowned and surprised himself by saying loudly, 'You can't tell me she's cancelled!'

He rushed quickly to his mobile and grinned triumphantly.

'Hey, it couldn't be better!'

He moved to his laptop which was already open on the glass desk, and logged on.

'There we are!' he exclaimed. This wasn't about Anjali – it was about Gemstone.

He opened up the email and read its simple contents, then clicked on the attachment and began to scan the first few pages.

'Yup, just what we needed.' He was delighted.

The backing of the deal was complete, post production was lined up….there were only a few tiny steps now to finish off Gemstone. He verified that the name Gemstone was employed throughout the document – yes, several hundred references, he confirmed with word search. The final switch to the real company name couldn't be done until all the pieces lined up.

Tonight, Anjali would help him review this document. Then he would send it off Saturday morning.

Next week, they could complete the final pieces with Gemstone.

'I knew he'd come through,' he let out a deep breath. 'Yeah, he came through all right. Bastard kept me on the line till the bloody end,' and he laughed loudly at the games he and Colin played with each other.

Now that he had his document to review with Anjali, the night could begin.

He returned to his dressing room and reached for a pair of slim fit light wool trousers. They were Italian, his favourite. The hotel had delivered them perfectly pressed. He didn't need a jacket tonight, just his shirt.

He picked up a large, flat rectangular box that had been gift wrapped.

'Perfect,' he said under his breath.

He ripped open the box with no regard for the beautiful wrapping, and opened the lid. Then, he undid the bow on a small black ribbon, and pulled back the tissue.

In the tissue was his favourite shirt in his favourite colour. Pure, crisp white. Executive white. White Knight white. Freshly new to replace the other. He grinned, back to being perfect with his beautiful bespoke shirt. He pulled it out and put it on, tugging it to perfection from the sleeves. He checked his image. Sharp, he thought, and he turned to sip the martini room service had brought earlier.

~ ~ ~ ~ ~ ~ ~ ~ ~ ~

Maisy was sleepy.

'Good night,' whispered Katherine. Maisy was so tired, there was no reply. She leaned down to kiss her softly then pulled the blanket up and turned out the light.

She tiptoed out and pulled the door halfway closed. 'Goodnight my darling,' she whispered.

Katherine didn't realise it, but she *had* been nervous without Edward in the house. In the back of her mind, over the last few nights, she'd felt a new threat squeezing in on her and Maisy. Now, with Thomas here, she realised how uptight she'd been. She hesitated at the door.

Thomas was downstairs. She was dithering because she had news to share with him; information she knew would upset him. Although changes to the dynamics of her relationships were already swiftly underway, this information would be a new catalyst and possibly draw a rift between her and Thomas. She sighed. Why did everything have to change?

She paused a moment longer at her daughter's door to hear her quiet breathing for comfort.

She headed down the hallway, and held the oak bannister as she descended the stairs. Before seeing Thomas in the kitchen, she would visit her mother's study first, to collect a few items. It was time now, to share everything with him.

Chapter 30 - Best Friend

He was in the kitchen, running the tap water. He needed a cold glass of water, his throat was too dry. His thoughts flitted from Katherine to his brother, to Katherine's mother, to the concerns Katherine had covered with him yesterday. Filling his glass, he paused and took a large drink. It was good they had talked yesterday, so much had been cleared up.

He heard her before he saw her, then cheerily turned around to say hello. She was standing in the kitchen entranceway watching him, and had leaned against the creaking door. She was watching him drink with a fixated look, as if he was a stranger to her. He had caught her off-guard and she moved her eyes to gaze outside as if she was guilty of something. She was carefully balancing a few items in her hands.

'Thomas, let's get a drink and sit over there,' she lifted her chin to point towards two wingback chairs in the conservatory.

He glanced to where she had indicated and said, 'Would you like a cup of tea or wine first?'

'A tea would be wonderful.'

'Hey, why don't you sit down and I'll bring it to you?'

She nodded a thank you and headed over to the chair.

He'd already boiled her a kettle, presuming she would want tea when she joined him.

In a minute, she had a cup of tea in her hands, with Thomas sitting close by.

'I can see you want to tell me something, fire away. Except, don't tell me I'm on your suspect list again,' he smiled at her trying to lighten the mood.

'No,' she laughed softly, 'but I do have news to share.'

She had tucked her items beside herself on the chair, and cupped her mug. She turned to see him better. The late evening sun shone on his blond hair and she could see, only just, that he hadn't shaved that morning. He was still smiling at her, his even white teeth perfect in his smile and a calm look in his eyes. He had his doctor demeanour on; he was focused on her, and patiently waiting for her to talk when she was ready. She swallowed, he didn't know what was coming. It was Edward's notes to the solicitor that she was worried about.

She laid everything out on the table, bar Edward's notes.

'You'll recognise most of this: mother's note; the first piece of cotton fabric I found in the breeze by the river, near the oak; my brainstorming list; and Edward's note to you. Here is the second piece of cotton fabric. I collected it from the oak tree today. And, I managed to pull my mother's shoe from the branches,' she hesitated.

He arched his eyebrows as if to question her hesitation.

'It was a bit hairy up there,' as she reflected on her momentary loss of balance, 'my poor mother, Thomas, it must have been terrible,' she steeled herself.

'Hey, let's just go through what you have here, we don't know for certain what happened. That's definitely your mother's missing shoe?'

'Yes, absolutely. I still need to find my mother's shirt to compare the cotton fabrics, that's a big gap right now in what you must agree is mounting evidence.'

His eyes rested on the shoe. He was visibly upset. She decided to delay showing him Edward's other letter for a few moments.

'Shall I tell you about my family's wealth? Those transfers that I've been discussing with the solicitors?'

He perked up. 'Yes, I didn't want to ask you until you were ready. What does it all mean?'

'Well, believe it or not, my mother was an extremely astute investor and one wealthy lady!'

'Wow,' he opened his eyes wide and shook his head. 'I can believe she was astute in her dealings, but was that all recent? I always had the impression that the estate was a challenge for your mother. Compared to how Colin and I had been brought up - that we were entitled with plenty of money around - your mother was always so careful to remind you of your current situation, and to keep you grounded. Didn't she often say that everything here was the remnants of old family money, that there was little wealth left and that current generations had to work to sustain it?'

'Yes, yes you're right!. She did say that but it was a total facade. I don't know why. The fact is that she had been managing a substantial portfolio, with the assistance of the family solicitors for decades. She took it over when my father died. Thomas, I'm ashamed to say, but there's a substantial amount of wealth. She was deeply involved with charities as well – it's a lot to take in.'

Thomas was still shaking his head in disbelief.

'As well as the normal types of investments, the family portfolio included vast amounts of real estate. I haven't had time yet to get my head around it and work through details, but I do know the properties are spread across several continents. If I wasn't in so much shock about everything, I might be excited – you know how I love travel and properties. But, it's so surreal just now – I don't understand it all yet.

'And the transfers, Thomas. It's disturbing. One of the stronger performing accounts in the family portfolio consisted of several good investments. The whole account was liquidated recently resulting in £12 million of cash...'

'Whoa!' He interrupted her. 'We're talking about substantial wealth here. Your notes mentioned this, but Katherine, I didn't understand it to be that kind of wealth.' He was serious.

'Well, Thomas, I'm embarrassed to say, but that's only the tip of the iceberg,' she held his questioning gaze, nodding with her eyes stretched wide open.

'It's crazy. We can go over it another time, together. About the account of £12 million, there was no reason to cash that in. Three tranches of money, each to the value of £3 million were transferred to three different 3rd party accounts: one to Bahamas, one to Panama, and one to China. And then, yesterday morning, a 4th transfer was made, again £3 million to the same account in China. Other than our family solicitors, Colin was the only one who had access to the portfolio. And of course, he's in China. The transfer was made yesterday, Thursday at 2:15 AM our time, which was 10:15 AM in Shanghai.'

Thomas' face was grim, and twisted with frustration. 'I don't know what to say. I read that yesterday when you shared your brainstorming notes, but well, we didn't have time to discuss it, you were off to collect Maisy. It's worse hearing you say it. What's my brother doing?' He brushed his fingers through his hair.

'Thomas...' she faltered. She'd have to show him Edward's notes to the solicitors.

He let her speak, but when she didn't after a few minutes he could see she needed slight prompting, 'Yes, Katherine.'

She moved uncomfortably and asked the obvious question, 'Any news from Colin?'

He dutifully pulled his mobile from his pocket and checked. He shook his head.

'Nor I,' she replied.

She took a breath and quickly jumped into the chasm she knew she was about to create.

'Thomas, the solicitor spent quite some time with me yesterday. And in fact, Anjali only stayed for a moment.' She let that sink in.

'The solicitor came to see me because he thought Edward's life might be at risk, and in fact, mine as well.'

'What? Why did he say that?'

'When I told him that the doctor was taking tests on Edward, that is, to check if he had any traces of prescription drugs in him, that he took or perhaps someone gave him, well that worried him,' she added cautiously.

He nodded. Katherine continued, 'In any case, the solicitor is suspicious that someone may have been targeting Edward.'

Thomas moved forward further in his seat, leaning closer to her.

'And this solicitor, are you sure you can trust him?'

'Yes, I can trust him. He's from the firm my family has used for generations. They manage our finances and are close to my mother and Edward. Regarding Edward, I felt so remorseful at the hospital when we visited. By then I knew that he couldn't be a suspect,' she said firmly. She looked down at the notes tucked beside her.

'Here, I think you should read this, Thomas.' She pulled out Edward's notes. 'These are Edward's observations which the solicitor gave me.'

'Edward's?'

'Yes, the solicitor said, and I'm repeating verbatim what he said: That Edward was, or still is convinced that my mother's death wasn't an accident, and that Edward believed it was foul play of the worst kind...'

Thomas took a quick breath in and reached for the notes she held out for him.

'...and so Edward documented dates, times, observations, and this is the information, this rather long note in his handwriting, of course all calligraphy.'

Thomas pulled his eyes from Katherine's and looked down at the document now in his hands. He read it twice.

'I can see Edward's concerns are similar to yours,' he was looking tersely at the note, 'and the smudged title of this list and the 'J's and 'A's in this section?'

His voice broke when he said that; he was challenging her.

She swallowed. 'James and Anjali.'

'Katherine,' he lowered his voice and it was angry, 'what do you mean?'

'I know, but, it could make sense, don't you think? Colin does have the motive, to get his hands on mother's money – to save his back – but I still can't imagine he would go that far. And as you said, maybe he still has money in the family estate and maybe his business is alright. I know he was working on a deal with Richard, so perhaps he had money to cover the family losses.

'But for James, how desperate was he – we know his whole reputation depends on that company and his breakthrough science. Do you think he visited my mother on the day and threatened her down by the river? Where was James that morning? He lied to Edward. I realise Edward checked whether my mother invested in James's business but as the solicitor said, it could have been through another financial vehicle that she did invest in.'

He was shaking his head and about to rebut, but she wasn't finished.

'And remember this,' she pointed to the threatening note given to her mother.

'It talks about 'eco' and James' business was all about green energy....'

Thomas sprung from the chair. She didn't realise how much strength he had – angry strength.

'Katherine I can't listen to this, I simply cannot,' he ran his hand through his hair again. He was shaking his head, his face etched with disbelief.

'James couldn't hurt a fly. He couldn't threaten a fly. I've known him for many years – you don't know him as well as I do – there's simply no way on earth he is the character for the villain in this plot,' his voice was deep with emotion and forceful.

'Katherine, why don't you open your eyes? It's Colin, it can only be Colin – even Edward's notes clearly describe that Colin was the most likely person to – to what? Murder your mother? We don't even know what Edward was thinking happened down there at the river. Colin had the greatest motive – he needed the money, the account he was talking to Richard about was actually liquidated – and most likely he transferred the money to where he needed it. He only had access to the money once your mother was dead. And now that we know all this information, the only mystery is how he did it, not the why. He needed the money, she wasn't forthcoming, he got rid of her to access the money through you. It was a risk, but a risk worth taking because he was sure he could bend you – like he always has!'

He was so angry, she had never seen him like this. Angry at her, angry at Colin. His words stung badly, despite her own suspicions of Colin. He grabbed his glass of water and strode to the kitchen.

She waited while he refilled his glass. He made his way back to the conservatory and was calmer but still very cross.

'Thomas, I'm so sorry I've upset you. And I do agree with you. My husband, your brother, is most likely the one. But we can't rule out James. And until we can speak to Edward to further understand his suspicions, I don't think we can be sure it isn't James. Colin is back tomorrow, or Sunday, and I'm afraid actually. I'm suspecting him to be the main villain whether pre-meditated or not, but who may have caused my mother's death. I don't think I'm grasping at straws. And it could also be James. We can't rule certain people out at this point.'

He didn't respond.

'The whole thing doesn't make sense. But then, when does murder make sense?'

Thomas was thinking fast, it had gone too far at this point.

'Katherine, I think we should go to the police.'

She looked at him in surprise and then her eye caught a movement beyond Thomas on the terrace. It was Sam. He walked to the terrace doors and knocked. He gave one a tug - but Katherine had locked them. She stood up, walked over and unlocked the wide heavy glass doors. Was it possible he heard their aggrieved voices through the glass, or perhaps interpreted their body language?

Sam pulled one open. 'Hello Miss Katherine,' he could see that she was distressed.

'Everything alright here, is Edward alright?'

'Hi Sam, yes, he is, Sam, he is, thank you. He's stable but there are quite a few tubes and monitors. He can't really move or speak but he is stable and simply tired, the doctor said.'

'Ah, an old man like me, he shouldn't be jumping into leaves, eh?' He smiled at her. 'When will he be back?'

'To be honest, we don't know yet. I'll ask the doctor tomorrow when I go.' She smiled in return and just like that, a light bulb lit up in her head.

'Sam, do you know if we had any visitors on Wednesday this week before Edward had his accident? I was out quite early and normally Edward updates me when I return, but of course, he couldn't on Wednesday.'

She sensed Thomas come closer behind her.

'Ah, well, it was a busy day - a lot of gardening to do and I was only out front a few times so wouldn't really know....I guess, yes we had one visitor around lunchtime, sorry I should have told you,' he replied to Katherine but he was looking straight past at Thomas.

Katherine followed his gaze and sure enough, he was looking at Thomas, now just standing behind her.

'That good friend of yours, James. He was a good man he was, helping in the evening. Took the children off me so I could get home.'

Thomas looked keenly at Sam, 'I'm not sure I follow, who was the only visitor on Wednesday around lunchtime?'

'Sorry?' He looked quizzically at Thomas.

Katherine held her breath.

Sam clarified what he was saying.

'James, your friend. He came twice on Wednesday this week. At lunch, and then later when he helped with the children. I'm sorry I forgot to say anything – I don't know who he was looking for at lunchtime. He didn't see me because I was busy. Had just started in the front garden among the shrubs clearing the undergrowth. By the time I'd picked myself up and came round from the bushes to talk to him, he'd already taken off in his car. I'm sorry now Miss that I didn't manage to ask him.'

Thomas was staring at Sam.

Katherine had difficulty speaking. 'Sam, please don't worry – thank you for letting me know.'

She searched how to bring the situation back to a safe place, 'You're working a bit late tonight, it's getting quite dark. Are you hoping to go to the hospital with me tomorrow?'

'Ah, a lot of gardening, as I said, especially at this time of year. I can't see Edward this weekend, we have the grandchildren over, but I'd be pleased to see good Edward on Monday, if that works for you, Miss.'

'Yes, of course, we can arrange that. Let's talk on Monday morning when you arrive here. Have a nice weekend Sam,' she waved goodbye and began to close the door.

'And to the both of you,' he waved back. Katherine locked the doors behind him.

She turned around and looked directly at Thomas.

'I know what you're thinking, Katherine. That James saw Edward on Wednesday and that you believe James could have given him drugs or such that caused his heart to fail.' He looked at her. There was disapproval on his face.

She didn't say anything, and cast her eyes across the garden. What did she believe?

He checked his mobile phone again. 'No answer yet from Colin. I think I need to turn in early, Katherine, I'm not in a good place right now. I need some time to think, on my own. We're talking about my brother and my best friend here....' he let his voice trail off.

Despite the early hour, she felt tired too. 'Shall I show you which room?'

'Oh, it's not the same one?' He tried to speak casually but it didn't work.

'Yes, it is.' She chanced a look at him. He was already watching her. Despite the anger in the room, their gaze exchanged a memory from a long time ago.

Her mother always kept a room for Thomas. But he had not stayed in that room for a very long time.

She couldn't pull her eyes from his. They were holding hers, and they were deep with meaning. He kept her gaze, walked close to her and bent down to kiss her cheeks good night. He lingered for a moment at the second kiss and whispered, 'I need to sleep on this Katherine,' and he walked past her, out of the kitchen.

Katherine could hardly breathe. She listened to make sure he was already at the staircase in the hallway before she let out a deep breath.

Chapter 31 - Priest Hole

Anjali walked into the reception of the Mandarin Oriental.

'This is beautiful. What a lovely place to have a work meeting,' she quietly said under her breath as she checked in. She had arrived early. Her plan was to relax, take a shower and dress for dinner at the hotel.

Her room was on the top floor, and the receptionist at the desk explained that she had to press her room card against the floor button panel in the elevator in order to access the top floor. At the elevator, it took a few seconds for the fob to work and she laughed lightly with relief when the elevator accepted her entry for the top floor and closed its doors. She was in a fabulous marble elevator with mirrored walls and before she knew it there was a faint ping and the doors opened.

She strode out from the elevator with her wheelie. There seemed to be only a few rooms on this section of the floor. She followed the room number directions on the brass panel opposite the elevator and quickly located hers. She wondered where Richard was staying and if he was here already.

Her hotel room door detected the key fob and clicked open. She quickly entered.

Stunned with what she saw, she almost forgot to pull her wheelie through so the door could close. Despite the obvious security of the hotel, it was a habit. She was always quick to enter her hotel rooms, cautious that someone may force their way in. She had travelled on business as a young woman and security was important to her. Ensuring she never had a room located near an emergency exit, on the ground floor or near an ice room, these were standard safety precautions she always took. And as bizarre as it sounded to her male colleagues, if it was late in the evening, she never entered an elevator alone with a man she didn't know.

She pulled her wheelie aside, put the double lock on the door, and then turned around to appraise the room. As she walked forward, she couldn't help but gasp. The room, in all its magnificence, was bigger than the ground floor space of her home. It was most definitely a suite and not just a bedroom.

The scent was incredible – there were flowers everywhere and cosy seating in several places. And the bed....she couldn't believe the size of the bed. Was that super king? No, she had a super king and this was significantly wider. And the pillows, pillows were everywhere. She suppressed a smile, how fabulously beautiful the room was.

There was champagne chilling on an elegant table with two glasses placed to the side.

'How perfect, nice hotel service,' she spoke aloud.

She wandered into the bathroom, and couldn't stop her smile from widening further. The room was a combination of marble and granite with mirrors, gold chandeliers and fixtures. There were two sinks, a roll-top bath, a large shower area and a section to the far left that partitioned off the toilet area. There was a vaguely see-through wall of smoky glass between the shower area and the bedroom. Hmmm, that's interesting, she thought.

Returning to the room she began to unpack, hoping to shower, relax and absorb her surroundings before dinner. She hung her dress in the shower room on the back of the door, so any wrinkles would drop from the steam of the shower. Going back to the main room, she noticed a card on the central table by the largest flower bouquet.

A welcome from the hotel, no doubt.

It had her name on it. She fingered the beautiful envelope, then opened it.

'Welcome to the Mandarin Oriental. A little treat from me - a digital detox - to thank you for all your help. Perhaps you'll stay a little longer in the morning and enjoy the spa. There are 2 gift certificates here - one booked for tomorrow morning, but if you can't make it, there's another one, perhaps for a future date when we can enjoy another work dinner together.'

It was signed, 'Richard'.

'Wait, what?' She took a deep breath in.

'Well, that's kind. It's definitely taking appreciation to a whole new level! I wonder if the guys on the team have the same types of perks?'

She picked up the Spa menu in the hotel information pack on the coffee table. Yes, there was an offering for men as well. Hmm, she didn't picture Richard as the type to give such perks to his team – but maybe he frequented the spa, that she could believe.

She checked the gift certificate. It was for the 'digital wellness escape', a one and a half hour treatment from the hotel's signature spa services. The description sounded superb: 'concentrating on the head, eyes, neck, shoulders, hands and feet, this restorative treatment aims to ease stresses and strains resulting from the frequent use of digital devices'.

'Ah, well, now that would be perfect. I do need it. I'm on my laptop and mobile all the time! In any case, it's a very thoughtful touch,' she could feel herself warming to the offer from Richard, and debated staying a little longer in the morning. Maybe he was considerate after all.

With her thoughts on whether she'd have time for a spa treatment in the morning, she headed to the bathroom to get ready. The bathtub was so enticing, she could maybe take one later tonight before bed. For now, the shower would definitely give her some much needed energy for the night ahead.

The wide rosette shower head was heavenly. She closed her eyes and her mind felt vacuous for a few glorious moments. The spray was heavy but soft on her head and the warmth spread down her body. She opened her eyes and tried the 'spa' options with strong penetrations of water on her back. They sprayed from several sections of holes discreetly patterned in the shower walls. Hmmm, lovely.

Looking at the shelf built into the marble shower wall, she spotted a collection of toiletries. How wonderful, she thought, and smelled the shower gel, shampoo and conditioner. It was all Parisian Diptyque and the scent was fabulous. She had brought her own toiletries but decided to use the hotels, how could she not?

Stepping out from the shower, she felt as if she'd been to the spa. She'd taken her time, and the steam had built up. She glanced at herself in the mirror and laughed. All of the mirrors in the room were perfectly clear – heated no doubt so the steam wouldn't build. She wrapped herself up in the sumptuous white bathrobe then moved into the adjoining dressing area. Diptyque body cream and hair mist were nestled in a basket of Diptyque tissue and dried lavender. She surprised herself by giggling – it felt like Christmas already! She tried the products out and did her hair for the evening. She hadn't been this relaxed in surely, years.

Happy with her hair she walked leisurely back into the main room and caught sight of the champagne. Should she? She better not, her mind needed to be clear.

She checked her phone for any messages. There were none but she thought it best to call home now and say goodnight to the children. Her call rang out for a bit before it was answered by James. The children were near the end of a Disney film so their goodnight was a quick one.

'I'm not being missed for sure,' Anjali chuckled to James.

'They do love their Disney films!'

'Yes, true. James, Richard has been so sweet. He obviously feels badly about asking me to work tonight. There was a complimentary gift card in the room to the hotel spa for a 'digital wellness' treatment. At least he gets how much I'm in front of my screen.'

'Making him money!' James interjected. 'I'm not sure 'sweet' is the right word to describe Richard. But, why don't you use the spa in the morning? I'm fine with the kids, you deserve it, and it's the least he can do for you.'

She agreed to wait and see how she felt in the morning, and they said their goodbyes.

She pulled her bathrobe tighter around her body, and walked over to the tall windows. She felt quite grand surveying Hyde Park from such a height, watching the cars and people, and just enjoying the view. She checked her phone. Still time to rest for a bit. She decided to stretch out on the chaise lounge.

How relaxing, she thought. I'm wrapped in a lovely robe, on a chaise lounge, with the scent of Diptyque head to toe on my body, thumbing through magazines from the coffee table, and there are no distractions!

She felt heavy with happiness and fatigue; her eyes were closing. She never relaxed like this, ever. Life was full on with work, the children, the house, and any hobbies like gardening that she could slip in. With the children still waking up during the night, most of her nights were disturbed.

Sleep, like a soft blanket, settled softly over her body, relaxing her limbs, and soothing her eyes. In a moment, her hands fell from the magazine, and she gently drifted off.

The alarm on her phone shocked her awake. It was almost eight o'clock!

'Thank heavens for that!' She congratulated herself for setting her alarm just in case. She must have been pretty tired. A short rest before a long night!

She popped up quickly and slipped on her dress. The wrinkles were gone, and no wonder! She had certainly steamed up the room! She spent a moment putting on some makeup then looked for her key fob. She slipped it into her evening bag that already held her iPad, mobile, small notebook, pen and credit card. She was set for a work dinner.

On the way out, Anjali caught her reflection in the hallway mirror and paused for a moment.

A bit dressy for work, but it was a working dinner. She put her hand on her stomach and smoothed down her dress: flat, flat as a pancake - you'd never guess that she had 2 young children. She checked the cashmere dress was hanging properly down her back, and then walked out the door.

She wasn't sure whether her dress was more evening wear than work wear. 'Ah well,' she sighed, 'It's too late now and it is the Mandarin Oriental, after all.'

~ ~ ~ ~ ~ ~ ~ ~ ~ ~

With Thomas up in his room, and Maisy asleep, Katherine had some valuable time to herself. First, she put her evidence away in the faux bookcase in her mother's study. Then, with a heavy heart, as she didn't want to talk with him tonight, she texted Richard. It was a simple message - did he know what Colin was up to as she needed to get in touch with him. She sat looking at the message before she reluctantly pressed send.

She walked quietly up the stairs to Edward's top floor. There was no way Thomas could hear her, but she wasn't taking any chances so it was a very stealthy, careful climb up the stairs. She froze when the stair boards creaked at Thomas' floor.

When she finally reached Edward's apartment, she hesitated for a moment. It didn't feel right invading his private space, but she needed the shirt. She tried his door, hoping in a way it was locked, but it wasn't.

Feeling very guilty - she never came into his rooms unless invited - she opened the door into his reception area. The first thing she noticed was how manly the room was. She had forgotten the full impact of her colour scheme and the furniture, but it was impressive and gentlemanly. They had worked on the renovation and style scheme together. She could see his office to the left and registered the overwhelming signature touches in the room. He had such a good sense of style. Her eye caught a painting through the doorway to his office. She couldn't take her eyes from it and slowly walked towards the image.

It was a beautiful, very like painting of her mother. It must have been one of her self-portraits, perhaps from her young 20's? But it had pride of place in his office, and as she had noticed, easily spotted from his reception area. She sighed sadly. Her mother had been such a beauty, how did it all come to this? She looked around his office space and her head was instantly bombarded with conflicting thoughts. Her mother's paintings were everywhere.

These were not hung when they redid the apartments, she thought to herself. He had amassed quite a collection over the years - my goodness, she thought. And then he hung them up, himself. They were mainly paintings of the house and gardens. She could tell they were her mother's. There were also several other self-portraits of her mother, and one of Edward. There was a painting, too, of his parents in one of their grand rooms, which her mother must have done when she was a young woman, given their age in the painting. And there were a few paintings of herself, and Maisy.

On his desk were several framed photos. They were all of her mother, laughing, posing, her face smiling and beautiful, teasing the photographer, and obviously loving life. Or loving, Katherine gulped, loving what else? In fact, she meant, who else?

It felt quite wrong but she couldn't help wondering. It was unimaginable that her mother and Edward had had an affair, but heavens, he certainly loved her mother. The evidence was everywhere in this room, his own, private office. They were the same age, and her father had been dead for such a long time. Perhaps after her father died? Her mother had never encouraged another love interest - it was a known fact in their circle, despite much attention from suitors over the years.

But....she knew he loved the family as a whole - maybe this was the same thing?

She worried that the shirt was here, in this room, and that if she found it, Edward would eventually know that she'd been in his private office. She backed out, careful not to move anything, and unable to take her eyes from the photos of her mother. She decided to leave his room for now. It would be so much easier to wait and speak with Edward tomorrow.

Confused by the photos, she tucked that worry about her mother and Edward's relationship to the back of her mind, and left the room. She couldn't deal now with another challenge to her understanding of 'how things are' and she was very, very good at pocketing concerns away to revisit another time. She closed the door to his room, and the door to her thoughts about their relationship and turned to leave. Let's leave this for now, she murmured under her breath.

She refocused her mind on the task at hand. She decided to check one other place where Edward may have stored her mother's shirt. It was a place well hidden away from any intruders, if that was truly a concern of his.

She crept down the flights of stairs to the ground floor and moved silently along the corridor to the library. She grasped the large cold brass doorknob, and carefully turned it. The door was old and moved slowly, with a heavy moan, like an ancient wise man. She winced with the sound, and paused to listen for any noise from upstairs. Nothing.

Once in the library, she turned a small table lamp on. Was it possible that Edward had hidden the shirt in the priest hole? The stately room was lined with many floor to ceiling bookcases. Three sections of the walls with bookcases actually hid small doors. The doors were designed to hold books, just like the remainder of the bookshelves, and so they seamlessly blended with the rest of the bookshelves. However, they cannily opened to hidden rooms behind.

One of the small doors opened to a backroom hallway which the servants would have used several generations ago. Normal in those times, the servants would have moved effortlessly around the house through hidden corridors and back rooms. Neither seen nor heard, unless they had a frontline role, their job was to ensure the family and their guests lived a luxurious life, like clockwork.

The second bookcase door opened to a small room that could hold about 5 people at a time. She thought about the history behind it. The secret room was a makeshift chapel that had been used in the time of the Protestant Queen Elizabeth around the mid to late 1500s. At that time, Catholics were persecuted and those wealthy enough had private, hidden chapels built to continue practicing their faith.

The third hidden door led to a priest hole. It was the compartment in which the resident Catholic priest would hide if he was being pursued by the Queen's men at the time. It was a clever hole, with a secret of its own.

Her mind raced through the setup of the priest hole. Like the others, the third bookcase had a small button function etched into the wooden border of the shelving and was not easily visible to the eye. Two of the buttons unlocked the bookcase doors so they could be pushed open. She remembered her grandmother telling her that they had fit a mechanism in the 1950s that modernised the locks and made the rooms more secure to hide documents and objects. The third button, controlling the priest hole access, worked slightly differently. With a press of the button, a small panel about half a meter square in the bookcase wall at ground floor could be slid open to reveal a tiny space: the priest hole. It was big enough only for a large child or small adult to crawl into, and a typical size for a priest hole. If discovered, and empty, the Queen's men would believe they had found the priest hole, and leave the premises without their priest. However, this space hid yet another secret.

Once a person crawled through the door, on the right hand wall of the compartment was another fake panel. By pressing a specific knot in the wood, the wall could be pushed aside like a pocket door. Again, only a small person could fit through this second opening. It led to a long slim room about three meters high and one meter deep. It ran the full width of both walls, about 5 meters long. One wall was a solid thick outside wall. The other, ran along the length of the servant's back hallway. Its presence was undetectable and secret. It was no doubt very cold in the winter, but would have been ideal for the stowaway priest to stretch out limbs in case of a long hideout.

Her mind wandered. Stories had been recounted by her grandmother, of priests who had used this very priest hole – and whose lives had been saved. The Jesuit priest, Nicholas Owen, had been sought after at the time to create these priest holes. The compartments could in fact be a labyrinth of complex passages, holes, and fake panels.

The fake wall behind a fake bookcase, also known as a double hide, was very effective. In one scary search, the priest hole had been found, but to the dismay of the Queen's men, no priest was found in that compartment. He had in fact, been stretched out behind the false wall, in the second compartment, and had survived for five days. Able to move his cramped legs, and feed on small pieces of food and drink stored there, he was one of the lucky priests to have lived through his ordeal.

These stories ran through Katherine's memory like a flash of lightning, quickly and automatically remembered whenever she used the library.

On her way to the hidden priest hole, she fetched a flashlight from the library desk. Then, she moved to the third bookcase and pressed the hidden button function. The very faint noise of a lock releasing was barely audible. She bent down and slid the small door open. She peeked into the hole and flashed her light. Nothing there – no shirt and no, no spiders.

As a child she was fascinated with the priest hole but always a bit nervous because of the spiders she sometimes found there. She and Thomas often used the space for hide and seek. No one else knew of the priest hole in the library, other than her mother and Edward. Colin wasn't interested in such historical novelties and as a child was never interested in playing with his younger brother and female neighbour.

She crawled in and closed the small panel door behind her. It was cold and the stone floor damp. Not wanting to stay any longer than she had to, she pressed the knot in the wood for the double hide. She slowly tried to slide the panel along to reveal the opening but struggled to budge this second small door open.

'It's over 500 years old, give it a chance...' she whispered to herself. And then, it suddenly gave way and with jerking movements she managed to force the panel aside. A gust of very cold wind blew towards her, and she flashed her light through the dark gaping hole. Nothing.

She edged forward. Halfway in the hole, and afraid to rub her hair on the edges of the entrance, lest a spider crawled on her, she gingerly flashed the light further down the small room.

'Yes!' She breathed out loud.

There, a little further inside the compartment, was a clear plastic storage box - with a shirt visible through it. This must be her mother's shirt! She had solved Edward's secret. Finally, she had her mother's shirt!

She moved forward slightly to reach the box and saw a small shadow scuffle away. Ew, she shivered, a large spider. Her hand went immediately to her hair and she swept down her hair along to her neck to check there was nothing there.

She pulled the box towards her, backing out and into the first space. She turned to exit into the library, and realised there wasn't enough room to turn around with her and the box in the tiny space.

'Awkward, heavens this is tight!'.

Well, she'd have to wriggle out backwards. She stretched sideways to open the panel door to the library then slowly backed out, bottom first.

Finally, with her body out and in the library she pulled her head from the hole. As the warmer air of the library hit her neck, she felt the hairs rise. But it wasn't just the warmer air, that spooked a tingle up her neck.

There was a noise. She'd just heard something - a noise like someone choking in the library.

Chapter 32 – The Mandarin Oriental

Ping. Hmm, he looked at his mobile on the table, and thought, why would she be texting me?

He read the starting line of the text and then opened it with a slight sneer. Hah, well *he'd* managed to secure a response from her husband and only just an hour or so ago. Perhaps Colin didn't want to communicate with her. He took a deep breath and looked at the tables around him. Some business meetings for sure, but most of the tables were occupied by couples dining and chatting. His eyes rested on a couple who were quite affectionate at the table. He turned his eyes away and coughing quietly into his sleeve, hid a smile. Yup, Colin was probably right now heavily engaged with another form of business….one she wouldn't approve of. He deleted the text message and focused his eyes at the front of the restaurant.

Let her figure it out herself. He had much more important things to think about tonight.

~~~~~~~~~~

Katherine whipped her head around to locate the choking noise and stifled a scream. There wasn't much light in the library, only the small lamp she had turned on at the far side, but she could make out that someone *was* there and coming quickly towards her.

Without a thought, she instantly shone the flashlight on the figure, and turned to defend herself.

What? The light shone brightly exposing the intruder.

'Thomas! WHAT are you doing? You scared the living daylights out of me! Why are you standing there!?'

Thomas tried hard to catch his breath. He was laughing so much he could hardly speak, and was choking slightly.

He pulled himself up and took a deep breath, trying to straighten his face. 'Me? What are you doing?' he exclaimed, 'You were hysterically funny backing out of that priest hole!'

She relaxed, at least she'd made him laugh. It was kind of funny. He seemed a changed person from earlier.

'I was looking for my mother's shirt,' she said meekly, 'in the priest hole.'

'And?' he teased her, still laughing.

She gently pulled the plastic box from the hole behind her and held it up.

'What an odd place to find it!' he stated.

'I thought on the off-chance, he might hide it here. Thank heavens he did! In fact, this shirt is pretty important right now,' she stated the obvious.

They both looked at the plastic box. A silence settled between them.

'Look, I'm sorry about my anger earlier. I tried to find you to apologise and talk about the next steps. It's getting complicated now and I think the solicitor could be right. There may be a threat out there. Of course, you weren't in your room. So I checked the kitchen, conservatory, your mother's study, and then I noticed the pale light down the hall in the library...'

'Oh, I see.' She cocked her head sideways at him. 'Thomas, it's ok, although I haven't had a fright like that for a long time! I'm sorry I angered you earlier regarding my suspicions about James. But I believe my mother's death wasn't the accident the police claim and I want to know the truth. I'm suspicious until I know more. And my next step was finding my mother's shirt - which you've caught me at, red-handed!' She grinned at him. 'Want to help?' Her tone was inviting.

He smiled at her and sighed, 'I think we should bring this to the police. Let's see what you have there, then let's talk about when we involve the officials,' he was reluctant to delay contacting the police any further, but could see that she wanted to check her mother's shirt.

'Ok, just wait here a minute.' She got up from the priest hole and smiling mischievously at him, rushed past him to her mother's study. There she carefully took out the two pieces of cotton she'd returned to the faux bookcase before heading to Edward's room earlier.

She hurried back to the library and turned on brighter lamps. She was nervous and excited.

'Thomas, here they are!' She moved over to where he was sitting. He'd taken the shirt out of the box and was looking at it with sadness.

She spread the two small cotton pieces directly over her mother's shirt. The two of them stared at the fabrics. Katherine squinted and looked closer.

'Oh my God,' her eyes were wide with confusion and she looked to Thomas for answers.

'What the...?' Thomas moved the cotton pieces but to no avail.

~ ~ ~ ~ ~ ~ ~ ~ ~ ~

The maitre d'hotel at the entrance of the hotel restaurant welcomed her. She gave her name and he flashed her a generous smile. 'We've been waiting for you, Madame, and I have a gentleman too, who has been waiting for you...' He smiled and beckoned her to follow.

The restaurant was simply beautiful. She had seen a few photos from their gallery page online, but this was stunning. The decor was perfect in every way. As with her bedroom, the floral arrangements were extravagant and the lighting and furniture intimate. The style tastefully boasted luxury. Quiet jazz tinkled in the background.

Richard watched her as she walked towards the table. He checked his shirt was tucked in and pushed his chair back. As he did so, he coughed. My God - her shapely figure was perfect in what looked like a cashmere dress. And her legs. He felt his pulse quicken, and instinctively smoothed his tie down.

He stood as she arrived.

'Madame is here,' the maitre d' introduced Anjali's arrival and pulled her chair back. She smiled at Richard. My heavens, he looks sharp tonight. She guessed that he'd dressed his best for the Mandarin Oriental, given its reputation and his special status at the hotel. The maitre d' helped her to settle and then placed her napkin on her knee.

'Nice to see you. Got here alright then?'

'Yes, thank you.'

Just then, two men arrived; the sommelier with a large champagne bottle - and another with the champagne stand.

The sommelier and Richard chatted amicably; they obviously knew each other well. Richard was shown the champagne label. He nodded approval. The gentleman then deftly opened the bottle while talking about the particular vintage and champagne house. He looked at Richard to check that he was good with the lady tasting. Richard smiled.

With a great flourish the sommelier poured Anjali a taste. It was a beautiful pink palette, with velvety-smooth bubbles on her lips as she sipped lightly. Anjali grinned at them both. The champagne was divine. He finished pouring both of their glasses and left with an 'Enjoy!'

Richard thanked the maitre d' without taking his eyes from Anjali. She realised he was watching her intently as she sipped the champagne.

He smiled charmingly at her, 'Shall we have a cheers?'

'To a relaxing evening,' he raised his glass.

''Yes, it's so beautiful here, Richard. What a perfect place for a working dinner. And let's cheer to getting this job done in good time!' She added.

They clinked glasses and the cold champagne slid down her throat. It was amazing. She had never tasted champagne like that before. She pulled the glass away from her lips, looked at the liquid, and took another sip, a slightly larger one this time. Ooooh, that was so nice.

'Like it?'

'Yes, that's lovely.'

He sat back and watched her enjoy herself. And so, finally he had her to himself. On his own turf, in his own way. And she'd discover tonight that his way was something she could easily get used to.

~ ~ ~ ~ ~ ~ ~ ~ ~ ~

Their starters were done, and he delicately tapped the corners of his mouth with his napkin. Several of his peers had passed his table and glanced admiringly at his dinner guest. One or two of them arched their eyebrows at him. Yes, she was stunning, and more so with the effect of the champagne and matching wine the sommelier had chosen to pair with the starters. Richard had chosen them: raw oysters sourced both locally and internationally to demonstrate their differing flavours.

Anjali had delighted in the starters. Her face was slightly flushed.

He watched her taking her last oyster, and thought to slow it all down....

'Anjali, are you ok if we do some work now?'

'Of course, yes, I'm intrigued,' she smiled, eager to get started, as she remembered why she was here. His conversation had been so engaging, chatting about people he had met at the hotel.

He looked up and waved for service. The maitre d' was immediately at his side. Richard quietly said something to the gentleman who then made a sign to a woman at the door. Within seconds she was at Richard's side and handed him two thick envelopes with the hotel logo on.

'Thank you,' he said to them both. The woman lingered and smiled at Richard who gave her a dismissive nod. In the meantime, others had arrived to clear the oysters and create space on the table.

Richard handed Anjali one of the envelopes. The hotel had printed two copies of the document he'd received earlier that evening.

Anjali took the envelope. She was serious as she opened it, turning to work mode.

'Anjali, as you know, we are at the final stages of an important transaction. Thank you for taking your time on a Friday night to assist with this, ' he paused to raise his champagne glass to her. She smiled in return.

'I'd like us to work through this document. I'm looking for any inconsistencies and having your mind working on this, with a fresh look, is just what's needed. Let me provide the background...'

He pulled a pen and small pad from his pocket and began to draw a timeline.

'There's a company which I invested in some time ago. It's referred to as Gemstone throughout this document. I had no trouble finding this code name, pretty obvious as it's been a rock solid investment, and precious as a gem....'

Something triggered in Anjali's head. She wasn't sure what. But....perhaps because it sounded so interesting. She lifted her eyebrows.

'Yes, the real name will be swapped in, but we aren't at that stage just now,' he replied. She understood – he was able to share the full details of the deal but not the name of the company at this point. That was typical in a transaction of this type.

'The investment or rather equity we put in was linked to a small amount of ownership, as normal. However, in my revised business plan, I decided I wanted more, 100% ownership in fact, and to buy the company outright.'

Her eyes opened wide with interest.

'This company is unique with fantastic projected profits and in fact, fits perfectly into my strategic portfolio. This document describes the next stage of our relationship with the owner of this small business.'

He smiled at her, and expanded on the context of the deal, slowly casting his net around her.

'There are complications of course, there always are. We've been working on several negotiations at once. The acquisition of this small business, Gemstone, where we already have a vested interest, has been one part of the deal. It's this company that has the technology we are after. This acquisition should be completed early next week.

'As well, I've a financial backer to assist me in both the purchasing of Gemstone and our plans for the business after the acquisition. He's a specialist in post-acquisition activities. He's investing himself in Gemstone, but he also has associates and contacts who will provide the complete production capacity, post acquisition; a way to turn the science and technology of Gemstone into a complete commercial offering for the market with a scalable production capacity.

'These associates of his, who focus on large scale production have provided, as of today, the plans for building an extensive production site. Their complete business plan and contractual commitments are within this document.'

Anjali was nodding. She understood the task at hand.

'We have high aspirations for Gemstone, despite it being a small company,' he paused.

She smiled and nodded again. It all sounded very straightforward.

'And there are interesting side notes,' he looked intently at her. She held his gaze, waiting for his next statement.

'The owner of the small company, well, he's in a bit of difficulty,' he coughed, to demonstrate his empathy and discomfort for the gentleman.

'His reputation is on the line. He's made some silly mistakes,' he played with his napkin, pointing to the middle of the timeline he'd scribbled there, 'there's no doubt that he's clever and his company has a unique and highly competitive technology which, to our delight and under our ownership, can be scaled and marketed for profit. That's for sure. But at some point he has,' he looked out across the restaurant, loosened his tie slightly and continued, 'falsified some of his findings. Of course, we identified that straight away, but this isn't even known at his own company, nor indeed in the sector where he is held in such high esteem. So, we've had that to deal with.'

Anjali reflected. How many times had she seen that in the businesses she'd assessed: Greed that compels people to be dishonest, and to unfortunately, falsify documents. But it was simply not acceptable. She reflected. It was amazing how many people wouldn't question foul play even if they suspected it; either because they were afraid of losing their job; or they were in for getting a piece of the profit.

The sides of her mouth frowned. That's why there were never very many whistleblowers. The whole system worked to protect itself. At work, she saw it everywhere around her. And in fact, these were the companies she stayed well away from. She was familiar with the types of deals Richard's team brought to him sometimes. Deals with a twist, not illegal but not completely above board either. She didn't approve, and certainly didn't recommend investments in those types of companies, but she knew it happened at times in their line of business.

'And the poor gentleman. He has a family and his reputation. Some financial troubles could be brewing with the company if he doesn't sell - so the timing is right. We're helping the gentleman out and, he's helping us out. Of course, our end of the bargain is infinitely better, but this deal will make him wealthy beyond what he ever could have achieved on his own. Of course as well, no one needs to know about the troubles he's been shouldering,' he smiled nobly at Anjali.

'I see, who's had a look at this already?' she asked. His answer would make a difference. Depending upon which colleagues had worked on the document, she'd know how much effort would be required for her final review and approval.

Richard provided several names and she nodded.

Not too bad, she thought. Given who worked on it and the size of the document, she flipped the pages with her thumb, we can easily get through this tonight. A late night, for sure. Now she understood why it was going to be so late, but it was certainly do-able.

She relaxed and smiled at him, 'Ok, we can get this done tonight.'

He grinned appreciatively, 'Wonderful, I knew I could count on you, Anjali,' and without waiting for her response he motioned to the waiter for a top up.

'A bit slower on the champagne,' she laughed, 'I know you feel bad bringing me out tonight, but my mind needs to be focused, otherwise we won't get through this!'

'Ah, no problem. A bit of champagne is good for the mind, don't you know?' he teased her.

She smiled and looked sideways at him. Then she pushed her bread plate further aside and pulling a pen from her small purse, she began to read through the document.

Chapter 33 - Night Visions

Their eyes were locked in disbelief. Thomas leaned over the fabrics. He played with them for a while and then leaned back.

'Katherine - the puzzle doesn't fit.'

She had been watching him move the fabrics around. When he stood back she tried herself to place the pieces so they matched up with the fabric and embroidered design.

'One of the fabrics is an obvious match. And it fits the ripped gash on the shirt. It's the one I collected high up on the oak tree. The other, it's close, but isn't a match. There's too much cotton here for the ripped part of the shirt!' She said to Thomas.

'And...?' He was watching her.

'And this means that it belongs to someone else. Despite being outside, it's a relatively new piece of fabric, you can tell. I found it there, where the accident happened. Someone else was down there at the river, Thomas.' Her eyes were wide and she felt a fear gnawing at her stomach.

'But that fabric could have been there from any time,' he replied calmly. 'It could be from another shirt of your mother's. She was always getting her clothes stained and tarnished from her river and forest walks. I can hear Edward saying it now. Or, it could have blown from miles away....it could have been there for years...' he could see her desperate look. She was so desperate to understand what had happened down there at the river..

'Thomas, this isn't 'old' fabric. It's still in fine condition. Look, I know this isn't like me, and I know neither of us go for this type of hocus-pocus. But I have a feeling, and it's a strong feeling. This belongs to whoever was down there at the river with mother.'

He could see she was serious. 'What are you thinking?'

She swallowed before replying.

'Colin. Colin has a few shirts just like this, Thomas. I think I need to look in his wardrobe.'

'But surely he would have thrown away a torn shirt, Katherine!' He was feeling exasperated - why couldn't he help her solve this. Why was the damn situation so perplexing.

'Yes, but he bought all his shirts in double,' she was leaving the library as she replied. He knew she was heading to Colin's room.

'It will take us some time to go through his shirts,' she whispered over her shoulders, and she sped up as she headed to the stairway.

~ ~ ~ ~ ~ ~ ~ ~ ~ ~

Dinner had been fabulous. She was definitely feeling more than a bit dizzy now. It had taken several hours to go through the document the first time. She'd highlighted issues but there weren't many. This deal was pretty solid. It was surprising that Richard needed her touch at all, it was much easier going than she thought it would be.

In fact, it'd been so easy to review the document that she'd managed to fully appreciate her dinner. Typically, working meals for her was total focus on the work, with food being an inconvenience. Tonight was different. Despite the pressure to get through the document, the focus had also been on the food.

Richard had insisted that he order the dishes tonight. He obviously had many favourites he wanted to share with her. So, she had just let him order for the two of them. The plates, however, kept arriving. He took such obvious pleasure in talking her through the dishes and asking her opinion, that she didn't mention it was too much food.

Then there were the wines. A wine appeared with each course of the dinner, regardless of the fact that there were quite a few almost full bottles already opened on the table. She'd been so careful to only take sips of each type of wine, she had to get through the document.

But once they were finished reviewing the document, she had felt a sense of relaxation come over her. The ambience of the room was so soothing and elegant, her work was done, and Richard was obviously pleased with the result.

Was this what Richard and her colleagues got up to on their 'all nighters'? Was it really about a final rubber stamp on a deal, no real heavy lifting and truly enjoying themselves with exquisite food and champagne? She'd heard the finance director moan many times about these all nighters - maybe he was telling some truth. She put her fork down and smiled at Richard as he commented on the food; he was obviously in his element.

He saw her watching him with a smile on her face. Ah, so I'm amusing her, he thought. Right, it was getting late, but was desert time, and Richard had a plan.

'Anjali, I know you adore desert,' he grinned knowingly at her. She raised her eyebrows and lifted her shoulders lightly, as if to say 'maybe'.

'So, we'll be getting a selection of their top desserts to share - how does that sound?'

'Delicious!' She laughed happily. 'Oh my heavens, so much food, Richard. But, well, I can't refuse that!' How absolutely delightful she thought to herself and hid a grin that wouldn't go away, behind the back of her hand. My heavens, what a lovely evening.

The table was cleared and it didn't take long before a great fuss was made of all the dessert plates placed decoratively on their table. Richard had moved his briefcase off the side chair and came around to sit beside her. The desert wine was being poured and the pastry chef had come from the kitchen to describe the plates with great pride. She couldn't believe the pastry chef had made an appearance. He knew Richard well.

She gingerly sipped her dessert wine. It was refreshingly sweet and yet simple, and so easy to drink she thought to herself. She couldn't help but catch Richard's eyes, laughing at the wonderful descriptions the pastry chef was running through. And then, they were alone to try the deserts.

Richard suggested she try first. She plunged her cutlery into an orange cheesecake decorated with tiny sugared mandarin slices and crystallised lemon and couldn't help but take a deep breath as she tasted it.

'Richard, this is absolutely marvellous, you should take a bite!'

He moved closer to her, such that his shoulder was rubbing hers, and reached over to take a piece of the cheesecake with his spoon. He tasted it remarking, 'That's very good, but try this one.'

He dove his not yet used fork into a chocolate and hazelnut torte and then turned to her, holding his fork close to her mouth, waiting for her to bite. She smiled and hesitated only a moment. Then she reached forward to take his offering.

He pulled back slightly to tease her and she couldn't suppress her soft laughter. She looked at him as if to say, smarten up. Then, he pushed his fork forward so that she could taste the desert.

She did realise that she was eating from his cutlery – well, not one he had used, but a fork he was holding. For some reason she didn't mind. She'd definitely offered food on a fork or spoon to colleagues in the past at work dinner parties, when everyone was relaxed and had a bit of wine, so it was no big deal. In any case, their work was finished, they'd had lovely food and wine, and she was off to bed soon anyway. Plus, Richard was known to be a big tease at times.

'What would you like me to try?' He challenged her, and topped up her dessert wine.

She shook her head for him to stop pouring, then grinned at the challenge and pointed to the berry dish close to her. It was overloaded with large, fresh berries and a type of swirled meringue.

'Try it and let me know how sweet the berries are in my dessert.'

He was disappointed she hadn't reciprocated by using her own spoon for his taste test, but was happy enough she was playing the game with him. He chuckled inside, thinking of a possible double entente: 'How sweet are my berries' said the actress to the bishop. I'll let you know how sweet your berries are later, he thought smugly.

He scooped a bite for himself but was too hasty. Several berries and fruit juice fell from his spoon to his crisp white shirt.

'Ah,' he said and couldn't help but laugh. His shirt was only just delivered today! God he was in a great mood - normally this would bother him - but he was laughing like a naughty school boy.

'Oh no!' She saw him laughing, and joined in. 'You'll need to get that in cold water right away!' She advised.

He studied the stain. 'Look, let's finish off what we want here then head up. I can get this in cold water and then we can discuss one or two more things.'

She looked at him quizzically, she thought they were finished.

He immediately sensed her reluctance. 'Actually, it's not about Gemstone. In fact, I've spent quite some time on your new business case, Anjali. I've been thinking a lot about it since Wednesday. There are a few items I'd like to ask you before the weekend, if you don't mind.'

She was impressed. He was already looking at the details of her opportunity? She sighed inwardly. She was tired, but he'd been so generous tonight and well, she was keen to hear his questions about her business case.

'Of course, no problem.'

'Thank you, perfect.' His eyes were dilated. He gently touched her hand to get her attention and although it was only the lightest of touches, it triggered his senses further. The anticipation was almost at a tipping point.

He gently pulled forward another plate for her to try.

Anjali moved her hand from his and repositioned herself a little bit further away from him to taste the dessert.

'Delicious, but I think that's it for me,' she sighed.

'No problem, let's go,' he seemed eager to leave, now that she'd had enough. He stood from his chair and pulled hers out, then put his hand just below her waist to guide her out.

The restaurant staff came to see them off, and Richard thanked them for their superb meal. He kept his hand on her lower waist and guided her to the elevator.

'That was a lovely dinner, thank you Richard,' she commented. She dug her hotel fob out of her purse.

'Yes, with lovely company,' he smiled at her and she blushed, studying him for only a moment then she looked away. He was so very good looking and gracious. Why wasn't he married?

The elevator opened as soon as Richard touched the button. He gently nudged her into the elevator, and held his card to the floor numbers then pressed the top floor. She noted that they were on the same floor.

'Thanks again for doing the final checks on the document,' they were in the elevator alone but he was whispering softly anyway, 'that was just what the document needed.'

She realised how tired she was, away from the glittering atmosphere of the restaurant and leaned slightly against the elevator wall. She hoped he didn't have too many questions, her head was dizzy. Despite sipping her wine, there had been quite a few wines, and it had obviously added up.

The doors opened. She fingered her fob in her hand.

'Hey Richard, I have a perfect lobby area in my room for us to work through the questions you have.'

He sensed her tiredness and pulled her closer. He purposely made it a friendly and casual gesture, but his heart was speeding up. They were almost in his room.

'Tell you what, mine has a larger lounge area and it will save me getting my questions then going to yours. Pop on in, and we'll go through the questions. It won't take long.'

'Ok,' she yawned. They walked towards his room, further down the hallway and he opened his door with his fob.

He took his arm from her shoulder, and directed her through the door. She realised how heavy and tired her body felt. She should be going to bed soon and hoped she could reply sensibly to his questions. She definitely had had a bit too much great-tasting wine.

Richard could sense her state. He grinned. His turf, his room, his way. He took her room fob from her hand, dropped it on the hallway table, then took her hand and arm.

'Richard, the flowers in both rooms are just lovely, almost extravagant.'

He led her past a small sofa in the lounge area, to the large table at the back of the room so they could admire the flower centrepiece. She placed her purse on the table and reached the flowers to smell their scent.

'The scents are amazing.' Her head felt clearer.

'Come on, let's sit here and go through my questions.' He brought her back to the seating area. It had a centre table, small sofa and chairs. He pointed to the small sofa. The table had a bottle of champagne chilling in a silver bowl with flutes on a silver tray.

He didn't offer her the champagne straight away.

'Ok, I've penned a few questions down here for you to check,' he handed her some papers from the table, 'are you ok to do that, while I find another shirt?'

'Sure, not a problem,' she was settled on the sofa and took his papers. She certainly sounded more with it, he thought. He'd definitely piqued her interest.

He actually had no intention of changing into another shirt, but he went to the dressing room anyway. He picked up a shirt from the cupboard and slowly returned to the sitting area. She was more focused now, he could see that, as she read through his queries.

She looked up as he approached.

'Hi, yes, would you like to go through all of these tonight? I can see why you needed them answered before Monday, some of them are quite fundamental.'

He laughed. 'Yes, they are, but that doesn't mean I'm any less interested in your business case. I still think it's an amazing opportunity,' and while speaking he put down his new shirt, and began to open the chilled champagne.

She noticed his movement out of the corner of her eye, but didn't resist when she saw the champagne bottle. It was the same as the first one they had enjoyed, when she had arrived at the restaurant, with the velvety bubbles. It had been so lovely. One more glass wouldn't be the end of the world, and she had already decided to lie in and enjoy the spa in the morning as James had suggested.

He poured them both a glass of champagne.

She settled back on the sofa to talk about her business opportunity. Her brain felt almost razor sharp again – she was so passionate about this deal, and his questions were very astute. She loved the challenge even at this late hour.

Richard leaned down to give her the champagne glass. He composed his face to look thoughtfully at her, but never intended to take no as an answer. 'Are you ok to go through this, so late?'

'Of course,' she took a sip of the champagne. Mmm it was so lovely, even after all the food and wine.

He watched her, and felt his pulse build. She was so close, so close to him. He decided to chance it, he just had to. He was after all, a chancer, isn't that what made him so successful?

'Before we start, I'd like to make a small speech,' he raised his glass and then sat beside her. She looked slightly surprised. She must have thought he'd sit in one of the chairs, he thought wryly. It was a cosy sofa and his leg pressed against hers. He turned his body so he could look at her better.

'To the most clever guy on my team – who looks smashing in a cashmere dress,' he teased.

She responded with a sweetly innocent, tinkling laugh.

He found her irresistible. But he had to take this slow. There was a way to do this, and that was to take it very very slow.

~ ~ ~ ~ ~ ~ ~ ~ ~ ~

Katherine and Thomas were in Colin's dressing room, looking through his shirts, when they heard the scream. It was a child's scream.

'Mummy! Mummy!'

Katherine looked at Thomas with a panicked face.

'Maisy!' They raced to her room. Opening Maisy's bedroom door wide, she could see her daughter in the dim light from the hallway, sitting up in bed crying. She quickly ran to hug her and sat down, pulling her onto her lap.

'Darling, it's ok. What happened? Are you hurt?'

When there was no response she rocked her, smoothing her hair back and telling her everything was ok.

'Sweet pea, Thomas is going to turn your bed light on, ok, so we can all see better,' there was no answer from Maisy only her sobs. Thomas switched it on.

'Mummy, Mummy it's the face, I don't like it!' she cried.

There was nobody in the room, it was exactly as they had left it.

'It's ok, darling, it was just a dream and I'm here now.'

'No, not a dream, the face isn't nice,' she repeated.

Katherine looked at Thomas who was frowning.

'Maisy, what face?' she asked.

'The face, the face over there,' and she pointed to the other side of the room. Thomas and Katherine looked to the art section of Maisy's room. Of course, there's nothing there, Katherine thought. What a scary dream she must have had.

Maisy slowly peeked out from her mother's shoulder to where she had pointed, and then cried, 'It's still there, it's there.'

Thomas moved to the art area. 'Maisy, I'll get rid of it, not to worry. Tell me where it is and I'll take it out of your room,' he was looking at the teddies.

With some effort, Maisy pulled herself away again, from the safety of her mother's shoulder. 'There,' she pointed definitively.

Thomas walked quickly to the culprit. It wasn't a teddy, it was a painting.

He looked at Katherine, but tried to keep the concern from his face, he didn't want to worry Maisy.

'Ok, I think you mean this, let's get this out of the room.'

'I don't like that face, it's a bad face,' she said.

'Sweet pea, faces in dreams aren't for real, it's alright,' soothed Katherine.

'It's not a dream, I saw that face and that car. That's NOT a dream, Mummy,' Maisy retorted still crying.

Katherine felt her hairs lift – she was aware of almost all of her daughter's activities – and had been unapologetic in her obsessiveness. What face, what car?

'Ok, Maisy, put your head here,' she gently pulled her daughter's face to her shoulder so she couldn't see and then indicated to Thomas to show her the picture.

He quietly turned it around. It was the painting Maisy had so painstakingly worked on that week. The garden wall, the red car, the face... This scene must mean something important to her daughter. She waved him to turn it away. Thomas placed it underneath several other paintings, well hidden.

She stroked Maisy, debating what to do next. She didn't want to upset her daughter but she felt a rising panic and had to ask the question. She said calmly, 'Ok, the painting is all gone now. You said it was real? Where did you see the face, Maisy?'

Maisy pulled her wet face back from her mother's neck and looking at her sadly said, 'Our garden, our wall, Mummy don't you know that?' Katherine stiffened, and she shook her head no.

She felt like she was watching a scene in slow motion – a scene with a menacing build to a tragic ending. What had Maisy said to her earlier in the week? 'A fancy racing car' and now Katherine understood, it was at their garden wall. She swallowed, not wanting to ask the next question. Maisy seemed calmer now but she had to ask.

'And when did you see that face, dear?'

Maisy wiped her tears from her eyes so she could see better. But she was struggling, she was so tearful and tired. She scanned her bed to find something.

She pointed.

Katherine looked at where her daughter's finger was pointing: it was to a teddy. Not just any teddy, but an adorable and innocent looking bunny.

Very gently she asked, 'You saw the face the day I gave you the bunny?'

Maisy nodded her head and cuddled further into her mother.

She couldn't help herself. She didn't want to upset her daughter, but a small guttural gasp escaped from her throat. The sound was like that from a wild animal, finally loose and sprinting from a trap with a painful utterance.

Thomas, at the other side of the room struggled to follow, but looked sharply at Katherine. Something was deeply wrong. He was lost in the exchange; something important was happening but he didn't know what. Katherine had understood something he hadn't.

Maisy pressed further into her mother's body for warmth. Katherine was staring at the bunny, but the look on her face was frightening. It was as if the devil had just walked by.

Chapter 34 - Stains

'Let's bring Maisy to the bathroom to wipe her face. A little bit of Calpol will help, I'm sure,' Thomas snapped Katherine out of her thoughts and led the way to Maisy's bathroom. Katherine nodded and followed him; she didn't trust her voice.

'Here we are,' he said and he wiped Maisy's face gently with the cloth.

'Is the Calpol here?'

Katherine pointed to the locked cabinet above the sink. She mouthed the code to him.

He prepared the Calpol and a little cup of water from the side of the sink.

'There you go, aren't you good,' he smiled as Maisy took her medicine.

Katherine cleared her throat.

'Perhaps you'd like to sleep with Mummy?' She said softly to her daughter, knowing this offer would most likely snap Maisy out of her frightened mood.

'Yes, please,' smiled Maisy, more calm now.

'That sounds like a plan. You two ladies head off to sleep now, and I'll go back to bed too.' He kissed Maisy goodnight, but indicated to Katherine he would wait outside. He lingered in the hallway and as soon as the two were in Katherine's room he sat on the chair outside.

Katherine tucked up in bed with Maisy and stroked her hair, singing softly. Within minutes Maisy was asleep, exhausted from her nightmare. Katherine was sleepy too. She let herself be lulled to a sort of sleep, but was jolted awake when Maisy moved her hand.

Katherine checked the time at her bedside and realised twenty minutes had passed. Slowly, she extracted herself from Maisy, and pulled the sheets around her daughter's little body. She tiptoed out.

Thomas was waiting in the long hallway, patiently sitting and reading a magazine that had been there. He shot up straight away when Katherine slipped out of the bedroom and put his hands on Katherine's shoulders, directing her towards the stairway.

'Come on, I'm getting you something to drink. Let's talk downstairs,' he whispered firmly.

~ ~ ~ ~ ~ ~ ~ ~ ~ ~

Anjali raised her glass to Richard's cheer as she laughed at his words. 'So you like my dress, you admit I'm clever, and you *think* I'm a guy! Thanks!'

She was relaxed, he was being funny, and the champagne was so nice. 'Right, let's get though the questions you have.'

She tapped his papers on her knees and leaned forward in the sofa to address his queries.

He breathed a sigh of relief. His leg was still pressed against her. The night might have finished extremely prematurely if she had minded him sitting so close.

'For sure, answer them in whatever order.'

She laughed at the first question on the list: 'How are you able to do such brilliant work, taking care of me and my business as well as taking care of a husband and children?'.

'Well, that's the strangest question of the lot - the rest I can easily deal with - this one is more complex!' She was in a chatty mood.

'Tell me about it,' he encouraged her.

She noticed he still had his stained shirt on. 'I will. You, however, need to get that in cold water,' she admonished him then continued, 'James is amazing really. He's pretty flexible and that helps. Of course, all that may change now. In fact I'm hoping he'll have more time for the children.'

He'd begun to unbutton his shirt, but paused - what did she say?

'What was that - did you say it would all change now?' It was impossible she could know.

'Yes,' she took another sip of champagne, she was so very relaxed now, 'it was such a big day for James. He closed a deal!'

Richard had his champagne to his mouth, but nearly spluttered it back into the glass as he registered what she said.

'What?!'

She looked at him quizzically, registering his serious tone, his face now in complete focus.

'Well, yes, I guess I can talk about it now, now that it's all done. He's sold his company. It was all signed this afternoon, and he's over the moon.'

Richard wasn't often speechless. He put his champagne glass down on the table. Is she playing with me?

'Anjali, that's great news. Are you sure the deal was signed, or perhaps he had signed some other documents to show intent to sell?'

Typical Richard, she thought, always interested in a deal.

'Richard, it's definitely signed and done. The deal was completed today.'

He looked at her and knew, now was the time, time to tell her. Maybe James wasn't as innocent as he thought, playing his wife like this as well as him.

'I have to tell you something very, very important,' he sobered his demeanour and looked sadly into her eyes.

She wondered what he would say to her. She tried to straighten her face. It wasn't working, it was definitely time to head to her room for bed. She put her glass down. After this, she'd have to take the rest of his questions next week.

'Gemstone – the documents you reviewed tonight – and the company I was talking about?' He nodded to her holding her eyes.

'Yes,' she kept his gaze, nodding back.

'That's E2E.'

He let the statement hang in the air.

She shook her head, and squinted her eyes, looking at quizzically. Was he joking?

'I'm sorry, what are you saying?'

He tried re-filling her glass, but she covered it.

'No, it's ok, I'm fine for champagne, no more for me. Richard what are you saying?'

That's too bad, he thought, so champagne is off-limits now....

'What I'm saying is that Gemstone is E2E, that's the company that we're closing on next week.'

'But, how is that possible?' She was totally perplexed and disbelieving.

How could James close a deal if Richard was his investor or acquirer, and Richard had not yet completed the deal? And why didn't James tell her - that her boss was investing? Why? Then, she heard him say something else.

'Richard, what did you say?' She licked her lips, they were very dry. She looked around for water.

'I gave you the background of Gemstone, the terrible situation the owner was in....' he was talking more quietly, almost sympathetically.

The terrible situation...? She swallowed. What terrible situation? Oh dear God no! The falsifications, the integrity of the owner, his reputation and financial situation...she remembered what Richard had divulged over dinner.

'Oh my God,' she gasped with her hand to her mouth and stared at Richard.

He gently put his hand on her leg. 'It's ok, Anjali, it's all being sorted. The company, you, the children, it will all be sorted.'

'Richard, I....I'm not sure I understand. What are you saying to me?'

'I'm saying that it's all going to be alright. I'll take care of it. I'll take care of you. James will be alright, but you'll be safe with me,' his eyes were different, looking at her as a prized possession.

She pushed back from him, and felt dizzy, very, very dizzy.

'I just, I need to digest this, I can't understand. I need some water...'

He gently pulled her back to rest her head on the sofa and hesitated. He ached with the need to kiss her - he couldn't believe how much he cared for her just now. It was all-consuming. It wasn't just passion; he wanted to wrap her up in his arms and comfort her.

His emotions surprised him. Was the timing right? Should he wait until James' credibility was completely trashed?

He delayed. He knew how the night would end, but he would enjoy the anticipation of the evening just that little bit more.

He squeezed her knee. 'I'll get the water, and sort my shirt out as well.' He amazed himself at his pent up energy, as he sprinted to get the water.

His veins were pulsing. He finished undoing the buttons on his shirt, pulled the hem out from his trousers, and filled two large crystal glasses with cold sparkling water from the hotel fridge.

He was watching her out of the corner of his eye. Her head was still resting back against the sofa. He moved towards her.

'Hey, Anjali, here you go,' he gave her the glass.

She opened her eyes immediately - thank God he thought - he didn't want her falling asleep.

She took the glass and watched him as she finished it.

He placed the other glass of water on the table and knew she was watching. He took his shirt off, slowly, waiting for her reaction. He knew his chest was appealing, and his arm muscles would have flexed as he pulled them out of the sleeves. Her eyes were focused on his chest. But they didn't seem to be registering. He pumped his chest up further and tensed his stomach, revealing his prided, toned six pack.

With his shirt in his hands he took the stained part and dunked it into his glass of cold water he'd placed on the table. He held it there and turned to face her, tensing his arms again and knowing she was still watching him.

Anjali had a sense of drowning. Yes, she knew, drowning in wine and champagne, she had drunk far too much. More importantly, she was drowning in information she wasn't in a position to absorb. She couldn't understand what Richard was saying and needed more information, calmly, so she could make sense of it all. And why didn't he put his other shirt on? Despite all the fearful concerns in her mind because of what he'd just said, her most pressing thought was why the heck was he so comfortable without his shirt on, really, he should put his clean shirt on.

Her eyes opened wide as she saw him leaning towards her to....to comfort her? A wave of claustrophobia came over her.

All she wanted was more water, more space, more information and for him to put his shirt on.

'Richard,' she backed further into the sofa, 'I'm sorry but I need more water.'

He restrained himself from embracing her and sighed inwardly. Had he plied her with too much alcohol?

He got up to refill her water.

As he did so, she looked despondently at the shirt in the glass. Despite the disturbing conversation they'd just had, a simple, unrelated thought popped into her head: such an elegant shirt and such a terrible stain, what a shame. She followed the fabric of the shirt. Something caught her eye.

Most oddly, along the full hem of the shirt, was the most beautiful white embroidery. She moved closer to look at it. She squinted and recognised it. Why did she recognise it? The memory was distant, but it was there. What was the memory?

'Here, Anjali, here's some more water,' he sat beside her, still topless, and moved to put his arm around her while she drank.

She pulled away from his overture, and turned to look at him directly.

'Aren't you cold? You should put your shirt on, Richard. Can you repeat what you said just now?' The water had been perfect. She was ready to listen and dispel whatever nonsense he was talking about. There was a total disconnect and miscommunication here. She waited.

'I'm a bit warm,' he grinned at her, 'and yes, I'll repeat it. Gemstone, remember, the company in question, rock solid, is actually your husband's company, E2E.'

'Rock solid' again, like he mentioned at the restaurant. Why did that phrase ring a bell? Her memory was chugging away and now it was trying to find the answer to two recent memories, but she couldn't place them. Why had she drunk so much?

'We are completing the transaction next week, so there's no way James closed a deal today. He must have been lying to you, as he has been, for sometime. His business isn't in a good place, he's falsified information, and he's in financial trouble.'

She froze.

He noticed her reaction and continued, softening the blow, 'But he has some great intellectual property; a discovery that will make a huge difference in my life, his life and many others, and that's worth my time and investment.'

He said to her gently, 'Look, I care about what happens to you...'

What was he saying about James and what does he mean, 'care'? What did that mean? She stretched away from him to check the stain on the shirt, to distract him so she could collect her thoughts better. She needed time.

'Oh dear, I'm not sure this is coming out! Do you have others to replace it?'

He absently pulled the shirt from her and frowned.

'Another shirt destroyed, ah well, don't worry about it. Yes, I can have another made,' he murmured.

A destroyed shirt, what about a destroyed life, she thought to herself. She was in a state of disbelief. What was he saying about her husband and about her life? She saw him looking at the shirt, he was thinking of something else, and then, she herself, looked at the shirt again.

A destroyed shirt. There was another destroyed shirt. Did she stain one of James' shirts?

She blinked and then she grasped at the memory, small pieces of remembered moments and conversations fluttering closer. It couldn't be. She leaned forward and looked at the hem of his shirt. Her eyes widened, then focused and just like that, she remembered...cotton embroidery, rock solid....and she knew.

Chapter 35 - Escape

'Thomas, Maisy saw that face and that car, the morning of my mother's death!' They were headed towards the stairs from her bedroom.

'How do you know that?'

'That's the day I gave Maisy the bunny. I gave her that bunny as a little gift in the morning. It was a sample I'd brought from work the night before. On the day of mother's death, I woke Maisy up, gave her the bunny, and then left early for work.'

'I don't get it.'

'On that Wednesday when I left early, there was no other car in sight. Colin then took Maisy to school. There would have been no red car at that time because Edward would have noted that. Then, later in the morning Colin left to pick up Maisy from school because as you know, she was ill. While Colin was gone, you came to the house to see my mother....did you see a red car?'

He shook his head.

'Edward, who knows everything that is going on, is also not at the house later in the morning. Why? He has left for your home to talk to you about the argument with my mother. He walked and waited at your house for you in case you returned. He could have been gone, maybe two hours?'

Thomas was watching her determined eyes.

'And they think mother died sometime around her swim or anytime up to an hour or two after. The only time Maisy would have seen the red car is first thing in the morning, which is impossible based on what I've just said, OR when she came home that day, in the late morning with her father...'

She put her hands to her face, and rubbed her eyes, trying to organise the thoughts racing through her mind.

'Thomas, that car can only belong to one person. Maisy has always been peculiar about his face, although it was such a long time ago,' her mouth tightened into an angry line.

'I think we may have a problem here, Thomas. What if Richard was at the house when my mother died? What if....'

'Oh boy,' he ran his hands through his hair, thoughts were whirling round his brain. Richard did have a red sports car.

'You're thinking it must be his car, and his face peeking from behind the garden wall, on the day your mother died,' he picked up her baton of thought as their minds both raced to the finishing conclusion, 'and that Maisy saw this and painted this scene. Colin would have known he was at the house too, of course, but he may not have spotted Richard in the garden.'

'Why was Richard in the garden - he never goes in the garden when he's here. You're right, for sure Colin would have known he was here - his car was right there for all to see - but only Maisy and he were there to see it!' Katherine whispered harshly.

They heard a noise, it sounded as if Maisy had shifted in her bed. Their whispers were too loud. Thomas motioned Katherine to follow him downstairs.

In the kitchen, he got straight to the point. A thought had occurred to him.

'Anjali is alone with Richard tonight. If he's dangerous, I think we need to tell her to leave, safely, now,' he was forceful. 'Here I was, worried that Richard possibly had some lecherous desire for Anjali, but he may be much, much worse than that!'

'You think Anjali could be in danger, because we've placed him here at the house on the day of the accident? That he could have been involved in my mother's death and may be dangerous to Anjali? I'm not sure we should scare her. Richard has only ever been professional towards Anjali. He would have hit on her long ago. He's not one to wait for what he wants. And I can't see what that has to do with solving my Mother's death, Thomas. Why do you think he is interested in Anjali?'

'I happened to see them going to lunch together on Wednesday. He was holding her too close for my liking, but that's his style, so I didn't bother saying anything to James. Look I'm not saying he's dangerous to Anjali but I'm not willing to take a risk. She shouldn't be there with him if we know he was here that morning.'

Katherine paced in the kitchen. 'I've been suspicious of James and you think Anjali is at risk because Richard is a sexual predator and now Richard is in the frame for my mother's death. And there's still a huge question mark over Colin. This isn't real life, Thomas. Are we over-dramatising this?'

Thomas absently put his hands to his temples and pressed them.

'Look, I don't think we should be taking any chances, it doesn't matter how ridiculous this is, and that's coming from a pragmatist. Let's think this through. We'll need to get in touch with Anjali and James for sure.'

'Anjali is the priority. Why don't I text Anjali, or call her? Thomas, what do you think? She'll have to get out of the hotel on her own, it's too far for any of us to get there in decent time. And for James, I know how you feel about him, but I'm not sure we should alert him. I still don't trust why he was here on Wednesday and didn't tell any of us. Don't forget, Edward suspected James in the death in some way.'

'Alright, we'll leave James for now. Let's sort Anjali.'

They decided a text to Anjali that didn't divulge too much would be safer - so as not to put Anjali at risk if she said something that would alarm Richard. Or indeed, if he saw the text. They both hoped that Anjali was already in her own room at the hotel, and that their suspicions were wildly incorrect.

Katherine texted: 'Hi Anjali, sorry to bother you. If you're still up, can you ring? It's urgent. Re my problem and the cotton fabric. Can you leave asap to help? Important. Katherine'.

They thought it could work.

'Thomas, why don't we wait fifteen minutes or so and see if Anjali texts back. She may be safely in her room and we're taking this out of all proportion. If she doesn't, we can get the hotel to put a call through to her room to catch her there. We should think about involving the police tomorrow. They will hopefully interview Richard. Plus, Colin should be back tomorrow or Sunday - they'll need to see Colin as well. James should also be interviewed, although I know you don't believe he could do anything harmful to anyone.' Katherine's mind was running a million miles and she was talking too quickly.

Thomas looked unhappy. 'Katherine, we should contact the police now. We are aware of another person near the scene of the crime. And neither he nor Colin mentioned that to the police.'

'No, let's give it 15 minutes to hear back from Anjali.' She was reluctant to involve the police too early, as they had already waved her concerns away. A thought dawned on her. 'You know, we didn't find a match in Colin's wardrobe, and we were done by the time Maisy screamed.'

'What does that mean?'

'Well, Colin could have the double of that shirt in Shanghai, or that second piece of cotton could match someone else's shirt. Someone who wears those luxury shirts.'

He knew who she was referring to, and it could make sense now, given Maisy's outburst.

'I can't see Richard having embroidery on his shirts, Katherine.'

Katherine wasn't so sure. Richard liked good design, and a flourish of embroidery would suit him to a tee.

~ ~ ~ ~ ~ ~ ~ ~ ~ ~

Richard had pushed his stained shirt away, not interested anymore and was waiting for her to ask questions. He caught her staring intently at the hem of his shirt, and smiled that she could appreciate his taste.

'Nice, right?' he asked.

She tore her eyes away from the hem as she replied, 'Yes....' She couldn't do small talk, not after what he had just told her, and not after the connection her memory had just made.

Her phone bleeped in her handbag. She looked around to locate her purse. There it was, over on the main table in his room. She got up quickly and moved towards it.

'Yes, in fact, exclusively hand-embroidered. My personal monogram. Hey, you're not answering a text at this hour, are you?'

He was getting restless and was aching for her body. He didn't want her phone to distract her and a message at this hour could only be bad news, the children, maybe?

'Yes, just a moment, it might be about the children,' she steadied herself as she walked to the other table, finding her mobile in her small purse. With her back to him, she read the text, and knew instantly something was wrong: why did Katherine want her to leave immediately?

She tried to keep her body still so Richard wouldn't suspect anything. Her eyes widened - could Katherine know about the cotton? She sucked in her breath as quietly as she could. Richard's shirt almost surely put him at the scene of the accident. Oh, God, she doesn't want me here. And, I don't want to be here.

Her mind felt hyper active and fatigued at the same time. What was going on! How do I get out? She squashed a nauseous feeling rising in her stomach. She spoke as calmly as she could.

'Oh dear, Katherine has an issue about some cotton for a new design. I'll just make this call quickly. You know her creativity runs even at late hours!' She needed to keep it light and relevant to the text, lest Richard check her phone. She was nervous now.

Richard tensed. He was almost in his dream world, so close to being with her. But there was something about her tone that alarmed him. He couldn't let her speak to Katherine now. What if Anjali divulged what he'd said regarding James. Katherine would surely advise her to speak to James first before she believed anything from Richard, and to go to bed. He didn't trust Katherine, she was too, too aware of his type, compared to Anjali.

'Text her back, Anjali, we have a lot to go over still.'

Anjali could sense a shift in his mood. He seemed pressed and anxious. And it was a command, not a suggestion.

'There are my questions regarding your business case and I'm sure you have questions about James,' he paused, 'and there's the matter of us. There's a lot to discover between you and me.' His eyes were changed. They were slightly menacing, and challenging. That nausea came waving through her again. Then he smiled at her. He licked his lower lip, bit it coyly and looked at her. It was an open invitation.

She was horrified. Was he actually coming on to her? Is that what the evening had been about? Panic mingled with her nausea and she felt her dinner lurch.

She suspected him of murder. Murder! He divulged hugely inflammatory information about her husband, which she didn't understand, and he was coming on to her! What had she done to encourage that?

She had to leave, that was certain. What if she tried to leave, would he stop her? She couldn't believe he was involved in the accident but the 'rock solid' comment and the matching fabric couldn't be coincidence. Did he murder Katherine's mother? Could he murder more than once?

I need to play it safe. Her mind was groggy and grasping for answers.

'Yes, of course. We need to talk. I'll quickly text Katherine rather than call her. Just a moment.'

Richard relaxed. Back on track. He thought she might bolt.

Anjali knew she had to move fast, tread carefully, and keep the communication line open with Katherine. God, if Katherine only knew what she had just figured out.

She replied: 'Can't talk now. I have the fabric match. Understand urgency. Will call you.'

Hopefully, if Richard saw her text he wouldn't suspect she was trying to leave – or was it escape?

There, it was sent. She felt relief. Now, to get out.

Richard was watching her. 'Right, come on over here, and let's pick up where we left off,' he was gracious but his voice was salacious. He was patting the sofa seat beside him.

It was so obvious now. How could she have been so stupid? Anjali's heart was pounding. Her senses became super sharp despite the alcohol. She heard her rising heartbeat in her ears and her mouth was dry again. She couldn't let him see her panic. She needed to find a way out.

An inner voice was telling her to fake it; to keep him on-side and then leave when he least suspected it - so that he couldn't stop her. But she was too desperate to leave and could barely look at him. The fact that he could be a murderer seemed so distant, the reality of what was happening now, seemed worse. He was seducing her and she had to get out.

'Hey, why don't we call it quits for the night?'

A shadow fell over his face.

'In fact, I can stay a bit longer in the morning, and cover your queries then, how does that work?'

He swiftly sat forward from the sofa. 'It doesn't work, Anjali. That isn't going to work. Now, why don't you come back here and we can continue as planned?'

He looked aggressively at her. There was no way she could run to the door and get there before him. No way. She'd have to walk past him in any case.

Surely she was overreacting. She would casually leave, he certainly wouldn't stop her? This was Richard, after all. She decided to try.

'Actually, Richard, I had such a wonderful night, and we've done so much work already, I really do need to retire now. The evening was very nice, thank you.'

She steadied her nerves and walked past him to reach the hallway of his suite.

She didn't dare breath.

He jumped up aggressively as she tried to pass. His body blocked her and he pushed her down firmly to the sofa, hurting her shoulder.

'Uh, Richard,' his sudden aggression caught her off guard. Her heart pounding, she rubbed her shoulder, trying to repress her fear.

'No, Anjali, you need to stay right here for a bit and rest. You look unsteady on your feet and .... relax, eh?'

He sat beside her and reached for his champagne.

She didn't dare move. How could he switch to this stranger – this person she didn't recognise? She had never felt so powerless; her authority and her right to leave had alarmingly disappeared in the face of a few minutes. This was more than bullying behaviour.

He took a gulp of champagne, seemed to decide something and set down his glass. He turned towards her quickly placing his hands firmly on her shoulders, pinning her to the sofa, before she realised what was happening.

'Relax...' his voice was gruff with emotion.

She was frozen.

How, she didn't know; but in an instant her mind understood what was required to escape. He wasn't letting her go. Her instincts took over.

She sighed suggestively and edged herself closer to him, pushing into his leg and thigh. She hated it. She could see him suppress a small grin.

She just needed him to sit back so she could grab a moment to think through her next steps.

Let him talk so you can think, that inner voice told her.

As uncomfortable as the subject was, Anjali looked meekly at him and gently nudged his arms off her shoulders. In a simpering, feminine voice she asked, 'Richard, I'm so upset about what you've told me regarding James, is it possible?'

Caught off-guard, he pulled away to look at her. Ah, she understands now, about James.

'Yes, Anjali, I'm sorry to be the one to tell you. But you understand, I'll take care of you...' he felt his aggressive passion abate to something more like tenderness. He put his bare arm around her, and pulled her onto his hairless chest.

She shut down her reactions and managed to control a disgusted shiver as her cheek touched his chest. Was it possible that what he said about James wasn't true? Richard said the evidence was all there - would Richard lie to her in order to win her over? Why was she so fixated on James when Richard could actually have been instrumental in the death of Katherine's mother?

She needed out. She needed to get to safety given what she now suspected. It was a balancing act, but she couldn't play this charade for too long. Her stomach was churning with sick feelings and it wasn't from the alcohol.

'Richard, this is too much to take in. I'm so disappointed in James. I feel nauseous. I should focus on something else for a short while. Then I can relax. Why don't I go through your questions? It will calm my stomach. And then, we can relax somewhere, perhaps, more comfortable,' peeling her cheek from his skin, she felt disgusting. She looked up at him, ensuring her eyes were soft and pleading.

'Of course, of course, I understand,' he replied gently. He trusted himself totally to get her in the right place. It just better not take too long.

She picked up the list of questions.

'The most challenging one,' she made as if to be wiping a tear away. If she was going to pull this off she would have to be pretty convincing, 'is question five – about the projected profit line.'

The effect of fake crying wasn't lost on Richard. He leaned forward to take advantage of the moment and embrace her again. He had a cunning, one track mind.

How he'd get her there in the end, through aggression or emotion, didn't really matter, he knew she would love it regardless. They all did, but she was his special one, she represented so much.

Moving his arms around her small waist and with possessive kisses on her shoulder he murmured, 'It's ok, Anjali, don't cry.'

He grinned as he kissed her. His adversary was well and truly trashed now, she definitely believed James was in trouble. He could comfort her, he always knew he would do, it had just been a matter of time. And she would stay now, for sure. She would stay the night and he would show her how much he wanted her. God, she was adorable and clever, but innocent. She was perfect. But she couldn't be nauseous, they had to get rid of that.

'As you say, let's just focus on these numbers,' and he drew his finger from her shoulder, down her arm to where she was holding the document.

She halted a flinch; her instant reaction was to pull away, but she managed to breathe in slowly and keep her body relaxed although her core was tight with repulsion. Keep him focused on work...

'I'm a bit hazy right now on the figures,' she twisted sideways and looked at him from under her eyelashes, 'shall I get my laptop from my room? It has all the details,' she gave him a shy smile, keeping her breathing slow to control her fright.

God, what was she like! His emotion was raw now, and it was getting difficult to focus on anything but her. He read her slowed breathing for passion. Alright – let's take the game one step further, he grinned deliciously. Let her get her laptop, we'll keep this game up for just a little bit longer...

'Yes of course,' then he instinctively looked at her mobile on the far table.

She smiled as calmly as she could.

'Don't worry I won't be distracted. I'll leave my mobile here,' and she very casually extracted herself, she didn't want to shatter his moment of trust.

She rested her hand on his cheek for a second, and smiled coquettishly at him. Keep his trust. Leaving her purse and mobile would reassure him she wasn't going anywhere. But her room fob was in her purse! Then she remembered he had dropped it on the hallway table when they first arrived. She needed to be sure he thought she was returning.

She stroked his cheek briefly.

'I'll be back to cover our,' she paused and finished in a softly sensual voice, 'business together.'

And then she was moving away from the sofa, backing away from him, before he could embrace her again. Keeping her eyes pinned to his face, she carefully felt for her hotel fob then picked it up from the hallway table close to the door.

He was completely aroused and greedy for what would come next.

She kept his eyes as long as she could. She didn't want to break the moment, fearful that he might stop her again. She had to leave the room. The whole situation was unbearable. She was at the door.

She grabbed the handle, and keeping her eyes on him, opened door. It was heavy. Only partially opening it, she slipped through, sure he would be on her heels.

She glanced sideways towards his door, too worried he'd be following, but he wasn't there.

And she was out.

Chapter 36 - Answers

They both jumped when the mobile beeped. Two heads crammed over the small screen to read the reply.

'Oh my God, she knows. Do you think she's telling us that Richard has a shirt that matches? How can she know that - but I'm sure that's what she's saying. Why can't she talk?' Katherine panicked.

'She needs an out, Thomas. We need to get her out of there. She's obviously still with Richard or she'd call,' she put her hands to her mouth.

'Ok, we call the police now.' Thomas' voice was calm and authoritative.

'I'll ring the Inspector, he gave me his mobile in case I had any queries or further evidence. He'll know what to do for Anjali. And maybe he'll take us seriously now that we have all this evidence, including the money involved,' Katherine replied. 'I'll text Anjali back, to let her know help is coming...'

'Be careful, let's get the Inspector on the phone first. He'll advise us. Will he answer even at this hour?'

'He told me any time of day, 24/7, his words exactly. He said that's the reality of his profession.'

Katherine raced to her handbag and found his mobile number. Her heart hung in her throat as it rang and rang. No answer. She tried again.

This time, on the fifth ring, he picked up. 'Inspector Budd.'

'Hello Inspector, it's Katherine here. My mother died recently - an accident on the river at our house. I apologise for calling you at such a late hour, but I need help urgently.'

The controlled panic in her voice had him on alert, 'Katherine, tell me where you are.'

'Yes, it's not me, it's help for my friend at the Mandarin Oriental Hotel, Hyde Park in London. It's urgent, this is what I know.'

~ ~ ~ ~ ~ ~ ~ ~ ~ ~

It took a few minutes to give the Inspector the main details. He already had involved others by the end of the call, and they in turn had began the process to deploy local police in the area. Before anything else, he agreed that they had to secure Anjali.

'We're heading out now to your house. We won't be much longer than half an hour or so. Call immediately if there's any news from Anjali. The police unit close to the Mandarin Oriental are on this already.'

~ ~ ~ ~ ~ ~ ~ ~ ~ ~

That soft ping of the elevator, as if everything was peaceful with the world. The doors opened to the ground floor. She tried to walk calmly but quickly across the luxurious reception. The receptionist nodded at her.

'Good evening, may I help you?'

Anjali shook her head and smiled faintly. The doorman held the door open for her. The cold air hit her like a wall, and then she was out.

She picked up her gait as she walked towards the sidewalk. She looked back once at the Mandarin Oriental. He wasn't there, and the doorman had gone back inside.

She turned and ran.

She had read about people running for their lives, and now she knew what it felt like. It was so late, there were no taxis, and she didn't trust the concierge at Richard's hotel to call a taxi and keep it confidential. Richard was powerful, and on friendly terms it seemed, with most senior people at the hotel. Who knew what the concierge would say if asked. She decided to run to the hotels further down the road and headed for their bright lights.

~ ~ ~ ~ ~ ~ ~ ~ ~ ~

Anjali had been away from the room for a little while, perhaps 5 minutes. Richard had lost track of time, as he himself had been side-tracked by some messages on his mobile. Where was she? Her mobile was with him, so he called her room directly from his hotel phone.

~ ~ ~ ~ ~ ~ ~ ~ ~ ~

Katherine was waiting to hear from Anjali and for an update from the police. Following the Inspector's earlier instructions, Thomas was calling Colin's hotel, to talk directly to reception. It was necessary that he locate Colin.

Katherine's mobile rang. She and Thomas looked at the phone with expectation.

'I don't know that number, it's a London number,' she stated cautiously.

She answered. 'Hello?'

~ ~ ~ ~ ~ ~ ~ ~ ~ ~

Thomas was waiting on his phone call for Colin's hotel to answer. The hotel suddenly picked up.

'Hello, can you put me through to the following person, and if there's no answer, may you please go directly to check the room. I've not heard from my brother for several days now, and there are family matters I must discuss.'

Thomas gave them his brother's details. The hotel confirmed that he was still staying there, and had not checked out. They put him through, but the phone rang out and then the hotel answering machine kicked in.

Hotel reception intercepted the call. 'He doesn't seem to be in. We will knock on his door, not a problem, can you hold on the phone, or would you like us to call you back?'

'I'll hold,' Thomas was firm, and he locked eyes with Katherine.

~ ~ ~ ~ ~ ~ ~ ~ ~ ~

There was static at the other end of the line. Katherine couldn't make out who it was, and was also trying to listen to Thomas on his call.

'Hello, who is this?' She asked again.

Finally, the line cleared.

'Hello! Katherine! It's Anjali,' she was sobbing.

'Anjali! Oh my God. Are you ok? Where are you?!'

'Yes, yes, I'm at a hotel down the street. I've convinced them to let me use the reception phone - only because I showed them my Mandarin Oriental fob, and explained I'd had a marital issue. They've called me a taxi - I don't know where to go to. I, I don't trust Richard, I think he was there, Katherine, at the river. I don't know what that means, but he must have been there. And he knows about your mother's note. And he told me such terrible, terrible things about James - that James lied to me, and he falsified information, that his company is in financial chaos, and he made a pass at me and I feel, I feel so disgusting...' she was completely panicked.

'Anjali, it's ok now. You're safe. Ask the taxi to bring you here, the police are coming to the house as well. Please don't trust anything Richard has said. Where's your mobile?'

'I had to leave it and my handbag with Richard. Ok, yes,' she was pulling herself together and talking to someone at the other end, 'the taxi is here now Katherine. The taxi is here, I'll head to your place, but I'll have to let James know.'

'Anjali, can you ask the taxi driver to let you use his mobile once you're in the taxi. And that we'll pay for that when you get here. We need to know you're safely in the taxi. The police will want to talk to you to understand what Richard said about James, and then they'll advise us what the next best steps are. So please don't call James until the police have spoken to you.'

'Ok, ok,' and she was sobbing again.

'Anjali are you ok? Are you hurt?' Did he hurt her?

'No, no, it's just, Katherine, it's all so terrible!'

Katherine was calculating in her mind, that it could be a few hours before James knew what was happening. She debated whether that was the right thing to do or not, but in her mind, James was still not in the clear, and she couldn't take any chances with Anjali talking to him. Whatever did Richard say about James?

'Yes, Anjali, it's all hard to understand, we'll talk when you're in the taxi. You're safe now. Head to your taxi, lock the doors safely, and call me immediately,' she didn't want to delay Anjali any further.

~ ~ ~ ~ ~ ~ ~ ~ ~ ~

Anjali thanked the reception for their assistance and moved quickly through the swinging doors. The doorman was standing with the door of the taxi open. She slumped into the back seat and pulled her long and shaking legs into the taxi. The doorman wished her a good night, and she managed a small smile then pulled herself up and leaned forward to talk to the driver.

She gave the address of Katherine's Cotswold manor.

'M'am that's pretty far and it's late. Are you sure that's the right address? It could take a few hours with detours on some of the roads. And this is well outside of London, the charge will be for there and back.'

'Pardon?' She was in another world. 'Yes, really I understand. It's not a problem. Let's go, please,' and she arranged to use the taxi driver's mobile. She rang Katherine to say she was in the taxi and leaving.

'Ok, Anjali, thank goodness. The police are on their way to the Mandarin Oriental, to question Richard. Did I understand your text correctly: that the cotton fabric we found by the river, the one floating on the breeze when we were together, that fabric and the embroidery on it matches a shirt Richard has?' Katherine knew everything hung in the balance, depending upon Anjali's reply.

Anjali's head was thrown back a bit as the taxi driver sped off, and she could hear police sirens from behind. She turned around, eyes wide open, and still fearful, to see police lights flashing from the direction she had just run.

'Oh, Katherine, I think the police are there already.' She took a deep breath, 'Yes, I can't be 100% certain, but it looked very, very similar. I believe the fabric we found that day is actually a ripped piece of cotton from one of Richard's shirts, and the embroidery, well it's actually a very small section of his embroidered monogram.' Her voice was shaky.

'Oh God. Ok. Anjali, the police want to speak to you urgently. What's the mobile number so they can ring you?'

Anjali gave her the number, and they hung up, so the police could ring.

~~~~~~~~~~

Katherine called the Inspector and explained that Anjali was already out, and on her way to the manor. She recited the mobile number.

There was relief in his voice. 'I'll call her immediately.'

Katherine took a moment to hold her tears in check. Anjali was safe.

~ ~ ~ ~ ~ ~ ~ ~ ~ ~

'Hello sir, I'm afraid there's no answer when we knock at the door.' The hotel reception reported back to Thomas.

Thomas knew what had to happen next. He was under instructions from the Inspector who was very clear on establishing fact.

'I'll need to call the police to assist me, if you cannot get hold of your guest. I'm now concerned about his safety and welfare. Please enter my brother's room to check on him, whether he's in need of help, and whether his personal items are still there.' He paused and then to emphasise the seriousness of the situation said, 'I'm deeply concerned and am involved with the police here, to reach my brother.'

'Sir, I shall put you on hold to discuss this with my Manager, just one moment please.'

Thomas put the phone on hands free, so that both he and Katherine could hear. They waited a painfully long several minutes.

'Ok sir, we will check on our guest. Are you alright to hold again?'

'Yes, thank you,' replied Thomas.

Katherine's mobile rang. It was the Inspector's number.

'Hello Katherine. I'm outside your front door now.'

'They're here,' she said to Thomas. She left him and rushed to let the Inspector in. Opening the door, she was surprised at the number of police cars outside. The reality of the situation dawned on her at that moment. She took a moment to look up at the dark sky and shook her head, wondering at the turn reality had taken tonight.

'Hello Katherine, good evening. Inspector Budd, pleased to meet you.'

His voice was calm and matter of fact. She shook his hand firmly, thanking him for his immediate response. She showed him and several other policemen into the kitchen and explained Thomas was on hold with the Shanghai hotel, pointing to the house phone. The phone was on speaker setting, and a calm surreal Chinese flute piece was playing.

The Inspector nodded.

'We've apprehended Richard now. And they also have the stained shirt and Anjali's purse and mobile. There was no struggle, the hotel was very helpful. They didn't want a scene,' he smiled, familiar with such situations.

'We also are with James at his home,' he paused. Katherine and Thomas hung on his next words. 'I arranged for plain-clothed police officers to question him. They are with him right now; I've just come off the phone with my detective there. They know what to ask him,' he said confidently.

'What has James said?' Thomas asked.

'I'm afraid we need to wait until I hear back fully from the team there. They've only just arrived there. Suffice it to say he was completely shocked and frightened. We didn't mention his wife at this point. He thinks she's still at the hotel working, or sleeping, I guess,' as he looked at the time.

He saw the pained look on Thomas' face and thought to provide some information.

'For someone who is a suspect, the team have said they've never seen anyone act so innocently,' he raised his eyebrows at them. 'So he's either an extremely good actor or completely unaware of the suspicions he has caused,' and just then an authoritative voice came back on the phone.

'Sir, we have unfortunate news to give to you. But we think we should wait until the police arrive, to provide further details.'

Katherine gasped and looked with panic to the Inspector. He indicated to both of them that he would take over.

'Sir, this is the police speaking from England. I'm also here, with your guest's brother and wife. We will require the details immediately,' he paused only for a fraction, nodding at one of his colleagues who had opened up his laptop at the kitchen bar, 'tell me what you know now, and we'll ensure that the reputation of your hotel is kept intact.'

The Inspector knew that the hotel had no obligation to share private information with him – a person the hotel couldn't verify over the phone. But threatening the reputation of a hotel was an excellent way to secure information.

'Just one moment, sir,' was the reply. They waited.

Within a minute, the voice returned to the phone. 'We have checked the hotel forms, and there's an emergency number to contact, should there be an issue. It says here,' and there was a pause as the person must have been trying to interpret a scribble, '...wife. I'll call this number, and if you do not hear from me, you are free to call back and also work with the local police. Thank you for taking the reputation of our hotel into consideration.'

Katherine piped up, whispering to the Inspector, 'Maybe it's my mobile, do they know the area code for England?'

'Sir, I appreciate your assistance. The number will most likely be a UK-based number, are you aware of the area code?'

'Yes, yes of course, thank you,' and the line went dead, as the speaker hung up.

They looked at each other. Before anyone could say anything, Katherine's mobile rang. The Inspector nodded at her to answer it, herself.

Katherine picked up the mobile. 'Hello?' She said.

'Yes, this is,' she answered.

She waited a few seconds, and turned pale. She closed her eyes, and then opened them responding, 'Yes, I understand. Just a moment please.'

She looked at Thomas and the Inspector.

'The man in that room is dead. They think Colin is dead,' she gasped for a breath and her mobile slipped to the counter.

A guttural sound came from Thomas as he moved quickly to hold her. She leaned on him.

'I'm sorry for you,' the Inspector said and he quickly picked up her phone.

'This is the Inspector again, we spoke moments ago,' he paused as they gave him more information. 'Yes, I understand. And the police are arriving? Please provide the details so that we can be directly in touch. Yes, just a moment please,' he turned the mobile on mute and turned to face them both.

'They have not confirmed the dead man to be Colin. They could tell me that the individual may have been dead for a few days. Apparently, his face may not be easily recognisable and I'm trying to ascertain why. They have said it could be an accident. This is the hotel staff, not the police, of course. This is all I know now.'

He looked at his two colleagues on their laptops and mobiles. 'We'll need to manage this sensitively. My colleagues will be working with other police units, and due to the international nature of this, with foreign affairs and the Consulate in Shanghai.'

Katherine pulled away from Thomas and looked at him, barely able to see him through her tears.

What was happening to her family? 'Do you think the individual is Colin?' she pulled a brave face and looked at both Thomas and the Inspector.

Thomas looked to the Inspector first before answering. The Inspector also was interested in his reply.

'Look, Katherine. We know how forgetful Colin is about answering our messages. It's possible that he's fine somewhere else,' Thomas tried to comfort her. He also wanted to believe this.

The Inspector watched them both, then his attention was drawn back to the mobile as he was told something else. He didn't hear what they said. He took the phone off mute and put it on speaker. 'Could you repeat that please?'

'Yes, Sir, of course. We have secured the passport. The police are here and they found the passport in his briefcase. I'm very sorry, Sir. They have just identified him as our guest, Colin.'

Katherine gasped and Thomas hugged her more tightly. She hid her face in his chest. Thomas' mouth was turned down and he gave a shocked look to the Inspector who studied them both.

'And,' the speaker seemed to be muffling the phone with his hand. They could still hear a harsh exchange in Chinese between the speaker and others with him.

'So sorry now, Sir, so sorry. I wasn't supposed to tell you that. Our police here say this is confidential. I must hang up now.'

'Wait, wait,' the Inspector quickly jutted in, 'can you put a police officer who speaks English on the phone?'

'Sir, no, I've been advised that our police will be in touch with the Consulate. May I take your number, they are asking for your number.'

The Inspector provided his number and despite his efforts for more information, they hung up.

Katherine turned her face so it wasn't hidden anymore and her eyes looked vacantly into the room. From where she was standing she could see a photo on the kitchen shelf of the three of them: her, with Maisy and Colin, smiling.

Her eyes began to swell up. She'd managed somehow to keep her emotions in check but tears were beginning to blur the edges of her vision. Her life as she understood it, was disappearing.

'Katherine, shall we bring the Inspector up to speed, on what you've found?' Thomas gently prompted her. Despite his shock, he knew the facts were still, very important. 'Are you ok to do that?' He pulled away carefully to check her face.

'Yes, of course,' Katherine wiped her eyes.

'I'll be just a moment, I have a few items to collect, actually,' she felt extremely sad but oddly her heart was beating. She was hopeful. Maybe this time the Inspector would consider her concerns about her mother's death. But now there was Colin. She had loved him so much. What about Maisy?

Colin! She screamed inside her head. What had he done and what had happened to him? She shuddered. What did they mean about his face?

Chapter 37 - Resolved?

Katherine stood at the front door, watching the lights of Anjali's taxi approach in the distance. She and Thomas had been in contact with her at various points throughout the trip. It had taken almost 2.5 hours with construction on the roads and she was almost at the house now, safe.

In that time, Katherine's evidence had proved to be extremely valuable to the police. The Inspector was still in the kitchen with Thomas discussing the events leading up to both deaths. The kitchen was buzzing with police talking on their mobiles to colleagues, video conferencing or working intently on their laptops.

Katherine moved quickly down the outside stairs as Anjali emerged from the taxi.

'Anjali!'

'Katherine, oh, I'm so, so sorry,' and they hugged each other tightly. Thomas had told Anjali about Colin on the taxi trip to Katherine's home.

Katherine gave her a thin smile. 'Let's get you inside. The police have a few things to talk to us about.' She gave Anjali an encouraging squeeze of the arm, but left the unstated hanging in the air.

Anjali looped her arm in Katherine's. 'That's fine,' but she was desperate to talk to James. Up till now, she'd been told not to. What was that about?

~ ~ ~ ~ ~ ~ ~ ~ ~ ~

The kitchen was a hive of activity; several different conversations were happening at the same time. The Inspector saw the two of them arrive at the kitchen door and indicated to a colleague to hang on. He walked towards them.

'Hello, Anjali,' he solemnly shook hands with her. 'I'm very happy to see you here. Come and take a seat while we talk you through a few things.' He looked around for an appropriate place to sit.

'Let's go into mother's study. It's quieter there,' suggested Katherine. The Inspector waved to catch Thomas' attention and asked that he follow them. He turned to his team and said, 'I'm looking to wrap this up here – thirty minutes to an hour – then we'll take this back to the office.'

They headed to the study and the three of them sat quickly, eager for the Inspector to update them. He addressed Anjali first. His voice was calm and reassuring.

'I'm sorry that we asked you to refrain from speaking to your husband. We realise how difficult that must have been for you. Thank you for supporting the investigation in this way,' he nodded seriously at her.

He then addressed all three of them, 'Thanks to the information we've secured over the last hour, we can confirm that James is no longer implicated in the death of Katherine's mother, nor in Edward's accident.'

'What? Oh my God, Katherine?' Shocked, Anjali pushed forward in her chair and looked at Katherine for an explanation.

Katherine was so relieved, but the situation was still serious. Even now she couldn't smile at her friend. 'It's ok Anjali, there was some confusion for a while. Please don't worry, I think the Inspector can tell us more.'

Anjali fell back into the chair and covered her eyes, trying to hold her tears to a minimum. Thomas looked emotional. He stood up and moved behind Anjali's chair, putting his hands on her shoulders. He and Katherine exchanged looks and the sense of relief was palatable.

'As well, we've determined why James visited your mother several times and was so agitated on his last visit, the week of her death. And more recently, we know why he was here, on Wednesday morning this week, the day of Edward's accident.

'Your mother, Katherine, overheard a conversation between Richard and Colin. We know this, because Edward mentions it in his notes. James told us this as well, tonight.' He looked at Anjali and gave her a comforting smile.

'It's been difficult to piece this together as she told James and Edward slightly different, although truthful, versions. She informed James that she overheard Richard talking to Colin about an energy company. Richard had said that a green energy company was 'on his books' in other words, part of his portfolio, and that he was going to take it over. But he needed Colin's contacts to help productise the green energy technology. It was clear from the conversation that these contacts were Chinese.

'She also told James that Richard was waiting on Colin's financial part of the deal. Colin owed a significant cash investment into the acquisition in order for the full deal to go through. She explained to James that she also was poised to invest hefty capital into the deal herself. Colin had advised her the return was 'indisputable', with modern, sustainable green credentials in the energy sector. It was this latter attribute that lured her in.

'James told us tonight that she communicated two worries to him on the Monday before her death. The first being that the producer of this emerging technology, post acquisition, would be Chinese and she wanted James' views on this; she didn't know whether such an arrangement would be unlawful - given that she understood the technology could be a valuable, national asset. She believed James could advise her on the national importance of this technology. Her concern was that the deal could be scrutinised by the new government watchdog - quite rightly - but she didn't want a risky investment like that.

'The second worry she shared with James, was that in recent conversation with Colin, the technology sounded alarmingly close to the technology James was developing at his own company. James had shared some high level information about his green energy tech with her, during their early meetings on sustainable, green energy. She posed a question to James: was there a possibility that the company

Richard and Colin were in the process of taking over was one and the same as E2E, James' company?'

The room was tense. Katherine had moved to the chair beside Anjali to hold her hand, and Thomas had a hand on each woman's shoulder. The developments were frightening and the suspense intoxicating, despite the macabre context of the situation.

'James explained tonight that he was deeply concerned about both of these pieces of information. Edward was correct in his notes; James was agitated, very agitated that week of your mother's death. James told us that on the back of that conversation he advised your mother to tread very carefully. He also immediately contacted his current investor, who was at the time, trying to buy his company outright. He booked an all-day session for later in the week, in fact the Wednesday; the very day of your mother's death. Feeling it would be a highly sensitive meeting, he didn't want his colleagues or Anjali to know about this. Edward's notes were right. That is why James wasn't at the office or his house on the morning of your mother's death.

'At this meeting James challenged his current investor, a VC firm. Given they wanted to buy his company outright, or be majority shareholder, he queried the ownership structure, who the parent company was and whether there was any connection to Richard's company and Colin. He was assured there was no connection. He also sought reassurances from the VC firm that his company's technology would stay in the UK. Katherine's mother had worried him.

'James had strong views about keeping the technology of such national importance, in the country. He was told not to worry, that such a situation wouldn't happen. However, the current investor would still not write this into the contract.

'This bothered him, but he didn't pursue it because in the days following your mother's death, another financing option had emerged. In light of the situation, James decided to focus on this new opportunity and negotiate financing with them. More on this in a moment.

'By the way, he also never took up an offer of investment from your mother. In his own words, 'he prefers not to mix family and friends with business'. Wise approach, I think, no?'

The Inspector paused to shift legs and move on to the next piece of the puzzle.

Katherine was listening wide-eyed, but kept checking Anjali, whose jaw was slightly ajar. She was evidently shocked about the revelations.

'To finish with James as a suspect. Yes, he went to visit Edward this Wednesday morning. He knew about Edward's investment acumen and visited to seek his advice. James was very close to completing his company's financing deal, and he had a few final items he wanted to check with Edward, as someone he could trust. We already had confirmation on that front from Edward, earlier today.'

'Oh!' An instant reaction from both Katherine and Anjali.

'Is Edward better?!' Katherine asked.

'Does this mean James isn't implicated in any of this?' Anjali's question merged with Katherine's.

'He isn't, that's right,' the Inspector nodded at Anjali, 'and yes, Edward is much better,' he smiled at Katherine. 'Edward contacted us from the hospital earlier today. Edward does have traces of drugs, but he was well enough today to clarify with us via a phone call that he was taking medication for treatment of anxiety. He's been taking these tablets, unfortunately, since the death of your mother,' the Inspector looked sympathetically at Katherine.

Katherine shook her head and caught Thomas' eye. He was frowning.

'I see,' Katherine said, 'So thank heavens, no foul play regarding Edward's health? Why did he call the police then?'

'No, it seems very unlikely at this time that there is any foul play. Edward was pleased that Thomas was staying at your house, Katherine, but still very concerned about your security. Concerned enough to ring us directly.' He saw Katherine's concerned face, and eyebrows rise. 'I'll get on to this in a moment. We were in fact, planning to make enquiries here tomorrow, on the back of Edward's call. '

The Inspector looked at Anjali, 'We expect James to be here shortly. He knows we're briefing all of you on our progress tonight.'

Anjali looked both relieved and puzzled.

He smiled at her. 'We have several police posted at your house. I believe your mother-in-law is there now as well to take care of the children. When James arrives, you can leave as soon as you like. We won't need to interview James any further.'

She couldn't stop her tears, realising how terrible the situation had seemed for a time, and wiped her eyes with her sleeve. Katherine gave her tissues from the coffee table.

Anjali tried to smile at Katherine and Thomas but she was still in shock. She struggled to swallow properly. She glanced at the door straining to hear if he'd arrived.

'I've asked the team to bring him here the moment he arrives,' the Inspector could read her thoughts. Although the evidence was coming together, he was still watching them all closely.

~ ~ ~ ~ ~ ~ ~ ~ ~ ~

Katherine was trying to process the information flowing from the Inspector. But it was like waves of information washing over her, which she couldn't properly digest. She felt she was watching from the ceiling. She was in her mother's study - and there was a police Inspector talking about crime and death. There were police congregated in her kitchen. Her friends and family had been implicated in the most hideous of crimes and her husband was dead. Not only that, he was dead under suspicious circumstances in China.

Her stomach muscles contracted with tension. She still didn't know how her mother had died. She took a deep breath and closed her eyes. What else did the Inspector know?

~ ~ ~ ~ ~ ~ ~ ~ ~ ~

Thomas could see that both Anjali and Katherine were pale. He as well, did not feel too strong at this point.

'Inspector, I wonder if we should pause for a drink, or some water?'

Katherine jumped into action, realising she was the host.

'Of course! Would anyone like a wine, whisky, or perhaps gin? Sparkling water or juice maybe?'

Just then, James appeared at the door of the study with a policeman. He rushed in to embrace Anjali, and broke the heavy spell in the room. 'God, it's good to see you Anjali,' he couldn't let her go. 'Good to see you all! I'll take a gin if there's one going! And I may need more than one!'

Thomas afforded a small chuckle as he clapped his best friend on the back. 'And me,' echoed Thomas, 'Anjali, anyone else?'

Anjali was still in James' embrace, and she muffled a reply, 'No actually, I think I've had enough to drink tonight. But plain or sparkling water would be nice. Are the kids alright, James? The detective is filling us in, but we could return home.'

'The kids are fine. They haven't a clue. The police were exceptionally quiet,' he grinned at the Inspector. 'Mum is a bit confused as to all the events of the evening, as was I for a while, but she's fine and there with the children.'

Anjali nodded.

'Inspector, would you like a refreshment?' Asked Katherine.

'Ah, a plain soda or sparkling water would be nice, thank you.'

~ ~ ~ ~ ~ ~ ~ ~ ~ ~

Katherine opened a drinks cabinet in the study whilst the others were talking. Anjali and Thomas were updating James on what the Inspector had said. James was also asking Anjali how she came to be at Katherine's house. The police told him she would be there, but not why.

She could hear Anjali steering the conversation to the police update, and trying to detract James from her own situation. Katherine poured a favourite gin of her mother's for James and Thomas; she thought her mother would like that. She poured herself, Anjali and the Inspector a sparkling water, added a lemon and served the drinks to each of them. She took her own drink and perched on the arm of her chair. She was too anxious to sit, with the knowledge banging in her head like an ongoing echo, that Colin was dead.

'Mother, we're almost there,' she murmured quietly to herself. Despite believing answers would surely soon come, she still couldn't relax. The climax was building and she was completely on edge. She was sure the Inspector knew.

~ ~ ~ ~ ~ ~ ~ ~ ~ ~

They waited for the Inspector to take his sip of water.

'And so, as I was saying, we won't need to interview James any further,' repeated the Inspector, nodding at James.

'It's worth saying that James has solid investors in his business now - a finance deal that is perfect for such important technology! James?' The Inspector looked to James to clarify the situation. Thomas raised his glass to James. They all raised their glasses and Anjali's colour was returning to her face.

With a pleased smile James replied, 'My new partner is the Department of Business, Energy & Industrial Strategy! I was approached as part of a new funding deal the government is offering green companies. The funding applies to national renewable energy projects and is part of a green finance scheme.'

'So in fact,' he looked at Anjali with a twinkle in his eye, 'the deal isn't with a new owner who has bought out my business, but with the government for a subsidy and some additional investment. They will be providing significant expertise, not just money, to help productise the technology. It's more than I could have asked for, and certainly enough investment to do what I've wanted, and importantly, it keeps my ownership intact.'

He was grinning widely with pride. 'However, given the potential of our technology and exclusivity of it, the government has been especially keen to ensure the tech and its production doesn't end up owned by foreign investors who could be 'bad characters' as they say. They've been very supportive in ensuring I keep ownership of the business which is just what I wanted.

'My current investor has twenty percent ownership already. They actually wanted to buy E2E outright and take complete ownership. It was basically that or nothing.'

He shared a confidential look with the Inspector, evidently wondering what else to divulge.

'And given they wanted full ownership or nothing, I'm quite certain they'll readily take my offer to buy back the 20%.

With the investment I have from the government, they'll get a decent return,' he reflected.

'It wasn't just that I couldn't retain ownership of my own company that bothered me about the offer on the table. They were also quite coy when it came to detailing the production plans post acquisition and ensuring that the technology would remain in the country. In fact the current investor...' James paused and looked at the Inspector again. They had obviously earlier been discussing the venture capital firm that was already invested in James' business.

'Ah, yes, I was able to share some quite interesting information with James earlier this evening. Shall I get to that later, James?' The Inspector looked out from under his thick brows and James nodded secretively.

'Back to Edward,' the Inspector reminded himself where he was in the complex developments of the evening.

'Katherine's mother divulged yet other information to Edward, as we know from Edward's notes and our call with Edward earlier. She overheard Colin and Richard talking about the risk with Colin's finances. She had reasons to suspect that Colin's family fortune was in a bad way, and that his business too, was on shaky grounds.'

Katherine looked at Thomas and said, 'That must be the same conversation I overheard.' She looked at the Inspector and explained, 'I also heard Richard and Colin talking – I couldn't help it, they were so loud. And then this week, I spoke to Thomas about what I overheard regarding Colin and his inheritance.'

The Inspector looked at Thomas.

'Yes, I knew as well,' Thomas sighed heavily. 'I knew because Katherine's mother also spoke to me about this. She was very concerned and thought I should know. She told me on the morning of her death, that she overheard the conversation. She wanted me to talk to Katherine and Colin about it.'

He knew he could never divulge what else Katherine's mother had spoken to him about. Without meaning to, he looked down at Katherine, then to the floor.

The Inspector noticed a nuanced hesitation. He wondered whether Thomas was withholding anything; perhaps a very private and personal topic with Katherine's mother.

Thomas lifted his eyes to look at those around the room. 'But I didn't feel an overheard conversation was enough evidence. In fact, I would have spoken to my brother about it, but I didn't want to worry Katherine with this, if there was some other explanation. I did leave our session angry with what Katherine's mother had asked. It was the last time I saw her.' Thomas' shoulders sagged and the impact his situation had on all of them was obvious.

He straightened up a bit and ran his hand through his hair adding, 'Edward knew we'd had an exchange of words that morning. He gave me a note this week mentioning it and wanted to meet. I felt guilty. I thought that maybe she was so angry with me on that Wednesday morning of her death that she hadn't been focusing on the river. I knew this didn't implicate me directly in any way, but it didn't stop me from feeling guilty. However, with Katherine's suspicions and evidence mounting, there was the growing possibility that there was a person there, with her, at the river.'

The Inspector nodded and said, 'Someone else was in the same boat as you, Thomas, and he's has asked me to share this with all of you. We had a good conversation earlier today when Edward called. He was surprisingly clear in his message, despite his health, and he had a lot to say. Edward had also exchanged angry words with Katherine's mother, but earlier in the week, before the Wednesday of her death. When she told him about Richard and Colin and the possibility she would invest with them, he was very disturbed at her lack of sound reasoning. Because of this he was still on unhappy terms with Katherine's mother before she died.

'Like you Thomas, Edward also felt guilty. He wondered if she was distracted because they hadn't spoken since the argument. They were, as I understand, the closest of friends.' He squinted his eyes and looked at Katherine. She shifted on her armchair. Did he suspect something about their relationship? She was back in Edward's office, looking around at all the photos of her mother and her works of art. The Inspector coughed and she was brought back to the moment. He was still looking at her. She smiled faintly back.

'Edward asked if I could relay this information I've just shared, to all of you this weekend. All of it, including his medication. He would prefer no more secrets. I thought this might happen tomorrow, however given the circumstances, tonight was the perfect time to do so. Of course, given our discussions with Edward today, I can advise you that Edward himself, isn't under suspicion in this investigation.'

There was a collective sigh, then a pause in the room, as they began to better understand the puzzle's pieces.

The Inspector swirled his sparkling water in the glass and continued. 'Back to the thread of deceit and suspicion, hmm?

'It dawned on Katherine's mother what was happening. Colin was in a bad place. As we know, Colin had convinced her to invest in this green energy company. But she hadn't yet made the investment.

'And now, we come to the other player in this affair. We were able to question Richard tonight. It's evident now, that Colin didn't have the funds for his part of the bargain. Your mother was on to him. In Richard's master scheme, after he and Colin successfully acquired the energy business, Richard would need a partner for the full production of the green energy technology. And for this, he needed Colin's contacts in China. They had the facilities and funds to quickly build production capacity.

'For Colin's part - well he wanted in for the prize - in other words, he wanted to be part of the deal because he saw profit, lots of it in the near future. And so, Colin was only willing to engage his contacts in China if he was part of the acquisition deal. Based on what she told James, Richard and Colin were of the view that there would be eye-watering returns on this investment.

'However, because of his serious financial difficulties, in the end, Colin needed your mother to put up significant capital for the whole deal to happen. We know from Richard that the deal was structured with Colin's money as well as Richard's and it was way too late in the game for Colin to pull out. We have him on record: Richard told us tonight that Colin didn't have the cash and was influencing your mother to invest significant capital. And I use the word 'invest' lightly here - it was crafted more like a loan from the sounds of it. The plan was to borrow the money from your mother and then to invest himself - your mother would have had very little or no ownership in the new company, despite what Colin was telling her. The ownership would have been almost exclusively under Colin's name, of course alongside Richard who in fact, did have the funds to invest for his side of the bargain. Colin told Katherine's mother that he was also investing, but in fact, your mother's money would have been all that was required - and would have counted as Colin's part of the bargain.'

They were all staring at the Inspector, spellbound as he unwound the truth, a large ball of yarn with surprising numbers of knots and twists.

'You are aware that a deal was on the table from the current E2E investor - a venture capital firm - to buy the James' business outright?' They nodded.

'What you won't know is that this venture capital firm *is* in fact, owned by a parent company. None of this is easily traced. Without getting into the details, there are 'shell companies' involved. Shell companies are inactive businesses, often with complex ownership, that allow financial manoeuvres that may be questionable, as in this case. Tracing the actual ownership of this VC firm is therefore, almost impossible. Of course, all of this is quite common when wealthy individuals want to hide investments and money.'

He surveyed the individuals, wondering if they had yet clicked – they hadn't, bar Anjali who had begun to shake her head.

'And its parent company is indeed owned...' he knew someone else was eager to finish that sentence, and so he hung back.

'...by none other than Richard,' said James with disbelief.

The Inspector pointed to him with his glass, 'Yes, by none other than Richard.'

~ ~ ~ ~ ~ ~ ~ ~ ~ ~

There were gasps in the room. Katherine didn't know why she gasped as well. Nothing could surprise her at this point. But that Richard was trying to acquire James' company, discredit him and go after his wife? She looked at Anjali who was clasping her husband's hands tightly. The same thoughts will be flying through her head, thought Katherine.

So her mother was on the right track – they were one and the same company – the company that James owned and the company that Richard and Colin were trying to buy outright. Her mother was correct to be suspicious about the technology landing in the hands of third parties in whom the government may take particular interest.

Where was this going? Who was the evil one – Colin or Richard? Or both? She found herself wishing that her husband was innocent, but worried that hard truths were still to come. Looking at the Inspector she knew he certainly wasn't finished.

Chapter 38 - The Truth

The Inspector placed his drink perfectly on the side table where he was standing, twisting it on the coaster for a moment, thinking.

'We unearthed this information when speaking with Richard tonight. Otherwise, we wouldn't have known Richard was the ultimate owner of the VC firm. Richard was desperate to get his hands on E2E, or 'Project Gemstone' as he named it during his acquisition and due diligence process. 'Rock solid' and 'eco-friendly' ring any bells?' All bar James nodded.

'Under questioning by police tonight, he growled at my detectives as if they were stupid. He wanted E2E because he knew the company brought with it not just the 'big bucks' but 'geo-political power' as he put it. Rest assured, Anjali, there was absolutely nothing wrong with James' company.'

James looked at him and then at Anjali, puzzled. It was obvious that the Inspector had not informed James about Richard's discrediting attack that evening, and had only clarified the ownership of the VC firm with him.

'A predator of his type will go to no ends to get what they want; what they believe is theirs already. What he told you about James' business? Well, we now know from Richard, that it was to discredit James and sever your relationship. He was delusional about the 'family' he was soon to set up with you.'

'What?!' James asked loudly. 'What's this about, Anjali?!'

'It's alright James, it really has no bearing on any of this. It did maybe several hours ago, but it's neither here nor there at this point. It's been a bizarre night. I'm fine now. Richard was up to some scary tricks, but there's nothing to worry about now. I'll tell you when we're at home,' she decided to underplay the nightmare of her evening.

She couldn't believe how calmly she'd just relayed that when not a few hours earlier she was seriously threatened by Richard's aggression. She would tell James later. They'd need to decide how to proceed with Richard; whether she should talk further to the police about this. She sighed without meaning to; it would be a difficult call, it depended she guessed on the outcome tonight.

She was sure the Inspector had more to say, and didn't want to delay him. Plus, Katherine looked on edge; she must be desperate to understand more. Now was not the time to discuss her own evening's trauma.

James looked unconvinced but he could see the Inspector was about to say more. He nodded cautiously at his wife, 'I'm not sure what Richard was up to tonight, but yes, we can talk about that later. I can see the Inspector has more to say...'

The Inspector moved to take a seat, he'd been standing for sometime.

'Thank you.' He looked around the room then his eyes settled on Katherine. 'I can confirm that on the morning of your mother's death, the events happened as follows:

'Katherine heads off to work. Colin takes Maisy to school. Thomas visits Katherine's mother, for a pre-booked appointment at her request, when, unlike either of them, they have an intense argument. Edward hears a heated discussion. Thomas leaves. Edward decides to walk to Thomas' house to see if he can help smooth things over. Colin returns from the school drop off to work from home.

'The difficult pieces were how Richard and Colin fit in from this point and of course, who was responsible for the note given to your mother,' he played with the rim of his glass.

'As well, Richard's face and car which Maisy so carefully painted... How did that fit in and how could that painting help us?' The Inspector put the question to the room. They were silent. It was obvious he didn't want an answer, he was simply preparing them.

'The note was almost certainly written by Richard, although he denies it. We believe this because Colin could have easily spoken to your mother that day to give her the pressured deadline.

'Not only that, but Richard enjoys a game, and the note, no doubt, was part of an appalling game plan.

'Katherine advised me that the post arrives daily without fail at 10:30. By then, Colin would have already left the house to pick up Maisy at school because she was sick. Katherine was at work and not on 'school duty' that day.

'We figure Katherine's mother must have gone through her post on Wednesday morning and read the note before her meeting with Thomas and therefore, well before Colin returned from school with Maisy. Thomas leaves the house after the argument. Shortly after this two things happen: Edward leaves for Thomas' house and Richard arrives at the house for a pre-arranged meeting with Colin.

'We have not yet checked this with Colin's secretary, and are assuming at this point, that Richard isn't lying; that there really was a pre-arranged meeting. When the team challenged Richard on his business acumen, and ability to finance the deal, it was obvious that he felt we were trying to impugn his character regarding his financial transactions and he divulged far more than he would have liked about the wider situation, in boasting about his cleverness.

'He told us that he was ready to 'sort out' her indecisiveness and thought being there the whole day would allow him and Colin to put additional pressure on her. Richard was acutely aware how necessary her money was for the deal to happen; Colin had nothing to invest. The note that would arrive with the morning post was as he put it, 'to unsettle her nerves and set the tone for the day'. But, he claims Colin wrote that note, posted it, and was entirely Colin's idea.

'When Richard arrives at the house Colin hasn't yet returned from the school. Richard is confronted by Katherine's mother about the note. She leaves him under no illusion and clearly spells out that she will not be investing in his and Colin's business opportunity. By this time, she must have decided to allow Colin to sink; rather than to prop him up financially.

'Richard has confirmed that she was extremely irate and insistent that she couldn't invest under a cloud of distrust and 'bully tactics'. He sneered at our officers that 'she didn't know what bullying was like, and hadn't dealt in the real world'. He also said that he was enraged by her impudence and frustrated that she wasn't enticed by the profit at the end, despite the means to get there. Richard was clearly condescending towards her approach to business and had no issue telling my officers of her 'hopeless business mind and bad decision'.

'The following reconstruction is based on pieces of information we have managed to extract from Richard and from evidence Katherine has found.

'Katherine's mother leaves Richard, who is in a dark mood. How dark, she would unfortunately soon find out. She herself is angry yet resolute. She must have assumed he would stay at the house to wait for Colin to return. We believe that at this point she writes in bold on the note, 'TRUST NO ONE', and slips the note into her locked desk drawer. Perhaps Richard told her that Colin wrote the note, if that is true. Perhaps she was frustrated that a family member would turn against her. Or indeed, perhaps she was forewarning Katherine who may find the note...was she concerned for her life at this point? We simply don't know. Either Richard or Colin, not that day but subsequently, tried to open the drawer no doubt to see if the note was hidden there, but they were obviously unsuccessful. We don't know the details of that yet, either.

'Even before Richard arrives, Katherine's mother is already dressed for her swim. She has her swimsuit on, her large man's shirt, and her shoes. Leaving the note safely in the study, she heads to the river for her short, Wednesday morning swim. Unbeknownst to her, she is being pursued.

'Unfortunately for Richard, in his indignation that we were challenging his financial dealings, and perhaps keen to settle that as perhaps he has more to hide there, he quite simply, in a blasé manner, let slip what happened at the river. And once that was out, the team was able to revisit the scene time and again in the two hours they had, to confirm the detail. It took awhile before Richard realised he was a suspect for the death, as opposed to shady financial dealings. Don't forget, he was also being investigated for tonight's situation,' he looked at Anjali, 'and so he was not thinking about covering up the situation at the river. It's surprising really, that someone of his intelligence didn't twig. He obviously didn't divulge any of this information when we first investigated so he knew, but under pressure, he certainly was more concerned about covering other things up. He didn't even want a representative there, he was quite arrogant with the police, wholly convinced of his innocence in the whole matter.'

He paused here, and the room took a breath. They looked at each other, shaking heads, Katherine's upper teeth were permanently holding her lower lip between her teeth.

'And so as I was saying, unbeknownst to her, she is being pursued. Just as she was about to take her shoes off to dip in the river, she catches sight of Richard. He's in a rage, on the path running towards the river, menacingly holding a large stick. She panics and rushes uphill, following the river path to where there's a large oak tree. It's some distance up river to reach the oak, about 500 metres. On the way, in her panic, she drops her dry towel. We know this from Richard's sneering account of the events.'

Thomas moved to squeeze Katherine's shoulder slightly; so that's what happened to the towel.

'Unfortunately, Richard is racing up the path behind her. She was perhaps running three minutes, maybe longer? It was uphill and although familiar with the path she would have been slowed down by all the thick roots on the ground. She must have been breathless with panic and intense running.

'She had her sight on the oak tree. Why? No doubt, she thought it was the safest place to protect herself. She would have calculated that there'd be time to climb a decent height before Richard arrived, but, she does not take the stick into consideration, or perhaps that she is tired.

'As she climbs, Richard reaches the tree. He claims he manages to poke her foot with the stick to make her 'get down' so he can 'talk to her' and in his words 'keep her safe - the tree was high'. We do know at that time there was a struggle of sorts. Unfortunately, we're still unsure of these exact details but we'll most certainly find out.

'Somehow, she manages to escape further up the tree. Richard does try to pursue her - we know this because he mentioned it indirectly when he divulged that she caused him to rip one of his favourite shirts as he slid down a section of sharp branches into spiky bushes. So he must have tried to climb the tree though unsuccessfully.

'We know that he was throwing objects at her - including the stick. That confession slipped out when he was angered during our questioning. So he must have stood below her spot and tried to scare her down. Again, he claims he was trying to 'encourage her to come down, it was dangerous up there'. We believe that she moved in the tree - perhaps numerous times - to dodge the objects. He was in a rage and she certainly would have feared for her life.

'At one point, she must have moved and slipped. Perhaps as she falls, her shoe catches in a branch... or it may be that she first catches her foot when sitting and leans forward to loosen the shoe to free her foot but then simply... leans too far and falls. We'll never know.'

He winced as he reconstructed the scene.

'We do know that her blouse rips in the branches. Her shoe remains in the tree. And she falls. On contact, her head hits the stone some distance below. She falls to her death, and is swept down the river five meters as recorded.'

'I'm sorry,' he looked at Katherine whose eyes were riveted on his face. He paused for several long seconds out of respect, and to ensure those in the room were following along.

'It was evident from our line of questioning that Richard didn't try to rescue her from the river. Richard has not divulged whether he thought she was unconscious or deceased at that time.

'Instead of pulling her out of the river, Richard runs back up to the house.

'We believe he was planning to leave the house thinking it was fortunate that Colin wasn't actually home. He thought better of going through the house, from where he came, and decided to try the door in the garden wall, which would bring him straight to his car. To his luck, the door was unlocked. But as he opened the garden door, Colin was pulling up in the drive with Maisy, back from her school. Richard peaked through the garden door and there we have it. That's the scene in Maisy's painting.'

'That painting,' he paused, 'was instrumental in solving this case.'

He stood up from his chair and cleared his throat. He stretched his legs and looked at each of them.

In a deep voice he stated firmly, 'We have this evening charged Richard with homicide.'

~ ~ ~ ~ ~ ~ ~ ~ ~ ~

A collective gasp echoed in the room. Anjali and James were perched on the edge of their chairs. Thomas's face was white. Katherine found herself quietly crying. Her husband was cleared, but her mother, she squeezed her eyes tight to rid herself of tears, how awful, how horrific. Her beautiful and loving, charitable mother. Although she had imagined a frightening death scene herself, hearing it like that, factually from the Inspector, and envisioning her mother's fright at being attacked was very difficult. And it was all, so final.

~ ~ ~ ~ ~ ~ ~ ~ ~ ~

The Inspector paused only a moment then continued, 'Richard denies homicide. He claims he was worried that she might try swimming in such an angry state and followed her to protect her. And that he was trying to get her out of the tree, given the danger. But he didn't think this through. In fact, he was so certain of his innocence that he easily walked into our questions, providing incriminating facts because of his arrogance and belief that he's beyond the law.

'He claims that Colin made the first three transfers. We're right now checking those accounts. I'm sure that we'll find the Bahamas and Panama accounts to be privately held by Richard and Colin. Richard may be facing yet more charges in the next few days.

'Katherine, regarding the third and fourth transfers to Chinese accounts, this will be more difficult to untangle. Richard claims the fourth transfer yesterday morning, must have been Colin moving forward with the Chinese partners, as apparently Richard wasn't aware of this transfer. More on this Chinese partnership in a moment.

'Katherine's mother did make an investment in a green company prior to her death, but this was a red herring. It wasn't to Colin and Richard's investment deal, for acquisition of E2E, nor was it direct to James' company. It was another business, totally above board. We were able to run further queries based on what Katherine told us this evening, and that account is a red herring.'

Katherine looked at him with sad eyes, 'And Colin, did he know? Did he know what happened at the river?'

The Inspector glanced at her solemnly, and then at Thomas, 'We'll never know for certain. However, Richard claims he told Colin that morning. He said that after Colin put Maisy in front of the television with a new stuffed animal she had cried for, that they'd then 'got to business'.

'Apparently, he told Colin that his mother-in-law had had an accident at the river, potentially life-threatening. Colin didn't challenge him and reportedly said she was getting old and shouldn't be swimming. Whether that was true, and whether Colin suspected foul play - we don't know. There was discussion about an ambulance and police, but it was decided between the two of them that Richard should leave immediately, and that they would leave her there.

'Colin did nothing. It wasn't until later when Edward returned to find she wasn't in her study, that Edward asked Colin if he'd seen her. When Colin said no and asked Edward not to bother him, Edward then wondered if she'd returned from her swim. As you all know, it was Edward who found her.'

~~~~~~~~~~

Katherine had to pull herself together, frozen with disbelief. She sat shaking with cold and looking at the Inspector, wishing him to say something more, more charitable about Colin. But nothing was forthcoming. She looked at the others, and their faces were pale. Thomas was still white, and looked chilled to the bone.

She swallowed. 'It's very hard to hear this.'

'Yes, I can understand that.'

'What about Colin in China? What do you know now?'

'Not enough. But we're working on this,' the Inspector took a deep breath and looked squarely at Katherine.

'Colin and Richard were working together. Richard was after James' company. But Richard also needed Colin. As we all know now, Colin had the contacts in China to productise James' technology for the market.'

James interrupted quietly, 'My suspicions were right, about the possibility of my company's Intellectual Property leaving the country.'

The Inspector nodded and continued, 'As we know, Colin was also investing in Richard's takeover of James' company. I mentioned earlier there would be more on this, well...

'Unfortunately for Colin, he had many investments over the years which have all gone sour. His family fortune too, is in a bad state. He turned to Katherine's mother for her money. In fact, Katherine's mother would have bailed out Colin. As I mentioned, he was structuring it so that her money was a loan to him, not an investment. In this way, he could benefit from ownership and the profit he envisioned.

'He was in China this week to sort the deal with his Chinese counterparts. It's early at this point, but it does look like a complicated business. Very complicated. The business dealings were complex on several levels and, Colin's death isn't straightforward,' he let that sink in.

'The Foreign, Commonwealth and Development Office also known as the FCDO will be in touch with you tomorrow Katherine. They'll be a valuable source of help. We're already liaising with the Consular Section of the British Consulate

General in Shanghai and they'll also contact you tomorrow. We are, at the moment, not convinced whether this is a murder investigation or not. They'll guide you through this and also talk about repatriation of the body.'

He looked at her sitting with her eyes closed. She opened them, and he continued, 'Given the possible media interest in this, the FCDO will most likely appoint a Family Liaison Officer, an FLO to assist you. I'm very sorry it isn't a simple case, and that it's not over yet.'

Thomas put his hand on Katherine's head and rubbed her hair gently. He exchanged looks with James. This could be tough going, he thought.

'I wonder if we should break for the night?' Thomas asked the Inspector.

'Yes, yes, of course, there isn't much more anyway I can say now. And the team is already packing up to go. Katherine, is there anything else you need from me?'

She shook her head, 'No. Thank you for everything. It's a lot to take in, I'm sure I'll have more questions tomorrow. Will I be able to contact you?'

'Yes, of course - we'll stick with you now till it's sorted,' he smiled gently at her.

'Thank you. I'll walk you out....'

The Inspector interrupted her, 'No, no, we'll make our way - I'll leave you to yourselves. Good evening, and thank you all for your support in this investigation.'

He dipped his head at everyone, paused to check there were no more questions, and just before he opened the door to leave, addressed the room one more time.

'It's difficult sometimes to understand individual motives. People who we think we know, we don't always know. Your mother, Katherine, was obviously a woman of integrity. She could take the measure of people and situations and understand superficial versus true commitment,' he looked at her and then his eyes rested on Thomas.

Thomas felt the Inspector's eyes bore into his. Could he know? Self-conscious, he gently removed his hands from Katherine, and without thinking ran his hand through his hair.

The Inspector then nodded politely to them all, and with a satisfied look left through the hall, following the last of his team out the front door.

Chapter 39 - New Beginning

The Inspector's departure left a moment's silence in the room.

From behind Katherine, Thomas raised his eyebrows at James and Anjali and indicated that it might be time to leave.

'Katherine, it's so much to absorb,' Anjali stood up and faced her friend, who was sitting with her hands clasped surprisingly gently on her lap.

There was relief and empathy in Anjali's face. She was relieved now that she understood James' involvement, but she struggled to comprehend how Richard and Colin could be so morally wicked. Katherine's face was unemotional, perhaps determined to keep herself together. She was worried for Katherine. Her life was about to change almost beyond recognition.

'Are you alright here tonight?'

Katherine nodded her head, but looked as if she hadn't quite heard the question.

Anjali contemplated whether she should stay or not. There was also much she had to share with James regarding Richard, and the sooner the better. The appropriate place would be at home when they were alone. In any case, Katherine and Thomas already knew most of what had happened. She spoke slowly.

'I think James and I should return home to the kids and relieve James' Mom. Perhaps it's best if we don't keep you up longer and talk through it all. It's simply too much to absorb at this time. We all need our sleep, well I need my sleep that's for sure,' she couldn't help but yawn.

Spontaneously, Katherine yawned in response. 'Yes, of course, it's time to head to bed. We all need our sleep,' she smiled faintly at Anjali and reached out to squeeze her friend's hand.

Anjali clasped her hand and pulled her up gently from the arm of the chair. They hugged each other emotionally.

James turned to look at Thomas and mouthed, 'You ok?'

As usual, Thomas ran his hands through his hair and then shrugged his shoulders. Familiar with tragedy and complex family emotions in his profession, nothing had quite prepared him for this. His hand moved to describe a 'so-so' feeling and he silently replied, 'Talk tomorrow.'

James nodded, then inclined his head to the door. Thomas shook his head and indicated he would stay awhile. James mouthed, 'Good idea. We'll leave now.'

James piped up, 'We'll pop by early tomorrow - shall we pick up Maisy so you have some time to work through this?'

'That would be so helpful, thank you,' Katherine nodded. They all began to walk towards door and into the hallway,

Anjali with her arm around Katherine. Thomas hugged them goodbye.

'I'll walk you out,' said Katherine. She accompanied James and Anjali to the front door and said goodbye. The last of the police cars were already moving down the long carriage drive. She waved goodbye to Anjali and James, waving until the lights of their car disappeared from sight down the dark country roads.

~ ~ ~ ~ ~ ~ ~ ~ ~ ~

Katherine closed the heavy door and turned the key in the lock. She leaned against the strong old door for a moment then turned around slowly. Thomas was far down the hallway by the study. He was leaning against the wall, hands in pocket, one long leg stretched across the other. He smiled at her gently.

Katherine returned a shaky smile, then slowly walked towards him.

As she reached him, his hands came out of his pockets and he drew her to his chest. She felt herself sinking as he pulled her closer and a ripple of shivers travelled the length of her body when he gently touched her hair. The tragedy of the situation and of truths that were further to unfold, melted away momentarily.

She breathed in his always-oaky scent and leaned her face back to look at him. Those grey-green eyes. She could see the deep meaning there and felt her body warm to him intimately as she stretched her face up towards his.

~ ~ ~ ~ ~ ~ ~ ~ ~ ~

He felt a rage in his body. Everything was in the mix: anger, frustration, passion, elation. He had to mentally control his physical impulses but it was an impossibility. He was so confused. Where did this leave him? Or her? He pulled her even closer to his torso and with his fingers laced in her hair he gently tilted her head back further so he could see her full face.

There was so much intense feeling in her intelligent eyes and trust. He instinctively sucked his breath through his teeth. Trust.

He pulled his eyes away from hers, and looked down the long hallway. She had trusted his brother - to what end? Anger overcame him and he instantly cooled. She had to be able to trust him. And how could she if he took this any further?

~ ~ ~ ~ ~ ~ ~ ~ ~ ~

She closed her eyes a moment to savour the sensual feelings pulsing through her. It was such a welcome relief. Everything had been so intensely unsettling recently and for so long her reserve had kept her emotionally intact. And it had been forever since she last felt like this. Had she ever felt like this?

In the moment she took to both realise and fleetingly experience these newly stirred feelings, she sensed his body stiffen. The moment was disappearing. Fast, like the final grains of sand in an hourglass.

He loosened his hold on her and she opened her eyes.

He was looking away over her head and there was a hard expression on his face. He realised she was watching him, and he looked down at her, breaking his determined look with a gentle smile. He stepped back and slipped his hands down to her waist.

'Hey, are you ok?'

She took a moment to control her emotions and pulled herself back from where she had been falling. Why had he moved away? She looked to the ground and swallowed quickly, hopeful that her emotion wasn't as perceptible as it felt. She knew herself to be strong and wilful, but in the moment and with all that had unfolded tonight, she struggled to find her controlled, default state of mind.

She pulled herself up to her full height and like a reflex, donned her well worn sheath of calm and principle. It was what she did superbly well for her public face.

She smiled cautiously at him, then wittily responded, 'Well, as fine as I can be, given the events of the evening,' hoping that this would bridge them both to a more comfortable place.

He laughed, she thought satirically, but also there was relief in his quiet laughter.

He took the opportunity to casually remove his hands from her waist when he laughed, trying to inconspicuously move away from her body, and regain some distance between them.

'This situation is surreal, that's for sure. It will be a difficult few weeks, probably months for us and will take awhile to understand Colin and recover from the shock.

Richard, well, I've got no words for him.' He paused, contemplating what the Inspector had said.

'I'll start tomorrow and try to unearth my family's financial situation. It's hard to talk about, it's all so new... Colin's death. I'm assuming I'll have power of attorney. I can't say I'm looking forward to this. It sounds like everything's a right mess. Hard to believe Colin isn't with us anymore. I just don't understand. How can that be?

'And I'm responsible for the estate now, I never thought that would happen. Maybe...well who knows, but maybe I can salvage something for the future. Perhaps save Colin from further public scrutiny. The press would love a story like this. Oh, god, Colin. I didn't admire my brother, Katherine, but I did love him.'

His face saddened as the future dawned on him. What had happened to his flawed, charismatic brother? What death had he faced? How badly were the family finances, would he need to sell the estate and what about Colin's business?

His mind quickly turned to his personal life as he imagined the next steps. What would his relationship with Katherine look like? What about the intimate feelings taking over his best judgement, and the physical impulses he was experiencing towards her? That had to stop. His mind opened to the wider picture. How would she and Maisy manage? His thoughts came back to the moment.

'Of course, Katherine, I can be here with you to take those calls tomorrow which the Inspector mentioned. Would you mind that?' he asked in a guarded way, but the emotion was still evident.

Katherine was slow to respond. Would she mind that? She swallowed again. The sensation from a moment ago reared up instantly. That, and more, was the answer that flitted across her brain. And if she articulated this?

It was an impossible situation. She'd had her chance, many years ago and she'd chosen a different path. It would be too awkward for everyone to admit what she was slowly realising she wanted. In any case, she wasn't certain Thomas was in the same place as her.

She unintendedly clenched her teeth. Best to keep it as it always had been. She didn't need any more complexities in her life just now. Nor, in fact, did Maisy or Thomas.

What she did need was Thomas as her brother-in-law to help her get through this. They were in it together, as usual, bound by Colin. She shuddered as the reality of his death sunk in further.

'Yes, they'll surely want us both involved. You, his brother, and me, his wife.' She felt cold and alone. 'I'm hoping you're still planning to stay this evening?' She smiled at him. She could really do with his company.

'Of course,' but he wasn't looking at her.

She was content with that and cautiously looped her arm through his. 'Cup of tea before we head off to sleep,' she suggested tentatively, 'it will be a demanding day tomorrow.'

'Yes, that would be great, after that heavy gin you poured,' he teased her. She found herself able to laugh, but felt on the edge still, of something dangerous.

They walked together to the kitchen. It was a familiar scene but with a different backdrop, as Katherine made their teas. The chat was light. Anything important was off-limits as they casually talked about how efficient the police were and the weather the next day. A short while later they shared a quiet moment as they each sipped their tea

Thomas was so comfortable in Katherine's presence. He listened to her talk about the Inspector. In a sudden burst of memory, a scene replayed in his head: the study, Katherine's mother and what she calmly suggested he should consider, that morning of her death.

'Thomas, I'm about to divulge some distasteful and unimaginable information about Colin. But before I do that, and before you become irate with me, which you will do, I'd liked to discuss a much more positive subject,' she paused.

Thomas didn't move, he had no idea what she was going to say.

'You and Katherine,' she said it emphatically, and kindly.

His stomach muscles contracted, and a new feeling of tension began to spread from his core.

'I adore you, have always adored you. For some reason, certain pathways have been taken by my daughter over the years. I believe your pathway has always remained the same,' she paused.

'You see, I know, Thomas. You've never stopped caring for Katherine,' and that was it, she had said it just like that. He began to interrupt her but she put her hand up to stop him.

'And I believe, pretty soon, Katherine will come to realise that she also, only really had one pathway that she should have followed; especially when she discovers this information about Colin. It will become apparent to her, if you heed my advice, that this pathway is still open to her.

'With all my heart, Thomas, and knowing how hard it is to find a lifelong love, my advice is to let Katherine know. Share your feelings with her. Sooner is better, or you may leave it too late to be able to act on it.'

It was surreal. His disbelief that she would step over the line and suggest something like this, and to be so disloyal to his brother, shocked him into an automatic and defensive reaction. He was quick to respond and was emphatically dismissive.

But that was before she told had him about Colin's affair, and his finances. And of course, before her death. Did he owe something to her now?

The memory as quickly as it came, faded, and he paused to consider his next move. Thomas chanced a look at Katherine, hoping that might ease his discomfort, and gently nudge him in the right direction. But what he saw surprised him.

Katherine looked calm, positive and not like someone who had just been through a horrific evening. The pallor of her face from earlier was flushed now with some colour and the expression on her face was contemplative, but not sad. It was easy. There was no sense to throw fresh revelations into the already difficult situation.

'Katherine, you look refreshed from the tea,' and then he risked it, 'what are you thinking?'

She looked up at him, 'A lot of things, to be honest.' She put her cup down.

'How I, or perhaps how we, will manage through this.'

She dwelled on that then continued, 'I think it will be sometime as you say before we understand everything. For Colin, there's the repatriation, the funeral, and protecting Maisy. If the media does catch on, and the FLO becomes involved as the Inspector mentioned was a possibility, we'll both have to keep our sanity.'

She looked at Thomas for his reaction. He nodded solemnly in agreement.

'I'm just grateful that we're such good friends, Thomas, and that I've a pragmatic and supportive brother in law to help with all of this,' she cautiously gaged his reaction.

He nodded at her. Inside he was pushing his emotions from a moment ago, at bay. He is the supportive brother in law, and he would have been foolish to take it further. What about the trust he had worried about earlier?

'Yes, we'll get through all of this together' he responded.

She studied his eyes. Despite his words, they seemed indecisive. She couldn't bear to have awkwardness between them. What was he thinking? He obviously wasn't divulging anything. Perhaps it was better this way.

She took a deep, resolved breath, it was much better this way.

She compartmentalised, an old trick of hers, and this 'almost thing' with Thomas was tucked away. Her stream of thought returned to the events of the evening and all that the Inspector had divulged.

'Thank you Thomas, your support is really appreciated,' and that was it, there would be no more talk about what might happen between them from this point.

'It's all so complex,' she said, 'I simply cannot comprehend how two such socially upstanding, publicly successful and responsible people could be so heartless and criminal. How did they ever think they could get away with it? God only knows how Colin paid for it,' her voice was dull and faltered slightly.

'As for Richard, for him to think he's above the law, it's commendable how the Inspector's team didn't flinch at that. They've been so professional and responsive tonight, and amazingly quick to untangle this mess. Thank heaven they took my evidence seriously tonight, Thomas.'

She took another sip of her tea before continuing, with a slight hesitancy.

'You know, it did occur to me that having Richard in the frame as a murderer – well I think that spurred the police to respond quickly to Anjali's frightful situation this evening. I don't mean to be disrespectful, but I do wonder if they would have responded as quickly to the type of situation Anjali found herself in, under normal circumstances? Richard should be held to account for that as well. He is without a doubt a predator, it's not just about my mother now, don't you think?'

Thomas was taken back. Of course, put like that he agreed with Katherine, there was no doubt. But he was surprised at himself. He'd been disgusted of course, when Anjali emotionally recounted from the car the situation she'd only just escaped, but he'd thought Richard was an ogre and a stupid cad; he didn't think of it in criminal terms.

'You're right Katherine. I took a second to answer you cause I can't quite believe I didn't think that, as soon as Anjali told us what had happened tonight. I put it down to bad behaviour, very bad behaviour. But that should be unusual, that shouldn't be normal, that a woman isn't safe in such a situation. She obviously wanted to leave, and he got physical. That's not right.'

'I'll talk to Anjali about this tomorrow. She'll be thinking about this situation for sure,' Katherine responded.

'I'm sure James will be of the same view. He'll be pretty angry when she fills him in on the events of the evening.'

The two sat quietly for a moment. Then Katherine absently drew a circle on the table with her finger and spoke again, this time her voice was positive and calm.

'You asked me what I'm thinking. Well, I'm also planning my next steps for my business. I've already met with my executive team to arrange for their management of the company over the next six to twelve months,' she smiled secretly.

'I've yet to ask her, but given Richard's situation, I was hoping to poach Anjali to help me with both the business and my mother's investment portfolio. She'd be perfect, don't you think?' She looked at him coyly, proud of her plans.

'Hey, what a great idea,' Thomas grinned widely.

'And I'd like to focus on my mother's work, understand the investments and the charities she supported. I've still so much to tell you...'

He raised his eyes in surprise, 'At this hour?'

'Ah, no,' she laughed, 'for another day. But, once we get through this, I'm thinking of doing several trips abroad.'

'Really?'

'Yes, really. Not to escape, but to discover. *Apparently*,' she exaggerated the word, they both knew it to be true, 'I have a significant amount of international property and I'd like to better acquaint myself with that,' she grinned and cocked her head sideways at him.

'And Maisy?'

'Well of course, I'll need to wait till October break, and manage this around Maisy but...'

'But what?'

'I already have our first destination planned,' she paused.

'Our?'

She took the plunge.

'Myself and Maisy, and of course, Maisy's uncle if he can spare the time?'

He felt the colour rise in his face.

She added, 'If nothing but to keep us safe given the crazy world out there...'

Ah so, he thought. Were they back to normal? The two of them, the three of them?

'Sure,' he replied calmly, anything he reflected, to take her mind off recent events. And his, he thought.

'Tell me what you've planned.'

'Well, an odd letter arrived in the post this week, addressed to my mother. It's from an olive estate in Puglia. In fact, it's a property in Mother's portfolio,' she smiled secretly.

'And...?' He was so easy to string along.

'It's actually a charity working with young people from around the world; young people who need a guiding hand. The skills they learn and the fresh air apparently has had huge benefits for these young people. The majority go on to be employed elsewhere,' her eyes were bright with enthusiasm.

'I'd love to hear more about that, Katherine. Why is the letter 'odd'?'

'Well, the estate manager has died. It was an accident,' she emphasised the last word.

'His daughter wrote to my mother. She doesn't believe her father's death was an accident.'

Thomas' eyes opened wide.

'I was hoping I could travel to meet with her. We've had a short phone call. She'd like to discuss several items with me in person, show me a few things. And so, I believe I will. It should be a quick visit. And Puglia will be warm and lovely in October. Maisy would love that, and, wouldn't you?'

He shook his head and grinned at her, 'Yes, Katherine, I would.' He stared at her for a moment longer and his grin grew wider.

'But a daughter who doesn't believe her parent's death is an accident? Really?'

She smiled at him, 'Really.'

Printed in Great Britain
by Amazon